A GHOSTLY SHADE OF PALE

A NOVEL
by
—Merle Temple—

A Ghostly Shade of Pale

Cover Design and Interior Layout Design:
Tracy Applewhite Broome
www.tracybroome.com

Author photography:
Stephanie Rhea
www.stephanierhea.com

Southern Literature Publishing
southernliteraturepublishing.com

*To Susan Jackson Temple, wife, best friend, and earth angel,
who was my shelter in the tempests, lived the real story, and made
endurance and triumph possible. She "walked in beauty, like the
night of cloudless climes and starry skies, and all that's best...
meet in her aspect and her eyes." —Byron*

*To Grandma Pearl Temple, who loved her little boy and made
me realize that history and all who lived it are just a good story away.*

*And to Judy Temple, whose warm, gentle, and fragrant breeze
from yesteryear breathed life and love into my windless sea and
made me believe that fairy tales can come true,
happy endings are not just for novels, and
epilogues are still to be written by and for the young at heart.*

—Merle Temple—

Reviews for *A Ghostly Shade of Pale*

"*Captures the South, the period in the 1960s...evocative of some of the great Southern writers...a taste and feeling for where you are... a lot of layers in a fascinating book.*" —*Allison Hope Weiner, Media Mayhem, Beverly Hills.*

"*I fell for his language as a fan of Southern fiction...the novel is part gothic, part mystery, part thriller and all stratagem...opens with a murder and doesn't let go.*" —*Gila Green, Israel, Author, King of the Class.*

"*The press is just beginning to jump on board to something that's about to get as hot as a drug deal gone bad with automatic weapons and kilos of cocaine flying around. He's lived the life and survived it — with his faith intact.*" —*Mark Stowers, The Jackson Clarion-Ledger.*

"*The drug war is on . . . and we should all be afraid. Merle Temple takes the reader into a 1960s world of violence and mystery, and creates characters that are chillingly sinister, especially the evil Fredrick, who may haunt your nightmares for a very long time. This story blends action with a literary style that only grows in the Deep South. Not for the faint of heart.*" —*Adele Elliott, Real Media Radio.*

"*Temple's first-hand knowledge of gun battles, drug deals gone bad, corrupt politicians, and law enforcement officials, makes the scenes and pages come to life.*" —*The Oxford Eagle.*

"*Suspense-driven...a compelling read from cover to cover...memories have their way with him so those raw emotions would surface and be laid bare on page after page of remembrances in order for his readers to feel what he felt...*" —*Southern Writer's Magazine.*

"*Temple has the ability to bring his readers to a very personal place, allowing them to resonate with him as an author and with characters in his novel...what an amazing story (he) has shared with his readers.*" —*The Daily Mississippian (Ole Miss).*

"*Gripping...*" —*Mississippi Magazine.*

"*Terrific! Recommend it highly!*" —*Paul Rogers, WBZM, Orlando.*

PREFACE

"The thief cometh not, but for to steal, and to kill,
and to destroy…"
—John 10:10

In the early 1970s the drug war was in its infancy. There still existed innocence about the prospect of "winning" and saving the young from addiction or death. The costs of government intervention had not been calculated, so firm was the belief in the rightness of the crusade. This was long before the government enacted laws that would jail millions for long, draconian sentences—long before $1 trillion in expenditures and a steady encroachment on civil liberties in the name of security. Drug use was still a symbol of protest against an unpopular war and the values of the older generation. Politics was almost inseparable from the first wave of drug abuse. Few would admit that treatment and demand deserved as much attention as supply and prosecution. The new prohibition agents…these happy warriors went forth to tilt at windmills and slay dragons, oblivious for the most part that they despised a weakness they saw in themselves, refusing to acknowledge that they were in danger of losing themselves in the pursuit of their grail. They labored in a cynical and treacherous "war" where all was an illusion, the line between good and evil was a moving target, and monsters were all about. They never realized the very real danger that they might "win," but in the process, emerge resembling those that they fought with all of their might. They never thought that winning could mean the undoing of the tree of liberty, or understood that no amount of arrests could relieve the biting point of the tenterhooks on which they twisted. This is their story.

"Michael and his angels fought against the dragon;
and the dragon fought and his angels..."
—Revelation 12:7

"I never knew a man who had better motives for all the trouble he caused."
—Graham Greene, The Quiet American

CHAPTER ONE

"I have seen the moment of my greatness flicker and
I have seen the eternal Footman hold my coat, and snicker,
and in short, I was afraid."
—T.S. Eliot

Reginald "Reggie" Morris stared into a dark night made white by large flakes of snow falling in crystal sheets. He thought briefly that it looked like one of the small globes he had as a child, the kind you could turn upside down and shake until the little Alpine village was blanketed with the deepest of snows. Something in the night suddenly screamed in its misery and then it was quiet. There was only the song of the flakes against the glass.

Reggie shivered and turned away, carelessly swirling the inch of amber liquid in the snifter. *Some New Year's Eve,* he thought. This abhorrent weather front had ruined his plans for another of the big parties for which he was famous. He had not even covered his lighted pool and now strained to see through the thick blizzard obscuring his vision.

"It looks more like Maine than Mississippi out there," he muttered to himself.

Many years the pool would've been fine for a Christmas or New Year's gala. His remote lodge was nestled high atop a rise

1

far from prying eyes in the deep forests of the Tombigbee River Valley near Columbus, Mississippi. Some nights Reggie could still hear the almost feminine shrieks of southern panthers that roamed the area as they passed through their large territory, marking their presence with unsettling screams. Perhaps one lurked out there in the cold at that very moment, Reggie considered. They always unnerved him.

He smiled grimly—*should be celebrating*, he thought. His man had won the Mississippi governor's race, and Reggie had cleared over $1.8 million in 1976. At least that was just what he would report to the IRS. No need to burden them with the cash transactions that he laundered through other business ventures outside his law practice. Reggie lived for the here and now.

He brushed a lock of his golden hair from his eyes, hair that matched his delicate almost feminine features. He pondered the events of the past week. All had not gone well for Reggie, a middle-aged man who frequently danced with his demons. Why was he not content to make money legally like ordinary people? Reggie shook his head and looked blankly into the swirling snow. Snowflakes were orderly things that behaved in predictable ways, unlike his "business." There were some transactions that had been disrupted recently, and he had unsavory people who held him accountable for their merchandise—merchandise that looked much like the fine white powder now building up against the cold sliding glass doors.

The incessant ringing of the phone extricated Reggie from his thoughts.

"Hello," he said, absently.

"Reggie, this is Howard," the Tupelo police detective grumbled in a deep voice.

"Why are you calling me at home on a night like this, you dumb hick?" Reggie asked, as he took another swig of brandy.

"Reggie, the DA has got me boxed in. I'm stuck and can't

move. I'm afraid that our bribe to get him to drop the coke case on your clients won't work. He's got pressure from the state narcs. I can't stop worrying about it—so I called you to share the pain."

"You should know better than to bring up things like that on the phone. Just get another beer from the fridge, watch Dick Clark ring in the New Year, and quit bothering me! Good night," Reggie said as he abruptly hung up.

Out in the whiteness of the storm, a man pale enough to pass through such weather almost undetected watched Reggie's house from a stand of cedar trees just beyond the pool house. He could see Reggie staring into the night, talking on the phone feeling so safe and secure. He observed Reggie much as the lowland panthers watch a rabbit in the snow. That night Reggie was also on the low end of the food chain and the predator who stalked him was one of those unsavory people who settled his debts suddenly and violently. The man rubbed the word "Legion" on his pale arm… for his demons were many.

Though safe from the unseasonable storm that raged outside, Reggie felt ill at ease and knew that he had to make things right or there could be serious repercussions. Some of the people for whom he did favors were criminals but could be reasoned with. Others, the would-be revolutionaries he squired around to left-leaning tea parties, were borderline psychopaths. Ordinary people saw only the usual pitch for utopia and the standard bashing of America. They cheerfully applauded the academic and hypothetical nature of the sermon. Reggie thought that if they could see these guys for who they really were, it would terrify them beyond their worst nightmares.

For some reason Reggie was scared tonight, and the brandy wasn't reassuring him. The more he drank and the harder he peered into the growing whiteness looking for God-knows-what, the fuzzier everything became. He felt very alone. Only Peaches, his beloved poodle barking at his feet, provided comfort. Peaches

3

wanted to go out. Reggie cracked an opening in the sliding glass door and admonished Peaches "Hurry back, baby! Don't freeze, now."

Peaches dashed to his favorite spot behind the pool house sheltered by a thicket of azaleas. Reggie threw another log on the fire, and walked back to watch for Peaches who normally did his business quickly and returned to the house.

Reggie waited and Peaches didn't return. He finally cracked the door a bit and called, "Here Peaches! Come here, boy," but there was no sign of him, only the wail of the storm like some disembodied spirit.

"Here boy. Come here, Peaches! Come to Daddy," Reggie repeated louder and louder. His voice got higher each time and despite the cold wind, little beads of sweat formed on his upper lip.

The snow came down harder seemingly in response to his cries. He could barely see the pool house. Reggie knew he would have to go in search of his little dog, but his heart was beating fast and hard. The brandy gave him enough courage to take down his overcoat and open the door against the swirling wind.

"Peaches? Peaches! Where are you, boy?" Reggie shouted in the loudest voice he could muster. His thoughts turned to the tiny pistol that he had left in the kitchen. He had never been comfortable with guns, but in a burst of sudden insecurity and vulnerability, he wished he had it with him now. The wind mussed his normally carefully coiffed hair, and flakes of snow stung his eyes making visibility almost impossible. However, as he neared the pool house corner, there was no mistaking the growing red stain that marred the purity of the snow near the edge of the pool house. Feeling ill, he fell to his knees beside the butchered body of his precious Peaches lying dead in the shadows of the bushes that his devoted pet had dutifully watered.

Angry and heartbroken—terrified—Reggie turned and

hurled himself in a lurching run for the house. The wind and the snow tore at him as he ran for his life. The tree limbs reached down for him like long arms in the blowing wind. Just as a rabbit thinks he has it made, sharp claws of the predator reach out of the darkness and deny him safe haven. And so it was once again—a pale man, covered in snow, stepped out from behind a tree beside the house and grabbed Reggie from behind with arms both real and strong. Reggie's scream was cut short.

The monster that waited in the night spun him around and pressed a stiletto against his throat. Reggie's eyes went wild when he saw who it was…Fredrick!

Startled snowbirds fluttered from the shelter of their roost, fleeing this madness of man. The snow-covered albino stared down at him through dead, red eyes, so red they appeared to bleed. "Where's my money, Reggie?" he demanded over the howling wind.

"I didn't know that the state narcs were going to screw it up, Freddie. How could I have known?" Reggie pleaded.

"That's what you get paid for. I'm on the move and need my money tonight," the abominable snowman screamed over the roar of the storm.

"Please! I have the money in my bank account—Howard will bring it to you Tuesday morning. You just say where," Reggie whined, oblivious to his sudden incontinence and the trickle that ran down his leg and stained the snow. Steam rose from the crystals between them as gusts whipped the white around Fredrick's face leaving visible only the madness of the monstrous visage before the horrified lawyer.

"You weak little punk…you and your fat cop buddy couldn't protect one deal from the state? The people who fronted me aren't going to wait and I'm not going to wait, but Hell is waiting for you!" the man threatened. A twisted grin passed his lips as he pressed the thick blade of the dagger harder against Reggie's frail throat, and in one swift move slit his throat open from ear to ear. Tiny bursting beads of purple-red lifeblood popped along the trail of the cold steel releasing the sharp metallic smell of fresh blood.

Reggie's look was one of astonishment—how could it end this way? He tried to speak, but it was only a cough and a gurgle as he turned and stumbled, falling silently into the pool. His last thoughts were of crying out to God as his lifeblood pumped out of him and of a scripture his mama had once read to him as a child: "Fear not them which kill the body..."

The splash of his thin body was lost to the roar of the storm. Fascinated, Fredrick stood motionless and watched Reggie's diminishing body slowly sink into a red cloud, eyes fixed in the forever-death stare. Like some modern vampire, he drank in the sight of the rich, red color of the blood pool, calculating a false compensation and cure for his own colorless hair and skin.

"That'll teach you...just like I'll teach that narc, Michael Parker. I'll teach all of you." He knelt and recited his favorite passage from the Satanic Bible: "Cursed are the weak for they shall be blotted out."

He carelessly wiped his blade in the white snow and then trudged off toward the woods. The snow and the wind followed him, filling his footprints—erasing forever any sign that he had ever passed this way. Only blood sacrifices to the dark forces of the evil one remained as the clocks in Reggie's now ownerless home struck midnight in a wormwood harvest.

CHAPTER TWO

"Hope is the feathered thing that perches in our souls."
—Emily Dickinson

Ten years before Reggie's violent passing, such brutality would've seemed unthinkable to Michael Parker, a young adventurer roaming the lush green woods and limpid streams of Parker Grove just south of Tupelo, Mississippi.

Michael explored a patchwork of contoured hills housing tin and timber tornado shelters, fished the sloughs of fertile lowlands for alligator-gars, collected arrowheads from civilizations long gone from those parts, and navigated rustling forest greenery that concealed the silent stares of muscled bobcats and the gobble-gabble of wild turkeys.

Michael's grandparents Eula and his young bride, Pearl, settled Parker Grove at the turn of the 20th century, and endless tales of valor and honor spun by Grandma Pearl about her daddy, Captain A.W. Patterson of the Confederate States of America became a mainstay for Michael and the foundation on which he would build his life.

He and his dog, Brownie, served as a captive but willing

audience of two for Pearl's stage where a bygone era of cotton, Confederates, and courage still ruled, and kernels of an elusive truth waited to be harvested from the old lady in the blue floral bonnet.

One lazy Southern afternoon as they played Pollyanna, Michael said, "Grandma, tell me again how Captain Patterson evaded Union troops and saved his boys."

"Oh yes, Papa was in Company H of Moreland's Cavalry at the Battle of Tishomingo Creek. He came upon the main body of Yankees and as he turned to ride and warn his boys, the Yankees fired on him, a rifle ball passing through his coat. He fell to the ground, crawling for miles through the tall grass to warn our boys in gray. He was promoted to captain. All his boys loved him. So did General Wheeler." As she talked, he could almost hear the sound of cannon fire and feel the ground tremble as generals ordered their troops to charge.

She paused and looked far away as if to heaven and with a break in her voice, she said, "Papa was really something. So tall, six-foot-one, eyes as gray as his uniform."

She blinked away tears that tracked down her furrowed cheeks and finally came back to the present. "Son, you'll find that there are causes worth fighting for…even 'Lost Causes.' Just follow your heart and trust in the Almighty." Michael nodded knowingly at stories he never tired of hearing.

***

He had just passed his eighteenth birthday. The cover of *Time Magazine* asked, "*Is God Dead?*" He read of racial strife, something called LSD and heroin, and boys going off to a place called Vietnam to fight Communism. It seemed contrary to the world he knew and his childhood heroes like Gene Autry, Roy Rogers, and Elliott Ness and *The Untouchables*.

"Honey," Pearl said, handing him a white peppermint stick

ringed in red that she kept for special moments, "none of that stuff has anything to do with us." She was upset that Michael had accepted an offer to go to Washington to work for the FBI. Pearl had watched Efrem Zimbalist, Jr. on the FBI television show and despite assurances that Michael was only going to be a clerk, she couldn't be consoled. Pearl dearly loved the little curly-haired boy who sleepwalked as a child and instinctively had come to her for safety in the midst of bad dreams. She told him that she would one day have to leave him. He protested, but eventually promised that he would never forget her or the boys who gave all they could—those who still lived in the hearts of loved ones where ancient battles yet raged.

A week after graduation, the family took him to Corinth to board a train for Washington. In a tearful farewell the young fledgling left the nest. Sad faces and long embraces transpired as the conductor called, "All aboard." Looking through the window by his seat, his rapid breath fogged the glass as he saw his own reflection and his last fading glimpses of Pearl. He thought he was seeking answers, but all he really wanted was comfort even as he left the solace of family.

Finally arriving at night in the great train station in Washington under the lighted Capitol dome, the hustle and bustle and grandeur were quite overwhelming for a country boy from the Grove in Mississippi—so many cars and people under what seemed the skies of an impersonal and unforgiving city. He felt sick en route to Mrs. Money's boarding house.

The equivalent of two years of college work was crammed into twelve forty-hour weeks of fingerprint training, and he soon graduated and began searching the vast collection of files in the FBI Identification Building for prints with loops and whorls.

He spent summer evenings sitting on the lawn of the U.S. Capitol listening to wonderful free concerts by military bands, and settled into a Methodist church near there. The church had been built where J. Edgar Hoover was born, and one Sunday, Hoover and a pack of very serious-looking agents came for the dedication of a giant stained-glass image of Jesus in a window that seemed to reach heaven itself.

It was then that Michael met and chatted with his *ultimate* boss, a man most career FBI employees had never met. Hoover had kind words for the people of Mississippi, always the consummate "politician" who kept his job through many administrations because of good public relations and incriminating files he retained on the nation's most powerful figures. When asked why he kept Hoover, President Johnson crudely remarked, "It's better to have Edgar inside the tent peeing out, than outside peeing in."

Then there were the parties, too many parties—too many eighteen-year-old kids from America's heartland suddenly on their own in the big city. He heard of the clandestine use of drugs and saw kids losing their innocence. While he shot pool one weekend, a girl walked in dripping wet from being thrown into the pool. Droplets of water rolled down her cheeks and balanced on her upper lip as she stood and watched him. He looked up into the biggest blue gamine eyes as Roy Orbison's *In Dreams* played on the jukebox. He couldn't speak or make his shot. He was captivated.

Michael and Memphis native Dixie Lee Carter became inseparable and innocence was lost, or perhaps discovered—hands clutching hands in darkened theaters where, for brief moments, they were Lara and Yuri in *Dr. Zhivago*. She brought the music that his temporal ears couldn't chart and stirred in him an emotional conflict that clouded his mind and confused his language. He was in love.

Adrift on their silver sea of discovery, the pretty girl gained a hold on him that he hadn't fully understood at the time, but her touch, loving reassurance, and wild ways were powerful. The mere sight of Dixie intoxicated him, and the sounds of her whispering in his ear had taken him to some twilight land where feelings supplanted logic—a place where he was lost without her.

But she eventually grew restless and seemed to need to

scratch an itch from some part of her that was wild and in contrast to the gentleness and innocence she showed him. She had become a soul in torment, and they parted ways for a time.

Nevertheless, with Vietnam and the draft looming, she was at the airport when Michael decided to retreat to his refuge of honeysuckle and cotton in Parker Grove. Dixie clung to him in the terminal, pledging to come home to Memphis to find him. Watching her from the plane, all the bad seemed far away. He could see her face pressed up against the glass at the boarding area window at Washington National, her tears flowing in concert with the driving rain. Their parting seemed a bit like the farewell scene in *Casablanca*—the first time he'd ever felt that someone other than his family might truly miss him.

Finally, with his feet firmly planted on Southern soil, his sights were set on enrolling at Ole Miss. The school had a deserved reputation as a party school, and he often joked with friends that he'd read both books in the school library. The parties did go on, but that was not for him.

He was hungry to learn and worked his way through college—laboring in factories and working as a ditch digger, movie usher, and delivery boy. He was eager to do more with his life, and Ole Miss was a better school than its reputation. The cake was deeper than its frosting of fraternity parties, Miss Americas, and SEC football. All those gritty part-time and summer jobs reinforced his dream and his push for his diploma.

In what spare moments he had, he wrote letters to Dixie Lee in Washington. She gradually opened up to him—revealing what some pop psychologists on public television might have called her "inner child." Dixie showed Michael forbidden places in her psyche which yearned to be set free and burned away by the bright sun of truth.

Sitting in the Grove at Ole Miss under ancient oak trees, he read a letter postmarked Suitland, Maryland—written, he could imagine, in the subdued lighting and seclusion of her

11

suburban apartment long after her roommates had gone to bed—transcriptions from the silent chambers of the heart of a girl laboring in the shadows to illuminate her own darkness.

She began to speak of better days—of mewling chocolate kittens and of swimming as a child on a family vacation near Gulf Shores where a bottlenose dolphin surfaced near her, puffing bubbles through its blowhole, staring at her with sentient eyes and a mermaid smile. Michael closed his eyes and knew that he had just touched the essence of the girl he had fallen in love with. *Come out, come out and stay,* he thought.

The letters were laced with contrition and pledges of unending love—rolling, melodic quatrains of life—but this day, the last letter turned dark and fearful and hinted at a relative, an uncle, and a family reunion long ago. "The big man with close-set eyes and thick hands must have known something about me," she said, "something bad." She said she heard her aunt say it was that wicked child's fault for tempting her husband. The letter ended abruptly, and Michael could see what he thought were tear stains that had fallen in salty droplets to mar the edges of the pale blue stationery in irregular dry pools.

A gray-and-white chickadee came down at just that moment as Michael sat in silence, the distant sound of the campus bell ringing a metallic call to afternoon classes. The tiny bird stared at Michael in beady-eyed curiosity from under its black hood and seemed to bear a message from beyond the temporal with its persistent "dee-dee-dee." Michael thought of all the fledglings that had fallen out of their nests high above all danger in Parker Grove, and how he ran to catch them before they were devoured by the monsters which inhabited the world below their cradles.

Here he was again—running to catch Dixie and whisper, "Read life's warranty again. This isn't how it was meant to be. Replace those defective memories with new ones we can make."

***

In 1968, about the time President Johnson created the Federal Bureau of Narcotics and Dangerous Drugs, the long-missing Dixie Lee showed up from DC. All was well at first. They took in movies at Loew's Palace in Memphis, ate at Leonard's BBQ, and prowled by Graceland late at night hoping to catch Elvis out on a nocturnal motorcycle jaunt.

Michael was excited by her return. Maybe they could finally marry as many thought they would. However, he soon learned that her old itch was still there, and a luckier suitor was to scratch it. They had agreed to date others when they were apart—he in Oxford and she in Memphis—a prescription for disaster.

After a late dinner in Memphis, he was about to tell her that his dog, Brownie, who hated snakes, had been killed by a diamondback when the music she brought stopped. "Michael," she said, "I've come to a decision. You're far away, and I can't depend on you. I've decided I'm going to marry Benjamin. He's here when I need him and has a good future ahead of him." Some insecurity gnawed at her—something he could almost touch, but then it was gone—lost in the lake of regret where Dixie swam alone.

Michael took a deep breath and closed his eyes—there was only the vision of old dead leaves rustling along a wintry forest floor. He felt as if someone had walked across his grave and their sea of love had become a tidal wave of heartbreak.

"Whatever. It's your decision," he said, stunned, wounded, but determined to show no weakness and to offer no pleading of his case.

"That's all you have to say?" she asked, as the water in her eyes made the blue sparkle, reflecting the street lights outside Michael's Mustang. Mascara pooled under her eyes as she bit her lower lip. *Affected? Or innocence aware…?*

"I think you've said it all," he said, words stuck in his throat, a catch of aching goodbye. He started packing his bag to load into his little red 1967 pony in the middle of the night, refusing immaturely to stay one more moment near her vitality and burnished hair.

13

The jukebox in his mind suddenly went silent, as it cued up all the *"She done me wrong"* songs that would now dog him. With news of her marriage ringing in his ears and the feeling of a stabbing pain in his heart, he wished her well and left. A tufted great horned owl, like a dismembered spirit in the dark, called, "Who…who," to him as he left. "Yeah, me, that's who," he answered as he left behind the nurse who gave him medicine that no doctor could prescribe.

He went on a long sabbatical from the serious matters of the heart. Dixie called his grandmother Pearl looking for him once after cancelling her wedding, but he had gone deep undercover by then in a new job and was a hard man to find. Pearl said that Dixie cried, and she told her that she would pass on her message when she saw Michael. Pearl whispered silently to herself—"My boy, my poor boy." She had offered him well-traveled tales and her best peppermint after the breakup, but his wounded heart couldn't be healed—then he was gone in search of dragons to slay.

It's not getting what you want, but wanting what you get, he thought. He doubted that Dixie could ever resolve the two. The picture in her wedding announcement had haunted him with a melancholy that he buried under a mountain of discipline and denial. It was too late—a timeline of events began that would forever change both of their lives.

Michael left Parker Grove for the frontlines of the new drug wars. There would be no more lazy days with Pearl, shelling black-eyed peas, watching *Hopalong Cassidy* on their flickering black-and-white television, no more gatherings around the crackling, distant broadcast of *The Shadow* on the antique RCA radio.

"Who knows what evil lurks in the hearts of men? The Shadow knows!"

CHAPTER THREE

"You are always nearer the divine and the true sources of
your power than you think. The lure of the distant and the difficult
is deceptive. The great opportunity is where you are.
Do not despise your own place and hour. Every place is under the stars,
every place is the center of the world."
—John Burroughs

The new counter-culture sweeping America had become personal and real to Michael when it claimed two high school friends who were dear to him. He had played matchmaker for Ricky, the captain of the basketball team, and Helen, a doe-eyed member of his church. Carrying messages back and forth between them, Ricky eagerly asked him, "What'd she say?"

In a moment of horseplay, he said, "Pocahontas said, 'Speak for yourself, John Smith.'" Ricky flushed red. Mock punching and laughter ensued.

Ricky and Helen had fallen hard for each other. They were the perfect couple—good looks, intelligence, and student union leaders. They had it all, perhaps too much, and in full youthful rebellion, they rejected the small town establishment—but had merely substituted one collective for another. Just as the idealists had embraced Lenin and Marx, only to be slaughtered by Stalin, these rebels would find the new orthodoxy confining in its debauchery and deadly in its recreational toys. They had married, gone off to college, and entered the new no-guilt, free love, "turn on, tune in, drop out" culture promoted by Timothy Leary, the disciple of Aleister Crowley, the 19th-century Satanist and drug addict known as "the beast."

Drugs soon ravaged Ricky, and the marriage failed. He was on a downward, slippery slope that ended one dark night when his "friends" dumped his drug-ravaged body on the front lawn of his parents' home where he died of an overdose as he rolled in the early morning dew and cried out in a purple haze for his mama. Michael wished that he could've been there to save him, but he had seen him in his new incarnation before the end and they were strangers. LSD had made it impossible to communicate as they once had. They no longer spoke the same language.

Gone were games and proms, girls and music, fast cars and milkshakes. Squandered were youth, innocence, and hope. All dead, just like Ricky. Now, just shadow-box figures in stills from dreams—forgotten times and places like Pearl's boys in gray.

* * *

During his last semester at Ole Miss, bantering with tenured leftists, Michael heard about a new state Drug Enforcement Agency being formed in Mississippi and applied for a job. Pearl was appalled, but things were heating up in the fledgling drug wars. Operation Intercept by the Feds had just closed the Mexican border in a poor effort to reduce marijuana smuggling from Mexico, or more likely, a public relations stunt. Too many bankers held a stake in the drug money that buttressed the balance of payments between the U.S. and Mexico.

Every vehicle crossing the Mexican border was given a three-minute search. The farce lasted all of two weeks. Mexico promised all sorts of actions they never delivered, and the drugs kept on coming, but the public was mollified and a giant cottage industry was born to "protect" citizens from themselves.

After Michael's initial application and battery of tests at the MBN (Mississippi Bureau of Narcotics), Mr. John Edward Collins, director of the agency and a bear of a man, promised to hire him when he got his diploma. If Collins had sported a houndstooth hat, he could have passed for Coach Paul "Bear" Bryant of Alabama.

"I'm willing to take an appointment now and finish later," Michael said, a bit too eagerly. The old man pushed back from the table and lowered his reading glasses.

"No, son, that degree will mean more to you than this job in the future," the big man said, with a knowing smile.

"Can you graduate by January, boy?" he asked, raising a skeptical eyebrow and deepening his gravelly voice.

"Why, yes sir, no problem," Michael answered with assurance, the same response if Collins had asked if he could sprout wings and fly.

"Well, you call me then and I'll hire you," he said in his matter-of-fact way as he rose to leave the interview room, his 15EE cowboy boots adding to his 6'5" height.

"No problem, sir. Thank you," Michael said. As he walked away, Michael wondered how he could possibly graduate in one semester when he still needed twenty-five semester hours.

Six exhausting months later, Michael departed the hallowed halls of Ole Miss with his undergraduate degree and a promised job in sight. It had been a time only for work, study and no play— none of the Ole Miss lasses brought the tender love songs, and he saw no "Lara" among them.

Though he'd neglected to get his offer in writing, the director was true to his word and hired him. Shedding his wholesome look and living in conditions totally abhorrent to his obsession with cleanliness was going to be a challenge, but one Michael seized with a vengeance. The new agency was ramping up quickly, and there was little time for training for young men who wouldn't know illegal drugs if they saw them and who were woefully unprepared for the social rules of the day.

Contrary to what some later believed, his generation was not all at Woodstock, and many of his generation were more comfortable with their parents' values than those of the counter-culture they were about to infiltrate.

The Bureau followed national trends. The Drug Abuse Prevention and Control Act regulated manufacture and distribution of controlled drugs and gave police authority for "no-knock" searches. State laws followed as horror stories of drug deaths and depravity abounded in the press. The marketing campaign was on, and he remembered the director's first speech in which he said, "Stopping the flow of drugs will be like trying to dam up the Mississippi River with a shovel." The old man whispered under his breath… "But, at what cost?"

* * *

The damp wind ruffled Michael's long hair as he walked the last block to the little duplex in Hattiesburg. His "hip" looks belied the fact that he had ever spent time in Washington or at prim and proper Ole Miss. No need now for his new suit, a graduation indulgence he couldn't afford, but one that had beckoned to him from the display window at Reed's in Tupelo. It was almost Christmas, 1970, and the loud music that issued from the little house was not exactly "Jingle Bells." More likely the University of Southern Mississippi hosts running lines of coke were interested in "Let it Snow, Let It Snow, Let It Snow."

He pushed his way through the unlocked door and soon spotted a young, red-haired beauty through the haze of marijuana smoke. Tammy Price, whom he met by chance at the student union, had become indispensable to a microcosm of the wider war on illegal drugs. She began unwittingly to employ her charm and good standing within the local drug scene to introduce a young undercover agent to a gathering of several drug dealers at a community flophouse.

If my friends could see me now, here in this den of iniquity, a marijuana smoke-filled room with mattresses in every corner, he thought. It reminded him of the opium dens described so well in the Sherlock Holmes novels he was so fond of. Young couples snorted cocaine, smoked joints, dropped pills or clung to their bongs to get high and then engage in casual sex. Somewhere in the background someone played an album by Cheech and Chong, and later, Jimi Hendrix sang about the allure of his purple haze. Partners changed regularly as did the "drugs of choice." He wondered if this was ground zero in the conflict theory that his sociology professors and Karl Marx spoke of. It seemed a vision of hell but he thought, *The game's afoot, Watson.*

Strobe lights flashed to the pounding guitar of Hendrix, and the devotees were a mile high. Tammy swept her long red hair back, clapped her hands, and shouted above the din, "Hey, everyone, this is my friend Jim. He's cool, and wants to get some good stuff for a party he's having."

Blank stares through dilated pupils followed her words as best they could. Swaying back and forth, a tall, bald young man named Skin with glassy eyes sauntered up and surveyed "Jim" up and down. Satisfied, he said, "Man, if Tammy says you're cool, then you're cool."

"Nice to meet you, man," Michael said, as Skin teetered at the edge of incoherence.

"Well, what do you want for this here party of yours?" Skin asked directly.

"Man, I'm looking for some good Acapulco Gold reefer, some acid, and some ludes, if I can score the stuff." Michael thought, *Well, go for broke.*

Skin scratched at a scab on his pimply face as he yelled across the room at a scruffy kid with a mop of unkempt, rust-colored hair. "Hey, Carl!"

"What, man?" Carl muttered. His eyes were already rolled up into his head and his voice slurred.

"You still got that orange acid for sale?" Skin inquired. "Tammy and her friend Jim need some."

"Reaching into his green army field jacket, Carl pulled out a bag of orange tabs and said, "Yeah, I got 'um. How many you want?"

"Depends. How much per pop?" Michael asked, thinking of conserving his supply of cash and careful not to throw around taxpayer money.

"Fifteen dollars a tab," Carl answered, seeming more focused as Michael placed a wad of money on the table before them.

"I'll take ten then, man," Michael said, counting out the wrinkled green bills.

An anemic-looking creep with long, greasy hair strode up to Tammy and put a bony hand on her bare shoulder. She removed the unwanted hand, but smiled and said, "Bobby, you can give Jim a deal on that primo gold weed you got, can't you, baby?"

"Yeah, baby, you know I'd do anything for you, my pretty girl," Bobby replied with a hint of some unlikely intimacy between the two. He leaned over and made a show of opening a duffel bag containing one-ounce bags of marijuana. Michael saw movement where his hair was parted in the middle that suggested fleas.

"Cool! How much you need, Jim?" she asked.

"Man, if I can afford it, maybe six of those baggies," Michael said.

"Just for Tammy, I'll let you have them for twenty-five dollars—no, twenty dollars an ounce," he said through a haze.

"You're so sweet, Bobby," Tammy said in an expert playing of these, her subjects, by the princess of this court.

"I'll take 'um," Michael said, and handed him $120 in cash.

"Jim, honey, I've been checking around and there ain't no ludes here tonight, but there's some speed and Dilaudid," Tammy said. "It's high though, sugar."

"How much are they? I'm running on fumes here. My friends only gave me so much money to cop party refreshments," Michael said, thinking he would like to buy the potent narcotic Dilaudid.

"Danny will sell you the speed at ten dollars a hit, but the Dilaudid will be fifty dollars a hit," she said.

"I can cover ten hits of speed and two of the big downers, and then I'm tapped out," Michael said.

She smiled and led Michael across the room to a scruffy, bearded character named Danny. The pubescent girl with him appeared barely conscious and in the throes of a deep, drug induced stupor. "This is my friend, Jim. He wants ten hits of speed and two of the big D."

"Yeah, okay, man, nice to meet you," Danny said, with an outstretched hand that Michael could see needed soap and water.

"Same here, man," Michael said, as he gritted his teeth, clasped Danny's hand, and then slid into the interlocking thumb-shake so popular.

"Thanks," Michael managed, as he handed the cash to Danny and took the illegal pills. *Are these wretched people the REAL bad guys,* he wondered, *or victims?* Somewhere, the real enemy waited, but he wasn't sure it was here.

"We need to go now. I got to get back to my dorm before I'm locked out," Tammy said.

They made small talk on the way back to the dorm, and she told him that some of her friends had been arrested for just trying to "relax" their baby. He knew where she was going with that one right away. One of the bureau's undercover agents had witnessed a couple "shotgun" their infant baby in her crib. They drew in as

21

much marijuana smoke as they could hold in their lungs, and held it. They then cupped their hands over the baby's face and blew concentrated levels of the drug into the baby's lungs. The couple was arrested, and the baby was taken from them.

Just then the Holiday Inn came up on the right. She looked longingly at Michael, batted her long lashes, and said, "Jim, you know…you don't have to take me back to the dorm if you don't want to."

He was caught off guard and struggled for a response. He couldn't lose this contact. Some undercover agents pleaded a case of some social disease in such situations. One female drug dealer, legendary in the business, had an unorthodox insurance policy. She wouldn't sell to anyone who didn't sleep with her first. Part madam, part drug dealer, and thoroughly New Age businesswoman, Mae was unique and hard to get at. The heavyset woman could've been the reincarnation of the miners' best friend in the gold rush days, supplying everything lonely miners wanted. Instead of cheap liquor, she offered expensive cocaine to lift the spirits. One agent had pleaded a bad case of venereal disease, but she just looked at him in true Mae style and said, "That's okay honey, cause I do, too." He made a quick retreat from Mae and all she had to offer. The last thing he heard was the hearty cackle of the madam who had flushed out another government boy.

Others just didn't refuse at all. Some thought the ends justified the means, and others simply couldn't resist the allure of free love. It would come back to haunt them in court cases. Neither academy instructors nor university professors had prepared their students and trainees with an understanding of the new subculture, where casual sex seemed to be as common as a handshake. All these boys who'd once felt lucky for a quick kiss at the end of a date, now groped along in the dark passages of this new world where minefields were just one false step away.

A breathless Tammy awaited his acceptance of an offer none had ever refused. Usually fast on his feet, he replied, "I'm flattered, but I want our relationship to be based on more than the physical. I respect you too much." The moment he said it, he cursed himself for its lameness.

Tammy looked at him as if he were an alien who had just beamed into the car. She said with wide-eyed amazement, "You're the first man to ever say that to me!"

"Well, that's just how I feel," he said, looking at her pale skin, her large, prominent eyes, and almost waist-length red hair. He thought that she was no doubt telling the truth.

"That's so sweet. You're wonderful, Jim."

He, now the agent of government paternalism, felt ill at ease with her obvious admiration, but she remained a prolific avenue of introductions. He bought from some thirty dealers, mostly small-time, but some trafficked heavily in LSD and other drugs dangerous to naïve students. Still, it began to nag at him when courts dispensed heavy sentences to placate an anxious public. *Are these the ones we want to take up prison cells, at least for so long?* he wondered. Some just needed rehab. All needed a Savior, and he knew that was not the state.

Guilt flowed through him as he walked Tammy to the door of her dorm and it wasn't lessened when she stood on tiptoes to peck him on the cheek. She seemed like a little girl again for that moment, except for her glassy eyes dilated by the pills of the night—one who might be capable of finding her way back to reclaim a life outside the commune where she sought identity and approval. He had to remind himself that she was a player, not some wounded bird he had found as a softhearted kid in Parker Grove. She would've burned him to the ground if she had suspected for one moment who he really was and never looked back. More conflict.

At least when the day of reckoning came, he would know that he hadn't slept with her. Probably didn't matter, though—sex was not of any real significance for Tammy. He laughed to himself as he realized what a relic he was—a dinosaur oblivious to the meteor burning brightly overhead and the extinction it brought. He remained the child of Puritan ancestors with a belief that such joining should be more than casual and remain an act between two people who love each other. Too much the idealist—a real man never passed up a good romp in the hay with a warm and willing body, agents told him. He envied his peers at times, but more often, pitied them. He knew that they would be lined up at his funeral to say how pure he had been, but whisper, "Sap" beneath their breath as they left the chapel.

After he left Tammy at the dorm and returned to his motel room, he looked at himself in the faded mirror for a long time. "Who are you," he asked, "Jim or Michael?"

He washed his hands until they were raw, wrote his reports, preserved his chain of evidence, and headed home from a lonely life on the road to Tupelo for the holidays. He knew that these low-level dealers weren't where the real action was, but for now he was a rookie and learning, he rationalized. Eventually they'd unbundle the complicated chain of smuggling, distribution, and corruption and strike at the heart of the drug problem. In the meantime, he would stay out of trouble and worry about all of that tomorrow as Miss Scarlet said.

Others wouldn't, though, he thought. He knew many agents who weren't dodging the arrows of temptation that eroded their core, putting them at risk of losing touch with who they were forever. Many were good boys, fresh from college. They hadn't sown any wild oats, and here they were—dropped in the middle of the wildest oats anyone could imagine. They were at a buffet table gorging on the gluttony of forbidden pleasures until there was nothing left of who they once were.

Some discovered too late that they were dessert. Some would die. Some would go to jail. It was no one's fault. It was everyone's fault.

It never seemed so complicated in Pearl's good ole days.

CHAPTER FOUR

"They set their mouth against the heavens,
and their tongue walketh through the earth. "
—Psalm 73:9

The strains of "Auld Lang Syne" still lingered in the frigid air. Evidence of revelers seeking the symbolism of renewal and second chances littered the streets of the fruited plains of Mississippi.

Christmas had come and gone, and a blustery New Year's Day, 1971, found Michael catching a quick nap after a long night on mean streets. The cold wind whipped the southern pines outside his tiny Jackson apartment as gas heater flames licked the top of the grates in a vain attempt to heat the drafty old abode. The leaks around his ill-fitting windows whistled and moaned with the arctic gusts.

He planned to steal enough rest to watch Ole Miss take on Auburn in the Gator Bowl later that day. Katie the Siamese cat slept peacefully on his chest. He tossed fitfully but soon found himself back in school in another of his vivid dreams. When he was fifteen, the school had a boxing club. There were official bouts and unsanctioned "pickups" on lunch breaks. The latter often got rough. He was in junior high and the Tupelo High in-crowd loved to watch these free-for-all fights for their amusement.

The contest that he relived in his dream drew a large crowd. It was such an obvious mismatch that a slaughter was assured. They'd matched young Michael, most courteous in "who's who", against Bobby Moreland, a street thug with a rap sheet, who was the odds-on favorite to whip the stuffing out of the choirboy. Bobby pranced around the ring soaking up the adulation of the boxing patrons who demanded a sound beating of this odd shy boy, no quarter given. Michael didn't have one supporter there that day, but he knew what his opponent didn't—they were using Bobby, a vehicle for their sport and voyeurism. Unlike Michael, he was desperate for their approval.

"Bah-bee, Bah-bee," the crowd chanted.

Bobby danced over to Michael and said, "I'm going to whip your butt, boy."

The money men laid odds and collected bets—fistfuls of green, all against Michael. The bell rang and Bobby came out swinging wildly to the cheers of the crowd, determined to end it quickly. Bobby was a street-fighter and a knife-wielder but not a boxer. Chin tucked, Michael ducked under wild haymaker swings, hands close to his head to deflect glancing blows. Several more of the ill-advised, looping lurches left the big boy off balance and exposed. Then Michael pushed up with his legs and upper body to deliver a vicious left uppercut that snapped Bah-bee's head back, followed by a hard right hook to his left jaw that turned him completely around. After that there was a flurry of unanswered blows. As reality hushed the crowd, brokers scurried to cover their wagers from disbelieving onlookers with blank faces.

Michael awoke with a start, fists still clenched. How long had he slept? The television blared in the corner of the darkened room and an Auburn player was running down the field with the football. Ole Miss was taking its own licking and the Auburn fans were howling for their team. Chanting as fickle fans had so long ago when the young hoodlum was down on his back and totally defeated. "My-cul, My-cul," they'd cried. However, Bobby was no gladiator like the defeated Ole Miss boys. He was destined to be on the wrong side of the law for his entire life. He'd never be a free man or live in a home where a kind old lady would give him peppermint sticks that would light up his eyes in innocent anticipation.

Michael felt that the dream was born of his recent brushes with an alien culture—he could see analogies between the Bobby of then and the drug culture of today. Both flailed wildly on their path to destruction. Lying to the girl still bothered him too, though he knew it was always impossible to do good without also doing some harm, and doing nothing was most harmful—wasn't it?

There would always be dreadful decisions to make, but he felt that his fierce independence born early in his life would sustain him in the choppy waters ahead as he sought the elusive high ground between what was and what was to be. He naively tried to frame it all as a subjective right versus wrong contest, but it was an elusive target—a faceless, unfaithful paradigm as he passed through the looking glass like Alice in Wonderland and found that up was down and down was up.

All of that seemed "long ago and far away" as he and Katie reclined in his favorite chair before the black-and-white television screen. The sleek feline peered into his eyes intently, which meant she wanted a treat. He rose from his chair, rubbing granular eyelids as Ole Miss crossed the goal line for the last time in the fourth quarter—too little, too late. His ruminations were interrupted by the ringing of the black rotary-dial telephone. He hesitated, but caught it on the third ring.

"Michael, this is Harry," said Harry Johnson, the scourge of his life then. Pulling back the receiver from offended ears, he recognized his acting supervisor's nasal twang at once. There was no formal structure in place yet since the agency was so new, and Harry was an early hire who had just inherited an acting role, an unlikely and untenable one at best. He didn't like Michael, viewing him as someone who thought too much, which troubles people who don't. The feeling was mutual, and Harry's voice, which sounded as if he had snorted helium combined with his swaggering macho pose, didn't help.

"We need you downtown at the Capitol tomorrow," he said in his nasal twang and a poor imitation of authority.

"I have reports to write and evidence to deliver to the lab, Harry," Michael replied with barely concealed mischief in his voice.

"Well, all that'll have to wait. There's going to be a big anti-war rally down here tomorrow and we're going to infiltrate it."

"I thought that was the FBI's job. Why are we watching political demonstrators?" he asked, partly to irritate the pompous Harry but genuinely puzzled also.

"Because the FBI asked us to," Harry snapped, muttering blasphemies. "This is national security…Commies, boy!" Michael had to pull the receiver back again from his ear at the shrill piercing notes of the strutting martinet.

After a deep sigh, Harry said, "Because anti-war rallies are riddled with drugs and drug dealers, and every radical from five states will be here."

"It seems high exposure for us as undercover operatives. They'll be looking for the Feds and some covers may get blown," Michael offered, uneasy at being used to watching Americans protest. Captain Patterson's blood still flowed in his veins.

"Just be here by eleven in the morning to get your orders," Harry snapped.

"Well, brother, I'll be there with bells on and flowers in my hair," Michael quipped as he tweaked his nemesis.

"Wear your beads, peace symbols and stuff, college boy. Peace and love," Harry said as he slammed down the receiver.

Michael laughed and placed a call to his neighbors who checked on Katie in his absence.

* * *

Nearing the Capitol building, Michael thought about the anti-war rally and the war that dragged on so far away. He had once supported the war and still supported the troops, but he was no longer sure about this endless conflict. He had lost friends to the war on the field of battle, and would lose more in a slow death in the aftermath of a war poorly prosecuted by politicians who lacked resolve, the key element of old men who send young men into harm's way.

He was a student of history and armed conflict and knew that politicians couldn't manage battles from afar. When they restricted their generals and their troops to imaginary borders and safe havens for the enemy, it was only a matter of time, Michael felt, before defeat looked you in the face.

Michael never imagined himself at an anti-war rally, and yet here he was, and the crowd was huge. This intrusion and surveillance of citizens assembling for political protest was still a burr under his saddle. Parking was at a premium, and vans painted in psychedelic colors seemed to be everywhere. The boys had longer hair than the girls. Bright red and blue balloons with peace symbols filled the air. A bare-foot girl with flowers in her hair danced by him blowing bubbles with her wand. Old military jackets and ponchos and beads seemed to be in—no mini-skirts in this crowd.

Cars covered in banners expressing anti-war, anti-American sentiments were all around the Capitol. He'd never seen anything like it. Protest was good, he thought, but polite, genteel people from the South didn't take to the streets. It just wasn't done—*was it?* The twelve out-of-state tags bore evidence to the makeup of most of the crowd. He finally parked and wandered through the crowd, attempting a cosmetic assimilation.

29

A circus atmosphere permeated the scene. Tents and tables were erected by every left-wing organization in the country. Young organizers sporting black armbands and megaphones marched to and fro barking commands. The Capitol police scurried about doing their best to maintain order. It was enigmatic to see those who hated capitalism hawking Ho Chi Minh T-shirts and vendors selling "peace melons" from the back of gaudily-painted pickup trucks. Those who espoused a buffet-style religion were present as well, offering a designer deity made in man's image along with hybrid versions of peace symbols and crucifixes.

"Come! Sample my wares," Brother Thomas brayed. "Pray to Mother Earth, to the Zodiac, the Zen masters, and to a God who doesn't judge you. Embrace the divine through organic mushrooms."

New Age entrepreneurs selling roach clips, pipes, rolling paper, beads, and sandals almost overwhelmed the protest itself. This was a parallel universe, and the smell of incense and lunacy wafted on the uncommonly warm afternoon breeze. Was it real or were all the diverse players merely pawns of those who had financed both sides of armed conflicts throughout history? Did it matter? Was it just an illusion?

Michael was both repulsed and fascinated, but Harry was right about the presence of drug traffickers. They were as thick as flies and mingled with the often-radical SDS (Students for a Democratic Society) and their offspring, the truly radical Weathermen with their homemade bombs for peace. Michael saw no middle-class people there, no homemakers, and no college professors. This was a gathering of the prime hive of the counter-culture collective. Drugs and politics were inseparable. One seemed to be a badge of recognition and honor to the other. He felt that he was peering into the abyss.

Historical consequences lurked behind every symbol and would last far beyond the moment. A mutant virus was taking hold all across America, he thought. Here was the germination of an alternative to an establishment that surely needed change, but not this revolution that would leave so many innocents in its wake. They were unleashing a plague upon the land, though most of these lost lambs in their "summers of love" didn't have a clue.

A scraggly, young, brown-haired female organizer with a headband spied him.

"You don't have a sign!" Her voice was like chalk on a board.

"No, got one for me?" he asked.

"Yes, your group leader should've handled this," the exasperated little secretary for the communes of the disenchanted said.

"What university do you represent?" she asked, looking at her list.

"Uh...Ole Miss," he said.

"Groovy, man. You're the first we've ever had from that school," she said, beaming. Remembering the frat rats and sorority sisters of Ole Miss, he had no doubt that was true.

"Who do you want to be against?" she asked with her prominent upside-down peace symbol defiling the American flag.

"Well, who do you have left?" he asked the glowing but befuddled young girl.

"You can protest corporate giants, organized religion, the military industrial complex, or the President," she said.

"Oh, give me the corporations. Everyone is protesting Nixon. I just saw a picture of him choking the dove of peace," Michael said with righteous indignation.

"Good choice. They're making money off the war and dead soldiers when they're the war criminals," she declared with heartfelt conviction.

He saw his fellow agents there who had also been given instructions to document known drug dealers and their associates, and if given a chance, to infiltrate drug circles through the anti-

31

war stage. He also saw those he figured were FBI agents trying to appear as street people and not quite making it. He noticed a group walking with a camera, and they didn't look local, nor were they the police. As Michael feared, some of these militant anti-war leaders were working counter-intelligence, trying to document government agents of all stripes to put their photos in underground newspapers.

A large red banner was unfurled before the mass of marchers. North Vietnam flags were clutched in the hands of the confused. Everyone finally assembled and marched down Capitol Street in a scene straight out of *Dr. Zhivago*—just before the dragoons of the czar charged the crowd. Michael's own mother wouldn't have recognized him—unshaven, long hair, army jacket, headband, and peace symbol—carrying his sign condemning ITT. The protestors were loud, and the onlookers waving a sea of American flags were equally vocal.

As they passed a young mother with her children, she shouted through some missing front teeth, "You dirty, little hippie Communist." He wanted to tell her, "No, it's just Michael, the quintessential boy next door," but he smiled and flashed the peace symbol. He instinctively thought of an old tune the British played when they surrendered at Yorktown, "The World Turned Upside Down." It was all too convenient—good vs. evil, right vs. left. All this was lost on the woman who shook her fist at him framed by a face full of hate.

As the rally was breaking up, one of his fellow agents became entangled in an altercation with the national anti-war people. Their leader, wearing dark shades against colorless hair, was a pale but intelligent-looking young man who projected a coldness that could be felt far away. Michael moved closer. The local crowd was dispersing and oblivious to this unfolding drama.

He heard his unconvincing friend protest, "Hey, man, I don't care who said they thought I looked like a narc. I'm just a former vet here trying to help. Know where I'm coming from?" At that, Agent Randall Gibbs turned and started down a side street as the camera team approached.

The leader dispatched two bearded men with black armbands along with a photographer. "Wait up, pig!" one said, and when he did, Randall looked back. At that moment the camera came up, but Michael thrust his sign in front of the camera and spoiled his shot. The larger of the two arm banded agents of peace and love turned as Randall scurried away.

"What're you doing?" the bearded goliath asked.

"Peace, brother! Just wanted to get my message on the nightly news," Michael answered cheerfully, trying to move along.

"We're not the news, smart guy," the big guy said through gritted teeth, his black eyes growing darker by the second.

Michael saw him flush red with anger as he stepped in closer with clenched fists and tensed muscles in his neck. Michael felt that he'd just run out of charm as the first big ham-like right fist cocked and came his way like a missile. This was a surreal trip back to his boxing days, but it was for real. If it hit him solid, he knew he was a goner. He turned his head to the left, chin tucked, hands around his head, but he still felt the glancing blow off the side and back of his head. It was enough to make stars explode around him, but also enough to make the big guy cocky and careless.

He came in again with a hard left cross designed for a quick finish, but Michael moved and caught a much diminished part of the blow on his right shoulder, which was enough to make his arm feel partially numb. The big man came again with a wide, heavy right hook punctuated by a grunt and muttered obscenities. Michael managed to sidestep it and found him open.

The man's jaw looked like the rock of Gibraltar, and there were no gloves for this match. From a semi-crouching position Michael launched a strong left hook at his paunchy gut, trying to drive all the way through the target to his spine. The big man let out a whoosh of air and moaned as he staggered and turned slightly to his right.

Michael followed with a hard right hook aimed at the man's left kidney, and down he went on his knees, moaning, "Oh man, I'm hurt bad. You hurt me bad."

He stepped back and no one seemed to know what to do. "Enough!" their hueless leader shouted. No more photos were taken and as they passed, Michael said, "Sorry, man. I don't know what his problem is." The man said nothing, but lowered his sunglasses revealing ice-cold crimson eyes framed by ghostly white skin. The eyes seemed to look right through Michael. He felt pure evil as those eyes followed him into the crowd. As Michael faded into the mass of dispersing protestors, he looked back, and the man was still watching as a predator watches the meal that got away. He knew somehow that he had made a serious enemy…that this might be the *real* enemy.

He saw the man later that year on television in an anti-war rally at the Washington Mall that grew violent. *Couldn't forget that face,* he thought. The man that the rally organizer introduced as Fredrick had a sick smile as he talked to his brothers and sisters in the crowd of high marijuana THC levels and low IQs. Michael saw past the fake smile and looked into those eyes filled with hate and determination, like something coughed up from the bowels of hell. He considered morosely that the guy fit in well in Washington. He might even make a good Congressman.

CHAPTER FIVE

"On rough nights, I go sometimes to the oak of Wotan in the still garden, to make a pact with dark forces...when an opponent declares: I will not come over to your side. I will calmly say, 'Your child belongs to us already. What are you? You will pass on. Your descendants, however, now stand in the new camp. In a short time they will know nothing else but this new community.'"
—Adolf Hitler

Fredrick, a transient sojourner in the murky world of drugs, politics, and geopolitical intrigue, sat motionless in the dingy flophouse room that now passed for home. The room was darkened to accommodate his sensitive pink irises and deep-red pupils. His milky white skin was translucent in the faded light. The crowds from Jackson were gone and the brash pig interloper now only a minor irritation.

He was lonely, barely breathing and mesmerized, his rapt attention focused on the far corner of the ceiling. There a green fly hovered ever closer to a wispy, cotton-like but deadly spider web. Sitting in the recesses of the silken trap she had spun was a dark arachnid patiently waiting for her prey to draw near.

Fredrick watched as the fly finally buzzed too close to the web of death. The sticky silk mesh grabbed the winged diptera, and even though he frantically buzzed and struggled, the hapless housefly was about to be turned into spider food as the frenzy of his death throes waned.

Fredrick's pulse rate soared as he watched with anticipation, spittle dripping from the corner of his mouth. Finally, with the housefly encased in the web, the black widow rushed forward to sink fangs of poison into her victim instantly paralyzing him—pretty tame really for the venomous predator that ate her lover just yesterday after mating.

Fredrick, often confined indoors due to his pigmentation, had been fascinated since he was a child with such life-and-death drama, the gruesome dance between predator and prey. It was primal to him, suggestive of his hunger for and obsession with death and destruction that emanated from the voices he'd heard for as long as he could remember. In his desperation, he once sought to silence the maddening chorus of cries with offerings of the macabre, but eventually surrendered in obedience to his constant and unseen companions.

When he was a young teen with a genius level IQ, psychiatrists told his mother Clarice, a well-bred and affluent woman from Memphis, that they feared her son was schizophrenic. Fredrick laughed. He was not insane. Why, he was the only sane man in an insane world he reckoned, and the only shrink he believed in was his fellow traveler on the dark path, Sigmund Freud, who led him to *Faust* and *The Fatal Sign*.

No, he thought as he watched the end of the fly, he only sought to please the primary voice in his head that he called "Lou, the illuminous one." All the other voices in his chorus were the minions, the so-called fallen angels, who served their Prince as he did. He regarded himself as Lou's chief of staff leading an army—the real army of young converts to sweep those who opposed his

Master into a lake of fire. Some days he fancied that he was Vlad the Impaler come to life as Dracula to seduce the weak in the Lamb's flock to take their blood before they could be covered by His.

The death thrust he witnessed was always rewarding, although over time, he built tolerance like an addict and needed more and more to sustain his rush and to satisfy and quiet the voice of the one he often prayed to as Mephistopheles. He graduated to helpless reptiles, then to dogs and cats as objects of his sadism and satanic rituals, and finally to humans, whom he considered expendable parasites. The progression was undeniable—to taunt, belittle, malign, deprive, hurt, punch, strike, wound, cut, and finally to kill for the honor of his Prince, and to defy the one whom Fredrick believed was the real devil…the one the world called God and His Trinity.

Through his dalliance with the anti-war groups in the 1960s as he searched for converts, Fredrick's brilliance and psychopathic qualities attracted earthly recruiters seeking to enlist him in temporal struggles.

The Communists reported to superiors that they could use him because he had no conscience and could kill without question or remorse. They were also impressed with his ability to cite passages from Marx's *Das Capital* never knowing it was not political for Fredrick but just the ode to Lou that had inspired Marx who was angry with God and wished "to be equal to the Creator."

The CIA recruited him to attack Western institutions in a Machiavellian plan to generate anger on the right and support for the war. They offered to fund him through their deep pockets, not from taxpayer funds, but from proceeds of the lucrative drug smuggling they operated through their gunrunning mercenaries. They also offered passports to hostile regimes where ordinary Americans could not go.

Their familiar refrain to superiors? He could be very useful because he had no conscience and could kill without question or remorse.

Fredrick considered both camps as fools, pawns in the game directed from inside his head, the only reality he recognized. He would use them all, attack all institutions of man to seek, kill, and destroy, and in the ensuing chaos his netherworld would ascend and triumph over this sentimental love professed by Jesus Christ— something only a mind without the true messiah could create or believe.

Once an object of pity, the brooding and mentally-ill young patrician had now morphed into a dangerous, volatile, and lethal man who fancied himself the seed of Friedrich Nietzsche and the superman come for the transvaluation of all values. He liked to say that Friedrich was his namesake, but in fact, Clarice had named him for an ancestral minister.

Undaunted, he celebrated the spider's kill and repeatedly cited Nietzsche's words: *"What is evil? – whatever springs from weakness. What is happiness? – the feeling that power increases. What is more harmful than any vice? – practical sympathy for the botched and weak – Christianity."*

He couldn't acknowledge that his role models and earlier disciples of darkness and madness had suffered tragic endings. Nietzsche ended up in an insane asylum, unable to speak for years except to recite Bible verses learned as a child. Voltaire died in misery, Hitler took his life in his bunker, and Aleister "the beast" Crowley's last words were, "I am perplexed." In the end, Marx, who had written in anger about God, called his own writings senseless rubbish and human excrement. Freud died in pain, obsessed with a story of a man who had sold his soul to the devil but lost the very thing which he damned himself for.

Fredrick could see the matrix but believed that he, unlike the fly that was now nearly consumed, wasn't caught in its web. The devil was at his side, whispering in his ear a message that only the tormented can hear.

Fredrick sighed as the spider, appetite satisfied, scurried back to her corner—the dance of death about to begin again.

How many would have to die to placate the voices that spoke incessantly to the fevered brain of this brilliant, but quite mad, young man from Memphis?

CHAPTER SIX

"A man should stop his ears against paralyzing terror and run
the race that is set before him with a single mind."
—Robert Louis Stevenson

Four black vultures circled overhead on layers of searing thermal updrafts searching for the dead or dying. Beneath them a bright-yellow car crawled along momentarily disrupting the buzzards' search for a meal and their mission to cleanse the earth of putrid carrion. The drive down the dusty rural road hadn't been pleasant, but finally the shotgun house appeared before Michael, shimmering in the Mississippi heat.

The hashish dealer sat sweating on his makeshift throne in his country home near Starkville surrounded by third-rate bodyguards, all dipping into their product and high as kites in the cloudless sky. They yelled at a hapless, malnourished hippie girl who waited on them. Bruce Ray Adams, an obese bearded man with a large penguin gut, stacked compressed bricks of hash as Michael counted out the money for the buy. The blocks of dope were like Fort Knox gold.

In between sales, Bruce and his small army of long hair and

poor hygiene sat on the front porch where they smoked dope and drank slugs of Jack Daniels from the bottle. All were armed and amused themselves by shooting snakes and other unlucky creatures that happened to venture by. *Pow!* "Got another 'un, Jimmy boy!"

"I hate snakes," Bruce Ray said. It was a surreal moment in time and a snapshot from an opera of insanity that Michael had become all too familiar with.

Michael thought briefly of Brownie and snakes, but remained silent.

This would be another quick buy and a productive day for an undercover agent. Michael had been summoned back to Jackson for special assignment, but had stopped for one last dance around a floor littered with white dust and green leaves of intoxication. Agents were still working solo as the Bureau built up the force and trained new agents, but being the lone wolf he was, he liked it like that.

On the other hand, he was ready to get back to headquarters and be debriefed. Things had gotten a little rough around the edges lately. After the march in Jackson, the nebulous alliance between revolutionaries and drug dealers had become startlingly good at disseminating information on how agents operated and who they were in real life. Their intelligence reports began to dog the agents like a bad rash. They had to improvise their looks and methods of operation to remain effective and out of harm's way.

He had just survived an encounter at Mississippi State University with a known dealer coming out of a Starkville movie theater. The dealer turned on him in front of a group of users and other dealers while he was looking for a buy. Clyde T, who looked like a poor man's Bob Dylan, pushed up against Michael and challenged him eye-to-eye.

"I think you're that narc that everyone's talking about," he bellowed. Startled, wide-eyed movie patrons exiting the feature scurried rapidly away sensing trouble. The distinct mark of his aversion to baths was all too evident as he said, "Yeah, go ahead and deny it, Mr. Narc."

"That's right, Clyde," Michael said with feigned surrender. "You're absolutely right. I drove up here from Jackson especially to bust you!"

There was a long pause. The onlookers remained deadly silent, but Clyde burst out laughing, slapping Michael on the back. "That's the one thing you could've said to make me believe you're not that narc. No narc would have the nerve to say that."

Another bullet dodged, but for how long? He needed to take a breather, perhaps get a new car, a new look, but he would make one last run at the big hash dealer who lived out in the country near Louisville. It was on his way to HQ.

As Michael counted aloud to Bruce Ray, "Six hundred dollars, seven hundred, eight hundred..." Bruce interrupted his would-be buyer with a loud belch, followed by a recitation of the latest blasts from the grapevine.

"Oh man, I need to warn you about this pig that's making trouble for us all over the state. He's taking down some good people," Bruce Ray said, slurring his words, tobacco juice staining his beard.

Michael resumed counting as Bruce Ray fumbled around. "Where's that flyer we got last night?"

"Oh, here it is," he said, opening the bible of the anti-establishment echelon.

It was an underground newspaper with an odd logo of a raised fist holding an upside-down American flag. "Man, it says here that his name is *Michael Parker.*"

Michael caught his breath and almost lost count. "Got any pictures of him?" he asked too casually.

"No, man, but we got a good description of him. It says he is about six-foot-two, hundred ninety, long brown hair, and mustache. He was last seen driving a Chevy Impala, yellow with black racing stripes," Bruce said describing the very car sitting in front of his porch just over Michael's left shoulder. Fortunately, the dealer was too addled to know what he was looking at.

"Hey, man, we're gonna kill that narc if we find him," Bruce Ray said through the haze of his drug stupor. All present nodded in enthusiastic agreement, clutching their pistols as a huge brown water bug scurried across the floor hugging a stray breadcrumb.

"Not if I find him first," Michael said with a grin.

"You're too right on," Bruce said, laughing like a hyena.

"Thanks for the information. I'll be on guard."

The hippie girl was busy rolling fresh joints for the crew. Prominent bruises were evident under her torpid eyes and on her bony shoulders. The track marks of needle use discolored the veins of her arms.

He knew it was time to leave, but he'd noticed a large stock of weapons in the little farmhouse when he had used the bathroom. In the back bedroom Michael saw crates full of what looked to be thousands of rounds of heavy weapon ammo and a box marked hand grenades.

"Bruce Ray, what's with all the heavy artillery? Are you going to war?"

"No, man, just holding some stuff for some of those political freaks that flop here now and then," he said with frothy dismissal.

"Are you political, man?"

"Nah, it's just business," Bruce stammered. "I don't even like those freaks, especially Fredrick, the one with the dead eyes. We call him the Anti-Christ."

Michael looked at him, and remembered the anti-war rally encounter with the "Ice Man," as Clay had dubbed him, the one the Feds were so interested in—the one they told him he was lucky to have crossed and lived to tell about.

Even through his haze, Bruce Ray realized that he'd said too much. He looked nervous, and said, "That freak scares me, man.

He ain't right in the head—all that talk about the devil and how he hates Jesus? Man, I ain't got nothing against Jesus or the United States!"

Michael took the hashish, bid Bruce farewell, and walked slowly and deliberately out the front door toward his car. They were watching him. He could feel it, and was worried that it might penetrate their fuzzy brains at any moment who he was. He had just put his hand on his car door when Bruce Ray called out his undercover name.

"Wait just a minute, James," he bellowed. He was still standing on his porch swaying unsteadily, 9mm at ready hooked under his belt. Michael had the door unlocked, ready to swing it open for cover. The dealer took a step off the porch and reached inside his jacket for a moment that seemed like forever.

Every muscle tensed, he asked, "What's up, Bruce Ray?"

He pulled out a packet of white powder, not a gun, and said, "Here, man, you're such a good customer. I want you to let some of your people taste this coke we got. If they like it, I can make you a good price."

Michael's heart rate slowed a bit from the flight-or-fight response mode and he said, "Man, you're just too good to me."

Bruce Ray laughed, took a blurred look at Michael and his car and said, "See you next time, brother." The rest of the crew waved, and the catatonic girl just gawked, beyond feeling after unspeakable abuse.

"Not if I see you first," Michael countered.

"Man, you bust me up," he said, laughing as he walked away.

No, Michael thought, *but I will one day soon.*

* * *

He took the evidence to the state crime lab, a musty old building that housed evidence of crimes from drug-trafficking to murder. If the lab and its forensic inhabitants of old could talk, oh, the tales of murder and mayhem they could tell. Some even said that ghosts had been seen looking for their dismembered body parts. Dr. Foster, a gray-haired forensics expert, checked Michael's material to preserve the chain of evidence.

"Well, it looks like you've been a busy boy, Agent Parker," he said. He logged each envelope of drugs noting name, case number, date, and time. He paused to peer at Michael over the top of his glasses and brushed away falling ashes from the Camel cigarette that always dangled precariously from the corner of his mouth.

"Business is good, Doc, too good."

"You and your friends are overloading my staff with all these drug tests. Tell your senator we need more funding," the professional bureaucrat said in a mawkish tone.

"I'll certainly do that," Michael said as he turned to leave, anxious to exit the smell of toxic chemicals which permeated the air of the old museum of crime.

"Doc, now don't you be sampling our evidence. Just use your chemical tests!" The lab general laughed, enjoying a moment of almost giddy abandon. Michael had once seen him with a gun under his laboratory smock and suspected that he fantasized about being a field cop.

Michael left for Bureau headquarters in the highly secret location of townhouses in a nondescript business area of suburban Jackson. There was nothing obvious to denote this as anything other than the other buildings around the Mississippi Bureau of Narcotics. He needed a new car, more money for buys, and to see what the emergency assignment was all about. He was scheduled to talk with his friend Clay, the intelligence guru who lurked in a remote corner of the complex tabbed the "bat cave" for its secrecy and mystique among the regular field agents.

Long-haired agents sat in the lounge, swapping war stories. As he entered the building, he passed Beth, their pretty security lady who said "Halt!" in mock sternness. "Who goes there?"

"Bond, James Bond, Moneypenny," he quipped in his best Sean Connery imitation.

"What's the code word?" she asked. "Spit it out, or you're subject to search."

"Goldfinger," Michael answered and smiled. As he passed, Beth flushed bright-red under her golden bangs, as red as the burnt-sienna dress she wore.

Going down the hall, he ran into Clay, a tall, lanky man with a receding hairline who had served in military intelligence in Vietnam. He had become Michael's best friend, mentor, and mother hen.

"Man, our sources say you're radioactive," Clay said.

"I know that, buddy," he answered as he touched himself and made a hissing steam sound.

"Very funny. I'm going to talk with the director to see if we can't get you pulled in for a while. Your testimony in court cases and your high-profile status in this communiqué from the political radicals merit some time off the road," he said, always the serious and ever-vigilant officer who had prowled the front lines of no-man's land in Asian jungles.

"No, don't do that," Michael said. "I'm fine, just need to move around in a different area for a while. I heard that they're sending me down to some rural county near the Louisiana border. Now, just how much trouble could I get into in Mayberry?" Black-and-white images of Michael's favorite program, *The Andy Griffith Show*, flashed across his mind's eye.

Clay chuckled loudly before he caught himself and recovered.

"Yep, some politico called the director and demanded that we send someone in there to catch the three or four dealers they have, but there are some rough folks down there who gave the ATF boys trouble in the old days. So be careful."

"Always, Mother!" Not an obscenity so often employed by players on all sides in this alternate reality, but one of affection.

"I do need to tell you about the hash dealer and his connection with this Fredrick, the stone-cold freak from the protest rally. There seems to be a bit of a symbiotic relationship between these hard-core radicals and plain old drug dealers," he said, concluding an hour's worth of debriefing with Clay. Little excited the intelligence folks more than a fresh eye from the field with new data to plow into their files, to refresh organizational charts that they were building to understand who was who and what groups were linked and how. Tracking the movements of these people was critical work, but it often made the libertarian in Michael uneasy. *What if the government one day tracked everyone in America? No, it couldn't happen, could it?* Intellectual indulgences were not encouraged for young agents still trapped in the left vs. right paradigm.

"We'll get right on this," Clay said, handing assignments to loyal intelligence analysts.

"Got any good reports for me to read?" Michael smiled and playfully reached for a file stamped in bold red letters--Top Secret. Clay snatched it away.

"Here's the read file to be returned before you leave with any thoughts you might have concerning the latest updates," he said. "Oh, say hello to Barney Fife and Andy for me!" Clay said through his goofy smile as he walked back to his desk.

As he left the recesses of spook central, Beth gave Michael a shy, covert smile that somehow reminded him of a girl he had thought he had left behind in fields of tears near Memphis. Old times are not forgotten.

CHAPTER SEVEN

"In the shadow of Your wings I will make my refuge,
until these calamities have passed by."
—Psalm 57:1

Armed with a new car, a new look from his barber, and a mind filled with Clay's intelligence report on this backwater village, Michael arrived in Tylertown. It was all that he had imagined it to be. *It may not have been the end of the earth, but you could see it from there,* he thought. It was a small town, far from the areas that traffickers in illegal drugs frequented. This should be a quick assignment and a brief respite from pressures elsewhere in the state, Michael figured. One narrow main street in and out of a downtown lined in ancient storefronts, hardware, clothes, feed and seed, one gas station and two red lights.

After he checked into the local no-frills motel, he went to the business of a man who had agreed to hire him and steer him toward some known dealers. Billy Hull was the owner of a local hardware store and a local church leader. He wanted to cleanse his town of the evil of illegal drugs. He was a partially paralyzed Vietnam veteran bound to a wheelchair, and Michael suspected that this was also a chance to feel relevant beyond his geographical and physical limitations.

"You must be Lee Roy Brown, my new assistant," he said.

"That's me. Bad, bad Lee Roy Brown," Michael replied. They shared a good laugh and he worked in his store a few hours a day, pretending to be Hull's sister's boy from Memphis.

They spent many nights sitting on his front porch under the starry sky and moon that highlighted the Spanish moss hanging from the trees. "Do you know what stars are?" Billy asked one night after a long silence. "They are just cracks in the curtain separating us from God. That's the light of the celestial city, son."

Long past midnight they told stories and discussed philosophy on a wide variety of issues, punctuated by an occasional interruption as Billy would pop a round at a pesky armadillo scurrying in the night. They were new to the state. People saw them swimming across the river from Texas by way of Louisiana, and Billy hated them. Michael told him they were prehistoric and would be around long after humans were gone. Billy didn't care. He hated them even more than the coyotes also migrating into the state at that time.

Billy leaned back after firing a couple of rounds, swept his long strands of brown-blond hair across his balding top and said, "We have a real informant who can get you close to some of the people selling drugs to our kids. The sheriff has charges on him and has cut a deal with him." The call of the crickets and croaking of tree frogs seemed to echo the voice of the troubled vet with the thin lips and hawk nose.

"Good. I'm ready to get started," Michael said, anxious to wrap this up and leave.

"You don't need to trust him, though," he cautioned. "He's reckless, wild, and has no judgment. He's not beyond ratting you out." Billy was leaning forward in his chair, his finger poking the night air, startling a gray field mouse that peeked out from beneath the moonlit porch steps.

"Gee, Billy, give it to me straight. Don't sugar-coat it," Michael laughed. Billy leaned back.

"No, it'll be fine," he said, taking a swig of a stale beer he nursed, "but just watch him. He does know some bad people, including the Jackson brothers. Ross, the elder, just got out of Angola Prison in Louisiana, and he's not to be taken lightly."

He paused. "I know that you think this is probably not the greatest assignment of your career. I've heard that you're an up-and-comer in the Bureau with lots of cases under your belt."

"I'm here to do my job, Billy." He really did want to help the folks who were low on the pecking order of resources, but yearned to finish quickly and return to his search for the elusive frontlines and his growing need to find answers to questions that his soul sought to ask.

"I know. I just want you to be aware that there are some bad people here, and for you not to underestimate them," Billy said with a deep sigh and shrug of his curved and degenerating shoulders.

Affection for this wounded warrior welled up in Michael. "Thanks for everything, Billy. I'll be on guard. I value your judgment, and will make you proud," he said. Michael was young and thought he would live forever.

Billy smiled and nodded, and then *Pow! Pow!* He popped two rounds at another hard-shelled, little creature that only he could see in the dark. Michael wondered who those shadows in the dark really represented to Billy, a man haunted by a jungle far from Tylertown.

Informant Carl Raymond met Michael the next day in a remote location near a dense forest that Bigfoot himself might well inhabit. Carl, a surly punk with a neat mustache, shoulder-length hair, and an oversized swagger, began to lay out his rules and his conditions.

"You don't look like much to me, Mr. Big Shot," he said. "I

may be able to get you in with some of the dealers if you do what I say and let me take the lead and—"

Michael cut him off in mid-sentence and in a gravelly-throated imitation of Clint Eastwood said, "Carl, let's understand each other. When we're working together, I call the shots. I set the rules. I control the scene. You will do *what* I tell you...*when* I tell you...and although you aren't worth killing, I will protect you if you're loyal to me. Never, ever try to screw me, set me up, lie to me, or leave me hanging out to dry. If you do that, I'll put you back in jail, or just dump you in one of these swamps for gator food."

Carl's mouth gaped open. His eyes bulged from their sockets. He swallowed hard and said, "Whatever you say, Lee. You're the man."

"Thanks. I knew that we were going to be fast friends." He would never have dumped him in a swamp, but Carl didn't have to know that. He respected the gators too much.

Carl went to work trying to set up deals. He got into it right away and fancied himself a sort of deputy agent after the heart-to-heart talk. He contacted Ross and J.T. Jackson, the local bad boys who regularly moved brown Mexican heroin and other popular drugs...drugs that were the choice of the rich white kids whom these enterprising black dealers catered to. Carl told Ross that his buddy was in town and wanted to buy some smack. Carl gleefully reported to Michael that it would be no problem. The deal was set for Saturday night with Ross at a local safe meeting place as instructed.

"Just like that?" Michael asked with a furrowed brow. "This old ex-con who is street-wise didn't question you about me and had the smack on hand? There was no haggling over the meeting spot or prices?"

"No, man, everything's cool," Carl promised enthusiastically. But it didn't feel right to Michael. Probably because he still wasn't concerned about this hick town, he let it go. His obsession with getting out early was now in full command.

Carl and "Lee" went to the local river party early Friday night expecting to swim in the river and make contacts with some known dealers. Michael removed and hid his weapon in the car, secure in the knowledge that danger was nonexistent here. The routine deal with the heroin dealers was set for Saturday night. For now they could enjoy the party, flirt with pretty girls, and eat fried chicken.

The sounds of the party were revving up. Kids dove into the creek they called a river, and boys chased girls and vice versa. They were just getting ready to put their swimsuits on when the Jackson brothers suddenly pulled up next to the car. Ross, a muscled, dark man, was behind the wheel, and Michael knew immediately that he was trouble. He was no kid, no punk dealer. If you could survive in Angola Prison, you'd seen it all. Trouble was oozing from Jackson's chocolate eyes.

Carl turned pale, and said, "Hey, man, what're you doing here? We meet tomorrow night." He swallowed hard but had no spit in his suddenly dry mouth.

Ross didn't comment, except to get in the car and look at Michael with narrowed eyes and a flash of gold teeth and say, "Changed my mind, honkies. We deal tonight."

Unarmed and feeling very vulnerable, Michael gave it his best no-big-deal look and said, "Where to?"

"Our house," he said. "Too many people here and people make me nervous, white boy." J.T., his quiet brother with the vacant eyes piled in the back with an increasingly nervous Carl.

For hours they meandered in circles as Ross watched the mirror for tails. Fading light gave way to darkness. They drove to where the highways and paved roads ended, and then exhausted the dirt roads that wound through endless swampy lowlands. The only sound that broke the silence was an occasional, "Turn here, go there," from Ross. Finally, long after dark, they pulled up to a narrow path bordered by tall weeds. Under low trees, branches caressed the car top, and the blues blared from a New Orleans radio station that Ross had found.

The late-night fog clung to the ground, and Michael felt uncharacteristically unsettled—he thought it rose like a scene from some horror movie where a lunatic emerges with a chain saw. The problem was that the lunatics were in his car. They finally came to a little shack on stilts perched beside a dark, wide bayou on the Mississippi-Louisiana border. Giant live oaks and willows, draped with Spanish moss that moved snake-like in the slight breeze, framed the shotgun house. Night hawks swept by looking to make meals of the giant bugs that were everywhere.

"This is it," Ross said gruffly. "Got the money?"

"If you have the good stuff," Michael said, and exited his car, reluctantly leaving his hidden Magnum under the car seat. A lone black cat hissed at him and ominously crossed his path.

No one said a word as they approached the dilapidated shanty. The last thing Michael saw was a small, armor-plated creature scurry from the shadows. He thought of Billy's warning and looked up, seeking his lights from heaven, but the canopy of the giant trees rendered the night void of any celestial illumination.

Michael could make out little as they entered the dimly-lit room. The only light was provided by a flickering kerosene lantern. Ross said, "Have a seat, man, and I'll get the stuff." He registered the edge in the criminal's voice, but could only continue with the charade and hope for the best. As they sat down on the couch with Carl, J.T. suddenly turned and shoved a shotgun in Michael's stomach. Ross emerged from the back room and raised a pistol to his forehead. Carl turned white and looked like he was going to pass out.

"What's going on, man?" Michael demanded in false bravado as the blood began to pound in his ears. "We came here to do a deal in good faith. Carl told me you are a professional." A knot was in his stomach, a lump in his throat.

Ross studied him. "Well now, my man, that's just the problem. Smack is hard to come by right now, and I don't know you. Why should I sell you what I have when I can just take your money, keep my stash, and drop you in the back woods? Nobody knows you, or will miss you, and they'll think that Carl just skipped his bail. No one will ever miss this little piece of rat poop," Ross said with an evil smile. Carl then lost control of his bladder.

Could it be the wild card that agents feared—no deal, just armed robbery and murder if necessary? Michael felt foolish and reckless for letting them into his car, but he wanted the deal. Still burdened with the false immortality offered by youth, he was also looking ahead to a deal he was working with the mayor's son for some PCP.

A tree frog croaked nearby and a barred owl cried "who-haw, who-haw."

"Well, Ross," he said improvising, "that all sounds fine and dandy, but you aren't looking at the long-term benefits to our continued business dealings."

"And what would that be?" Ross asked as he sat in a chair directly in front of Michael, who was now in recovery mode. Ross stared at the agent with eyes that were crazy. The smell of the burning kerosene was suddenly overpowering, and the sounds of rats scurrying by provided a soundtrack for the macabre.

"I have contacts with an unlimited source of white kids experimenting with heroin. I have the market but not the product. You have that. We both have something the other wants. I can be your bridge to sell your smack, and you don't have to expose yourself," Michael said in a level tone, making it up as he went.

Ross smiled at his brother, closed his eyes and nodded knowingly. "You are a smart little white boy, now, ain't you? You a college boy?" he sneered through broken yellow teeth with ill-fitting gold catching lantern light.

At least he was talking.

"I'm a man who wants to be rich by the time I hit thirty," the agent said, gaining confidence. Carl was crying softly beside him and beginning to rock back and forth.

"You have possibilities," Ross said, with a wicked smile. Looking at Carl, he said, "What's wrong with you?" Carl just rocked and whimpered. Ross then laughed maniacally. He looked at Michael. "Man, you need to be careful who you hang out with."

"I'm beginning to realize that," he answered, meaning every word.

"Let me think," Ross said as the passive and silent J.T. held the shotgun on the man Ross said no one would miss.

Periodically, Ross swallowed small blue tablets of unknown origin. Stimulants most likely—the man got wilder by the hour. By midnight, Michael had begun to assess his options, which were slim to none. An old clock in the corner chimed loudly, announcing midnight. Carl nearly jumped out of his skin. He'd be no help in a sudden move, and J.T. and his shotgun were unwavering.

Fortunately, they hadn't conducted a body search. Inside Michael's right boot was clipped a State Narcotics shield. It was a dangerous move, but one that prevented a beating by some local police officer looking to rearrange the face of a hippie to satisfy his perversion of power. If these cretins found it, he was a dead man and might be anyway.

Ross disappeared, presumably to relieve himself. When he returned, he positioned his pistol on the table right in front of Michael and grinned. Satisfying himself that Michael was not stupid enough to go for the now empty revolver, he leaned forward brandishing a Gillette double-edged razor blade in his hand. He stared deeply into Michael's eyes searching for any hint of fear.

Without breaking his lock on Michael's eyes, he moved the blade to his lips, put the blade into his mouth, and crunched down on the cold, sharp metal. He broke it and began chewing the blade. Michael watched in disbelief as his captor stared at him, calmly chewing the razor blade as if it were some sort of candy. Finally, he swallowed it in a sickening gulp that made Michael want to toss his supper.

Ross grinned and blood gushed from each corner of his mouth. Red, bubbling foam dripped from his chin, and he looked like some horror from a bad vampire movie. Michael finally blinked. Here he was in the middle of nowhere trapped by an insane criminal who dined on razor blades. It was surreal, and shock and disbelief spread over the young agent as Ross placed his fingers deep in his mouth, pulled out a handful of bloody discharge, and held it dripping near Michael's mouth. He said, grinning through bloody teeth and brown lips reddened by his self-inflicted damage, "Want some, white boy?"

"I don't believe I'd care for any," Michael said with ironic formality.

Ross laughed, coughing and sputtering as blood streamed down his throat. He wasn't done, though. Maybe Michael needed more convincing. The sweating black man grabbed a full box of long-stemmed kitchen matches and ignited the whole batch into a large, open flame. He moved his head back and inserted the burning mass past his bloody lips and into his mouth. Michael looked on in amazement as the flames licked at Ross' face and nose, illuminating the deep cuts inside his mouth. After what seemed an eternity, Ross closed his mouth and swallowed the fire. Act One was over.

It was at that moment that Michael believed it likely that he was going to die. That awful realization released a reaction in his brain that he had heard of but had never experienced. His whole life flashed before his eyes in a kaleidoscope of images bombarding his brain. He saw himself as a toddler with Grandma Pearl, images that he could not consciously recall. He could almost smell the smells and taste the tastes of times resurrected in his mind. It was frightening but beautiful, and he didn't want it to stop. If this was anything like what some drug users described as a good trip, then he could see the attraction, but this trip was driven by a mind preparing for eternity. The scenes faded as rapidly as they had formed and he was left with only a diffuse sadness for all that had been and might never be again. He said a silent prayer, praying not for deliverance, but just—one more sunrise before he shed his mortal coil.

When Michael returned to the here and now, Ross was still there, bloodied, but somewhat calmer. The stimulant that fueled his bizarre ritual also protected him and the blood flow had stopped, at least externally. Or, perhaps the fire had cauterized his wounds.

Ross looked at Michael and said, "Let's take a ride." The ever-silent J.T. rose and took the pistol, pressing bullets into the empty chamber. Carl's eyes widened and his heart pounded in his skinny chest—he knew he was going to his execution. Ross drove the car, and J.T. sat mute behind Michael with the pistol. Carl slumped in the corner of the back seat, whimpering like a lost puppy.

Ross broke a long silence, asking, "So, you think we could make some money, boy?" His hands were tapping the steering wheel to music only he could hear.

"I do, if you can just get me the stuff at a reasonable price," Michael answered.

"Hmmmm," he murmured. "How much you think?" He dodged a possum crossing the road, bounced out of the ditch and back onto the dirt road.

"Ross, the possibilities are unlimited."

The unlikely group drove on through the night until a bright, new dawn cracked through the thick foliage lining the rough road. Mosquitoes sought shelter in damp recesses and blood-sucking flies awoke and swarmed by the thousands escorting the car as the first timid light peeked through the canopy of the forest. Michael's simple prayer had been answered.

As the sun rose higher, Ross broke the silence. "I think we can deal. I like you. You are not like this weasel," he sneered, motioning to Carl. Presently, Ross pulled into a rutted lane that led to a dilapidated shack owned by Philip Snodgrass, a local backwoods bootlegger. Ross explained that he needed some hooch to wash down those tasty razor blades.

J.T., distracted as Ross left the car and lumbered toward the house, hoped he would return quickly with something to drink. He was sleepy after the long night and the little .22-caliber pistol in his lap did not provide much comfort. Seizing the opportunity, Michael slowly retrieved his .357 Magnum and pulled it up to his chest.

His heart rate increased and blood pounded in his ears, but time slowed to a crawl. He went through it in his mind—he could already see himself turning to shoot J.T. without warning, then rolling out the left side of the car using the hood to aim and steady his shot as Ross charged forth. He fished a pair of earplugs for swimming from his pocket and wedged them into his ears. If things went sour in the next few seconds, his ears could rupture from the blast of the Magnum in an enclosed space.

He slowly turned to J.T. who looked half-asleep, and said softly, "Hey, J.T." J.T. looked up and his eyes went white and wide when he saw the nose of the Smith & Wesson between the seats aimed at his chest. In his Clint Eastwood voice again, Michael said, "Now J.T., I really don't want to kill you, and discharging this Magnum inside this car would probably rupture my eardrums and the hollow points would blow a hole out your back the size of a basketball. So, just drop your little .22 peashooter outside the window—carefully now, by the grip,"

J.T. looked with wild eyes at the nose of the Magnum, the hollow points clearly visible. A click of the hammer being pulled back provided further emphasis. He was done, Michael thought, but Michael was wrong.

J.T. turned to drop the little Saturday night special outside the car window, but at the last second for reasons only he would ever know, the suddenly animated marionette whirled and fired the Saturday night special at Michael. There was a sudden flash in the dark and a pop sound as the gun discharged, but the projectile lodged in the car seat's raised headrest beneath Michael's face. Almost simultaneously, Michael fired the Magnum dead into the center of J.T.'s chest. The sound was deafening, and Carl was screaming as blood and tissue splattered all over the inside of the car. The thrashing man smeared the windows of the backseat in a ghastly mural. J.T.'s body slumped forward and the last of his life flowed from him.

Carl continued screaming, "Oh my God, oh my God!" Blood ran from his ears. Ignoring his useless informant, Michael opened the door and swung out behind it for cover. He could already hear sounds of reaction coming from the bootlegger's house. It was still quite dark and Michael strained his eyes, searching, waiting. There was a crash as Ross broke through the front door of the shack and came running up the hill like the old fullback he was—cutting, feinting, doing what he could do to make the goal line.

He had a .32 semi-automatic and was firing in short bursts as he ran. One round passed over Michael's head and another made a pinking sound as it hit the car door used for cover. Ross was fifty yards away and closing in quickly. Michael squeezed off two rounds that lit up the darkness, but true to that gun, they were high and to the left.

Ross cut back again in response, closing to thirty-five yards and firing. Shards of glass from a ricochet rained on Michael as he rose again and sighted Ross, unleashing two quick rounds. The massive black man stumbled and lurched backwards, tried to regain his balance, and then dropped like a stone. He had been agonizingly close to the end zone.

Michael sat down with his back to the car door, reloading from spare rounds clipped inside his boot with his badge. Ross wasn't moving, but the large trees cast him in shadows in the early morning light. Then, Ross' mangled body was clearly revealed in a gory palette as several outside floodlights came on, and the old bootlegger appeared with a shotgun. "State Police!" Michael shouted. "Drop the gun, and get back in the house!" The old man looked at Ross, sized up the situation, and decided this wasn't his fight. He dropped the scattergun, and retreated to the house.

Michael stood up slowly with both hands on his Magnum. J.T.'s blood was on his arms and in his hair. Carl's screams and cries were a rumble in the background. The smell of gunpowder and death hung in the air, overpowering all else. Michael was numb, but taking no chances. He approached Ross cautiously—the floodlights from the house revealed all that he needed to know. The first round had caught Ross high up in his left shoulder. The second had hit him on the right side of his chest.

A bloodbath, he thought. *A bloodbath. Two people dead. Madness!Madness! For what?* He had never killed anyone before. Death comes calling suddenly—just when you think you have it made. Why did J.T. shoot? What if the headrest hadn't been raised or there'd been no headrest? Michael had hesitated tonight as the inevitable conflicts arose. Does he kill them before they kill him—despite the fact his faith taught him not to kill? His NRA instructors told him while he worked out such conflicts, the bad guys would be blowing his brains out.

He reached Ross, and he was unconscious on his back. There was still a bit of life in him, though—his respiration was rapid and weak, accompanied by a gurgle. His breathing stopped and started several times before he succumbed to his massive injuries. There was one last, gasping inhalation. He would not be going back to Angola. No more razor blades, the only flames—in the lake of fire.

Michael's hands trembled as he fell to his knees and vomited until there were only dry heaves. He was shaking violently—some kind of shock, he thought. He staggered back to the car, looked at what was left of J.T., and thought that neither the Bureau nor any used-car dealer would ever be able to sanitize that car again. Carl was lying on the ground in the fetal position. He had somehow managed to stem the flow of blood from his ears, but was still crying and rocking in a catatonic trance.

"Carl?" No answer.

"Carl?" Louder.

"Yes, sir," he sobbed.

"Are you all right?"

"My ears hurt and I can't hear so good. J.T.'s guts is all over me," he wailed.

"Can you get down to the house? Ask the old man if you can clean up and bring me some wet towels. It looks like there's a phone line running to the house. Call the sheriff. Ask for backup and paramedics. Then ask them to notify the Mississippi Bureau of Narcotics director that Michael has been in a gun battle, and...I'm okay. Two are down."

"Yes, sir," he said. As Carl neared the house, Michael walked to a nearby well house that had a water hose attached. Hopefully, he turned the valve wide open, and there was a stream of good cold water. He washed his face and hair thoroughly. Feeling better, he removed his shirt and washed his chest down with the cold water. He continued until the last traces of red gore were gone but knew that this episode would stain his soul forever.

He was surrounded by an eerie stillness, but after what seemed like forever, the first squad car pulled into the drive with others close behind. Wailing sirens and flashing blue lights sent questionable neighbors scurrying for cover. The word was out— the cops had finally gotten old Snodgrass and they might get his moonshine customers, too. However, the old man was fine and standing on his front porch with Carl taking in the show. Didn't get shows like this back here in the bayou.

A number of big-shot cops, including the district attorney, pondered how they might claim responsibility for taking down these major criminals. Michael couldn't care less about politics at that juncture and gave open and honest interviews about the shootings. Officers took statements from Carl while ambulances arrived and removed the bodies. An hour or so later, Collins and Clay arrived and took charge of the scene. Collins talked with the sheriff and DA in hushed tones. They shook hands, patted each other on the back, and nodded solemnly as only grizzled old veterans of the lawman's club could do. It was an exclusive fraternity.

Michael sat in a squad car sipping a Coke when Clay tapped on the glass. "How are you?" Kindness and concern were in his words and sadness in his eyes.

"Things weren't so pleasant in Mayberry," he said, still fighting waves of nausea and periodically leaning out the door to retch.

Clay nodded and turned to give Michael a moment of privacy to wipe his face.

"I can see that, but you did what you had to do—what any of us would have done under the circumstances."

Michael fought nausea again.

"I just don't know why the kid tried to shoot me. Why? I was trying to arrest him quietly. Doesn't make any sense," Michael complained, shaking his head in disbelief.

The soothing gentleness in Clay was a welcome balm to a traumatized soul.

"You're lucky. He could've killed you. It was just a matter of inches and it wouldn't have mattered how young he was. I've looked into the dead eyes of many Viet Cong soldiers younger than him, and sometimes there are just no answers. We're going to have to terminate your undercover operation and pick up everyone pretty quickly. This is going to spread like wildfire in the press."

Deputies walked by and gawked at this curiosity in their county. The stories old men at the general store would now have to tell, stories which did not need their usual exaggeration.

"Could you call my family, Clay, and tell them I'm all right before they hear it on the news? I just don't think I could manage right now."

"Got you covered. I'll patch through HQ in a few and alert your folks. You just sit and take it easy now. Be advised, you will draw some time off and counseling. It's standard and mandatory. So don't argue." Clay was taking charge.

Michael closed his eyes, remembering that he was not alone in this mess, remembering Billy. "I know. Clay—there are other concerns. Please call Billy Hull and tell him what happened. Provide him with some protection."

"Will do. We'll send an agent to his house tonight and make certain there are no repercussions from any friends of these people."

"One more request. Get Carl to the hospital and tend to his ears. The kid's at risk, too—see if the sheriff is okay with us giving him some money and getting him out of the area *permanently*."

"Consider him gone," Clay said.

In the days that followed, the media talked of little else and tried to reach Michael, but Clay had him where no one could find him. Within a week of the awful night of death, over a hundred dealers were arrested from Starkville to Hattiesburg. It had to be done before they saw the old pictures of Michael that the press was circulating and just vanished.

Tammy Price, Southern Mississippi drug queen, was heartbroken when agents called on her at her dorm. She thought "Jim" was so nice—she cried. How could he be a government agent? She had sold a drug that was not illegal at that time and wasn't charged, but after her friends learned who she had brought into their midst, she was socially persona non grata, and moved away to live with a questionable pharmacist after declining an offer to work as a willing informant in other areas of the state.

Bruce Ray was in disbelief when arrested. Agents seized drugs, guns, and ammunition. Clay suggested that he talk with the

Feds about the 20,000 rounds of automatic weapon ammunition and grenades seized and whom he was dealing with. He told Clay that he never would have hurt Michael and that he wasn't a bad person.

"What about the underground flyer and what you said you were going to do?" Clay asked.

"That was just the drug talking, man. That ain't me." The Feds began working him hard on Fredrick. Bruce told them that Fredrick had been there at his place the day after the shootings in Tylertown. The FBI told Clay that Fredrick was a key leader in a truly radical branch of the Weathermen who were using drug profits to supplement payments from the KGB to fund their little revolution. It wasn't clear if the FBI knew of his relationships with other federal agencies or if it was all part of the game.

Sensational headlines were repeated around the state as more and more drug dealers realized that they'd been nailed—trials , pleas, and more headlines followed in front-page news. One thing was apparent to all involved—Michael's time as strictly an undercover agent had come to an end. He was named the first resident agent for a field office outside of Jackson to work with Clay, develop better intelligence, and to raise the public profile of the Bureau by bringing private and public pressure to areas dominated by organized crime. It was time, the Director felt, to move away from targeting street dealers which did little to cut off the source of drugs but threatened to overwhelm the penal system.

The director decided that Michael, who had been in seclusion trying to sort it all out, needed a further break resuming his duties and secured a seat for him in the ten-week Drug Enforcement Administration (DEA) Academy in Washington. Nothing would stop the nightmares until a note from Pearl arrived just before he left for Washington.

"Son, His grace is sufficient. I want you to have this prayer found on the body of one of Papa's soldiers in 1865. I pray that one day you will be able to pray this prayer. Love, Pearl."

As he opened the stained and crinkled paper and read the soldier's dying prayer, he felt a longing for places that he'd never been and people he'd never met. "I asked You for strength that I might achieve, I was made weak that I might learn humbly to obey. I asked You for health that I might do greater things, I was given infirmity that I might do better things.

I asked You for riches that I might be happy, I was given poverty that I might be wise. I asked You for power, that I might have the praise of men, I was given weakness that I might feel my need for You.

I asked You for all things that I might enjoy life, I was given life that I might enjoy all things. I got nothing I asked for, but everything I could have hoped for. Despite myself, my unspoken prayers were answered. I am among men, most richly blessed."

CHAPTER EIGHT

"Thou believest that there is one God...
the devils also believe, and tremble."
—James 2:19

An unobtrusive "government-gray" van with untraceable license plates zipped along Interstate 55 early the morning after the news broke about the gun battle in tiny Tylertown. Wisps of early fog not yet burned away by the sun broke away and yielded to the brisk pace of the ghost vehicle with darkly tinted windows which clouded the men inside and their motives.

Their agenda was as foreign to the inhabitants of rural Mississippi as the latest reports in the *National Enquirer* of UFO sightings. No need to look any further. These were the real aliens.

The young driver was only twenty-five. Muscular, square-jawed, Tommy was a "jarhead", a Marine fresh from two tours of duty in the steamy jungles of South Vietnam. He'd survived the second tour and some fierce fire fights only by the sedation and shield of LSD, the awful home brew of rice alcohol cooked in ancient kettles, and by ingesting drugs gleaned as payment for cooperation with the smugglers of Air America.

It was there that he was first recruited for black ops. A gung-ho but disillusioned young anti-Communist, the men in dark glasses convinced him during long drug-fueled seductions that they were the guardians of the real world plan and that he could join them to serve the "true America."

Tommy hated "Gooks"—or so he thought. After more than twenty sanctioned kills as a sniper and countless other discretionary targets of opportunity, he had begun to see the faces of those he had coldly dispatched or "lit up" at a distance. They now visited him nightly, beckoning him to join them in the hell that he had condemned them to. Only the drugs his new friends furnished would muffle the tortured cries of the dead.

Now, here he was in Mississippi of all places. When he left the confines of Langley, he envisioned assignments in Paris, London, Rome, or even Moscow. He felt he was nothing more than a glorified babysitter today.

I didn't sign on, he thought, *to squire around freaks like this.* He accepted that the "greater good," as his control agents called it, was served by using such deviants, never pausing to consider that those same handlers might view him as a freak as well.

That "greater good" stuff had been invoked a lot lately to him, just as in Nam. The meeting they had just left in the port of New Orleans was populated by shadowy figures, agents of foreign governments and resistance forces, all supplied by his employers. Both sides were the users and the used. Little talk was ever heard of liberty and patriotism.

Guns, drugs, gold, artifacts, and secrets were the currency of these clandestine realities: mercenaries loading guns going south and unloading drugs coming north. His paradigm was exploding. Good guys violating the Constitution and using profits from illegal drugs to fund black ops was hard to rationalize for someone with Tommy's Midwestern values.

Once, his control officers watched him at a remote airfield

as crates of armaments were unloaded. A single grenade fell from a box and landed on the pavement of the remote air strip. Instinctively, the young Marine yelled, "Grenade!" and fell to the ground, his hands covering his ears. For a brief moment, the sounds of choppers and the smell of napalm swirled in his head.

"At ease, soldier," the man in the mirrored glasses said, lifting him up. "That war isn't yours anymore. We're doing what we must. It's a dirty world, and we use dirty people to prevail. Those stuffed shirts in Congress would never give us the money to do what must be done, so we improvise. While they're out kissing babies and chasing skirts, you and I are saving the free world, Marine!"

Sleeping next to him today, his passenger was almost prone in a reclined bucket seat. A book he was reading lay open on his lap.

Tommy was no prude, but this guy and his blasphemous reading material made the Okie's skin crawl. Occasionally during their trip, the silent anarchist beside him would look up, swallow hard, and lick his lips to say of the book's author, "Marquis de Sade was one of us. The simple passions give way to the complex, the complex to what some would call the criminal tensions of murderous emotions. The greatest satisfaction truly comes from corrupting, torturing, and finally killing the weak strains that infect the earth. We cannot allow this natural pleasure to be interrupted by some so-called divine deity in our minds."

Yeah, he thought, *better keep this fruitcake asleep. Can't take too much of that drivel.*

The news break was coming on, so Tommy reached over to change the dial to soft, comforting music to soothe this savage beast next to him.

Just as he touched the dial, a ghostly pale hand shot out and grabbed his hand. "No, don't touch that!" the de Sade fan shouted.

The local broadcaster continued: "WBRQ has learned that two men died in rural Walthall County, just outside Tylertown last night. Ross and J.T. Jackson were apparently killed in an exchange of gunfire with a state narcotics agent identified as Michael Parker. Details are still coming in. Stay tuned to WBRQ, News 104 for the latest updates."

The pale hand clicked off the radio and clinched into a fist so tight that the blood surging through his bulging veins burned a candy-apple red against his white skin.

"Is there a problem, Mr. Hammel?" Tommy asked.

"Someone I know," Fredrick hissed through gritted teeth.

"The dead or the living?"

"Both. Ross was recruited by prison outreach in Angola. He was a black gang member full of rage, a useful idiot we had plans for. A sleeper whom control planned to use for smuggling and suicidal insurgency to marginalize civil libertarians against government surveillance and crackdowns."

"Too bad," Tommy said. "I'm sure the agency can easily replace him. Sounds expendable."

"He was," Fredrick muttered through dry, chapped lips that he constantly moistened and picked at. "He is."

"What's the problem then?" Tommy asked, sensing potential problems or vendettas leading to rogue actions that his bosses so abhorred.

"It's not him. It's this Parker. I know him. I've seen him and read about him in some of the druggies' underground papers that you government boys sponsor. You and your pathetic weather pimps."

Pausing as he fished for a tube of Chapstick, he said with chilling finality, "He is in my way!"

"Why waste energy on him? He's just a low-level drug agent rousting dopeheads. He's nothing to us—less than nothing."

Fredrick didn't answer. The agency's mission wasn't his. When he first saw Parker, he knew that he was the embodiment of all that the pale psychopath hated. He was an enemy of Fredrick's messiah.

His master showed him that this Parker was a follower of the carpenter from Galilee. Fredrick's seething hatred for a man he barely knew was irrational, but wars had been started over less. Murders were ordered by governments for imagined sleights and for the basest of favors for useful dictators.

Fredrick also had a sixth sense about people he lumped into four categories: use them, convert them, ignore them, or kill them.

What cinched it for him, though, was the fight. Not that his man was embarrassed, or that the incident was of any real consequence, but when Parker passed him, he saw the cross around his neck that had fallen from beneath his shirt during the fight.

The sight of the cross unleashed Fredrick's demons and left him physically ill. He tried to suppress his rage lest it distract him from larger missions. It had subsided, but now this!

This Parker had come too close to Fredrick's web of madness for the second time, and like the spider he enjoyed watching, some primal drive had been engaged, the murderous urges that de Sade advocated.

I will remember that face, he thought, *and ask my government handlers to access state files.* The long brown hair, the facial hair, and such, could all change. Everything in him told him that he would see Parker again.

His driver brought him back to the present moment as they approached the Canton exit on I-55. "Do you want to check on the storage cache at the Adams house?"

"Yes," Fredrick said. "The Black Liberation Army in Georgia can use some fresh supplies, and we need to debrief Bruce Ray if we can find him semi-coherent. See what they know about this intruder who keeps putting his feet in the door of my master's divine house."

The van whipped in front of a semi to take the exit, passing on the left a farmer on his tractor and a crossing guard escorting elementary school children to their tiny red-brick school house. All were ignorant of the agents of death who had passed so close to all that they believed was still America.

CHAPTER NINE

*"Such is the irresistible nature of truth that all it asks,
and all it wants, is the liberty of appearing."*
—*Thomas Paine*

Twilight settled over Memphis. A grizzled traveler in the underworld that catered to the vices of man looked out the window of his worn old nightclub with its tin roof, fiberglass walls, and sawdust floors. He peered up at a blue-black sky broken by huge cotton-candy clouds made pink by the rays of the sun beneath the horizon. A bright moon rose to his left and the brillant evening star to his right. A flock of Canada geese flew across the clouds toward the moon, honking their tribute to life.

The man sighed deeply. He and his club, like the neighborhood, had seen better days. As far as he could see, there was nothing but blight and condemned houses and warehouses. He was surrounded by decay and these new punks and would-be gangsters who respected no one.

He felt boxed-in. Leaning forward, he sucked on the knuckles of his right hand and winced as the pain came again from the old leg wound. Somewhere in the background, he heard the rattlesnake buzz of someone wanting entrance to the club. *Someone is always trying to steal my shade,* he thought. Not today. Today, he was looking south.

Sonny Walker, a veteran entrepreneur catering to the vices of man, wanted to get rich by moving his gambling and clubbing operation out of Memphis, away from the scrutiny of rival gangs and elected crooks. His idea was to leave behind the expensive politicians and slip below the radar of the Feds in the Promised Land of rural Mississippi. The redneck schmucks had no chance with him. He planned his move to just south of the Memphis city limits where politicians were cheap and elected sheriffs were hungry for a cut of the big-city action. South of the Tennessee border was ripe for drugs, gambling, booze, and fast women. It was a no-brainer and he could almost smell the money. Profits had plummeted in his old digs in Memphis.

He had a dream, much like Bugsy Siegel had a dream for a wide spot in the desert called Las Vegas. Sonny's Vegas was to be the stretch of Highway 61 south of Memphis that ran through Desoto and Tunica counties in Mississippi. This desolate area could be his Vegas he wagered, although few of his friends believed any sane person would come there to party and gamble.

While Michael was in Washington, Sonny was buying prime land dirt-cheap. His first big project was a club in a no-man's land, just a whisper from Memphis and a short ride for thrill-seekers and high-rollers. His friend's lack of enthusiasm did not deter Sonny. He told them that one day he might even get Elvis to perform there as he now did in Vegas. That's when his buddies knew he was dreaming. The trouble was that Sonny was not the only one who had foreseen this land of plenty. His opposition had bought up the politicians before Sonny got there and informed them of how insulting Sonny's offers would be versus the enormous potential take.

So one day as Sonny was gleefully preparing to open his

club near Walls for business, some old friends came calling from Memphis along with the local police. The scam was obvious from the start.

The local welcome wagon of county authority arrived to greet Sonny with all the greasiness of Strother Martin in *Cool Hand Luke,* ready to dispense "justice" and to tell their church deacons how they kept this bad boy from Memphis out of their county. Next month, they could buy their wives that new car and their mistresses a new fur coat with the fruits of today's "public service."

Tom Hughes, the local building inspector, dapper in a yellowed straw hat, drawled, "Mister Walker, you are in violation of numerous county codes, and I'm afraid I am going to have to cite you." Strike one.

Bill Johnson, a tanned and weathered county commissioner, dryly added, "Yes, you will have thirty days to appear before our commission and show cause why your license should not be pulled." Strike two. They had done this before, these clever boys in their wrinkled seersucker suits.

Smelling a rat, Sonny tried to object, but his complaint was cut short...

Red Tate, the chief deputy sheriff and consummate redneck, dipped a pinch of snuff and said, "I think it's all over anyway, boys. Mr. Walker has a previous criminal record and that precludes him from having an alcohol license in our county. We don't want his kind down here!" Strike three, you're out! Next batter.

Eventually, Sonny's new detractors moved on, leaving the furious club owner with a stack of written citations and implied threats. He thought to call his lawyer in Memphis but was interrupted by the impatient blaring of a car horn out front. What now?

Tony "Ace" Connelly, a dark-complected Cajun formerly of Louisiana and owner of the Ace of Diamonds Club in Memphis, waved his cigar from his red Cadillac convertible. He had a vapid but nubile girl at his side with bleached-blonde hair who looked at Sonny with the glassy eyes of a junkie. Sonny walked over to the car fingering the little pistol he kept in his hip pocket for insurance. He nodded, but said nothing to the driver with whom he had been rivals for a long time and whom he knew to be a truly evil man.

Ace, a connected mobster with deep-set bitter eyes under shabby brows, smiled at Sonny and tapped cigar ashes on his boots.

"Sonny, you need to sell me your setup for a 'fair' price and get out now. Walk away while you still got the legs to carry you, old buddy," Ace advised him matter-of-factly, like a judge passing sentence as he blew smoke in Sonny's face in a gesture of contempt for his once formidable rival. Sonny fought back against a rising, seething anger as Ace mocked him. An old dog sitting nearby smiled at Sonny in sympathy, and the empty girl laughed— an empty laugh.

Sonny Walker was a practical man and knew he no longer had the muscle that Ace brought to the table, so he walked away while he could. He even made a slim profit on his investment, but he was Mrs. Gertrude Walker's little boy and held a grudge like his knife-wielding bootlegger mother was famous for—the one that had sent her to Parchman Farm. Revenge on Ace and the syndicate of clubs owned or allied with his mortal enemy became all-consuming and he had an idea—a good one. He had read about the exploits of a cop named Michael Parker. He would find this crazy kid who supposedly was coming to Batesville, see if he was for real, and look for a way to get even through him. Dealing with cops made him sick, but he was old and needed leverage. As much as he hated the police, he hated Ace times ten. No sir, Ace was not going to steal his shade and get away with it.

* * *

When Michael arrived home from endless hours of field exercises and dull classroom lectures in the confines of the DEA

Academy, it felt good to be outside the Beltway and its endless crunch of traffic and to be back on familiar turf. Washington hadn't changed much and he found too many memories of *her* there, too. It wasn't home. The people, like the weather, were warmer in Mississippi.

Michael's first stop was home in the Grove. Pearl had been sick. The dreaded day she warned him of as a boy—the day she would leave him—seemed suddenly very real. Her once vital mind now drifted a bit, but she was alert when he came, and they shared her prized peppermint sticks.

She told him a story that he pretended he had never heard as Annie Pearl once again held court with her boy. She asked him again to promise never to forget her though there was no chance of that ever happening. Leaving her was the hardest thing he ever had to do, but his family told him that she was better and could hang on forever.

While he was alone in her room, he began to tell Grandma of the horrors of Tylertown, and she patted her boy's hand as he cried again, not so much for that night but for this day and all that was slipping away from him.

* * *

Looking out at the crowd before him at the Batesville Breakfast Rotary Club, nestled in the banquet room of the Townhouse Motel, he was eager to be out in the field, but the director said that public relations was an important tool in the war on drugs and corruption in Mississippi, not to mention funding in the legislature. He grudgingly accepted the Rotarian's invitation to speak, to make nice as Batesville was where his new office would be.

Still, he hated the formality of it all and especially the pious fawning of some of these well-meaning folks. He was especially uneasy with those who read about Tylertown and told him he was a hero and wanted their picture with him. They chatted and passed the bacon and eggs around the table until the speaker called them to order.

Michael surveyed his audience—mostly middle-aged white men, overweight and balding, serious pillars of the community stuffing their faces with food their hearts could probably ill afford. He smiled as he wondered who first said, "See that chicken there? I'm gonna eat the next thing that drops out of its bottom." Good way to laugh away any stage fright.

"The drug wars will be long and costly," he told them. "Much will be asked of us."

Borrowing from the director's speech, he said, "Stopping the flow of drugs into the state is akin to damming up the Mississippi River. The beast is a many-headed snake. As soon as we lop one off, three more appear. What we must establish is firm ground, a hostile anti-drug reputation, and a low tolerance for drug trafficking and the drug money that threatens to corrupt our system of government. In addition to the obvious danger to our children, the greatest risks reside with the money organized crime uses to buy up elected officials and public safety officers. We cannot retreat in the fight against those who believe government is for sale and that morality is a trap for suckers." He didn't mention the need for funds for treatment of addiction, and the strain on the judicial system and prisons, but he had begun to question the wisdom of betting all on enforcement actions.

Waitresses in bright-blue aprons hurried through picking up plates as he continued. Portly bankers appreciated them as they walked away with their trays, anxious for a few moments off their feet.

"We can't do this alone and we ask for your continued support and prayers. I encourage you good folks to call me if you have any information that might help us. Thank you."

Thunderous applause followed. Red-faced men leaned back, plucked their matching red suspenders and nodded to each other in approval. He was preaching to the choir—one of aging businessmen who, despite some ethical challenges of their own, felt that they were the good guys and wanted the criminals in prison. There would be much talk at their homes tonight over the supper table about the scourge of drugs and the earnest young man at Rotary today.

Former Judge Hal Davidson, who invited Michael to his club, rose to sum up. "That was a wonderful speech, Agent Parker. We all feel safer knowing you are on our side fighting the scourge of drugs in our communities." As he listened to the judge drone on in politician style, there was something about him that made Michael's skin crawl. He was a pretender, a user of such causes, now mounting a run for governor if rumors were true. Somehow, that wasn't comforting. His perfectly coiffed silver hair, silk suits, and crazy green fish eyes seemed to mask a persona altogether different from the public image he tried so hard to create.

As the crowd broke up, the members filed by to thank their speaker. Predictably, they slipped him their insurance cards, schedules of their church services, and bank rates as they shook Michael's hand. Michael had come to collect these little advertisements that spoke of a gentleman's success. "Networking," they called it. They offered him generous discounts because he was a poor, underpaid cop and to curry favors. He politely declined them all.

Judge Davidson, beneficiary of many such fine breakfasts, waddled up to Michael.

"Mighty fine, son, mighty fine," he said with a deep Mississippi accent. "Mah-tee fine. You know I could use a quality, clean-cut young man like you to chair the Davidson for Governor Youth Campaign." His carefully invented façade was marred by a facial tic that was pronounced when he was agitated.

"I'm just a narcotics agent, sir, and happy to be one at that."

Fish eyes studied him. Davidson was unaccustomed to his offers being refused. He then saw potential votes leaving the room and snapped back to full campaign mode.

"Well, we'll see what opportunities the campaign brings," he said, and was off shaking hands. Michael took a long look at him as moved through the crowd. The hairs on his neck stood up—such darkness. The man just left rancid residuals in his wake.

Needing some fresh air, Michael walked around the quaint town square, so prominent in many old Mississippi towns. There was a hardware store, several clothing stores, a drugstore, and in the center of the square, the town's police station. Several men sat on a bench in front of the station, making small talk. Sparrows fluttered about by the dozens with a few pigeons that bobbed their heads as they scurried to recover popcorn from an old man on the bench.

He realized that re-entry into the larger world wouldn't be easy. In fact, he'd been amazed to see people going about their business, going to churches, raising their children and just living normal lives. His life hadn't been normal, and he sensed it wouldn't be as long as he was lurching about in search of dragons to slay. There was no shortage of dragons and evil in the world and there never would be, but his problem was that he never lived in the moment. He was always somewhere down the road looking back and critiquing his own performance—rewriting the lines, trying to change or control his destiny— a modern-day Don Quixote dreaming the impossible dream.

It was a short walk to his office where his thoughts were interrupted by the loud ringing of the black Western Electric telephone. "Bureau of Narcotics," he answered as he turned down George Klein's rock 'n' roll program on WHBQ Radio out of Memphis.

"Agent Parker?" an unfamiliar raspy voice asked in almost a whisper.

"Yes."

Silence and a rustling sound, maybe something over the phone mouthpiece being removed.

"My name is Sonny Walker from Memphis. You don't know me, but I read about your appointment in this area, and a mutual friend told me that you are a straight arrow," Walker said with a certain dry professionalism and air of authority.

"And," he added, "you ain't been here long enough to be bought off!"

"Well, thank our mutual friend for me."

A slight chuckle and the sound of a barking dog, then a thud and a yelp.

"I have some information that is critical for you to know about. I'll meet with you if you wish. Lay it all out, you know. Don't think you will be disappointed."

"I'm listening."

Honking horn, sound of traffic. A payphone?

"Ah, all I can say on the phone is that there's an organized crime push into Mississippi from Memphis." There was a pause and then Sonny continued, "And I can deliver them to you on a silver platter—fried or filleted."

Never look a gift horse in the mouth—or do you?

"Why would you want to do that, Mr. Walker?"

He laughed. "I'm sure not a civic-minded person or a chamber pimp, but they done me wrong, and I want to set it right, see?"

Michael knew it was almost never that simple and thought for a minute before he knowingly took the bait. "I understand. When are you available?"

They set a meeting for midnight that night in Memphis, arranging a mutual "how will I know it is you" signal and greeting.

Late that night, Michael found himself sitting in the dark, unknowingly humming the tune "Midnight in Memphis" as he awaited Walker's arrival. The fog was heavy on the dead-end street and the lone streetlight did little more than cast an eerie glow into its thickness. An emaciated male calico cat that had seen better days wandered up to his window, and he threw him some scraps.

Sonny was late, but that was typical of nervous informants. This section of Memphis—near Whitehaven—was still safe at night, although he had to shoo away a young man who asked if he was "looking for a good time." The sight of the gold shield sent the creature of the night scurrying into the shadows. Michael glanced at his watch and wondered why they now called them "gay." He didn't seem very happy.

Night bugs of all varieties swarmed around the streetlight, buzzing and popping and falling on his windshield. Twelve-thirty and still no informant, but there was a scraping noise, and two thugs came strolling by looking for trouble. However, the sight of the Magnum on the dashboard quickly ended any plans of mischief, and they moved off, looking for safer prey. Finally, close to 1:00 a.m., he arrived. The big car stopped, waited, and finally flashed its lights twice, then once. The reply of two quick flashes was given. *Such B-movie theatrics*, Michael thought and smiled.

As he approached Michael's car, he could see that Sonny Walker wasn't what he expected. The sixtyish man was dressed conservatively, and seemed almost too placid for his role in life. A bit of research had revealed that Sonny had pulled time in Tennessee after a run-in with ATF agents led to illegal liquor and weapons charges. He was the owner of two clubs in Memphis, and from the looks of him, not a happy man despite his riches. The tall, silent, sallow informant rarely made and never kept eye contact. His calm demeanor had vanished, and he was obviously uncomfortable being in Michael's car after midnight in the suburbs of Memphis. Nevertheless, he sucked up his concerns and the meeting proceeded down at the end of a lonely street behind an abandoned gas station, just a stone's throw from Graceland. The car window was down and the sweet Southern fragrances suggested that somewhere in the distance someone was cooking barbeque.

"Sonny, a pleasure to meet you," Michael said, as he nodded and firmly shook Sonny's hand. "What you got for me?"

"Well, you cut to the chase, don't you, son? No foreplay at all. I like that. I want you to know right off that I ain't no snitch. Some people done me wrong and it ain't right. I ain't no saint, neither, but these people, they are bad to the bone."

"You don't like the police much, do you, Sonny?"

"Well, I ran into some who weren't too good to me, and this limp of mine, well, I owe to one of them," he said, rubbing the leg that ached, especially when the storms came. It had become a reliable weather indicator.

"Then, don't think of me as police. We are just Sonny and Michael, and I'm the instrument of your revenge," he said with the boyish grin that Clay kidded him about and which Grandma Pearl adored. The chemistry between these two unlikely allies was beginning to form and a new universe of possibilities beckoned from this dusky suburb of Memphis.

Walker stumbled and mumbled at first, but the more he talked, the angrier he got and the faster he talked. So Michael quietly turned on the switch of his small tape recorder and the tape spindles rolled, capturing Sonny's angst and mood changes. Michael couldn't keep up, but he couldn't shut him up, either. There was a real rage fueling the guy as he laid out how the local sheriff had been bought by Ace Connelly and his syndicate of club owners and would-be wise guys.

When he was finally done with his ranting, Michael said, "Look, Sonny, I know you're upset, but I want you to go through the whole thing again—slowly and just the important facts. Okay?"

Sonny's hands were shaking as he lit a cigarette. For a moment, Michael thought he could be an illusion, a fur ball coughed up by the wandering calico cat.

"Sorry, okay. Agent Parker, excuse me, I mean, Michael, what they're going to do is bring down three clubs: One here, one here, and the other there," he said as he pointed to a worn Mississippi road map he produced. "They have some backing from outside sources and will be drawing from Tennessee, Mississippi, Arkansas, and Louisiana—old Dixie Mafia boys, investors they call them. Several of Ace's backers is I-talians, if you know what I mean. Once the clubs are open, they'll have hard liquor, amphetamines, cocaine, and other illegal drugs for sale and some fencing of stolen goods, maybe a little money laundering. The waitresses will all be selling themselves along with the drinks and dope.

I seen them girls, son. They got thighs like beer barrels and shoulders like Tennessee linebackers, but the real money's in the gambling. I'm talkin' illegal slot machines, high-stakes pool tournaments, dice tables, poker—the whole nine yards."

Sonny was firing words again like a machine gunner now reloaded with a fresh clip, targeting enemies real and imagined, and Michael thought he seemed to have a good familiarity with these vices himself, but just nodded as the old criminal meandered along, singing his song with endless verses—*It's Crying Time Again.*

"They'll have 'juice machines' in the walls, magnets to stop the dice—clean them plowboys that come in there outta their last penny. Wives and kids'll never see them little paychecks. Any money left and they'll try to get them hooked up for a trip with them girls to the adjoining apartments. If they won't go, that's when the free beers come out—special beers laced with scopolamine to mess up whatever little brains they got left. Then the girls can cheat them at dice or just roll 'um and steal their money. Any complaints, they just call the sheriff and he sends some boys to lock 'um up for drunk and disorderly conduct," he concluded with a self-satisfied grin. "Whatcha think?"

"Sonny, you sure know a great deal about their business," he said, thinking this had probably been Walker's own business plan at some point. Sonny stifled a yawn against the back of his nicotine-darkened fingers.

"Son, I have been around some in my life, lived longer than you and seen more—lots more. I was in McNairy County, Tennessee, where there was once pretty much the same setup," Sonny confessed.

"Was that Buford Pusser's crowd?"

Sonny looked at Michael with an arched eyebrow and then nodded.

"Yeah, some of that stuff's true, and some ain't, but the setup worked like a charm. Money flowed there and it'll flow here. Once they get established, these clubs will be used to coordinate thefts, hijacking, prostitution, gambling, drug smuggling and distribution, and shakedowns. They'll launder the money through some legitimate businesses that Ace and his backers have across the river. Some of the old McNairy County boys are in this, too, I hear."

Listening to him reel off this valuable intelligence, the time flew by, and it was all Michael could do to maintain an air of nonchalance. "Sonny, all you've said is that Ace's crowd is *going to* commit this, that, and the other crime. I can't move based on that."

Sonny scratched at his scalp for a moment and said, "Tell the truth, a lot of it is already a goin' on and the rest ain't far behind." He grabbed at his last cigarette, visibly drained, but relieved that he'd told all and released the hatred within that poisoned him.

"Okay, Sonny, you will furnish me information on who is doing what, when, and where?"

"Yes, son, I will, as God is my witness. An eye for an eye," he said with conviction. He even placed his hand over his heart in a mock pledge of allegiance—he, this new convert to the justice of the Old Testament, and even what man called "justice" in the temporal world.

"Hate him that much for hurting business?" There was a long pause as a fat green leaf, illuminated by the streetlight, floated moth-like from a nearby tree and settled on the hood of their car.

"No, not just that. His goons caught my nephew delivering some stuff to my new club, and used him to send me a message. He's still in Memphis Baptist Hospital in a coma, and I have to see his mother, my baby sister, cry over her only boy every day." Sonny leaned out the window, sniffed the air, and dabbed at an embarrassing tear.

"In the old days, I wouldn't have come to you. When I was younger, I would have dealt with this in-house. Now, I just don't have the kind of muscle that these punks do. So, I call you and put my trust in you—not the law, but in you." He seemed resigned to his fate and totally committed to what would've once been an unholy alliance to him, and at that moment—as ferocious as a kitten.

"I won't let you down, Sonny, and you won't be sorry. Do you need any money for expenses?"

Sonny vigorously shook his head.

"No, I can't take your money, and I know you don't mean it as an insult, but it would sully the sanctity of this deal," he said, squaring his shoulders and projecting his chin.

Gangster ethics, Michael considered.

"Fair enough, Sonny." They shook hands, and agreed to meet again in a week with a laundry list of names to add to the ones already given, along with a time and events calendar.

As he was leaving, Walker paused and leaned in the cruiser window and made hard eye contact this time. His breath betrayed his weakness for Budweiser.

"You're still a young man and we heard about what happened down south, but still, I just want you to know that these boys play for keeps," he advised with an air of sincerity. The concern on his face was real.

"Thanks. I'll keep that in mind," Michael said as he watched him walk off into the fog and bugs still fought over just whose streetlight it was. He thought that the powerful dynamics of politics and revenge weren't all that much different. Either way, someone paid dearly. He was excited, but also a bit apprehensive about his new partnership with this Bible-quoting outlaw.

Mockingbirds at home in the country or the city began to sing and herald the arrival of a new day, and somewhere, a rooster crowed. He realized that he'd forgotten to eat that day and inhaled several burgers at a local Krystal on the way back to Batesville. Despite the early hour, the phone was ringing an ominous greeting as he opened the door. He rightly guessed that it could only be Clay, and he sounded somber. *What have I done now?* he wondered.

* * *

A sudden clamorous wind blew in from the direction of Parker Grove, whistling under his office door and blowing away any illusion of order in the world and the innocence of angels. His eyes began to overflow with water that marred his cheeks and tracked down his face. His shirt seemed suddenly to choke him as his heart raced, and breaths came in rapid, shallow gulps. The now scant weight of the .357 Smith & Wesson beneath his coat could no longer indemnify him. The finality of goodbye echoed across the great divide and the Grim Reaper sealed the sepulcher of all that was with a boneblack gravestone and a distant calling— "Dust-to-dust."

The early morning dew still lay heavily on the orange day-lilies she had planted. The liquid whistle of a rufous-sided towhee echoed from the hollows below the apple orchard where he once fetched apples for Pearl. Their blooms were just about to open to the morning sun. The rabbits she fed were munching on the monkey grass in her flower bed outside her window.

In her bedroom, where she'd dispensed lessons in lost causes, entertained challengers in games of chance, and awarded love and peppermint, which to her were one and the same, Pearl Parker heard the summons that all must heed one day from the eternal conductor calling for those who have tickets beyond the reef.

Her nurse said that just as the first rays of a vigorous new sun began to burn away the night and signal life and renewal, Pearl pursed her dry lips for moisture. The nurse placed a moist swab to her mouth and rubbed a bit of Vaseline on her chapped skin.

Pearl hadn't spoken for weeks, but she began to sing in a low, slow, whispery voice. "I...wish...I was...in...the...land...of cotton." Then she opened her vital gray eyes wide, smiled a little girl's smile, and said, "Is that you, Papa?"

A look came over her face as if she could see something that those trapped in the world couldn't see and knew something they couldn't know, but one day would.

Then she was gone. Her Captain and her Pilot came to take her home. Back up, Lord. Annie Pearl is coming up to bat. This time, she's swinging for the fences of heaven.

CHAPTER TEN

"O Death, where is thy sting?
O grave, where is thy victory?"
—1 Corinthians 15:55

He got up early that last day at home and followed the worn path of Bermuda grass down to Pearl's final resting place. The morning sun was low behind him, and several purple-green dragonflies cruised the area. Creeping plants threatened to overtake the path he walked, and despite the sun, the incoming lampblack clouds forecasted a gray day.

Even now, a few scattered drops fell in front of him, sun-touched and almost mercury. An old cinnamon-colored gentleman passed him, a groundskeeper out to tend the hallowed earth before the heat and humidity set in.

Ancient pitted gravestones of pocked granite with faded words like "Beloved Son" and "Loving Wife" populated Gray's Cemetery near the town of Nettleton. A pale gray-brown squirrel that lived there came down from its nest to watch Michael.

Faded flowers from the graveside service now littered the grounds, blown by an ill wind and stinging memories in this yard where so many cherished loved ones had been laid low over the years—where most who had mourned them were now mourned there themselves.

The service had been a fine one. Pearl would've been proud. She was laid next to Eula, who had long preceded her as a young husband lost to what they called consumption. Their places were part of a larger plot where Captain Patterson and Pearl's mother, Rebecca, rested.

Everyone came clothed in the dark attire of grief. In hushed tones and downward glances, the director, Clay, and a contingent of agents filed by Michael and his parents to pay their respects. Only Collins and Clay truly made the eye contact that spoke volumes of hurt for those left behind.

The young pastor, fresh from seminary, couldn't really know much about death—or life, for that matter—but he did an admirable job of speaking of the day that the Lord would come and wash away everyone's tears, when pain would be no more, and all wrongs would be righted. He also had done his homework and managed to capture Pearl as girl, wife, mother, and grandmother.

After the service, Michael roamed the hills and hollows of Parker Grove. It was there he would find Pearl and the faith that had shined so brilliantly in her eyes. She had a joy the world didn't give her and that the world could never take away. He fished and on impulse, stripped off his clothes and dove into the snake-infested waters where he had learned to swim and did long laps up and down the pond until he was exhausted.

On the way back to the house where he grew up, he stopped in his father's watermelon patch and broke open a huge red-meated watermelon and ate it there under a lemon sky, just as he had a thousand times as a boy—another solemn ritual of affirmation and goodbye.

Spent from his swim and full of watermelon, he stopped by Brownie's grave under a clump of emerald pines where the warm brown needles covered him like a gentle comforter in all the seasons of eternal rest. Michael told him that Grandma was gone and that he missed them both. Then he sang the tearful *Old Shep* and began to cry silent tears. Brownie was gone where the "good doggies go."

The sound of the large raindrops now slapping against the fresh red earth around Pearl's grave brought him back to the final way station surrounded by a rusted cast-iron fence with spiked tops that pointed to heaven.

Despite the growing intensity of the rain that tried in vain to wash away his grief, he stayed and talked with her for a long, long time. Then, he finally reached in his pocket and took out a wad of folded white paper. He carefully removed the liner that he had taken from the King Leo tin, revealing two sticks of prime peppermint.

He laid one on her fresh earth and sat and ate the other to mend his heart so caked with grief.

* * *

He returned to the hot gloom of his office filled with stale air and silent laments. Under the door was a sympathy card signed simply, "Sonny." He'd forgotten about Sonny in his sorrow, and needed to tell Clay all he had learned. Clay had been laying off him, giving him time and space, but now he needed distractions, to resume pushing the stone up the hill where the effort becomes the goal, running to avoid the Grim Reaper, hiding in flimsy castles constructed to halt the relentless march of time and pretending not to hear the grains of sand sliding through the hourglass.

Just then the phone rang and the doctor of distraction hung out his shingle. Clay's welcome voice spoke pleasant greetings and asked more polite inquiries, then dove into the real purpose of the call.

"The FBI called and passed on some rather sensitive intelligence involving you."

"Me?"

"Yeah, you know your hashish dealer? Well, he's been singing his black heart out—put the Feds onto a prison group associated with this freak named Fredrick, the man you encountered in Jackson, and a group of radicals in Alabama."

"Radicals in Alabama?" he asked, laughing. "Are we talking good ole boy Neo-Nazis or Bubba Communists?"

"Funny, really funny! They intercepted a letter to this group. It was sent by a prison gang and they stated that you're on their hit list."

"What'd I do to deserve such an honor?"

"Several of the people you bought from were cutting a share to the movement. The seizure of all of that ammunition cache didn't make for happy campers."

"Clay, I've got some big fish to fry right now. What am I supposed to do, hide out in my bunker?"

"Well, be on notice," he said in his fatherly way. "The Feds will monitor further chatter through their sources. The prison will let us know if any of these guys are paroled, so we can put a tail on them. God knows the damage they are doing from the inside."

"Okay, well then, I guess I can tell you my news now," Michael said.

"All right, but you need to listen, take these things seriously," Clay said in despair.

"I don't worry, buddy. I have you watching over me."

When he finished telling Clay about the setup, the informant, the nasty boys from Memphis, and the newly employed public officials, Clay could barely contain himself. "Man, that's fantastic. We can come in and help you document everything and burst their bubble at the right moment. First, let me check it out with my Klan informants in the area," he continued.

"Klan informants? Why would you have informants in the Klan and what would they know about this?" An image of flaming crosses burned in his mind.

"Well, these fellows aren't the bombers or the violent types, just the big talkers, redneck wannabes. They're a little long in the tooth but still connected," Clay said.

"One thing you have to remember," he continued, "is that no matter how we may disagree with the Klan on some issues, they believe that drug trafficking is a tool of the Communists to bring down America. They'll feed us any information they can get their hands on."

"Who knows, Clay? They may be right. The ultimate evil may be in Moscow, Havana, Hanoi, or Beijing, or...it could be as the conspiracy buffs say—some of our own bankers and government agencies. The intelligence community gunrunners to Central America come back loaded with coke, weed, or diamonds—freelance opportunists, or money for black ops?"

"Maybe both, but it's our job to bring down the Mississippi boys," said Clay.

* * *

Over the next week, Clay talked with his sources and they pretty much confirmed all that Sonny had said—now classified as 1A intelligence in Clay's world, intelligence data from multiple reliable sources and with priority to act upon it. When the director saw the full report from Sonny and Clay's people, he authorized all available resources to be put at their disposal. The director had requested a face-to-face with Michael prior to any formal police action.

Collins sat in his office and pulled on a new pair of cowboy boots and peered at his agent. "You ready for this, boy?"

"Yes, sir, I am," Michael said, meaning it.

John Collins was getting older and he was tired, really tired. Couldn't even remember when his back didn't ache. Perhaps this was the beginning of a relationship in which the director could foresee the eventual passing of the torch if his young protégé was worthy. Now and then he called Michael at 3:00 a.m. to mess with him if he could find him home. The director would greet him in his deep, gruff voice, barking, "Hey, boy! What're you doing?"

Michael, sleepy, flustered, and unsure why he was being scrutinized, would garble some response about working on important reports or planning raids. At times, Collins couldn't suppress his laughter and Michael soon caught on. The director became a father figure to him and he wanted the "old man" to think he never slept—not far from the truth. Collins knew he had awakened his field agent, but it was a measure of affection that he had difficulty expressing in other ways. So different from his young agent, he had raised a lot of heck in his day and came up the hard way, but always said that boys like Michael were the future—if there was to be a future.

While the MBN agents laid their plans, Ace and his crew of young miscreants were hard at work in their quiet invasion of Mississippi. Three clubs were up and operating in short order. The initial focus of the MBN was called the Full House Club, a blue and white building with attached apartments in a drab little town named Cotton Row, near where Elvis once owned a ranch for awhile. Aptly named, the town was little more than a wide place in the road, not twenty minutes from Memphis.

Ace had renovated an old club, at least functionally. The finer external amenities weren't what drew the customers. It was the lure of the hidden, forbidden pleasures that lay within. It might've looked like a dump on the outside, but on the inside he'd spared no expense. The men who came there to gamble found big-time pool hustling and all-night poker and dice games. Those who came there for women and drugs found them in one package. The waitresses, who hawked amphetamines table to table, sold more personal charms in the seclusion of the apartments.

MBN agents put full-time surveillance on the club for forty days and forty nights. They watched the comings and goings of the club from a special van outfitted with the latest in photographic

equipment, video/audio recorders, and directional mikes—
carefully hidden outside the van to pick up, record, and enhance
nearby conversations. It was parked in front of a bait shop across
the road where pickup trucks, boats, and other vehicles were
routinely left unattended for days. Teams were rotated in and out
in the wee hours and kept the cameras rolling.

They captured evidence of the comings and goings of the
strange mix of people who frequented the club by night and lived
quiet lives by day. Agents also documented several drug deals, some
made just inches from the van where agents sat motionless despite
the stabilizers to mask movement within. At least twice, drunken
patrons emerged with a "waitress" and wandered close to the van
to complete their transaction while leaning against government
property.

And so it went. As the days passed, the agents began
to get a fix on the key players and their modes of operation.
Robin Rhodes, a businessman who specialized in coin-operated
machines, was identified as the broker. He acted as the bagman,
carrying bribe money to local law enforcement. The pictures of
unsuspecting cops helping Rhodes unload his illegal slot machines
and subsequently receiving tips would be hard to explain, not to
mention the large dice tables the deputies set up. Pictures of two
judges and the area's chief local law enforcement officer being
hugged by Ace in celebration would guarantee front-page material
and keys to conspiracy indictments.

It was a rich, though routine surveillance, but on occasion
there was the unexpected. Once, during a lull in activity, Clay and
Michael were manning the van around 4:00 a.m. Things were
mostly quiet, but a beat-up blue car with Tennessee plates passed
by several times and caught their attention. The four passengers
hung out the windows and took a closer look at the van each time.
On the fourth trip by, they slowed down and Michael said, "I think
these little street hoods are going to try to jack our van."

They disappeared into the darkness, only to reappear shortly and pull in behind the MBN van. What to do? Michael said, "We can't risk ruining all of this by arresting these punks and causing a commotion."

The car doors opened and all four passengers emerged. They tried to appear nonchalant, openly carrying the tools of their trade—crowbars, door jimmies, and a sledgehammer. There was the murmur of voices and the sound of metal on metal as the hoodlums began their work.

Clay whispered, "Michael, follow my lead." With that, Clay launched into his best falsetto voice. "Oh, Charlie."

"Come to me my lovely vixen," Michael said in a husky voice.

"Oh, what a man!" Clay replied breathlessly.

Stifling laughter, they bumped and banged the sides of the van. The team of would-be carjackers froze, then broke and ran for the idling car as if the devil was after them. The last the agents saw of them, their fishtailing car was throwing gravel and bellowing an oil-laden cloud of smoke as they sped for the state line.

Laughing until his sides hurt, Michael asked, "Oh, man, where did you come up with that voice?"

"Well, there was this time in Saigon when I was in military intelligence and had to pass for a female Caucasian," he said

Laughing hysterically, Michael said, "The Vietnamese must've thought you were the ugliest American woman they had ever seen."

Clay laughed about the war, something he rarely ever spoke of, but tonight he laughed the goofy laugh that had become his trademark. Now and then, he would answer his radio as Goofy One.

"I hope they didn't hear your laugh."

"Oh, they found it very erotic," Clay said, and again they broke into uncontrollable belly laughs, the tension melting away. Then Clay looked deadly serious and said, "You know, I have always wondered about something."

"What?"

"Well, in the cartoons, why does Goofy stand up while Pluto remains on all fours? They're both dogs!" They began to laugh again at nothing—at everything. Two friends, immortals of the moment, doing what they firmly believed must be God's work.

* * *

Time passed and business at the Full House Club was good. Persons of interest poured through the doors. Busy agents ran through film and tapes like there was no tomorrow, driving the financial bureaucrats crazy. They had documented at least a dozen known organized crime figures from the Mafia, along with their loose confederations of contract professionals. The traffic between the clubs and the adjoining apartments was nonstop, night and day. Johns staggered out, often leaning on the women who had just robbed them. Deputies showed up when the good ole boys were tapped out and found they'd been cheated or robbed. They were given a rough ride for their drunk and disorderly behavior, and now and then a tap on the head with a blackjack—a reminder of what was to come if they didn't quiet down and accept their fate. Everything Sonny had predicted was unfolding like clockwork and being recorded for posterity. You couldn't make this stuff up.

CHAPTER ELEVEN

"It's déjà vu all over again."
—Yogi Berra

So many ice chests, too much junk food, and urgent trips to makeshift latrines as the calendar turned ever so slowly and methodically to a ragtime rhythm. The long, languorous vigil had depleted the observers at Cotton Row of their salt and light. The initial jokes and the novelty voyeurism faded as the unbroken line of passengers in the passing parade filed by, so many appearing vacant of life—desperately and utterly alone. More seemed amoral—devoid of mercy, tenderness, and shame—evoking nausea of the soul in the virginal hearts of these new centurions.

It wasn't getting any cooler in the sweltering van, but fortunately for the weary agents, the clock was ticking for the operation. After a month of documenting crimes and building a mountain of probable cause, the team of agents was nearing critical mass in terms of intelligence gathered and a foundation for enforcement action. They were waiting for the right moment to move and some catalyst that would trigger a full-blown assault on Ace and friends. The Bugsy Siegel of this new frontier supplied that.

Sonny said there would be a large Fourth of July party at the club and produced the fliers circulating in certain Memphis circles. Drugs would flow, racketeers would abound, and the best pool hustlers and their stake horses would be there for a big winner-take-all high-stakes tournament. Drug dealers, gamblers, prostitutes, public officials, and organized crime figures would all gather under one roof at the same time. The Full House would be as hot as the Mississippi summer sun that night. Clay and Michael decided to raid the party and provide the fireworks. They had one week to plan and gather any last minute evidence. They adhered to one maxim: There is never enough evidence—never!

"Clay, we have some time. What do you think about taking a little risk? Let's slap a bird dog unit under Ace's back bumper and follow them into Memphis and pick up some new intelligence. We might uncover some hidden associates that never risk visiting the club."

Clay was always eager to try out his latest tracking devices and once had to recover one in a dramatic confrontation with a suspect who discovered the directional finder under his rear bumper. He causally walked up to the nonplussed man holding the bird dog and said, "Oh, good. I see you found my bird dog. Thank you." Clay just took it and walked off.

"Well, it's a calculated risk, but if we're careful, it could yield some important information. Maybe even a big fish," Clay answered with a look he might have given regarding a recon mission in Nam.

"No guts, no glory," Michael offered.

"Course, we'd have to follow Bureau guidelines and inform the authorities in Memphis that we're crossing into their jurisdiction," Clay added somberly.

A momentary silence and nodding of heads was followed by uproarious laughter. Best to assume every cop in Memphis was on the take. It was not true, but the odds were so bad, better to assume that all were compromised. After all, as a blinking neon sign on the church up the road said, "We are all sinners," and Memphis was no Garden of Eden.

***

A row of ruffled, chalky clouds ringed the moon over the Full House. It was just past 1:00 a.m. when Ace and several of his drivers, soldiers, and girls came out—laughing and drinking. They piled into two big, black Lincoln Continentals and sped north toward Memphis. A few minutes later, Clay's gray Ford sedan fell in behind the revelers. The other team of agents was waiting at the Tennessee state line, prepared for the first trade-off. Both cars had locked their directional finders on the frequency of the bird dog, carefully hidden on the underside of the lead Lincoln's chassis.

Eventually, the mobsters took a hard cut onto Shelby Drive and then slipped into the heavy traffic of the interstate. Several exits later they turned onto Winchester where they proceeded slowly, presumably trying to avoid cops not on their payroll. The two cars finally turned into a short drive to a gated compound surrounding a large Victorian house that looked like the Corleone spread in *The Godfather*.

The house was well maintained and the surrounding gardens manicured. It was no ordinary house. The occupants of both cars piled out near a small stone walkup located just inside a gated parking circle at the entrance. Whiskey bottles fell to the stone pavement, shattering as women shrieked in their highest girly voices. Powerful security lights cut through the darkness of the Memphis night, but were switched off after the party entered, returning the compound to darkness. Night vision gear would be required to continue surveillance.

The team of agents waited—something night owls became good at in their business. They made all the tag numbers and logged them into Clay's efficient data management system. By 3:00 a.m.

the agents were settled into their surveillance position across the street and two blocks down. Faint sounds of music were heard now and then from within—then nothing. Though the house had been quiet for some time, it came to life suddenly and the sounds of men and women laughing grew louder. Was there something to celebrate?

Clay and Michael remained fixed to their night scopes, hidden by the deep shadows of a giant oak tree that had likely seen much in its many centuries of standing sentinel over this piece of earth. A fresh breeze blew from the north, rustling leaves and providing relief from the suffocating heat and humidity. The laughter continued, but the agents could make out little at first.

"Good golly, Miss Molly," Michael exclaimed in a newfound attempt to avoid profanity but with genuine shock. Clay was focused on the house with photographic attachments to his night scope as he tried for some low-yield pictures, like those he often presented at staff meetings showing grainy green images that he swore were of a plane being unloaded at a small crop-duster hangar after a long flight from Honduras.

"What?" he asked.

"Do you see the man with a woman under each arm getting in the Lincoln?"

"Yeah, he looks familiar," Clay said, clicking away with his automatic drive that inhaled film at a rate that Bureau accountants found extravagant and obscene.

"That's former Judge Hal Davidson, now prospective candidate for governor!" Michael exclaimed.

"Holy Moses," Clay said, in his own attempt at swearing off obscenities.

The fish-eyed politician, who had wanted a good young man for his campaign, was staggering drunk, supported by a pair of scantily dressed women who appeared to be more than potential contributors to his campaign. Even in the grainy green of the night scope, the man was disheveled and unsteady on his feet. The two girls poured the bulk of a man into the back of the Lincoln with the bird dog, then hopped in on either side with their john. Ace materialized from the darkness, bent down, said a few words to Davidson, and handed him a fat envelope. The two men shook hands, and it was over. The driver shut the door and pulled away from the compound lights into the black veil of night now darkened by congealed clouds that covered the moon.

"Take him, Joe," Michael whispered cryptically into the mike. "And retrieve the bird dog if we lose you."

"10-4," Joe Sheffield muttered, already gunning his powerful cruiser.

As Michael's attention returned to the house, there was another flurry of activity and a small knot of people moved toward the gate. The occasion was obviously over, and there was Ace— shaking hands, kissing women, saying good night to his guests. As the revelers came into focus, there was an immediate disconnect. These people didn't look like they belonged here with Ace and his hooligans. These, for all appearances, were well-dressed, ordinary citizens. Michael shook his head—they had either made an enormous mistake or hit the jackpot. The group said their own goodbyes and climbed into two waiting cars—an expensive Mercedes sedan and a custom-painted jade Cadillac limousine.

As the two cars pulled away, another man joined Ace in the driveway and they became engaged in a heated discussion. Michael blinked and blinked again at what his tired eyes said they saw. It couldn't be, but it almost surely was—Fredrick! His ghostly appearance was even more bizarre in the green light of the night scope. After seeing the judge, this was too much—like Christmas, Fourth of July, and somewhere over the rainbow, all rolled into one. Michael's heart raced. What was this odd mix of people all about?

"Clay, do you see who I see?"

"I see a man who seems to fit an established profile," he answered. Meaning he didn't know who he was.

"It's the Ice Man, Clay."

"Here? Interesting," said Clay, who was seldom surprised by anything when he was working his gadgets. If a flying saucer landed in front of them, Clay would calmly photograph and log the date and time of the event with an explicit description for the official record—Men from Mars.

"Who did you say again?" he asked when he was through recording data. "What? No joke?!"

Ace and Fredrick lowered themselves into the remaining car parked in the driveway—a sleek, mint-colored Jaguar, and pulled onto Winchester with a well-tuned exhaust note.

"Let's stay on him, Clay," Michael urged.

With only one unit and no bird dog to track, they had to take some chances. After a few turns, the Jag settled on a route that led to Ace's main Memphis club, the Ace of Diamonds. The agents held back, successfully obscuring their tail until they reached the club near 4:00 a.m. Despite the time, the club was still rocking and a mix of expensive cars and shabby farm trucks filled the lot.

Michael laughed—two drunks were "watering" a well-meaning protest sign against the club planted in front of a dirt-poor Baptist church down the street. The preacher should have used waterproof paint. They staggered off, still zipping their pants as the agents passed the club and pulled into the church lot.

Michael said, "There they go," as Ace and Fredrick were met by their comrades at the front door of the club. "Clay, I've got to go in and see what's going on. Okay?"

"Are you crazy? He knows your face, and you're on their official hit list."

"Father Strickland, I'll wear a wire and if anything goes wrong, I know a former honorary colonel in the South Vietnamese Army who would come charging in, guns blazing. Besides, he's only seen me once when I had long hair and a beard. Tell me, do I look like the same person?"

"No," Clay scolded, "but you're also risking some fallout to our upcoming raid."

"I know, but it's a risk that's worth it. I'm not known by criminal elements in Memphis, and I just want a quick look around.

"All right," he said in resignation, "but if I hear anything unusual, I'm calling backup and coming in—firing on all cylinders."

"Just wait for the signal," Michael said.

"What?" he asked.

"Goofy is just a dog," Michael said, and they laughed a nervous laugh.

Entering the glitzy, gangster elegance of Ace's main headquarters was a study in contrasts. It was replete with burly bouncers everywhere. A lighted dance extravaganza illuminated the dance floor in a tribute to the disco area. Sparkly streamers hung from the ceiling, and scantily clad waitresses moved among the patrons.

There was a large bar area framed by ornate teakwood where four bartenders worked steadily to keep the booze flowing from spigots dispersing a foaming golden elixir. The eclectic mix of patrons reflected the mix of vehicles in the parking lot. Businessmen dressed in expensive suits sat side by side with farmers in bib overalls mixing Red Man with Jim Beam. Several Mafia types straight out of central casting and regular hoodlums milled about with prostitutes on their arms in this ellipse of illusion where you were who you pretended to be, and women with hollow saffron eyes were anything you wanted or paid them to be.

Michael recognized one of the suits as an influential Memphis businessman—a likely target for shake-down and extortion. He was about drunk enough and several of the girls were eyeing him. If they were lucky, these rich thrill-seekers would look out their Union Avenue office windows tomorrow with hangovers and no sleep, and perhaps fret about the consequences of nights when they took too many wrong turns and could never find their way home.

Michael noted that the several private "conference rooms" stayed busy—groups entered and left, possibly for business, to run lines of coke, or for various forms of human actions covered by the blanket admonition on the nearby church sign blinking an electric blue and silver in the night—"Repent."

The DJ fired up Sly and the Family Stone's "Dance to the Music," and drunken farmers and stockbrokers joined strippers on the dance floor. Michael was chuckling at the antics of a hefty dancer wearing a Caterpillar cap when he felt a powerful hand clasp his shoulder. Cursing himself for losing his concentration, he turned to look directly into the same pair of cold, savage red eyes he had seen on the streets of Jackson. There was no doubt now. It was Fredrick, backed by two large men who looked more competent and deadly than Frederick's former bodyguards. Several female companions reeking of smoke and cheap perfume whispered to one another in the background—the chatter of shrews in the oldest profession.

Emotionless, the ghostly figure said, "I know you." He evoked the image of a pale scorpion unchanged in millions of years, prepared to strike as that is all it knows.

"I don't think so, pal. I never forget a face, especially one like yours." One of the big, thick guys edged closer, but Fredrick waved him off as Michael discarded the idea of asking him about his bad case of pink eye.

"You weren't following me, were you?" he asked with squinty eyes as his lips sucked in, following a tongue that flicked lizard-like, ever moistening the perpetually dry orb that was his mouth.

"Not unless you were coming up Park Avenue."

The disco beat pounded, and few took notice of this little drama except Fredrick and his entourage of muscle and females.

However, they were eyed by the club beef, but they never moved, indicating that the Ice Man was special and had his own rules here.

"Why do I think that I know you?" he asked rhetorically, studying Michael's face.

"Hey, man, it's dark in here, and it's late. We're all probably a little drunk, and I just have one of those faces." He was almost nose to nose with him, and there was the scent of a strange mixture of Brut and ether.

"I don't think that's it," he said, almost touching Michael from head to toe and even against his cream lips, a visible trace of what could be powdered cocaine dusted his mouth.

Michael saw him tense and grip something in his left pants pocket--maybe a stiletto by the brief flash of a metallic blue handle. He had the strangest feeling that Fredrick was a spider, and he was a fly that had just lit on the edge of a very carefully constructed web.

"Anyone here know you, will vouch for you?" he asked. The red eyes were highlighted in the dark like burning demon spheres burning a hole in the night.

"Oh, I'm sure that there are some of the ladies here who would remember me," Michael replied with a grin, knowing that Clay must be about to bust a gut in the car, and was probably begging for the signal, his no-cursing pledge broken and shattered.

A musical voice lilting out of the darkness said, "Sure, honey, James has been coming around here for a year or more. That is, when his old lady lets him off his leash. Come to Momma, big boy."

It was like those moments when you change channels on your television and certain words and cadence of speech rend the fabric of time to play a reel from yesteryear—walks on the Mall, the sounds of "Stars and Stripes Forever" wafting down East Capitol Street, the lighted dome of the Capitol against the dark of the city and a baby bird in free-fall from her nest too bruised to ever fly again.

Yes, that voice—Michael knew that unmistakable voice from past whispers and purrs in the dark of night. He turned in the direction of the voice, and there she stood. Dixie Lee Carter was looking directly at him, dressed to kill in a glittering crimson red dress that framed her long, golden hair, looking like a million dollars and swallowing black beauties with champagne. Even though he felt as if a mule had kicked him in the face and he might throw up, he asked, a bit too casually, "Miss me, Dixie Lee?"

"I miss your money, honey," she said and then the other girls around her laughed. However, Fredrick did not see anything funny. He looked hard at Dixie Lee, and Michael saw the fear flicker through her. Satisfied that he had delivered his message, Fredrick turned to Michael and looked him up and down. He was a study in cold, calculating deadliness and was not satisfied, but he walked away and disappeared into a private room in the back of the club where he obviously had bigger fish to fry.

Michael knew at that moment how a convicted man in the electric chair must feel when they rush in with a reprieve from the governor with one second left. He turned and studied Dixie's pretty face through the smoke as the surging disco music pumped through his body. Colored lights blinked in rhythm with the beat and cast an eerie glow over her perfect features. A bit perplexed by Michael's fixed stare, Dixie danced a couple of steps, twirled around and said, "What?"

"Sorry. Just mesmerized by your beauty, dear," Michael quipped, thinking this was quite the night for surprises, and this one had proven timely. Still trying to calculate what the meeting of drug dealers, domestic terrorists, ordinary citizens, and the probable next governor of the state was all about, he wondered how he would handle this little incendiary chili pepper that had been lobbed to him. He was moved by her mere presence—she was like a smoking grenade in his sweaty palms. Too many worlds were colliding. *Someone has a sense of humor up there*, he thought.

"Want to dance, James?" she asked. Only moments ago, she was just a ghost in his dreams, but now, here she was—no apparition, but an all too real flesh and blood spirit materialized to haunt him again.

"Only if we can slow dance," he said, as a relatively tame song came up.

"Sure, whatever you want," she answered. He followed her to the dance floor where he held her again for the first time in years. His hand found that comfortable place in the small of her back that hadn't changed. As his fingers interlocked with hers, he felt the years wash away in the swirl of her familiar smell and feel. He felt dizzy for a moment, but recovered. They danced silently for a moment and her exploring hands came to rest on the 9mm that hung underneath his left arm.

"My, my," she breathlessly remarked. She paused briefly but began to caress the weapon. Dixie Lee was leading this dance, and held all the cards at the moment, so he did what he always did—waited.

"I've missed you so, Michael. It's been so long." Her breath was hot and moist as she whispered in his ear, making the four years without her seem like four days.

Lamely, he said, "What's a nice girl like you doing in a place like this?" As she breached his defenses, Fredrick was almost forgotten, irrelevant.

She pulled back and looked deep into his eyes. "Me? What are *you* doing here? These people would kill you if they knew who you were." *Those eyes, those eyes*, he thought.

"Would you believe I'm just finally taking a walk on the wild side?" he asked.

"No," she said flatly, blue eyes softening as she laid her head on his shoulder, the perfumed hair intoxicating him.

They danced until the music stopped, and she looked at him and said, "Take me home, Michael." He hesitated and looked around. Two big brutes seemed to have the front door covered. He doubted his boxing skills would impress them very much.

"The only way for you to get out of this joint safely is to leave with me now," she said, giving an exaggerated shrug and pooching her lower lip.

"I'd be delighted to escort you home in that case. We have lots to catch up on." So many questions rattled around his brain.

She grabbed a bottle of champagne and bid everyone good night. They all yelled, "See ya, Dixie." They walked out to her green 240Z. Dixie Lee pitched Michael the keys. She slid into her seat, exposing her long, graceful legs and red high-heeled shoes.

"You mind driving me to my midtown condo?" she asked. He didn't have much choice.

He opened the door on the driver's side of the low sports car and then briefly paused in the darkness to alert Clay. "Goofy, Pluto is okay. I'll call you at the motel when I see how this plays out. Good night!" He hit the off switch on the body mike and laughed as he fell in behind the wheel. He could almost hear Clay's teeth grinding.

He took the long way around, a special route to the tall buildings of downtown Memphis. Both remained in silence, enjoying the beauty of the night, until the lights of Graceland launched old memories. "Remember when we used to come down here and try to catch Elvis coming out at midnight?" she asked, laughing with her hand resting on his shoulder, and then on his leg in an odd familiarity that unsettled him.

"Yes, a lifetime ago, it seems. Wonder what Elvis would make of us now?"

He told her that he would drop her off and take a taxi to meet other agents, but he knew he would stay if she asked him. She did, too.

As they finally entered the large complex of gated condominium units, he paused at the sights. Dixie Lee's condo overlooked the skyline of Memphis, offering a gorgeous view of the Mississippi River as it snaked around the little city. Michael was both impressed and disturbed. She lived well and had a view to die for, but where did all the money come from? Michael scolded himself. Did he always have to be the cop?

Dixie asked him in, and he fumbled nervously with her door key, feeling like the inept teenager so long ago in Washington. Dixie left to powder her nose and Michael passed through tall French doors onto the condo's private balcony. He imagined he could smell the river and hear the muddy waters lap the shore. Somewhere, the sound of jazz drifted up to the balcony. Feeling far away from crime and criminals, Michael took a deep breath and gazed upward at a star-filled sky, those little breaches in heaven's curtain that his friend in Tylertown had described to him. He felt happy, content, and safe and didn't mind that it couldn't last because it couldn't. Could it?

When he returned to the tastefully decorated great room complete with a wet bar, he was greeted by a snow-white Maltese named Geordie. He gave Michael the once-over as he raised his brows and tilted his head, first to the left and then to the right. His intense little dark eyes were sizing up the new guy. He sniffed and appeared to reserve judgment. The bedroom door was partially ajar and Michael could see that Dixie had a large bed that looked extremely inviting. He figured he could fall asleep there in about two seconds, given his current state of exhaustion. Her bedroom also opened up to a private patio and hot tub with a view of lighted buildings and twinkling street lights that seemed to be the pulse and heartbeat of Memphis. Some quick mental arithmetic put the cost of the place way out of his range.

She emerged from her dressing room in a one-piece lounge suit, zipped up the front, accenting her svelte legs and ample bosom. Her hair was longer than Michael remembered and cut to suit her face, highlighting her large eyes and pouting lips. She walked with assurance, a female tigress in her den. He didn't know if he was the male tiger or some wounded thing she had dragged into her lair to play with. All of what he had seen raised profound personal and professional questions, and he knew he was walking a fine line. Sure, at some level he wanted to be alone with her, but he also had to know what she knew, how she had access and familiarity with Ace's people and ultimately, how it might help his case. Ever the cop.

Sure, Parker, he thought as he watched her ease across the room like a cat, exuding a sensuality that was still too fresh in the memory bank. Michael bit his lip, and the taste of blood refocused his mind. *Watch it, boy. This woman's pureness is more in question than ever. Do you really know her? Did you ever?*

Dixie Lee switched on her expensive Bang and Olufsen sound system and "Bridge Over Troubled Waters" oozed out of multiple speakers. She walked out onto the balcony with her drink and he followed, watching her. *"Sail on, silver girl, sail on by."*

"I just love it here," she said, throwing her head back with wild abandon.

"You've done all right, Dixie Lee. I'm impressed."

She turned to him as the song played, *"When you're weary, feeling small…"*

"Are you, Michael, or are you just full of questions?"

"Both, I suppose," he said, turning to face her and seeing that look in her eyes that once could melt him, limpid pools of blue that a man could drown in.

"Do you suppose it's destiny that has thrown us together again?" she asked.

"I believe everything happens for a reason. Pearl told me you called home looking for me that time," he said matter-of-factly or as some guilty admission that he knew she had sought him.

"Yes, but I waited too long, didn't I?" she asked in a little-girl voice, her fingers intertwined with his on the rail.

There was the rumble of thunder in the distance and a cool breeze caught her long, blond hair, lifting it from her shoulders. Michael thought she looked even more stunning with the gossamer cloud swirling around her face. His heart pounded, and the floor seemed to sway beneath his feet.

"Who's to say, Dixie? Everything is timing. Our timing was always just a bit off."

"The good times were very, very good, Michael," she said.

"Yes, they were," he answered. "I loved you once upon a time, but as I recall, that wasn't enough for you. Benjamin...was that the name of the man you wanted to marry? Was he enough?"

She came toward him, and put her hands up to his face. She dipped two fingers in her drink and placed them on his lips. The taste of salt from her margarita lingered. "No, I never married. I tried to find you. I left messages, but you never called. It's not too late. Your goodness always drew me back." Was this an act? A contrivance? She was not only inside the walls of his castle...she had scattered his armies.

"My so-called goodness wasn't enough to sustain your love, Dixie Lee." All the old anger and hurt came back then, and Michael lost a modicum of his usual control—"How can you afford this, this *place*? What on earth do you do for a living? Are you working for Ace and his crowd?" Finally, he stopped himself and looked at Dixie, really looked at her. There was hurt, but not surprise in her eyes which looked almost turquoise in the night light.

"That's a fine way to treat a woman who saved you tonight," she said, as two simultaneous tears overflowed her lower lids. Stepping back from him, she said, "So, you think I'm a gangster's call girl or even something worse?"

"I saw you in a very bad place tonight taking uppers with your expensive champagne. You seemed to have access to some very bad people, and now this. What do you expect me to think? I'm a cop."

She turned back toward the river and bowed her head. Somewhere, the horn of a distant river barge blared a bass note in the night.

"Michael, I went to that club for the first time with my boss, an older corporate manager who I worked for as his executive assistant. He introduced me around, and we partied and danced there off and on for a year. Yes, I take some pills now and then to get me up or bring me down—to make me forget. They are easy to get there, but you probably know that. I have sort of a lifetime pass there to see some of the best bands, and I love to dance," she said in a monotone of confession.

"I got that pass along with clear title to this condo when my boss went back to his family. It was a perk given him by his company, and he just mailed the deed to me one day, and I haven't heard from him since—don't want to." She stepped back inside to a long couch where she sat with her legs tucked under her, facing him with woebegone eyes. The Maltese looked concerned, sensing his mom was hurting as he snapped his head from Dixie to Michael and back again.

"I got involved with him one night after a trip to the club. There was supposed to be a group of us, but he maneuvered it to just be the two of us. I didn't understand it at the time, but I believe he had something slipped in my drink. The next thing I knew, I was back here in bed with him. He was good to me at first, but then became abusive and beat me when things weren't just right when he came here. I don't know why I stayed, Michael. I had called, and you were busy with the career you always wanted. I guess it was too late, way too late. I don't know. I have a job at AT&T as a service center supervisor. I just love it, Michael. He's been gone for about eight months and I'm alone, drifting, searching for something, for someone… someone like you." She looked up at him from under long lashes and he felt her longing and loneliness.

He desperately wanted to take this wounded bird into his

arms and make it all right. But the professional side of him needed information, didn't trust her, and was skeptical. Her story was likely a partial truth, but a big part of him was not her prosecutor but her defender.

"What is your former boss's name?" he asked.

"Frank DeVaney, Vice President of Turner Manufacturing and Transportation," she answered quietly, looking at the floor now. Was she assuming a posture to be punished now by him for her sins or seeking some sort of absolution?

Testing her, he asked, "Who is Fredrick, Dixie?"

She shuddered involuntarily and rubbed her arms where goose bumps ran.

"That guy is sick and weird. His name is Fredrick Hammel. He once went to Memphis State University. He came from a wealthy family near here, but he moved off into the radical underground and came back as this sort of sadistic disciple of the devil. He has hurt some of the girls who worked for Ace before."

Michael considered that was consistent with what their investigation had uncovered. "Why would Ace allow that freak to hurt his property?"

"Money. From what I heard from my former boyfriend when he was drunk or sniffing the angel dust, Ace makes deals with Fredrick's group—weapons, drugs, explosives, political protection, and there's some kind of reciprocal arrangement," she answered.

"How could your...friend possibly know all of this unless he was one of them?"

"He wasn't exactly one of them, but he was into Ace for some large gambling debts, which maybe adds up to the same thing. He couldn't pay. He wanted to live and clear the books, so he used some of the company trucks to transport illegal items, or so he told me when he was drunk."

"Ever see a sleazy politician from Mississippi at the club?" Michael asked.

"Oh, you mean that Hal guy. Yeah, he was always trying to hit on me and every other female in sight. He liked them young, I heard—real young. Ace has big plans for him and Mississippi if he's elected governor." She looked up, saw Michael looking at her and blushed, looked away, then blushed again—a sanguine red.

"You are a fount of information for someone who doesn't associate with gangsters," he said, still not believing as he clenched his teeth and fought against the presence of her, her shape and sway. *Is this Dixie? My Dixie?*

"I listen to the girls down there, but picked up most from Frank who was scared of all of them, but liked to pretend that he was better than them. He told me one night while snorting a line of coke, 'I'm not like that scum. I'm chairman of United Way.'"

The darkness of night had begun to yield a bit as morning threatened to break, and stars were almost absent, their evolving backdrop blinking them out of terrestrial view one by one.

The sun wasn't far away and Dixie had said all she was going to say. Michael asked to use her phone and then dialed Clay. "Hey, it's me. I'm all right, and I've learned much," he said.

Michael pulled back the phone as a stream of profanity erupted on the other end.

"Don't you ever do that to me again!" Clay retorted.

"Promise. No more dance clubs for me," Michael said, meaning every word.

"Okay, geez. We're getting in a complete rundown on license plates. The other agents followed Hal to a hotel near Southaven, Mississippi where he checked in with the two wholesome women," Clay said. "He has yet to emerge, but the boys have the bird dog from Ace's car and are still on him. The tags on the Ice Man's cars are coming back as belonging to an attorney in Tupelo named Reginald Morris. We're still processing information on the other license plates."

"Clay, please run the name Fredrick Hammel with the Feds,

and Frank DeVaney," Michael said, not satisfied with the sketchy information he had on the two.

"Do you want to share everything with the FBI now?"

"Not yet, unless you think it imperative, but I do want to line up IRS Intelligence agents to go with us when we hit the club."

"Ah, the Al Capone strategy," Clay said, referring to the "get 'em any way you can" plan.

"Yeah, did you see all those slot machines with no tax stamps they unloaded at the club? Not to forget the information regarding traffic we have from surveillance for the IRS boys to extrapolate taxes owed. Man, they have police state powers that make us look puny," Michael said. He also thought that they had powers that terrified the libertarian in him, but for now, they were useful, he thought. *No one ever thinks the government will use their power on average citizens, only "bad guys."*

When he finished the call, he turned back to Dixie Lee, who had exhausted the last of the dope's false energy. She was asleep on the couch, looking so familiar, an old friend he had missed even if the love part had gone bad. On impulse, he walked over to her, bent down and lifted her from the couch. She stirred, but didn't awaken. He took her to her bed, removed her shoes, and tucked her in. As the sun's first purple light brushed the dark skyline, he kissed her lightly on the forehead and stroked her soft hair. She purred like a kitten and smiled in her deep sleep. He walked back to the couch and fell into a hard asleep, dreaming of cops and robbers, lost loves, and second chances as a flock of raucous early morning fish-crows flew by cawing loudly, accusing him of hurting the pretty lady with blueberry eyes.

Some time later, somewhere far away, someone was banging and beating on the door to eternity, begging—no, demanding to be let in. Michael was trying to sleep, and wished they would stop. The noise grew louder and louder until he realized that it was someone banging on Dixie's door. He pushed through the last layers of sleep and heard it—a key turned in the lock. The door burst open, but banged hard as the gold Sears and Roebuck security chain caught it.

"Let me in, Dixie!" a man shouted. "Let me in my apartment right now, you little tramp." There was a crash as the big man put his shoulder to the door and ripped the security chain from its bracket—screws flying, dancing across the floor.

Michael rubbed the sleep from his eyes as he rounded the corner to see Dixie Lee facing a man in his early to mid-forties. He was a big guy, old athlete gone to seed most likely who now pretended that his golf games kept him in good shape—obviously not a gangster, more likely the corporate friend and good community citizen. Geordie, the Maltese, was barking ferociously at the man. He had his own truth.

"Frank, please leave," Dixie pleaded as Michael sensed at once all the ugliness and pain that was between her and this man.

"No, I won't leave. I give you this place and the doorman tells me that you brought a man up here, you little tramp." His hair was thinning on top, but he kept it long over his ears, and he was red-faced with a bit of gut over the belt.

Dixie snapped back, "My name is on the deed, Frank, and this is what you wanted. I haven't seen or heard from you in months, and now you break in like you own me?"

"Grrr," came Geordie's growl, followed by rapid, high-pitched barking.

"I'll come back whenever I please and take whatever I want," he shouted just as Michael quietly entered the room. The intruder grabbed the girl with one powerful hand and kicked her little dog across the room. "I'm gonna kill that little mutt!" he said, as Geordie yelped in pain.

"What's the ruckus out here?" Michael said, yawning. "I'm trying to sleep."

Dixie looked on the edge, and the man looked over the edge, possibly drunk or high. Both looked at Michael as if he were an apparition suddenly conjured up into what had probably been their

116

private little hell for a long time. Normally, he would have shown his badge and told Frank that he could leave or go to jail, but with Frank's connection to Ace and crew, there was too much danger to Dixie Lee and the operation.

Therefore, Michael tried charm. "My name is James," he said, sticking out his hand, "an old friend of Dixie's. She let me crash here on her couch last night."

"I don't care who you are. Get out!" he ordered imperiously. "Dixie and I need some private time to talk," he said, grabbing her hand roughly as if she was mere chattel, a thing to be abused to assuage his insecurities and self-loathing which he exuded like some pungent odor.

"Uh, Frank, is it? I'm afraid I can't do that. Dixie promised me breakfast, and we were just about to go down to IHOP for some pancakes. I love their pancakes, don't you, Frank?" He could see the flared nostrils and the jaws clench so tightly that it threatened to crack the man's pretty dental work.

Frank looked at him like he was crazy and turned to grab him by the shoulders to send the upstart on his way. What was it about his charm that seemed so lacking lately? As Frank reached with both hands out wide in an attempt to sloppily manhandle him, Michael stepped back and aimed the heel of his right hand at the bottom of Frank's nose with a hard, upward drive. A sickening snap followed as bones crunched in his nose, unleashing a torrent of blood. As Frank withdrew, Michael placed a nice right round kick of his heel into the soft tissue and cartilage of his right kneecap. The big man went down like a ton of bricks, just like academy instructors had promised, except this time, he had a little white ball of fur named Geordie fastened to his ankle, growling and shaking with all his might.

Sure, maybe Michael could have done it with less enthusiasm, but this was lesson number one, and he intended for Frank to remember it. Dixie Lee was stunned, looking first at Frank and then at her old love. There was no sign of compassion for old Frank. The cop in Michael had seen too many abused women, and wouldn't have been surprised if she went to Frank, but she didn't, and he was glad for her. Maybe, he was glad for himself as well. A clock radio popped on somewhere and radio host George Klein was promising to put the *"Geekers in your speakers."*

Michael walked over to the prostrate and moaning corporate exec, and bent down to assess the damage to the man who was sweating cold beads and breathing heavily.

Frank groaned, "You broke my nose and my leg. I have to speak at the chamber dinner tonight."

Michael examined him closely like a sympathetic physician.

"Oh, it isn't that bad, Frank. You just go on home and clean up. Ice down that nose, use a little of your wife's cover-up, and you won't look half-bad. You may limp a bit, but just ice the knee, work it some, and it'll be fine. It's not broken, at least so far."

Frank just moaned and mopped his nose as he tilted his head back to stop the blood. Michael turned to Dixie, whom he thought looked like the girl he once knew, taking the first step away from the vexation of her tormentor.

"Dixie, please call the doorman to help Frank to his car," Michael said, as he reached down to help Frank up and to the elevators.

The fight was gone from Mr. Community, and he steadied himself against his tormentor as they hobbled out to the elevators with a wet towel on his nose.

The bing of the bell and the flash of light marked the approach of Frank's coach.

They waited for Charlie, the doorman, to come up, and Michael looked at Frank. "I'm sorry we got off on the wrong foot here, Frank," he said, "but before your friendly doorman arrives, let me make sure we understand each other so this unfortunate accident isn't repeated."

118

Somewhere in Frank's bruised head, Michael knew would be a festering, *"I'll get you for this,"* that must be nipped in the bud and ripped out by the roots.

Frank just groaned in pain. "If you come back here and bother her, or if I find out you have harmed her in any way, I'll be back, and this licking will seem gentle. I will also tell Ace that you are talking to the Feds about what your trucks really carry, and you know what Ace will do." There was genuine terror in Frank's face for the first time.

"Don't think about going to Ace with this because my sources will whisper in his ear about what a loose cannon you are. Then, just in case Ace doesn't kill you immediately, tips will be left with the Memphis Commercial Appeal about your double life, and there goes the marriage, the chairmanships, the country clubs and such—and yes, the IRS will show up. It would be most unfortunate. Do we understand each other?"

Frank had been told all his life that he was special, privileged and superior, but now he looked at Michael from behind his swelling nose with wide bloodshot eyes turning more black and purple by the minute, and nodded like a born-again Boy Scout.

Charlie, the stocky doorman, arrived, but was somewhat reluctant when the elevator door opened. He summed up winners and losers and supported Frank by the waist and helped him inside. "Take him down, give him an ice pack and put him in his car," Michael directed.

Charlie asked as he hit the garage level button, "What happened?"

Michael responded, "No big deal. We were practicing that new disco dance, and he couldn't seem to get the moves—just two left feet, I guess. Maybe the local Arthur Murray dance school has some openings."

Charlie responded with an unconvinced, "Right," and the doors closed. There was every reason to believe that Frank would never be back nor ever say a word to anyone. The blueblood bully would lie awake at night praying that no gangster or federal agent would ever show up at his door, and that none of his old fraternity brothers would ever find out and see him for who he really was and take from him the very silver spoon that had been in his mouth the day he was born. Michael felt something warm and wet on his bare foot and when he looked down, there was his new best friend, Geordie. The little dog looked at him with unabashed acceptance and the beginnings of deep affection in his big eyes and in the rapid wag of his stubby snow-white tail.

Dixie Lee stood silently, watching Michael beside the shattered door. She came to him and hugged him and cried softly into his shoulder, years of torment and anguish pouring out.

"I'm not a bad person, Michael," she pleaded as she lowered her face into her hands. Her flaxen hair gleamed in the morning light, as she began a tender but dry sniffling.

He sat with her and squeezed her hands softly. "I know," he whispered. "I know."

Dixie began to talk—haltingly, at first in little-girl whispers, punctuated by gasping, choking half-sobs.

She spoke, she paused, she considered, reconsidered and she resisted before a final embrace of all that strained to come forth. A gut-wrenching emission of half-mocking laughter deteriorated into a Nile of tears as she gnawed on her lower lip…reddening the left corner.

She rambled, avoided, retreated, and charged the ghosts of her life in a babbling self-interrogation and examination of things gone wrong, good and evil, wrongs to be righted, and people she desperately wanted a second chance to tell only that she was sorry—for what, she was not sure. Gone were her effervescence and affected nightclub charm. Only nervous, blue, vulnerable eyes peered out from behind a veil, dissolving with each passing moment.

As she talked, somewhere far away muffled sounds drifted in—arguments in adjacent apartments, pieces of television commercials wondering "where the yellow went", and a distant police siren. The fluttering near the window of a sooty chimney swift searching for sanctuary seemed a metaphor for the tortured woman Michael watched now in the subdued lighting of the apartment.

Dixie spoke of family—her sisters particularly, reddish-blondes who looked like her—her Baptist church, long since abandoned, and a pastor who seemed to be speaking to her every Sunday—too close to home. Brief smiles punctuated embraces of simpler times—a lifelong collection of butterfly charms... monarchs and swallowtails adorning her childhood bedroom. Rambling, she asked him if he knew that she could type 100 words a minute now.

She remembered and recounted whispers about her and Frank around corporate water fountains with yellowed handles. Then, she scurried to safety behind stories of her gardens, gold and purple pansies in late Southern winters, and the fragrance of red azaleas that winds carried across gardens she tended so lovingly in the springs before she moved here.

Ancient tablets were brought forth from behind heavy doors that were rusted shut...concealing a gateway to a distant realm to which only she had the key—a key reluctantly used and now revealing smells and textures of darkness that made Michael want to retch.

This man, Frank, had become the long-dead man now reincarnated in some kind of twisted nightmare—the long-gone abuser of little girls who still preyed on the weak, now returned from the grave to tell the woman-child that she deserved no better—a male of no gentleness, a brute of lethal vileness, a thing and entity that reveled in cruelty. He was at once a charmer who elevated the broken bird with lavish attention only to withdraw and heighten the savagery of the clenched fist disguised as a helping hand—a hammer to render her subservient and unquestioning.

All attempts to extricate herself brought only a pounding of her self-image and a promise to get her fired from her new job due to his power—pure masculine power with no semblance of the feminine so essential to balance the delicate dance in a world he'd redefined as only the abused and the abuser—selective affection applied only as hot and cold partitions in a game of expendable gifts to exploit the terror in an expendable woman.

During that long, tortuous purge, the strangest and most wonderful transformation began to take place. Michael realized that he was witnessing a long-overdue birthing process. Dixie was emerging from a womb of sorts. The old Dixie began to melt away before his eyes. The walls seemed to close in where her pain seemed unbearable, just before she burst into the blinding light at the end of the narrow, dark tunnel ahead. She gasped her first fresh breath in a vivid new world where the grays and blacks gave way to a rainbow of bright colors. Truth, hidden in her darkness, now began to light her path.

She had calculated a false freedom when she first left him, but now she had taken her first deep, cleansing breaths as a free woman, once utterly and awfully alone in a rented world—now a butterfly come forth from the shell of the cocoon of despair and hollowness that had imprisoned her for so long.

The soft hum of the condo's air unit brought them gently to real time, and the gentle breeze moved the drapes around them. There was almost an audible bump as the now rotten poison apple she had tasted so long ago fell away from her countenance to the grounds of a new landscape filled with fruit as in the original Garden. Distant hymns of redemption played.

Her eyes were puffy and swollen. She appeared drained and languid. Bright-red blood showed in the corner of a gnawed and bruised lip that involuntarily trembled, but Michael thought that she never looked more beautiful.

Was it real? Could it have been so easy? There was nothing—absolutely nothing—easy about what he had just seen. This would have made the angels weep, first in empathy at pain and then in joy as chains were broken and the lonely inmate came forth from her tomb like Lazarus.

The quiet, solemn vigil of the small white dog with the crying eyes at his lady's feet bore testimony to it all. The air suddenly seemed fresher, cleaner, as if a stain had been washed away.

Dixie wearily wiped away her tears, smearing her mascara, forming gothic black smudges under her eyes. Reading his eyes and his heart, she said, "Thanks for not judging me. You're still my knight in shining armor, aren't you?"

He smiled and said, "Shucks, t'aint nothing any red-blooded Southern gentleman wouldn't do."

After a long, silent moment of squeezing her hands and fighting off his own tears, he called Clay and asked for speedy Bureau taxi service. Clay said he was already on his way.

He really wanted to stay and talk for hours of simple joys and of hope and faith, but he knew they both needed time to think, digest, and consider second chances.

He told Dixie that duty called, but that he'd be back if she wanted to see him or needed help. She cried a bit more and said that she did want to see him. She then said something that touched him way down deep, giving him goosebumps to his toes. "No matter where you have been or where you go, you always remain here." She placed her quavering hand over her heart and held it there as she stretched up on flexed toes in a childlike truth, gazing at him through big tear-filled eyes that now flowed again when the well should have been exhausted, and said, *"Deep in the heart of Dixie."*

Michael caught his reflection in the gilded mirror as the elevator counted down the floors. His eyes were swollen and puffy. His hair and clothes were disheveled and he needed a shave and shower. He thought that he looked pale, older than he remembered, and considered that the past twenty-four hours had been a little too much. He felt like a ship lost in churning shoals without sails or lifeboats. Maybe he needed a new plan. Maybe he needed to pray.

CHAPTER TWELVE

*"I...will sacrifice, I will endure, I will fight cheerfully
and do my utmost, as if the issue of the whole struggle
depended on me alone."*
—Martin Treptow

Back at the Ace of Diamonds Club, Fredrick had been put up in one of the apartments in the rear of the club that Ace kept for "special" clients. During the night, Fredrick began to awaken with convulsions and shrieks of that which the frightened women attending him thought was "madness." Fredrick rose and demanded lights everywhere. He normally couldn't bear bright lights, but now seemed afraid of the dark. He shook violently, his pale lips turning blue.

He grabbed the attendants and cried, "He's been here. He!"

Sweat running down his ghostly face onto his blue lips, he stood swaying to and fro, reeling off garbled phrases and quotes from the Satanic bible. He used words from a language no one knew in a voice not his. It was hoarse and wild...not really speech, but eruption. His red eyes were feverish with fear, then excitement. He seemed possessed by demonic forces, with him as a temporary vehicle, prey for things the hapless girls at the club could not see.

"He's been here! Help me!" he would cry and roughly grab them as he waved a stiletto madly.

"Who? Who's been here, Mr. Hammel?" they asked. "Is it the devil?" one terrified girl asked.

"It was him… him…with her!" he screamed.

The girls, frightened out of their minds, looked at each other. "Who are you talking about?"

Then he became quiet suddenly and fell onto the bed, where he twitched and then was still. They approached him carefully, but the duality in him had disappeared. They sighed with relief, but suddenly, he sat up one last time and asked, "There! In the shadows in the corner! Who is there?"

He closed his eyes, swayed and whispered, "Oh, it's you."

A smothering, pulsing presence of evil then filled the room, and the girls started running and never stopped.

* * *

On occasion, you are caught driving down the road in thick fog, unable to see beyond your front bumper. You know it isn't safe, but you feel your way along, hoping for relief, for clarity, for deliverance. Life can be much like that, and when the thick soup unexpectedly breaks, you suddenly find that you can see beyond the immediate, round the bend, over the horizon into the future. Your vision is clear, and there they are—the beasts near at hand and the Promised Land just beyond. Those moments of exit from sensory deprivation can be illuminating and intoxicating. The last twenty-four hours had been like that.

The full candle power of a sun that didn't seem 93 million miles away was breaking over Memphis, illuminating the good and the bad. Michael had a short wait for Clay in the lobby of the Riverside Condominiums, where the headlines of the morning edition of *The New York Times* caught his eye. "U.S. and French

Drug Agents Break the *'French Connection.'*" Corsican gangsters and the U.S. Mafia had long operated the route out of Marseilles for heroin smuggling, supplying the bulk of the U.S. demand. It sounded like a huge success. *Prices should be going up on the street for smack, law of supply and demand,* he thought. *Good—or was it?* On the other hand, that would only drive up profits, fund new smuggling routes, and provide more money to buy protection and corrupt police. Was it only the independent operators who were indicted while the protected and the sanctioned continued untouched, providing fuel for an unaccountable shadow world?

He couldn't think about that now. It made his head hurt worse than it already did. Folding the paper under his arm, he walked up to the yellow curb to wait for Clay. The ochre-orange sun was up now warming the earth and illuminating the silver and black concrete towers around him, the mirrored exteriors reflecting and magnifying the sun. The beauty that was the city in the purple hues of early morning had faded in the harsh light, turning yellow-red with each passing minute. Honking horns and screeching brakes shattered the silence of the night as people hurried to the pedestrian jobs that they hated. Exhaust fumes replaced the smell of the river and the fragrant magnolia trees that grew in abundance. His senses were assaulted and his head pounded. He had had too little sleep, but none of that mattered—he was full of adrenalin and the whispered promise of what was to come.

Just as Clay approached, a late working girl wandered up and looked at him as a possible "one more for the road". She was young, too young, with a wide, soft face with lots of baby fat. She had a wide expanse of hips and a small roll of fat just above her belt. She began to assume a mock pose of seduction that was more grotesque and tragic than sensual. Michael felt an overpowering sense of sadness and declined as gently as he could, saying, "My friend is picking me up. I must go," then added, "But it's hard to say no to a beautiful lady like you." The girl actually blushed.

Michael jumped into the gray sedan and Clay skillfully merged into the pressing traffic, leaving the young girl to live in her own private hell.

"Okay, tell me everything. I want to hear all about this Dixie," Clay said, with a mischievous smile as wide as the river. "Don't leave anything out."

Michael hesitated for a moment, wondering where Clay had spent the night, but let it ride. "You got me, Clay. See this bruise on the heel of my hand? She was so wild that I had to fight her off. It was touch and go for a while, but my chastity is intact."

Clay looked at him and, shaking his head, said, "Oh, if it was anyone but you, I wouldn't believe it. But with you, it's almost plausible. You don't have anything to share with your buddy?" he begged as a tiny old Pinto whipped in front of him and he sat on the horn.

"No, I never kiss and tell. Now, for God's sake, please tell me where we are in all of this."

Clay began to reel off a verbal intelligence report with the efficiency of someone with a photographic memory and a keen sense of organization. He could paint a picture, an artist without a brush. His matrixes of connecting intelligence analysis, combined with the input of his counterparts at the IRS, the FBI, and the federal drug boys, provided a good treetop view of the swamp they found themselves in. He was himself but a tad more animated, even more excited than usual.

"A loose confederation exists in Mississippi between a few key independent drug dealers, several major mobbed-up dealers and smugglers, and a very radical faction of the Weathermen called 'the Angels of the Apocalypse.' Fredrick Hammel is the eastern director of this organization based out of Memphis with safe houses within Mississippi. The FBI has pegged him as a major figure involved peripherally with at least two bank robberies and the 'Winter Soldier' meeting of anti-war activists and a plan to assassinate key pro-war senators. Fredrick is known to associate with groups like the Vietnam Veterans against the War, and is believed to be a conduit for and launderer of money from the Soviets and the North Vietnamese," Clay said as a transfixed Michael listened as this James Bond movie plot script unfolded. A gray-and-white possum with an oily sheen darted from a stand of trees near an overturned silver garbage can. The sneer on his face could have been a judgment on it all.

"The spooks at Langley say that the KGB's top priority has been to damage American power, judgment, and credibility. KGB chairman Yuri Andropov managed the Soviet anti-Vietnam War operation and financed many groups including Fredrick's crowd. Andropov said that they have 'damaged the U.S. foreign-policy consensus, poisoned domestic debate in the U.S., built a credibility gap between America and European public opinion through disinformation operations, and believe that Vietnam is their most significant success,'" Clay said.

"Fredrick frequently travels to Paris, where he has met with leaders of the North Vietnamese Communist Party and some American sympathizers in the anti-war crowd. Memphis is familiar turf for Fredrick given his background, and Mississippi offers a neutral zone where he feels the enforcement community is incompetent. His wealthy parents still live in Memphis, but have little contact with their son. They indulged him as a child. Oddly enough, his privileged childhood evolved into a full-blown hatred for capitalism and for Christians and a penchant for violence and blood. He often quotes from the Satanic bible. He tested at the genius level, but on the other hand, has been plagued by mental illness and instability, and there were periods where he was on lithium. He is classified as dangerous, delusional, and unpredictable."

Michael said, "Go on," thinking about the deadly character he had crossed.

"Crazy or not, he is cunning and has a knack for using capitalism to further his anarchist goals. The drug trade has been a lucrative source of funding for rebellion. Some of the drugs are smuggled into the country courtesy of mercenaries working for the CIA who aid so-called 'freedom fighters' with weapons for whatever side we back at the moment. These 'soldiers of fortune' then bring back cocaine on return flights. Some of these pilots are left-leaning counter-culture types and have formed an alliance with Fredrick and his Communist backers to use that influence to obtain high-quality drugs to smuggle into the country, helped by rogue CIA insiders. A group of narco-terrorists in Colombia seem to be emerging as a major supplier of cocaine that we see, and there is again some alliance between these thugs, Fredrick's group, and many enterprising coke dealers," Clay finally concluded out of breath as he took a long drink of a cold Coke from a bag of ice on the floor of the sedan.

Michael wanted to ask for a scorecard, who was good—who was bad—and who just ugly. "So, how does that fit with the local scene and guys we are more familiar with?"

"Ace Connelly is a target of opportunity for the IRS boys and the FBI. He is laundering money through his clubs for two Mafia families. He also has some arrangement with Fidel Castro for using Cuba as a safe haven for wanted mob figures and for drug shipments. It's believed that Fredrick facilitated these meetings with Castro and that somewhere in the midst of this trading of favors, this symbiotic relationship emerged between the local mob and the radical political fringe." He shrugged his shoulders as he changed lanes again, and said, "Yeah, I know. This is strange stuff, and I had to ask myself, 'How did we get in the middle of this?'" He coughed and took a large white pill for his nagging health issues. His color was not good, and his winces at sudden pain punctuated his narrative.

"The gangsters actually hate Communists, but business is business. Ace met Fredrick when he was a young boy at Memphis

State University. Fredrick was a student leader of the left there, such as it was, and Ace cultivated a relationship with him, using him to distribute drugs to local counter-culture groups.

"That arrangement has evolved to the use of this trucking company and others for the smuggling of drugs, guns, and stolen goods across the country and into Mexico. Ace now controls full or part ownership in three clubs in Mississippi as well as his clubs in Memphis. He used some muscle to expand here but also political influence. Former Judge Hal Davidson, whom we watched the other night, has made overtures to local officials on his behalf. Davidson has also laundered money for Ace by arranging for relatives and supporters to donate, in name only, large sums of mob cash for the support of his race for governor. He returns some to Ace in the form of *consulting contracts* for his campaign," Clay said.

"He also does some legal work for Ace for large fees that are rebated to Ace and his affiliated organizations and front men. Your friend Hal's a savvy politician, but short on smarts when it comes to women. Sex, booze, and money are his vices, and he doesn't care how he gets them. That's how Ace got him—through call girls and gambling excursions to Vegas where old Hal dropped a bundle and became indebted to Ace. We have identified the two prostitutes who spent the night with him. They are call girls run by a Memphis pimp on Ace's payroll. Truth is—Hal couldn't get out now if he wanted to."

It was all just too much, but Sonny had warned Michael that these were bad, bad people. Still, he was afflicted with a grain of the denial that most Americans labor under—a belief that these things couldn't happen in the sweet land of liberty.

"Documented?" Michael asked.

"Yep, Ace has audio clips, movies of him with underage girls, and documentation of him taking cash—seemingly a frequent thing. They have big plans for him if he becomes governor, and may expand to the Gulf Coast to challenge the Marcello family out of New Orleans," Clay continued.

"There appears to be only marginal connections between Hal and Fredrick at the club. He has told Ace that he cannot abide Communists or traitors to his country." Clay stopped and laughed a hearty laugh that shook his whole belly and shoulders.

"What a patriot," Michael said, and they both laughed again, but inside, Michael felt the need of that shower more than ever. He was feeling really tired and asked Clay to stop at a small coffee shop in a sketchy neighborhood, an old trolley car refurbished as a colorful diner—good coffee and food where you couldn't go too wrong by arresting most of the clientele.

He thought again of the dumpling-faced girl on the street. She probably ate alone in just such dives all over inner-city Memphis every day before her pimp took her money and beat her for holding out on him just to keep her a broken slave in his harem. Michael inhaled his eggs and bacon and listened while Clay ignored his food.

Clay resumed his now whispered diffraction of his crime story. "However, Fredrick does use a Tupelo Columbus-area lawyer on Ace's payroll for defense of organized crime figures. Reginald Morris seems to be an up-and-coming player way beyond his turf in Northeast Mississippi. The IRS is looking at him. He has been observed flying into some remote getaways near Sardis Lake with Ace, several local politicians, and some Italian imports. Oh, yeah, they have a picture of him with Fredrick. He actually has Fredrick holding this little white poodle that Morris seems very attached to and takes with him everywhere."

"No joke? I'm curious, does Reggie fly in alone?"

"Why, you know him?" Clay asked.

"Just that he had a penchant for big parties and was very friendly with some local cops."

"Funny you should mention that, his almost constant

companion on these flights is a local detective out of Tupelo named Howard Floyd. They say he is up for chief of detectives and maybe head of a regional narcotics unit." Clay waved off an approaching waitress who had the best red hair money could buy and a mouth full of Double-Bubble gum, which she smacked over the plates she delivered.

"That's the one. He had a reputation in town of being quick with his blackjack and slow to refuse kickback. I interned over there in the sheriff's department before I left Ole Miss and the deputies warned me to watch out for him. He used to tip off the bootleggers every time he learned of a raid—that was back when Lee County was dry."

"Well, he's in a different league now," Clay said. "Associating with organized crime figures and narco-terrorists is a giant leap from tipping local bootleggers."

The trip through the old hometown scrapbook and Clay's rogue's gallery was so fresh, Michael could almost smell the spoor of fleshly usury and decay.

"Well, they said he was ambitious."

"Yeah, I guess so. Oh, by the way, Fredrick's people owned the ammo stored at your hash dealer's pad. It was about to be moved to a site for an armed robbery in Atlanta. Fredrick was facilitating a cell of the Black Liberation Army over there that routinely kills police as an initiation rite," Clay said, shaking his head. "You know we've hit the mother lode. We said we wanted to stop wasting time on the street level!"

"Yeah, buddy, but are we up to it? Suddenly, I feel very small and insignificant," Michael said, looking longingly at Clay's untouched eggs. Clay consumed three cups of strong coffee, but lived on the adrenaline of the chase.

He shoved his plate at Michael, and continued. "Well, we've been given the green light by the Feds to move on the nightclub, see who we get in our raid and what we can squeeze out of them. IRS intelligence agents have signed on to come with us. The big pool tournament is coming up this weekend providing an opportunity, and we'll take advantage of it. Obviously, we have to get busy, but God knows we already have plenty of probable cause for search warrants."

The erstwhile veteran table lady brought Michael another basket of biscuits from the kitchen because she "loved to see a man who enjoyed his food." Even sticky gum remnants on the basket couldn't deter Michael.

Michael gobbled down Clay's breakfast and laid a ten on the table to cover the two breakfasts and a tip. Both remained quiet as they made their way out through the crowd of mostly black patrons. Traffic had increased, and the Memphis reflected from uncountable mirrors and windshields was almost blinding. Clay forced his way into the stream of traffic amidst what Michael preferred to believe were waves of good will and one-fingered salutes to Clay's skills as a driver.

The discussion resumed as the big car headed south. "Our boys in the van say that the traffic has already picked up at the Full House Club. They've noted license plates from a dozen states visiting the club in the last twenty-four hours. Most are staying in Memphis and partying at Ace's clubs, but definitely coming down to our place. Some are private pool hustlers and their stake horses. Some are mob favorites, and some are professional gamblers and known drug runners. Your informant left word on our secret line for you that they've brought in ten thousand amphetamines for the tournament and party for however long it lasts, and the girls will be dealing table to table. A bunch of undeclared cash will be in the club for betting. The IRS wants that and the slot machines without tax stamps. They also want to seize the books of the club. The informant said that there will be a bunch of heavily armed people in the club for the tournament to protect the cash and their investments."

"The tournament starts Friday night, you say?"

"Yeah, boy," Clay said, grinning.

"Then, let's rack 'em up—eight ball in Ace's side pocket."

The gray ghost turned on Elvis Presley Boulevard dodging a yelping yellow dog that ran in front of them and leaving behind the imbecile drivers hurrying so diligently, arriving wherever they were going only by the grace of God.

* * *

There was a flurry of activity as they began the logistical process of obtaining enough agents to make the raid flawless and overwhelming in force. Defensive and offensive weapons were chosen—meeting places, command rooms, motels, and jail facilities reserved. While MBN agents processed their requests, Clay and Michael set out to write their affidavit for the club search warrant. The final document was five legal pages long and contained overwhelming evidence supporting the raid. It laid the foundation for the probable cause to enter the club and conduct a wide-ranging search for illegal drugs, weapons, contraband, and stolen goods.

The next problem was to find a judge who would not tip off the Cotton Row "businessmen" or their protectors at the sheriff's office. Since the local elected justice court judges had a history of tipping off the subjects they signed warrants on, a circuit court judge was found who had a reputation for honesty and reliability.

Clay and Michael traveled to the far end of the judicial district to meet in chambers with Judge Otis White, a sixty-year-old jurist, a man to be admired and respected. The gray-haired jurist, still in his black robe from court, looked over the warrant and affidavit and said, "Boys, this is the best probable cause I've ever seen for a search warrant." He signed his name, looked up at the anxious pair, and said, "Godspeed to you boys. Give 'em hell!"

Armed with the enabling warrant and encouragement, formal preparations went full speed ahead. A bank of rooms was acquired at the Howard Johnson Motel in Memphis. Rooms were filled with agents from various agencies, and they were kept busy, focused, and almost out of trouble. Rock and disco music drifted down the halls as backdrop for card games, bad stories, and coarse jokes.

Agents, brought in from other areas, lacked a certain sense of ownership in a case that was not strictly "theirs." They acted almost like hired guns or mercenaries and too much time waiting could result in a shoddy performance when the real thing arrived. They could get sloppy, or they could get mean depending upon their personality. Some tried to sneak women into their rooms. One platinum-haired woman in black slacks, a white blouse, and large black sunglasses was intercepted by Clay on the way to an arranged meeting. A stewing pot will eventually boil over, and Clay repeatedly said, "The sooner we saddle up, the better." He was right.

Sonny's input was constant, apprising Michael of who was coming and when, who would be packing heat, and who would be holding drugs. No one was more excited than Sonny, and he provided a flow of information concerning critical details—where the cash was kept and what the affiliations were of individuals representing different crime organizations. He suggested an optimum time to strike in order to catch as many fish in the net as possible. Yes sir, for Sonny, this was payback, no more stealing his shade in his old age.

Michael wanted to call Dixie Lee, but the days flew by— every moment was precious as the raid planning continued. She would have to wait and wonder for now. She had a number for emergencies, but hadn't used it. She was leaving it all in the visiting team's court. Still, the feel of her face in the snug of his neck as she held on to him lingered and had no cure.

The antsy agents waited until the second night of the tournament on Sonny's advice. It was a tough wait for the agents, but finally, their synchronized watches counted down the last ticks. On Saturday night just before midnight, a small police armada left Memphis to descend on the club now full of stern men, loud women, and hustlers with custom cue-stick cases. The Full House Club had Lincolns and Caddies lined up and down both sides of the highway from Memphis. The lot was packed, and two deputy sheriff cars were present. Four teenagers parked cars for big tips and would have to be scattered before agents went in.

Agents arrived at the Full House, stepped out of their vehicles, and scurried to their assigned positions, disturbing late night masked raccoons who saw the armada, abandoned their own raid on club trash bins, and retreated into the woods. There were last-minute checks of weapons, ammunition, and communications equipment. Agents armed with 12-gauge Remington pump shotguns covered all the doors, silently awaiting Michael's signal.

Michael wanted everyone to settle into position and be ready for whatever was to come. He wanted to savor the sounds and smells of the place. The Full House Club could just as well have been an old saloon or brothel on the edge of Tombstone or Deadwood. The throaty laughter of women, the spin of the roulette wheel, and the shouts of excited gamblers filled the air. The smell of whiskey was raw, repulsive and alluring. How many bottles had already been consumed? How many lines of coke, how many pills and joints by the boys who blew smoke in this unfolding vignette—an endless game on a stage in a place no one had ever heard of—a sinking ship where all the deck chairs were about to be rearranged.

Michael took a deep breath and nodded, grasping the door handle with sweating hands. He slowly opened the door and entered the Full House Club unnoticed. There was no gunfire—nothing. No one turned. No one paid him any attention—gambling, sex, and drugs continued unabated by those whose senses were drugged by pills and booze—a surreal moment. Serious faces framed the borders of six pool tables, a few couples moved on a small dance floor, and others drank at tin tables, sitting in wire chairs. Waitresses produced black and red capsules from aprons as they bent over the tables taking orders.

The dimly-lit dive was a haze of blue cigarette smoke that burned Michael's eyes and irritated his nose. Every square inch of the Full House Club was packed with patrons—there was no place to move and no oxygen to breathe—just embers of dying cigarettes and dark bodies moving in the dim light. The area along the red naugahyde-padded bar was covered with men ordering drinks and waitresses in red aprons and black hot pants holding trays of foaming beer high over their heads as they maneuvered in the crowd. Michael's watering eyes took it all in. He saw the six agents sent in to keep him from being bushwhacked, two of them next to big bouncers near the door. So far, so good... Now!

On his signal, automatic weapons were shoved into the rib cages of the burly bouncers, freezing them on the spot. Everything slowed down then, seeming to move to the rhythm of Michael's heartbeat. The pounding music was a distant buzz. Heads turned slowly, ever so slowly, as Michael announced, "State Bureau of Narcotics. You're all under arrest! Nobody move!" Silence, then a record dropped in the jukebox, and Merle Haggard began to sing about the night the bottle let him down.

Thunder? Shots? No, the rumble was from wily patrons dropping heavy weapons to the floor to avoid carrying concealed weapon charges. Suddenly, he felt like a big target standing at the front door with a bull's-eye painted on his forehead. He pulled his own weapon and moved to the shadows just as a small army of agents flooded the room.

There were screams and yells as people were thrown to the floor or ordered, "Against the wall, hands in the air!" Theatrics ensued that Michael didn't like. Somewhere, there was the smell of tear gas as a woman tried to gas an agent with a small pocket dispersant. The caustic fumes reddened the eyes of nearby agents.

A few, who weren't wise or too drunk to care, resisted and loud "whacks" registered as they were slammed down on dice tables and cuffed. The floor was slick with spilled beer, vomit, and a few tooth fragments, and the "innocent bystanders" protested like babies. All of the agents were tense, some scared, and a few just mean, thoroughly enjoying the opportunity to hurt those who they believed normally held the upper hand, but there was no serious damage to good procedure. They'd been cooped up, but not too long.

The two deputy sheriffs in the joint for the protection of Ace and friends were politely ordered to leave immediately, and they seemed all too eager to comply, dropping their beers and their women along the way. They could be counted on to run squealing to the High Sheriff and all of the beneficiaries of the largess of Ace and friends.

Michael turned to face the Ace of Diamonds himself who was fuming. Anthony "Ace" Connelly looked at him with visceral anger and hatred in his eyes. Michael smiled and handed the angry proprietor his copy of the warrant.

His face contorting into a blood-fed reddish pulp, more fist than face, Ace snapped, "What're you doing to me? Do you know who I am?"

"We're serving a warrant on you, Ace. I'm just here looking for crimes in progress. Know of any? Better not answer. You have the right to remain silent and have a lawyer." Mean eyes followed Michael through the crowd as agents processed patrons for trips to jail amidst a blur of girlish squeals and slurred protests.

Ace and Michael were surrounded by busy agents going about their work, frisking guests, looking for weapons, drugs— any contraband. The IRS boys were clotted around a bank of slot machines busily making notes. Ace glanced at several Mafia thugs that he was particularly concerned about and was met by cold, threatening stares. He blinked and swallowed hard. If the cops didn't kill him, these men would.

A large man about thirty, slender in an immaculate suit, who looked as if he had never seen the sun, with an accountant's demeanor, joined Michael and Ace. "Ace, I would like to introduce you to Federal Agent John Cook of the IRS Criminal Intelligence Division."

One nail in Ace's coffin. Michael thought, *If I had a hammer, I'd hammer in the morning, at midnight, too.*

Cook stepped up and said, "Mr. Connelly, I also have papers to serve on you. My agents are now seizing all of the slot machines in your club. None have federal tax stamps on them. Your club's books, receipts for tonight, and loose cash will also be confiscated. We'll compute and extrapolate the estimated federal income tax that you'll owe the government from the time you opened this club until this moment. You will be informed in writing. I can tell you that from what we have seen, it'll be substantial—something with high six figures." Ace's eyes closed, and he didn't look well. His mouth went wide as if to scream, but nothing came out.

Compute and extrapolate! Man, you have to love these tax boys when they aren't auditing you, Michael thought. Money was the soft underbelly of gangsters, and Ace couldn't conceal his pain. Michael left Ace with Agent Cook while he continued his standard "taxman cometh" speech. It was time to inventory the catch. Several girls were being handcuffed in the corner and Michael noticed that one of the waitresses was cuffed way too tight. Her wrists were already reddened and swelling.

He took his cuff key, smiled at her, and said, "Let me loosen those up for you a bit, Miss. Can't have us accused of police brutality to a lady." She looked up at him from under her mane of rust-colored hair, blushing, surveying him through long, dark lashes and a ton of makeup with which she had tried in vain to cover her large freckles.

"Thank you," she said. *Treat a pro like a lady and you make a friend, or an informant, for life,* he thought. He asked her name and directed the arresting agents to hold her at the jail. He sensed an opening and decided to interview her sometime before dawn to see what she knew and what they could trade.

A weary but pumped Clay walked up. "Michael, we got thirty-six people cuffed and waiting for transportation. More are being processed."

"What are the charges so far?" Lines were formed and the shuffling step of people who were restrained could be heard. One loud threat to sue everybody was cut short.

"Seven waitresses arrested for possession of amphetamines." Clay answered. "The rest are for drug or weapons charges, and a couple for resisting arrest. Oh, we have two more on outstanding felony warrants that we identified earlier from surveillance. Counting the guns on the floor and the ones we caught holding, we have seized over fifty semi-automatic weapons tonight. Two were fully automatic. Cook's boys have seized almost two hundred and forty thousand dollars in cash from the pool tables, the bag boys, and the stake horses."

"Oh, the field drug kits also test positive for drugs in a stash of beer cans we found separate from the others," Clay said with a goofy grin as Ace, momentarily forgotten, looked as if he was about to have a serious cardiac incident.

"Drugs in the aprons—drugs in the beers! Ace, this is just getting worse by the minute," Michael said. A loud *bam-bam* across the room caught Michael's attention. Three agents were employing sledgehammers—destroying the wall near Ace's dice tables to expose his series of dealer-controlled magnets used to stop the loaded dice in mid-roll.

Michael stood aside and watched Ace's handcuffed waitresses

and gangster guests in their shiny suits and slicked-back hair being marched off one by one to waiting vans. The tax boys paraded past him with box after box of records and stacks of cash. Ace's business license was unceremoniously taken from the wall. Michael had a fleeting pang of sympathy for Ace, but it passed rapidly—he was dangerous now. He had been financially broken, humiliated, and worst of all, made to appear the fool in front of his dangerous and psychotic friends.

"Ace, the good news is that we are not going to arrest you tonight, since you're not holding any drugs or weapons personally. The bad news is the FBI will be by to see you with federal indictments from the grand jury for racketeering, conspiracy to traffic in drugs, and prostitution. Some of these girls you use look to be underage, and that could be a violation of the Mann Act—white slavery. Just go now, and make nice to all the people who are going to be really, really upset with you. Get back to Memphis and don't come back. You aren't welcome here," Michael said emphatically.

His eyes were bulging, and he alternated between tears, a dry gagging sound, and a hiccup. The angry man looked like he was burning Michael's face into his brain as he backed toward the door wagging his finger. "I'll be seeing you," he muttered.

"In all the old, familiar places?" Michael asked, grinning broadly.

Ace stormed out and roared off toward the Tennessee state line in his Cadillac, peeling rubber and fishtailing from side to side until his taillights disappeared from sight.

Clay said, "You have just made yourself an enemy. We have not seen the last of him."

"I'm afraid you're right. What are the early reports from the county jail?"

"Pandemonium and disbelief. The sheriff is flabbergasted to see so many old friends he promised to protect now locked in his own jail. The new inmates are mighty unhappy with him, and wonder why they paid him all of that money!"

"Any glitches tonight?"

"Oh, only one—the tax boys found a kid with needles and drugs in the bathroom and were about to arrest him when we came by. Kid claimed that it was only insulin for his diabetes."

"What?"

"Yeah, really! When the IRS played narc and asked him who got him hooked on that stuff, the kid said, 'My doctor!'" They laughed uncontrollably, and the stress flowed out of them through their laughter. The place was empty. It was over, at least for now. Clay and Michael grasped one another's hands, two boat rockers out kicking butt. Life was good. After all, they were doing God's work—weren't they?

Off to the east, the first hint of the paleness of a new day was suggested, and already in the now empty parking lot of the club that they had watched for so long, they could sense that peculiar pre-dawn stillness that silently judges the nocturnal folly of men. Michael closed his dry brown eyes and prayed a prayer of thanks and that God spare him from his worst fear: that he would pass through this world, learning little, and leaving nothing.

CHAPTER THIRTEEN

"No, I won't back down. I won't back down. You can stand me up
at the gates of hell, but I won't back down."
—Tom Petty

The DC-9 skimmed along the blue-green waters near the coast of Alabama as a radiant sun lifted over the Gulf of Mexico. Below the plane, with no markers except for the numbers on the tail, dolphins breached the placid waters and a flock of brown pelicans flapped and glided in unison toward Dauphin Island off the coast of Mobile.

Returning from Honduras and El Salvador, they flew low to avoid radar detection even though the sun now illuminated the faded silver bird, and the sound of its engines could be heard for miles. It was standard protocol. Besides, no Coast Guard cutter or Customs jet would dare intercept this old reliable workhorse for she had diplomatic immunity.

As the plane hummed and vibrated along its clandestine flight plan, Tommy the Quantico alum and journeyman CIA operative, worked his way to the rear of the plane where the small makeshift passenger area housed its lone traveler strapped in a worn bucket-seat with cracks in the blue-gray fabric exposing yellowed foam padding.

Tommy had been in the forward area working the arcane Morse code receiver and transmitter that some within his intelligence unit still preferred. Hunched over and steadying himself on crates and electronic cabinets, he copied decoded cables for his passenger's eyes. As he approached, Fredrick was reading. His breathing seemed to be rapid and shallow, and he was tapping his right foot and whispering, "Yes, yes."

"Excuse me," Tommy said. "We have information, read-only messages from our media monitor group. It seems that there was a raid near Memphis involving one of Connelly's clubs. It's too early to tell how it will impact us, but it doesn't look good."

Fredrick did not look up. Then Tommy said, "An early interview was held with this Parker you said you know."

Fredrick lowered his book and looked into Tommy's eyes with a serpentine glare, almost flicking his tongue to taste the air, probing Tommy's words and his mind. It always unsettled the Marine in a way the ghosts of all of his victims in war could not.

"Well," Tommy said, "the locals will handle it all. No need for us to be concerned."

Fredrick sighed or perhaps hissed, "No, Satan rocks me in his cradle. He will not allow Jesus or his agents to be impediments to truth. All will surrender to his fervent dance and pay their dues and cross the River Styx in Hades on his punctual ferry. This blood of their Christ does paralyze and confuse man, but we will prevail. Even as we speak, my brothers poke pins in Parker's voodoo dolls."

Tommy's skin crawled at the dark process of alchemy that exuded from this creature seeking the transmutation of everything to his obsession or madness. Tommy turned to go, but he saw the book in Fredrick's lap, an ancient text called *The Christian in Complete Armour* by William Gurnall.

This seemed an odd choice, to say the least, for this manic disciple of the occult. Tommy had read the reports of the disturbance at the club in Memphis and the terrified bar girls who fled Fredrick's insanity. He could not fathom why his handlers continued to invest so much in this unstable psychopath, but that was part of his job to make sure that Central knew the moment Fredrick's liabilities exceeded his assets to them.

"I thought you hated these Christians," Tommy offered to Fredrick. "Why are you reading this book?"

Fredrick raised his eyes once again to gaze at this man he viewed as a simpleton. *So typical of the banal fools, these barking government poodles,* he thought. *Repulsive, unworthy of my intellect and gifts.*

"Thomas," he said as a mentor to a child, "this Gurnall captured the essence of the Christian army in battle in this essay for the 1600s." He stopped and rubbed the fresh tattoo on his arm that he received in a back street parlor in San Salvador.

"He shows how his warriors can resist Satan and sit in this meek army of the Christian God. His words are offensive to my ears, but his descriptive formula for this armor shows me two things. First, this Parker does not yet possess this armament and he is vulnerable. Second, it shows me the weak link, the chink in what shields he does have. These Christian warriors, their cities, and their fortresses were always weakest or lost through their women. This is where this Parker can be destroyed. He limps along with his sentimentalities, unfit for battle."

Tommy said, "Well, you know we can't get sidetracked by these personal obsessions," but there was no response. Fredrick was back in his shell, communing with his own demons.

Tommy turned and walked away as the plane engines droned on. He thought that he must try again to tell his control agent that this depraved and twisted contractor that they thought they had created was not their creation and was a ticking time bomb.

* * *

Michael slept poorly and dreamed often, the events of the past twenty-four hours providing grist for dreamland's mill. He had developed an inability to reach a deep REM state and too often awoke weary still and frustrated. His dreams, like his thoughts, were dramatic, theatrical even, little plays where good always triumphed over evil, and the good guys wore white hats. It was the world that Pearl bequeathed to him—gone but not forgotten.

Chivalry was still manifest. Wasn't it? *No, he told himself, this is not a game. It is enough all by itself, no need to make more of it than it is. No need to erect castles on shifting sands. No need to make evil more sinister than it is. Cruelty is cruelty all by itself. Could a random accident, fate, or chance dictate all of this? Is there only the moment he could never seem to live in? Where ends truth? Where begins fiction?*

He felt silly. He was no avenging angel or the Archangel Michael himself come with the armies of the good. *No, just act out your part as the curtain comes up, then take your bows at curtain call even as the applause dies, and they carry you off so new gladiators can enter the arena.*

Stop making complexity out of simplicity. Stop seeking meaning within the confines of a meaningless existence.

Yet, there it is again—that feeling, that call to shelter, to stop being angry that Pearl died and with her—faith. Put on the full armor and stop feeling guilty, always feeling guilty for imperfections, real or imagined.

Things had gone eerily silent on the grapevine except for one source with access to new low-hanging fruit to pick. Ruth, the young waitress from the club, provided a bushel. Michael struck up a rapport with her and arranged for some favors if she would be his "fly on the wall" in Ace's clubs. The morning he first debriefed her at the jail, she showed a nervous habit of constantly running a comb through her thick, rusty-red hair with a crackle and pop of static electricity with each stroke. As soon as the fiery-haired beauty accepted his offer of no jail time in return for information, he knew the raid had yielded a valuable new ally in what threatened to become dangerous times. She began to contribute crucial new information about the clubs and the hoodlums who frequented them.

A federal grand jury in Memphis had been empanelled to look into indictments of Ace and his associates, and Michael had already gone in for round one of testimony and would likely be called back. He couldn't wait.

Clay's sources in Memphis Narcotics said that Ace had to reimburse some angry guests at his party who were parted from their money, and some suspected of being snitches had suddenly disappeared from the nightlife in Memphis—looking for Judas in all the wrong places. Ruth told him of a bizarre gun battle at one of Ace's other clubs in the county. Someone came by on a motorcycle, blasting away at the club and its occupants. He emptied his weapons and reloaded for another run. That run, the men inside were ready and blew him off his bike. The raid had unleashed the tendency these folks have to turn on each other when things go bad. Someone has to pay, and the cops are dangerous. So, for now, there was a sorting out—a survival of the fittest in their world.

Michael placed a call to Dixie Lee and told her to stay away from Ace's clubs. Every time he heard her fluency of heart, he reconsidered his fear that it was too late to love and turn back the hands of time. Excited, bubbling over and sensing a new lease on life, she thought she could pick up useful information for him, but he told her it was too dangerous. There was a real risk that they might connect the two of them from the night at the club. He asked himself what other informant or source would he protect in such a manner? She agreed to his request, but the woman was hardheaded, stubborn—difficult to sway from an idea once she had her mind made up. He feared she was trying to prove how "good" she was in order to erase the old script of their lives.

The good news was that her former boss had not been back. Frank was transferred out of Memphis after he showed up for his speech the night of the encounter—hung-over, bruised, and swollen. His attempt to cover it up with his wife's concealer base only made it more grotesque. After his speech, Frank told an associate that socialites don't suffer fools well—don't tolerate anyone who might offend their sensibilities or arouse their suspicions that he (hence, they) might be consorting with "undesirables." It seemed that his community influence was on the wane, and there were rumors of trouble at home. His corporation couldn't get him transferred out of Memphis soon enough, and his access to trucks for criminal activities ended. Dixie was free of his prison.

"So, I feel safe here now in my Memphis and my condo, Michael. I haven't felt so good in a long, long time. I miss you. Can't you come see me, just for a little while?"

"I'd love to see you and God knows I need the break, but there's too much stirring in the aftermath of the raid. I'll see you when I can."

He could imagine her pouty look and pouched lip and the way she fluffed her hair when she wanted her way.

Predictable answer, she thought. "Michael, Michael. Okay, I understand, but for heaven's sake, be careful with these people. You know how dangerous they are. They ran wild in Memphis and aren't going to take being embarrassed down in Podunk, Mississippi, very well, darling!"

What a new resin of joy now flowed in her every word. Darling?

He laughed. "Dixie, I'd like to thank you on behalf of Podunk, Mississippi, and all her fine citizens for that comment."

* * *

Days on the calendar began to fall away like dying leaves in an autumn wind. He slept, took long runs trying to sweat out the impurities of life, and shared impromptu meals with his parents and friends, but the slow pace of their lives was maddening to him. He didn't see Dixie that week or the next, but he did take it easier on himself for a period.

He caught up on his reading and even took in a movie he

had wanted to see, *The Godfather*. It was during this time it dawned on him that he didn't have hobbies like most people. He didn't have the money or the time for golf or tennis—any of those games rich guys played. When he was a little kid, he liked to go fishing with his older cousins on Sunday afternoons after family softball games. He wondered whatever happened to his cousins and if he might someday wet a line with them again. He felt guilty that he had never told them of the secret power of Pearl's peppermints. A profound sadness came over him—perhaps it was time to see Dixie...perhaps... Further thought was interrupted by a ringing telephone. It was Clay. He was in Jackson collating evidence from the Full House Club raid.

"Hey, buddy, enough R and R. Time to go to work again. You remember my sources in the Ku Klux Klan I told you about? Well, I'd like you to meet them tonight behind the old VFW club in Byhalia. They called and have some information they want to deliver in person. They want to meet our famous agent." He chuckled.

"Tonight?" *So soon*, he thought.

"Yep."

"All right, Clay, but Klansmen—really?"

"They aren't bad people, just sentimental, old men still fighting the Civil War. If you'll cut them some slack, they can provide us with some valuable information," he said. He paused and said, "Oh, I told them that your great-grandfather fought in 'the cause' and you would be honored to meet them. That clinched it for you."

"Okay, okay, Clay. I'll be there."

He gave Michael their names, code names, and descriptions and set the meeting for midnight—as usual.

A bright-orange milkweed butterfly floated up to him and lit on his shoulder as he left the field office in Batesville to gas up for the new nocturnal adventures Clay had awarded him. The slender, diaphanous visitor was vivid and flawless in color and construction, yet almost pellucid in form. It opened and closed its wings in a slow, purposeful rhythm, a brief grounding moment and distraction for a young state agent caught up in the ugly underbelly of life.

Michael then came face to face with none other than Hal Davidson on the town square. The butterfly hurried away, and Michael followed the bouncing beauty of orange and black. He was transfixed for a moment, wanting to call it back.

The judge, tapping his feet and clearing his throat, seemed more agitated than usual. "Well, son, I hear you've been a busy boy," he said, staring through his vacant fish eyes, always seeming to be looking at someplace beyond the person he was engaging.

That broke the butterfly's gentle spell and the old combative Michael returned to the ugliness before him.

"Well, we just had to clean up some trash dumped in our state by mistake, Judge."

Davidson seemed to be nodding and preening in agitation, thinly concealing some real rage.

"Yes, yes, well, you know that I'm one hundred percent behind you, and still think you could be valuable to my campaign, and I'm not talking volunteer status. I'm doing quite well with my fund-raising. I'd be prepared to offer you a generous salary and fringe benefits that would make your state compensation seem pretty paltry."

Yeah, Michael thought, *and I hear there are generous fringe benefits.*

"Judge, I'm afraid I was meant to be a poor, obviously crazy, lawman, and not a politician. Such a position would be out of my league—you'd probably fire me within a month."

A patchwork of red spider veins spread across Davidson's face, visible now in his agitation.

"You are crazy but crazy like a fox, boy," he said with a bit of anger flashing, then the quick cover of a crazy smile. Manic? Schizoid? "Sometimes, I think you're just playing with me."

"No, sir, I would never sit at your poker table. You'd bluff me every time."

The judge replied with clenched jaws and a frown, but Michael smiled and said, "I'm truly honored that you would consider me for the political game, but I simply don't know how to play."

The judge fumbled with his blue suit coat and straightened his floral tie.

"Well, let me know if you should reconsider." Determined to win, or at least have the last word, the judge skated over to thinner ice and continued, "I know your grandmother has passed, and I suspect you could use the money for her medical bills."

That thrust in the fencing contest pierced Michael's cool façade. He stilled his erupting anger and responded, "Judge, I am honored that a man such as you would concern himself with my family's welfare, but I take care of my own. Never fear. Have a good day."

Researching the opposition, huh? Michael thought. *Trying to buy or intimidate me. We must be on to something really good. Maybe too good.* That thought caused him to consider that he'd not been very careful lately and *that* was dangerous. Chiding himself, he went back to his office and carefully swept the place for listening devices and bugs, tiny electronic "ears." Then, he scoured his apartment. The only bug he found was an enormous cockroach crawling on the coffee pot at the office, and it wiggled its giant antennas and swore that it knew nothing about crooked politicians or organized crime. Unlike the judge, the roach was honest and was released without further scrutiny.

By the time he arrived at his destination, a giant pockmarked harvest moon peeked down through the canopy of old trees around him. Healthy rats scurried from beneath garbage bins as he approached. Michael sat behind the remnants of the old VFW club near Byhalia, Mississippi. It was near midnight and he felt unusually apprehensive—trusting the Klan, even the geriatric Klan, was a step his mind just could not take.

He hummed a tune to take his mind off the wait. "Well, she comes around here, about midnight. She makes me feel good. She makes me feel all right." He could not remember more words to "Gloria" and searched for another song—any song with midnight would do. After "Walking After Midnight" with Patsy Cline, he was getting desperate, thinking of leaving… A screech in the distance put a quick end to his indulgences. Two dim headlights cut through the darkness as an old red pickup came lumbering up the service road toward where he was parked. More rats squeaked and pulled long tails behind them into the dark as the cloud of dust kicked up by the truck clouded their retreat.

The battered truck was barely visible in the pale light of the moon and the distant pole light left over from better days at the club. The truck stopped and made the appropriate light signals. He answered in return. Two blinks to their three.

Two older men got out and ambled toward his car. Michael fingered his weapon and stepped out to meet them. The one leading the way looked about sixty-five and his partner close to seventy. Michael was taken aback by their appearances. Both looked like they could have just come from a game of checkers at a rural country store. They wore plaid shirts and jeans. The heavyset one had blue suspenders to hold his prominent gut. They looked more like kindly grandfathers than cross-burners or anyone who might have useful information. However, he knew looks could be deceptive and he trusted Clay.

The older man, who smelled of tobacco juice said, "You must be Agent Parker. You're just as described but even younger. I'm Harold and this here is Ernie."

"Howdy," said Ernie, a painfully gaunt man with thinning gray-brown fine hair and a rural Mississippi accent. "It's nice to meet you. Colonel Strickland speaks highly of you." They referred to Clay's honorary rank in Vietnam.

"Thanks. What's the mood up here near the border?"

In lightning moves and deadly accuracy, Harold took a moth out of the air with a gob of tobacco spit and then grinned at his accomplishment, showing brown teeth. "Right tense, right tense indeed," he said as Ernie watched, grinning his approval. "They's some folks who are sorely upset at you, Agent Parker." Harold then looked even more absurd as he adjusted a brand new shiny hairpiece that looked as if it came off a bargain rack and was as black as shoe polish.

"Oh, they'll get over it in a while," said Michael.

Harold looked at Ernie and shook his head.

"Nope, I don't think so. You're young and don't know these ole boys like we do. We done been around these parts a long time and know lots of people. They are talking serious about hurting you bad, boy," Harold said in all earnestness, a bit of tobacco juice on his chin.

Poor old guys had been watching too many bad B movies, he thought.

"Harold, these guys are basically businessmen—crooks sure but business people who owe cuts to other bad people. Hitting a state agent would bring down the wrath of God on them. It would be very bad for business. I don't see them doing that, unless it's some hothead, freelance operation."

Harold was now getting exasperated and the fat in his jowls jiggled as he talked.

"No, no, it's past good judgment, son. It's about retribution and saving face. It ain't about logic, son. It's about dominance," he said. "Who's gonna be the big dog in the yard, or the top rooster? They're out to mark their trees, boy. You know, hiking their legs. So, we've come to make you a bargain tonight," Harold said, with indisputable barnyard logic and frankness. Ernie's head was bobbing up and down in agreement.

The smaller man jumped in the fray.

"We like you and Colonel Strickland, and I guess you know that he agreed to never ask us nothing about the Brotherhood of the White Knights. We believe that these evildoers—all drug dealers—are carrying out the work of godless Communists who are trying to destroy our nation by enslaving our children with drugs," Ernie said, with a simple honesty and conviction, gesturing with his hands like a symphony conductor.

Michael nodded for the old cross-burners to rant on. He remained silent and fascinated, thinking—*just when you think you've seen it all.*

"We know some of these people by past association when we were younger and more active. We know that you know the ones most likely to be threatening your life and threatening our way of life. So, son, we just want you to give us the names of these people. We promise that you will never have to worry about them again." As if to make his point, Harold squashed the nicotine-poisoned moth that fluttered uselessly on the ground with his big boot. A slow, sickening crunch followed as he ground him into the ground, driving home his point with a blank stare and simpering smile.

There was finality in Harold's voice that spoke of conviction, however dark, and Michael's initial amusement with the two characters rapidly faded. There was flinty hardness in the old men's eyes that reflected years of fighting battles without compromise— an eye for an eye and a tooth for a tooth. He wondered if they knew Sonny.

Several names came to Michael's mind for these boys' list of evil doers, but this was highly irregular to say the least and might even make Michael an accessory to God-knows-what, even murder. Why had Clay sent him on this mission?

"No, no," he said. "The law will take care of these people. I appreciate more than you know your willingness to help and to protect me. You are patriots, I can tell, but I must pursue them through the law." Michael was forceful but respectful in his reply, and knew these guys already had their own list, easily fashioned from articles about the raid in the local newspaper. Likely, they also already had a plan and were looking for an official blessing.

"You sure?" Harold asked, as he glanced at Ernie.

"Yes, I'm sure, but I need to hear whatever you are hearing and any names and such. Please let Clay or me know as soon as you can. I appreciate you guys coming up to meet me. It has been a real honor," he said, trying to show respect and keep all lines unbroken, all eyes and ears open.

The talk continued for a while about the local scene and whom to trust and whom not to, and the two old men told a few stories about things past, excluding Klan activity of course. Finally, they said they had other *business* to take care of and left at about 2:00 a.m. as a hungry old possum and her babies headed for the dump.

Michael sat and watched the ancient pickup disappear into the night, absorbed into a growing fog. Alone in the dark, he wondered if he had imagined the whole thing. The two old Klansmen seemed too much like character actors from a movie about a time long past. The encounter filled his mind as he tried to process it all and he drifted off to sleep when he arrived home.

Burning crosses! There were burning crosses as far as Michael could see and they turned the night to day. The screams were bloodcurdling as Ernie and Harold, clad in white robes, urged hapless blacks into the flames with pitchforks. No, they were not all black—there in line, awaiting the inferno, were his all of his cousins from the days of fishing. They…

Michael tore at the sweat-soaked sheets, but the horror ended when the screams of the doomed were replaced by an incessantly ringing telephone. He was both relieved and annoyed. Who would be calling in the middle of the night? Clay? But the bedside clock said it was 10:30 a.m. It was Ruth, his waitress-informer, in full panic mode.

"Michael, I need to talk with you," she whispered, sounding agitated, afraid, and like a little girl calling her daddy.

He shook the sleep from his head and said, "Okay, Ruth. What's up?"

"They're going to kill you!" she stammered, increasingly agitated and genuinely worried for the man who'd just shown her a little kindness. A familiar sound? Combing her hair?

"Now, Ruth, calm down. Exactly who is going to kill me?"

"All of Ace's club managers met here at the club where I am now, over on the far side of the county. They met to see how much each would have to kick in, and who they would hire to do it."

"Ruth, are you sure?"

"I heard them, and they are mad, real mad," she said, whimpering, her voice rising and falling, breaking and failing.

"Any names mentioned?" he asked.

Coughing and clearing her throat, she began again, "No, that's all I know, honest. They would kill me if they knew I was calling you," she said with real fear in her voice.

He didn't want to believe the girl, but he did—she was telling the truth. "Thanks, Ruth. You take care, and keep me informed. If it gets too hot, you get out. Do you hear me?" He heard someone knocking on a door in the background behind her. Someone was calling her name.

"I will. I will. And I'll call again soon—promise," she said. Then she was gone. It was the last time he would ever talk with her.

Michael looked at the receiver in his hand. The Ernie and Harold of his nightmares and late-night encounters had somehow known about this in advance. Had he played that card well or just eaten the Queen of Spades? It could go either way.

* * *

Michael was enjoying a cup of real coffee and good doughnuts from a local restaurant as he sat poring over paperwork.

There were new cases on the horizon and he did not have enough resources to get through the Full House Club investigation. He was almost relieved when the telephone rang.

"Agent Parker?" A monotone, almost robotic voice. Disguised?

"Yes."

"You don't know me. You did some pretty good damage at the Full House, but there are some people you missed, some more you would like. Am I right?" The voice sounded a bit like Hank Williams, Jr.

"I'm listening," Michael replied.

"I can give you what you missed, the pieces you need to wrap it all up if you're really interested," he offered, bragged, and almost taunted in a swaggering tone.

"Why would you do that?"

"Let's just say because I'm a good citizen, and I figure you would reward me," he countered. Check and checkmate.

"There could be some compensation if you deliver what we need."

"Let's meet then," he said. Eager? Too eager!

"Where, when, and who are you, by the way?"

"James Tiller's my name. We can meet in Memphis, where I live?" he asked.

"No, not in Memphis," Michael said, feeling strangely uneasy.

"Okay, then we can meet in Desoto County on your side of the line," he offered.

"No, I would rather meet in Tate County," Michael said, not wanting to meet in the county where Ace and crew owned the locals.

"I can't meet there in Tate. I got troubles there, you know. I know a good private place in Desoto County out in the woods where we won't be disturbed at night," he said. Danger? Going too fast. What game is he playing?

"No, I won't meet you out in the woods or at night. I will meet you in Desoto County today at the first exit south of Memphis at the old Gulf service station, now closed—Horn Lake. It sits just off the interstate. Know it?"

"Yeah, I know it. Can you meet me there at two p.m.?" he asked.

"Yes, I'll see you there."

"Mr. Tiller?"

"Yeah?"

"You'll be coming alone?"

"Yeah, just me. See you there." A little laugh! Cat and mouse?

Michael hung up and digested the call for a moment. He didn't feel as good as he should have about such an offer. The name Tiller rang a bell, but the context remained elusive. Something about the tone in Tiller's voice wasn't right. Maybe it was all the talk of retaliation, but if this was a gift horse, he decided not to look him in the mouth but in the eyes near Memphis. He called Clay, but he was at a conference. He left word that he was headed north to meet an informant and left it at that. He just had time to make it if he got on the road right away.

He drove out to Interstate 55 and headed toward Memphis, unable to shake the feeling that he was throwing caution and instinct to the wind. Finally, he pulled the 9mm out of his shoulder holster, put it under his belt buckle, and closed his blazer over it. He fiddled with his state police radio, but it was still on the blink. He was flying blind today—no calling the cavalry.

As Michael neared Memphis, Clay received a frantic call in Jackson from the now breathless informant, Ruth. "Agent Strickland, Michael gave me your number if I couldn't reach him," she said, near hysteria.

"Yes, Ruth. What is it?" he asked.

"Please find him and tell him the meeting is a setup and they're going to kill him."

She abruptly hung up, her last transmission from gangster

land. Clay had seen the earlier note, tried to raise his friend on the radio and could not. He was sweating and his hands were shaking. *How am I going to find this wayward lamb? I am going to kill him if these guys don't,* he thought. All he could do was alert the cops. He was not really religious, but he said a prayer for his impetuous young friend.

There wasn't a cloud in the steel-blue sky over Horn Lake. Michael pulled in at the old Gulf station south of Memphis on I-55, and a car with Tennessee plates was parked there, engine idling, an oil-laden cloud of smoke almost enveloping the car. Crushed beer cans littered the area near the car. Otherwise, the lot was empty. The station was boarded up. Weeds sprouted profusely from large cracks in the concrete. Lizards scurried across the broken pavement. Litter thrown out from patrons of nearby fast food restaurants blew across the sun-baked lot in a gust of wind. The scene had a surreal feeling, a set for a Hollywood gangster movie, but this grand theater was not Hollywood.

A large man got out of the car. He was a white male, age thirty to thirty-five. He had long, dirty-blonde hair, a scrubby beard, and looked to be about 250 pounds. His shirt was hanging loose around his waist, a favorite method to hide the bulge of a gun under the belt. He wasn't alone. A second man of similar appearance got out. He might have been a few years younger, and a red scar that ran from his left eye to his lips added to his rough appearance.

As they approached the car, Michael was faced with two choices—hightail it out of there, or stay and see what happened. He decided to stay. No guts, no glory?

"Agent Parker?" the first one asked. "James Tiller. This is my brother, Robert. I asked him to come. We are a team," he said. James had huge hands. No, not hands really but giant paws with broken knuckles.

James slid in beside Michael, and Robert opened the back

door and sat down behind Michael and to his right. Somewhere a voice screamed at him from within about the difference between stupidity and risk taking. All the bridges of retreat were burning. Their added weight made the springs creak on Michael's car.

They made small talk for a few minutes. James Tiller glanced left and right, and said, "This is too public. Let's ride out in the country where we can talk, private-like, pardner." He had a crooked nose that someone had once rearranged.

Michael said, "We are not going anywhere. Spit it out or get out." They clearly had their own agenda, but what was it?

"Got any money on you?" Robert asked him, a bit of spittle at the corner of his mouth clinging to heavy stubble. He was slightly slurring his words.

"Why would you want to know that?"

"We need money," he replied with a guffaw as he rubbed the back of his hand across his nose and back, a tiny droplet of blood there. Cocaine?

"Look, we're not going out in the country and you get no money until you give me something I don't already know," Michael said emphatically, his voice sharp like a new razor, brown eyes turning almost black.

Then he recalled where he had seen the Tiller name—an old police report. "Aren't you the Tiller brothers who were arrested for assault and armed robbery?"

"Yeah, and you forgot rape," Robert giggled with an evil laugh that made Michael's skin crawl. A tattoo on his right arm read…"Mother."

"Give us some good-faith money. Just remember, we know where you live, boy," James threatened with the sale of a base brutality.

At that moment, Michael knew that he had wandered into a trap. So slow, so foolish. He looked longingly at a passing police car and considered sitting on the horn, but didn't. So near, yet so far, but he knew there would be no cavalry. This mess was of his doing, and it was his wagon to pull. He faced them and visualized what was to come as he steeled himself.

If they found him dead in his state car, he wanted them to find at least one of these thugs dead and a thickening blood trail leading off from the other. He was confident that he could shoot James, maybe twice, and then swing on Robert. Yes, he could do that, but figured he would take a round from behind in the interim. He wiped his sweaty palm on his pants and said a silent prayer as he opened his coat and placed a shaking hand on his 9mm. *Steady, boy.*

"Look, I don't know why y'all are here, but it's obvious that you aren't here to give me information. If you're here for what I think you are, I'm armed. Let's get on with it," he said as he tensed and waited. Agents less troubled by ethics would have just shot them on the spot with no warning, but that wasn't him. He feared God, and the deaths in Tylertown were too fresh in his memory. Too many mocking ghosts came in the night already—too many.

"We have our guns, too, boy!" James said.

"Don't doubt that, just want you to know I have mine and I'm prepared to use it. So, either do what you came to do or get out of my car," he said with feigned calmness, eyes darting from one brother to the other, finger twitching on the trigger of the 9mm.

"What do you think we are here for?" James asked.

"I think you're here to pump me for information, to kill me, or hurt me—teach me a lesson," he answered, now honed in for any sign of quick movement on their part. The ticking of the second hand on his wristwatch sounded like Big Ben!

"Man, we just got off on the wrong foot. C'mon, let's ride out in the country so we can talk in private," James said too easily, smiling at his brother.

"No, I like it here just fine. Now get out of my car, or let's get it on," Michael said, moving the safety off the cocked 9mm with his right thumb.

"All right, but you got us all wrong. Meet us tonight—in the country, and we'll have something definite to give you. You're too nervous. We just want to help you. You don't have many friends up here, boy," James offered.

"Fine. Just get out, now!"

They exited the car, bulging nervous eyes never leaving his gun hand, and slowly backed across the hot pavement to their rusty 1958 Chevrolet. It started with a rattle and sped away toward Memphis. Michael uttered a deep sigh of relief and eased the safety back on the 9mm. He held out his trembling shooting hand, and steadied it by sheer will, knowing that the presence of such men who held no value for life and to be so close to death, robs you of something and demands a price. Michael drove to a nearby payphone.

Lightning crackled through a darkening sky. The afternoon heat and humidity had generated a thunderstorm and it grumbled in the background. Big drops of rain spattered on the phone booth as he dialed Clay's number. He knew he was about to hear about his foolishness, but he'd already learned his lesson. Maybe.

"Where've you been, Michael? Man, we have been going crazy trying to find you." He explained about Ruth's call in return for a rerun of the potentially deadly showdown at Horn Lake.

"When are you going to stop this Lone Ranger stuff?" He lectured him like a father, but finally calmed down. The old Clay returned. "While you were out playing Russian roulette with your life, the DA got a call telling him that he was next after they killed you."

"Knowing the DA, I bet he about wet his pants," Michael said. Clay laughed, and the tension began to dissipate.

"If you're willing to meet them again, I'm going to send a team to meet you and the DA at the Airport Ramada in Memphis tonight at eight p.m.," Clay said.

"That sounds fine. When they call, I'll set it up accordingly. You're not coming?"

"No, got to go in to see the doctor later today," he said too casually.
"What's wrong?"

"Nothing, it's just routine," Clay said.

"Probably ate too many foot-long chili dogs on stakeout with you at the Full House Club." Clay laughed, and so did Michael, but he felt ill at ease, much as he had when he approached the meeting with the Tillers. There was a sick feeling in the pit of his stomach, reminiscent of the night in Tylertown. A feeling of dread had gathered around him like the dark clouds he now watched above the phone booth as God sent torrents of righteous rain to purify an almost field of death on the edge of what Michael felt must be the Twilight Zone.

He returned to his office and made some calls to other informants to get the lay of the land and everything was abuzz in Memphis. As night drew near, he drove back to Memphis from Batesville. He received a radio call from the Desoto Sheriff's Office saying that someone wanted to talk to him and asked if he could call the number. *Fine, radio is working now*, he thought. He pulled off the interstate, and called the number.

James Tiller answered, and said they wanted to meet. Michael told him it was too noisy at the payphone—he'd call him back as he got closer to Memphis when he could hear.

Criminals of the Tiller brothers' notoriety didn't use police dispatchers to casually relay messages, unless they were very friendly with the cops. Michael arrived at the Marriott, and the team laid in their plans. The DA was there, packing a gun he had no clue how to use. To say the overwrought Ole Miss Law School graduate was nervous would be a gross understatement. The plan was simple. Michael would meet with the Tillers and be the bait to lure out the rats. MBN agents, including expert marksmen, would be there to provide protection. Orders were to shoot if the two criminals even looked like they were going for a gun.

Michael knew these boys would indeed shoot—they were known to be trigger-happy and it didn't comfort him to know that he'd be at approximately ground zero when they cut loose with the AR15 rifles. That was why he hated being bait. If the robbers didn't shoot you, then the cops might. These boys felt that they had all the probable cause and moral warrants needed to deliver justice. If one of the Tiller brothers scratched his behind, Michael knew that it would be all over for them. Fine, but how many rounds would discriminate between good guys and bad.

He reluctantly called the number the Tillers left. Busy signal. He dialed again and it was still busy. This went on for a couple of hours and when the phone finally rang, there was no answer. A trace of the number came back to a private number registered to a Mr. Tony Connelly at the Full House Club. Everyone knew then that it was for real, and figured the Tillers probably got a bit nervous about the delay and suspected something was up.

The DA said he was moving state charges against everyone charged at the club up on the schedule, and he was going to have the club condemned by the fire marshal. He didn't like being threatened. He was out of his element carrying a gun, but now a player with ownership, not a spectator in the abstract.

They left it at that. The Tillers would have to wait for another day. No charges could be brought on what all knew had been contracted to be the end of the MBN's local field agent.

Michael declined offers to ride back with the other agents for a late night meal at their favorite truck stop. He needed something more, and thought he knew where he could find it.

He dialed her number, and a sleepy Dixie Lee answered, "Hello."

"Want some company?" he asked. Tender, a bit wounded.

"Yes, yes, I would. How long?" Nurse Dixie to the rescue.

"I'll be there in about thirty minutes." Check in at Dixie's ICU, where old times are not forgotten. He could already see the dark-blue flecks in the corners of her brighter blue eyes, and the way they changed color altogether when she was flushed with emotion.

"You don't sound so good," she said.

"It's been a long day. I looked across the great divide and tickled the Grim Reaper. Tell you when I see you," he answered wearily. He knew now that love was not a conditional word, that it didn't change with the weather but also that storms of late had churned all of it up from whatever watery grave he had consigned it to.

"Okay, I have lots to tell you, too. Don't be mad. I went down to Ace's club. See ya! Can't wait," she said, and was gone— only a trail of impish laughter, residual teasing and mischief of days of yesteryear.

He was already halfway to his car parked under a Methodist church marquee which read, "All saints have a past. All sinners have a future."

CHAPTER FOURTEEN

"The moving finger writes; and, having writ moves on:
nor all thy piety nor wit shall lure it back to cancel half a line,
nor all thy tears wash out a word of it."
—Omar Khayyam

The clappity-bump of the seams of the old concrete
pavement on the road to Memphis kept rhythm with some distant,
celestial symphony dictating Michael's mood. A passing blue-
and-white jay defiantly dropped an unacknowledged present on
his windshield as the intense driver wrestled with a plethora of
emotions on the way to Dixie's apartment.

With all he had to ponder with crime bosses, politicians, and
the searching of his heart over Dixie Lee, he was perplexed to
find that one image was fixed in the front of the passing parade
of memories—an old black-and-white picture of Pearl and Eula
that always sat on the table near her bed. The tintype photo
captured them immortal in the process that produced a dark and
life-enhancing gloss by squeegeeing down the wet picture on a
ferrotype plate.

Eula and Pearl were dressed so eloquently given their
economic status, appearing elegant, almost regal in the picture,

167

which conveyed a type of intimacy that spoke to all who saw it. Photographs from those days may have seemed primitive nowadays, but they seemed to seize not just the image of the people, but their very souls housed within their fragile temporal vessels.

The photographs were like the love letters written by Eula to Pearl which she shared with Michael—written with care, intimacy, and grace—almost poetic in a style that should shame the modern butchery and trivialization of the English language. The letters were full of words by people who kept an ancient covenant to use words to endear, to paint on rich canvases, to uplift—and never to debase.

Thinking of the picture reminded Michael of days fetching figs, muscadines, and plums for Pearl to transform into her wonderful jellies and jams—searches for wild blackberries, stealing moments alone to cut grapevines in the dense forest of Parker Grove and swing through the woods like Tarzan himself. It was there, amongst the vines and grandmother chores that the young ape boy discovered the ancient beechnut tree that clung to the banks of a sandy brook shaped by runoff from the hills above.

There, carved in the tree like tablets of old, were the initials of Eula and Pearl—together forever through all time, just like in their picture. As he heard again the gentle rush of the water in the stream, he knew what his heart strained to speak to his mind. A touch of continuity urged him to pick up the torch from Eula and Pearl. In the aftermath of the resurrection he had witnessed in a Memphis apartment where a young ugly duckling in spiritual distress had begun her transformation into a beautiful swan, he wanted to carve his name on trees of life with Dixie. He wanted to leave happy photos for their children and grandchildren to learn from.

Dixie Lee opened the door to her condominium wearing a powder-blue jumpsuit that framed her in a pastel softness. She didn't need heels to almost match him nose-to-nose or magic potions to cover any flaws, for now there were none. Like the grape-blue hyacinths and the white spirea that young girls pick for bridal wreaths in spring, she smelled clean and fresh with a hint of what he guessed was Chanel No. 5. Her shiny hair fell loosely upon her shoulders, and her blue eyes sparkled, radiating happiness.

The full blush of renewal and unrestrained joy flowed from her like a powerful force of nature, and Michael found this new incarnation of an old love altogether irresistible but strangely unsettling for he knew that he was at a crossroads. It was a moment of decision, and all the rules were being rewritten and new paths lighted. When he was near her, he could barely breathe, so much of his reserves focused on her and how she made him feel more than he was or ever thought he could be. The picture of forever was suddenly before him trumping all else.

Michael had been to the edge too many times, peered into the abyss, and felt lucky to be among the living. Was it some primal urge to validate life he felt, or was it just the realization that he might not be so lucky next time?

All he knew was that his near-death experience gave him a sense of urgency, a desperate yearning to get it right this time. He reached out and brushed her sun-kissed hair from her eyes, cupped her face in his hands, and kissed her gently on the lips while they were still in the doorway. She kissed him back and clung to him there, sealing the entrance against all intruders. A longing to rewrite old scripts and shed emotional poverty erased forgotten boundaries for two people who had lived only on the periphery of life. All else faded in their embrace, and Michael began to speak to her of all of their tomorrows, whispered promises of unending nights as confidantes, best friends, and husband and wife.

She hadn't changed unless it was possible that she had become even more beautiful, aged like fine wine. There was a new light in her eyes, a gleam that spoke of something he hadn't seen before. Perhaps, he considered, it had always been there—lying and waiting, a tender trap for him. If so, he was now a willing victim. There was no going back, no will and no path to do so. They had burned all those bridges and condemned those highways. He was content to live forever in this moment and in this life with this woman and no other.

Following her silhouette to the couch in the now dimmed interior lights and clutching her warm, soft hand, he began to woo her, to honor her, and to tell her as Eula had told Pearl that life without her would be unthinkable. If only, if only— he had some peppermints.

* * *

He awakened in the wee hours after a timeless river of exploring the depths of Dixie's soul had washed any lingering doubts. He gently touched the face of the beautiful woman sleeping peacefully in his arms on the couch where they had talked until time and emotion had drained and exhausted them. He felt happy and at peace, the first he'd known since Tylertown, but it was tinged with a sadness or anxiety as an old mental photo of the two of them drifted by—he, looking up from his aim to sink the nine-ball and seeing a vision of his future before him—a soaked Dixie with a large droplet of silver water clinging to her perfect nose.

He walked to the window, and stood transfixed by the beauty of the lazy brown Mississippi in the rosiness of early light. Inexplicably, the great river that flowed below seemed to speak to him—"No matter how careful you are or what you do, your life is just a passing moment on this planet, no more significant than the fall of a sparrow. Eventually, you shall see." He stepped back from the window and there was only the howl of the wind. He wiped a smudge of pink lipstick from the corner of his mouth that seemed to remind him that he was hers alone, and smiled as the early rumbles of an awakening city drifted up on a sudden breeze.

When he returned to the couch and watched the rhythmic rise and fall of her breathing, the sallowness of color in the room gave way to a tyndall blue scattering of morning beams diffused by the mist-laden light of the den that had been their confessional and sanctuary, casting a halo effect around the woman he loved. Dixie reached up and brushed his cheek, and asked, "Michael, am I dreaming? I have prayed so long for this."

"No, I'm not a ghost or an apparition, just all too mortal as life has reminded me," he said.

"Are we only about that—your mortality?" she asked, tenderly brushing his cheeks and tracing the contours of his face, a flash of searching and questioning from the lady looking up from the oatmeal-colored divan.

"No Dixie, we transcend all of that, but it reminded me of the old quote, 'It's later than you think.' I don't want to wait any longer," he said, tracing her long, graceful lines along the nape of what Solomon might have described as her gazelle neck.

"It wasn't just your words last night, Michael. It was your heart. You've finally let go and let me in. Something's changed you."

He touched the texture of her slender throat and rubbed the blue-green opal that hung there on a silver chain. "I know. You've changed, Dixie, and you've changed me. I love you," he said as he leaned down and crushed her to him in a moment of affirmation as old as mankind, casting aside forever all the wrinkled dreams of their former lives.

"I love you, Michael. I won't hurt you again. I swear," she promised as her voice cracked.

"Hush now, don't cry. The past has passed. Let's look forward and purge the ghosts of yesterday. Deal?"

"Deal," she said. She snuggled into the curve of his arm as the long night of earnest declarations begged him rest, and he drifted off in a cloud of iridescent colors and sparklers played from the opal and captured in her eyes.

***

His sluggish slumbers ended when Dixie placed a tray of steaming food on the coffee table before him. It smelled great and he couldn't recall when last he had eaten, the emptiness evidenced by the deep growl in his belly.

"Wow, what a feast! If I'd known you could cook, I would've proposed a long time ago!" he joked, as she hit him with a pillow. They laughed, and he said, "Thanks, I'm famished! Food never tasted so good." Life seemed richer, colors brighter. The birds sang louder. Somewhere outside, they must be erecting a giant billboard, *"She loves him. She loves him not. No, she loves him!"*

"You're welcome. Do you want to hear now what I learned at the club?" she asked, beaming with a vitality that was almost electric.

His anger with her over her risk-taking had subsided. "Yes, go on." *Surrender, give up, boy.*

She went to the Ace of Diamonds just after the raid on the Full House Club. Everyone was in a foul mood. The place looked like a fortress with new faces, nervous people. Ace stayed in the back room and received visitors from out of town all night. Some of the meetings weren't pleasant, she could tell. The girls in the club told her that the cops had hit Ace in Mississippi, and he was giving envelopes full of cash to some of his angry visitors. She said Hal Davidson came the third night. He was sober for a change and wouldn't have anything to do with the girls. Ace acted as if he was giving him instructions. Dixie said that the loss of the trucking revenue followed by the club raid had put Ace between a rock and a hard place. She thought he was strapped for cash. Some of the bands complained that they were not paid for their appearance, but were afraid to confront him outright.

She paused, frowning in thought, resting her chin on her right hand just behind long, shapely pink nails.

"Oh, let me think. Don't want to forget anything. I remember now! A prissy lawyer from your hometown of Tupelo showed up with a guy who had a badge hidden under his jacket. The girls called the lawyer—Reggie. There was a long meeting with him and then Mr. Creepers arrived. You know, the devil himself, Fredrick. He went into the ongoing meeting with Ace, the lawyer, and that cop from Tupelo. Fredrick didn't seem happy when he came out, but with him, it's hard to tell," she said, taking a deep breath.

Michael remained quiet and listened politely, though his fear—real dread for her safety—was returning.

She continued, breathless, a picture of bubbly exuberance, saying that it certainly wasn't a night for business as usual and Fredrick may have wondered why she was there. "When Fredrick left, as he was going out the door, he turned in my direction and gave me a long, hard look, or so it seemed. I smiled and waved and he just stared. Made my skin crawl.

"Strangest thing, he walked halfway to me and said, 'Is that you, Delilah? Or is it Gomer? Is he Samson or Hosea? Maybe Gideon come to pull down the altar to Baal?' I didn't know what to say, and then he left. What does it mean?"

A sense of foreboding and some of the blackest thoughts he had ever felt swept over Michael.

"Dixie, you must promise me you will never go there again. These people can't link us, or you'll be in real danger," he pleaded, finally realizing he was gripping her wrists too tightly.

"But I want to help."

"You've helped me. I learned a great deal from what you've just told me, but you must stay away now. Promise me?"

Dixie gave him one of her sly, disarming looks as she snuggled her head into the nook of his neck and said with a giggle, "Only if you will squeeze me tight—right now, this very second!"

He tilted her chin up to him as he looked at her with arched eyebrows, and said in his best Sean Connery imitation, "Oh,

Moneypenny, the things I must do for my country!" As they clung to each other, laughed and celebrated this second chance, this new land of innocence, he thought that the sun, moon, and stars were in her eyes and the new light in her washed away the coal gray and black, leaving only a diamond named Dixie.

***

Michael finally reached for the phone around 11:00 a.m., knowing that it was past time to check in. He dialed Clay's private number, and was surprised when Peggy, Clay's data analyst in the intelligence division, answered. Something was wrong. The tone in her voice conveyed mourning, defeat, and abject grief.

"Peggy, where is he?" he asked as he heard her sniffling.

"I'm so glad you called. Clay's so sick. He has cancer," she blurted out with a sob. The word hung in the air—cancer, a toxic and deadly thing.

"What? No! There has to be a mistake."

"No, he was diagnosed yesterday. They first told him there was nothing they could do. It's spread to his lungs, his ribs, all through his chest. It's hopeless, they said. They say he only has three months to live." She began to quietly weep for the boss they all loved so much, the western buff and former denizen of Southeast Asian jungles—this good and decent man.

"Hopeless?" he interrupted.

"Maybe not," she said. "Late last night, a specialist agreed to try something drastic—a radical new procedure, and surgery's been scheduled three days from now."

"Why are they waiting at all?" he asked, his anger breaking through the enveloping shock and anguish.

"That was the earliest Clay would agree to it. He said he had unfinished business to tend to. He's disappeared and won't answer his radio. No one knows where he is, not even his wife.

We're all so worried." Peggy began to weep again and he could hear people comforting her in the background, fumbling with inadequate words.

"Peggy, Clay would want all of us to pull together and keep the shop running until he's back. He *will* be back. You do believe me, don't you?"

"Yes, I want to," she said meekly.

"Start preparations now for an extended leave for him, and find a way to get reports to him through a shuttle of top secret documents for him to approve—everything you can do to keep it normal and make his return real. We can't be weak now. We can't lose him. He needs us, and we need him," Michael said, so sure of himself and defiant in the grips of his pain and insecurity. Or was he? He was already compensating as he did when he felt control of the script of life slipping away from what he felt was the original draft.

"I will, but where do you think he is?" she asked.

"I don't know, Peggy. I'll have to think on it, but he must want to be alone. He'll show up. Clay doesn't cut and run from anything," he said.

As he hung up the phone, it all came back to him—all the stories Clay had told him about being out on intelligence missions in Vietnam, the planes spraying defoliants to eliminate the dense jungle to expose the enemy. They had used toxic chemicals, including Agent Orange with little regard for American troops. Clay said he would get drenched, soaked with the stuff. He said he could taste it, smell it, and feel it on him for days after he showered. He knew that it couldn't be right or safe. It never quite left him, and it happened repeatedly as the Air Force tried to conquer the jungle and flush out the Viet Cong—spraying chemicals sold to them by war profiteers. Now, Clay had joined the long list of good Americans dead or dying from exposure to the stuff.

Dixie came up behind him and was stroking his hair as his

eyes filled with bitter tears, giving him a steady pat-pat and a there-there that harked back to earliest memories of mother comfort.

"I'm so sorry. He's very important to you, isn't he?" So tender, salve to an open wound. Words drifted from Ben E. King on her stereo, *"Stand by me..."*

"Yes, he's the best friend I ever had. I trust him with my life. This just can't be real. This can't be the end of the road. There is so much more we're meant to do as a team. I know it's our destiny. Where can he be?"

The clock ticked, minute by minute, hour by hour, yielding no news in a vacuous vigil. Days passed, and no word came from Clay. Michael was restless and tried to immerse himself in work. He checked with his informants and got the same story everywhere. Nothing was moving. It was eerily quiet.

MBN moles believed the plans to hasten Michael's departure from this temporal world had been abandoned. He thought that very strange for people who had seemed so determined, and so did the informants. They had no explanation, and he had other things to worry about now. He felt frustrated and wanted to lash out, but there was no release for his pent-up emotions. He was angry at God—irrational, petulant, and blind—unable to see or hear for the noise of bitter emotion that churned in his broken heart.

He left Dixie after promising to return to make plans for their life together. He arrived at St. Dominic's Hospital in Jackson, Mississippi, at 6:00 a.m., the morning Clay had scheduled surgery and sat where he couldn't miss him. The old brown-bricked hospital with the giant cross stood near Interstate 55 on a hill. He had thought of it as little more than a landmark, but today it had new meaning.

At 6:15 a.m., Clay, his wife Carol, and their young daughter came down the dimly lit hallway. Clay rode in a wheelchair and his illness was evident—his color was bad and his face was gaunt.

Had the disease moved so quickly or was it the emotional stress of knowing and facing dangerous surgery?

He spied Michael right away, lit up, and laughingly said, "Look what the cat drug in! I thought you'd be in Memphis dodging bullets or cupid's arrows to your heart."

"No, no, I've not lost the faith. I am merely giving the gangsters time to recover and find better hit men. It seems the sporting thing to do, after all," Michael said in false bravado and nervous humor. The smell of hospital disinfectant mixed with the scent of floral arrangements at the candy striper station punctuated the air.

Carol was obviously distraught but graciously walked away with her daughter for a moment. Alone, he knelt beside Clay's wheelchair and quietly asked, "Why didn't you call me? Are you all right? Where've you been?"

He looked away quickly. Evasive?

"I had something very important I had to do...something I might not have gotten to do if God isn't with me today."

"You might not approve if you ever find out," Clay added. "You are such a Boy Scout, such a purist," he added, shaking his head in mock resignation.

"No, not true," Michael answered. "I always defer to your wisdom and the crystal ball you keep in the inner sanctum of the bat cave!"

They clasped hands like the night at the Full House Club, and Clay said, "We really gave them hell, didn't we?"

"They never knew what hit them, buddy." Then, it was time. A pretty nurse came around the corner in her starched white uniform, white shoes, and white support hose—a *swish, swish* of nylons as she walked. She smiled and said, "Mr. Strickland, we need to prep you." Crisp, sharp efficiency, or was sharp the operative word?

"I'm coming," he said.

"You know what that means, Clay? She's going to shave your privates." They both laughed.

"Yeah, forget the cancer," he said. "If she makes one slip, I'm a dead man walking anyway."

They laughed and shook hands again, masking the pain behind their foolishness as they always had. Michael watched him roll down the hall and prayed that he would see him again in this world. The *squeak, squeak* of Clay's wheelchair followed him into the gloom of a dimly lit hall outside the OR.

Clay's family, some of his staff, and friends sat quietly in the surgery waiting area while Michael paced the floor. Restless children popped drink cans and dropped cookie crumbs on the floor of an old carpet, and fear was etched in anxious faces as the big wall clock ticked on…and on.

Well-wishers came and went, and around six hours into the surgery, Brad Allman, a bespectacled shaggy-haired boy, Clay's new number-two man in the Intelligence Division, joined the waiting party. Brad was an efficient young agent once dubbed 007 before he surfaced topside, and was extremely loyal to Clay. He expressed his concerns to the family and sat down by Michael.

"Any news?" he asked in a low voice.

"No, just waiting. It can't be easy on Carol."

Brad looked as if he knew a secret he was dying to tell, but wasn't sure. The shadows of sorrow clouded his countenance, and he emitted a mirthless half-laugh as he rubbed the bridge of his nose in a nervous twitch.

"I was ordered by Clay to stay at the Bureau and keep things running, but I had to come by," he said. "There's something I want you to know in case things don't work out. I'm not supposed to tell you this, but I want you to know why Clay delayed his surgery." Michael became alert, all ears.

"What was so important?"

"Your safety," he said, now rubbing his eyes.

"What? What are you talking about?"

"Clay set up a meeting with the bagman for the clubs in Desoto County. You know, the guy who furnished the slot machines and picked up the kickbacks for the sheriff?"

"Yeah, I know who you mean—Rhodes. Why did he do that? Why was that so urgent?"

"Clay didn't know if he'd make it through today, and he wanted to fix it for you."

"Fix it? Fix what, how? I'm not following you, Brad." A pregnant drop of sweat fell from Michael's nose and spattered on an antiseptic hospital floor courtesy of a pungent Pine-Sol.

"Clay took Rhodes for a drive in the country and asked him if he knew you. Rhodes said he knew of you. Clay told him that you were a good, young agent, a patriot and his friend. Rhodes was arrogant and told him that he didn't see his point. Clay told him that the point was all of this talk of retaliation had to stop. Clay told him firmly but gently that he had a list of names in his safe in Jackson and if anything…anything at all happened to you—if lightning struck you, if a bus hit you—it didn't matter how you died. Clay would ask no questions. Then he looked and said, 'I will come back and start at the top of the list, and your name's first.'

He said Rhodes' eyes bugged out of their sockets. Clay's suddenly animated guest started swearing how much he admired you and that he never wanted to see any harm come to you. You were a fine boy, a great public servant, and so on. He was still blathering on when Clay just stopped out in the middle of the country and told him to get out and left him in the middle of nowhere. When Clay said drove off, Rhodes was hugging a scrub green pine tree, puking."

The informants were right, Michael thought. The contracts had been cancelled. Even in his darkest hour, Clay was thinking of others—always the quintessential big brother and protector. Now he had saddled up for one more charge at the enemy, perhaps his last. Michael wondered what he had done to deserve such a friend. *Please God*, he prayed silently, *don't take him from us yet*. He bowed his head when Brad walked away and began to quietly, reverently weep for such a friend.

About an hour or so after Brad left, a weary surgeon came to the waiting room. His green scrubs still soiled from delicate work that would waste and weaken most people, the young man looked as if he had been to the brink himself and needed a stiff shot of whisky.

He spoke slowly, choosing his words carefully after the exhausting seven-hour surgery. "Mrs. Strickland, Clay is stable. He is going to live. We think we got it all, or at least we hope so. He is a very strong man." Carol began to cry tears of relief, and Michael put his arm around her shoulder while he grasped the hand of Jennie, Clay's little girl, who didn't quite understand all that was happening.

Carol said, "Oh, did you hear that? He's going to be all right."

"Yes, our prayers have been answered," Michael said.

The surgeon with the tired but kind green eyes said, "I do need to tell you that we had to take as much of his diaphragm as we could for Clay to live. We had to remove most of his ribs, and we placed a wire mesh in him to protect his vital organs. He'll have to go on a regimen of chemo and radiation, but we feel good about his chances."

Those words drove home how close they had come to losing Clay. They also inferred that more hard times might lie ahead. Right now, that didn't matter. Clay would live to fight another day. Knowing him, he would defy the doctors and be back at work in record time.

Call it a hunch. Call it providence.

CHAPTER FIFTEEN

"I will allure her...speak kindly to her...I will give her vineyards...
and the valley of Achor as a door of hope."
—Hosea 2:14-15

A dirty silver rain pelted the roof of the high school gymnasium and the wind rattled the ill-fitting doors and windows installed by low-bid contractors. The day was as gray as his mood, Michael thought as he looked out at the senior class of Tunica High. There was no discipline left in Tunica High, and he was unable to hear himself talk over the din of the unrestrained discourtesy of students talking.

Disinterested teachers and administrators with flat eyes dulled by dogma stood idly by and made no attempt to intervene in the commune where self-esteem and feeling good trumped knowledge. Worst of all, he had spotted known users and dealers of drugs—laughing like it was all some big joke. This was the doctrine of the subculture he saw in the Jackson anti-war gathering now migrated to infect the incubators of learning.

Many of these teachers had stumbled through four years of college, albeit in a drugged haze. Here they were now as role models for impressionable youth. Anything goes. Do your own thing. Some were actually dealing to their own students or using alongside them. He knew that he was witnessing something profoundly wrong—a cancer that would forever change the schools where he had flourished under the best of teachers before this pandemic that might disarm the American spirit and sever the once unbroken line of promise inherent in each new generation.

Today, the underpowered sound system he was using to address the graduating class strained over the din of the storm, but he gave it his best shot. He hoped to reach at least one of these kids with his closing "words of wisdom" in one of the final speeches they would hear but few would likely remember.

"You will be faced with choices throughout your lives. You'll come to many forks along life's highway. Some roads will be inviting and paved with smooth, fast lanes to a future that requires little courage. This is the path of no risk—the path of least resistance. Another road may appear less inviting, even dangerous, but that little country road could be the path that leads you to the day that you look in the mirror and still know and like the reflection you see. *That face* will understand that materialism without morality and prosperity without accountability make for an empty life."

There was polite applause and a murmur of approval among the parents and older teachers, but the younger teachers and students went away sullen or ho-hum, so boring. How could someone so close to their own age preach such drivel about personal accountability? What was he, some kind of Holy Roller? Besides, they had graduation parties to go to…

A water-drenched and wind-whipped futility followed him to his car. He sat there, soaking wet, listening to the drumming of the rain on the state car, ruminating over the future of the next generation. His thoughts were soon interrupted by the crackle of the radio. His mood improved immediately. It was Clay. He'd been back for a month and ahead of schedule by at least six months, but the time he was away still seemed an eternity. Cases went on, but without him working in tandem, progress on the growing conspiracy case stalled. Dixie Lee had been a safe harbor throughout it all.

As the spheres in the heavens rose and set, candlelight dinners and wedding plans illuminated their days and nights of joy and redemption far above the dark noir of dramas below. Seeing Clay so close to the edge had made Michael feel his own mortality, and time with Dixie Lee became precious. The holidays had been rich with parties reminiscent of Norman Rockwell paintings as he squired Dixie around and savored quiet moments with those who offered unconditional love. All that was missing was Grandma Pearl. How he wished she and Dixie could've met. What a joy that would've been to see those two women together—dazzling lights that no darkness could ever extinguish and a zest for life that he could draw from forever…

Clay's chemo and radiation treatments continued. He practiced a form of self-hypnosis he had mastered long ago in Vietnam to help manage the pain and side effects of the chemo. Some days it worked, and some days it didn't. Clay was stoic through it all, never complaining. Michael felt that he complained more about every little ache and pain than Clay did about his cancer.

Michael thought about all that had transpired since Clay's illness. He was wounded deeply in a physical way from the massive surgery, but he was as mentally sharp as ever or more so in his determination and sense of urgency. He didn't tell Clay that he knew what he did for him, just merely remarked one day in the hospital that the threats had suddenly and mysteriously ceased and how perplexing it was. Clay just said, "Well, go figure."

He had a room full of plants and flowers from agents, friends, and family and a corner filled with strange code-like names from the invisible army of informants whose loyalty he commanded. One peace lily card was not signed, merely addressed to Colonel

Strickland. It didn't take a rocket scientist to guess who the two old guys were who sent that token of esteem to their "Colonel." Despite it all, work went on and people rushed to and fro seeking answers to questions they didn't know—always hurrying that they might not be late for their own funerals.

* * *

He was jolted from memory and musings when Clay spoke again.

"Michael, can you land line Delta 9?"

This was code for secure line transmission to his unlisted private line via a scrambling device that he and Clay used to foil the wire tappers in government who were always trolling for political dirt to blackmail people. He knew it was important and rushed to find a secure phone. He dialed Delta 9 for a channel where he and Clay could talk. Any interceptors only heard static.

"Lone Ranger here," he said when Clay answered.

"Got things to discuss, buddy," he said.

"How are you?"

"Fine, but the hypnosis is wearing thin," he said with a brief reference to his condition before he dove into business. "First of all, I'm really upset with you."

Michael was taken aback by Clay's unusual angry tone. "Why?"

"I just got the report of who applied for the first permanent promotions in the new, formal structure, and every incompetent rooster in the agency applied but not you…"

His voice echoed a bit on the secure pathway and came and went like the ebb and flow of electronic surf.

"Well, does that mean I'm not an incompetent rooster?"

"No, wisecracker, it means that you should've been at the top of the list and I want to know why you passed on this test."

"I'm not ready by my own standards. I need a little more time in the field to feel comfortable leading and developing others."

"The others don't give a hoot about being ready. They aren't ready, and many never will be. They just want the job—the power, title, prestige, or whatever. This is your best shot. There are six openings available. The next time you have a chance, if you have a chance, the odds against you will be enormous," he argued with irrefutable logic and a deep disappointment uncharacteristic of him. Perhaps it was a new sense of urgency born of his illness. Michael felt guilty because he didn't want to let him down.

"I know all that, Clay, but this is not my time, and besides, I like the long odds. I march to my own drummer."

"Well, tell me a secret that everyone doesn't already know!" he said, exasperated. "All right then, reluctantly on to item two. You know that your friends are pleading out in Federal Court in Memphis?"

"So I heard. It seems that they're cutting their losses, and the Full House Club seems abandoned. The other clubs are suffering too, it appears. I drove up to one the other night, parked out front, and just sat there. Within twenty minutes, everyone left," Michael said, laughing. "The manager asked me to give him a break, said I was killing his business. I sat there until he locked the door and went home."

"You earned the right to be cocky, and things have quieted down, but you should still be careful," he advised. "We hear the same information as you. They are moving on, and the IRS and FBI have Ace in such a bind that I don't think we have to worry too much about him for a while. Between the Feds, his accountants, and expensive lawyers, he's a busy boy."

"Do you have any word on Fredrick? He's the one who still worries me."

"The Feds have been reluctant to share too much information about the revolutionaries lately. It makes me wonder if they haven't flipped him. You know how they are," he said.

Yeah, he knew how it worked—information for freedom to operate, freedom to cross borders loaded with coke, guns, or worse in a shadow world where arrogant men, carrying the teak talisman of life and death, orchestrated an unseen tangle—where truth has no currency and justice only means "just us."

"We did pick up enough to know that the weapons cache seizure, the raid on the Full House, and the cases on some of their 'share the wealth' dealer associations truly interrupted the flow of cash to the militants. They are struggling to get more from their benefactors overseas," Clay said, pausing and grimacing in obvious pain.

"Your lady friend's sighting of him in the club is the last known visual contact we have. There are rumors and rumors of rumors, but nothing concrete except a lingering hatred of you. I think the FBI has wires on Hammel's parents' home in Memphis and several known flophouses. Could you get her to make some subtle inquiries?" he asked.

"She's not a Bureau informant. She's game-playing for me, and I told her to stay away from the club. Fredrick gave her a hard look the last time he spotted her. It's just too dangerous."

"I know, buddy. I know you want to protect her. Just ask her to keep her ear to the ground," he said in a fatherly way, not quite yielding.

"I'll see what she can do from a distance," not quite meaning it.

"Your friend Hal seems to be running hard for governor. Although it is way too early to officially announce, he's picking up lots of money from the worst sort of people," Clay said. "I think we'll hear an official announcement in the next few months. He hasn't been back to the club that we know of and is being a bit more circumspect since the raid and subsequent trials. He's out making the rubber-chicken circuit at the moment and drawing support from a strange mixture of rednecks and the black community.

He's portraying himself as a populist, man of the people. One prominent civil rights leader said, *'He is a cracker we can deal with,'"* Clay said.

"Man of the people, huh? I've seen his kind of people," Michael scoffed. "What about Reggie and Howard from Tupelo?"

"Well, it seems that Reggie is the go-to lawyer for drug dealers, and has a propensity for buying up local judicial, prosecutor, and police influence. Howard seems to be his mole, a sort of bagman for his activities. He's an independent operator who has gotten mobbed up by osmosis." An intercom blared in the background with Collins' demanding voice.

"Gotta go. The director is calling, and he's in a foul mood today."

"Part of the perks of being in headquarters," Michael said, laughing.

Rows and rows of small frame houses with peeling white paint and spindly, sickly trees framed the road home. Michael watched the little houses, typical of small Mississippi Delta towns, as he drove to his apartment. Maybe he was just depressed because so much had happened, and yet, it wasn't over. Not by a long shot. The beast had been wounded in the first skirmish, but there was more to come. So much press had been given to the raid at the Full House that it made it too hot to handle for most of the organized crime groups affiliated with Ace and crew. Many of the wise guys arrested at the club had been thrown in the slammer for sentences ranging from months for firearms possession, to parole revocation and hard time in state and federal prisons for violation of parole or probation guidelines on previous convictions. The Feds were working Ace over on taxes owed and were busy pursuing racketeering and conspiracy charges against him as they bargained with his people who were arrested at the club.

Some asked what good it did to arrest a few gangsters for carrying concealed weapons or possession of amphetamines in small quantities or simple-minded waitresses for amphetamine possession and solicitation of prostitution. To someone who had served five years of a fifteen-to-twenty-year sentence, the prospect of going back to serve the remainder of the sentence for parole violation was a powerful incentive to give up bosses and opt for the Federal Witness Protection Program.

Waitresses like Ruth had proven to be invaluable sources of information, and some were testifying before federal grand juries—but not Ruth. She'd disappeared. Ace was tapped out for money for lawyers and IRS bills, and virtually finished no matter what happened in future trials. The Mafia families he did business with would no longer come near him. So, did the good guys win? Yes, this time, but it was only a drop in the bucket, and that begged the question—who are the good guys? Everyone get out your secret decoder ring and junior space cadet radios for orders from HQ.

No charges were brought yet against Fredrick. But as long as he was out there somewhere, Michael was uneasy. Garden-variety gangsters were deadly enough, but it was business with them. Fredrick was an empty vessel, a psychopath lacking in any vestige of restraint. Perhaps the Feds had a lock on him, but it didn't seem likely that he would ever cooperate. Would he run? Given his background, seeking asylum behind the Iron Curtain didn't seem likely. He was who he was, but he also liked the finer indulgences of capitalism.

Michael's dark ruminations were soon forgotten when Katie, the cat, met him at the front door. An ideal companion for him, she was a loner who loved with a loner, and sat beside him while he typed his reports. Made for each other, she didn't have much use for anyone except him and only tolerated his neighbors who cared for her when he had to disappear for a while

She sat beside him at his desk, and rubbed against his arm as he looked at the lines of poetry he had written. Okay, it was a start, Michael thought. Sometimes he thought his poetry was

"O.K.," but it wasn't something that he shared with his less-than-sentimental peers. It had always been a release for him—a very private release. He had written poetry for Dixie Lee in Washington and was inspired to try it again.

Hearts aflame with what seemed to a unique, first-ever in the history of romance love had always done thus—even when the talent was as sparse as the water Michael once used to prime old artesian well pumps in the river bottoms of the Grove. Like the pumps, the effort can tap into something pure and refreshing.

The last lines of iambic pentameter that he mailed to her also included a little silver cross necklace, with a note saying, "I pray this rhyme is good enough to be worthy of you. If not, please wear this cross anyway and think of me and my love." He had wondered about the poems and felt embarrassed, but when she called, she said in moist whispers of trembling timbres that they were wonderful and promised to always wear the cross. She saw the cross as a sign of her personal redemption and loved the poems. What else really mattered, Michael wondered?

Out of gratitude, she invited him to come to Memphis for dinner and to watch the second run of the "Elvis Aloha from Hawaii Concert" special with her. It was to be beamed around the world and they had missed the first broadcast. Michael's friends on the Memphis police department told him how Elvis liked to play cop, rode with them now and then, and even pulled over local speeders with his badge from the Shelby County Sheriff.

They said that Elvis once even fronted them the cash for a drug buy one night when they could not come up with the money. A study in contrasts, Elvis was so ingrained into the fabric of America that he seemed immortal. Michael's mother had taken him to see Elvis in 1956 at the fair in Tupelo. After that, Elvis had seemed like family.

In 1948, Michael quietly entered the world at the Tupelo Hospital just as Elvis and his parents packed up their old Plymouth and left for the Promised Land in Memphis. Now, with Dixie waiting for him, Memphis looked more and more like Michael's Promised Land.

* * *

In the meantime, Michael knew it was time to focus on a number of garden-variety drug dealers who operated without political connections, motivated by greed and the hedonistic lifestyles they led. Three agents worked deep undercover in Michael's district. His banker friends had arranged manufactured savings passbook accounts showing large sums of phantom money in their undercover names. Anyone who checked would be told that they were valuable customers of the bank. The bank president had been most accommodating in providing the fake passbook and cover story.

Being the proper fiduciary agent, he did feel compelled to tell Michael, "Ah, you know you can't really draw out this money." Withdrawal was never contemplated, but the fake documents had great flash value on the street. The bank board could rest easy.

The undercover agents were little more than inexperienced college kids about to come into harm's way and be subjected to a long list of temptations. They could shoot with the best, but Michael wondered if they had the moral fortitude to survive what lay ahead of them in this new Babylon.

Today he was to meet Jimmy Smith, Doug Rogers, and Ralph Ryan in Grenada for a little show-and-tell with the dealers they'd been courting. Doug was the oldest and largest of the agents—he was a mild-mannered, fair-haired kid who could tear a Memphis telephone book in half. Ralph was the leader. Jimmy was the quiet one, the follower. Ralph was also quiet by nature and had lived a sheltered life. However, the freedom of the Bureau had transformed him into one loose goose. He had dropped his childhood sweetheart-wife for the pretty and kinky girls on the road. Michael worried that he no longer seemed the same person that he was in the academy. The dealers they were to meet had connections from the Delta to Memphis and could move large quantities of drugs.

Grenada was best known to legions of crappie fishermen for the big lake nearby with the same name. However, its location along Interstate 55, halfway between Memphis and Jackson, made it a popular meeting spot for drug dealers and criminals of all sorts. Michael pulled into the parking lot of the Interstate Motel in Grenada and waited. He came in his personal car, a 1972 red fastback Mustang with a black interior that he and the bank owned. Michael wore a casual suit over a bad shirt with ruffles, open to mid-chest, showing lots of chest hair. Heavy gold chains and slicked-back hair completed the look of the '70s disco lounge lizard.

He backed into a parking place under a dimly flickering neon sign that proclaimed "vacancy" to no one's surprise. Following a short wait, headlights cut through the failing light and three cars pulled into the parking lot. Pleased that the cops and robbers had arrived at the same time, Michael exited the car and leaned against the Mustang, a twin of the one Sean Connery drove in *Diamonds Are Forever.*

The motley crew piled out with a drop-dead gorgeous creature in a halter-top that was scarcely there, the bare minimum legal cover that left little to the imagination. The dealers had come to meet the financier behind their "friends," the man they believed to be a young, wealthy politician who dabbled in the dark side by fronting family money for drug deals. The agent's bulging passbooks had proved to be effective bait, like shiners for Grenada Lake crappie.

Ralph approached Michael and said, "Hey, bro, what's happening?"

He gave the new cultural handshake with appropriate hand slaps and such, and Michael reciprocated. "My man, what's *happenin'*?"

"Dude, this is Rosemary Taylor. Rosemary, this is Mark, the man we told you about."

"I've heard so much about you," the tawny-haired, lean and limber Rosemary said. She gave him a feeling women must have when men undress them with their eyes. Likely, she was just looking for the money, but her hazel eyes were full of come-hither seduction. Michael actually felt uneasy and suppressed a compulsion to check his fly.

"Likewise, Rosemary, but their description of you fell short of the mark…"

Ralph laughed. "Watch out! I told you he was a charmer."

It was soon obvious that Rosemary was more than decoration. Despite their size and appearance, her companions were like her puppets and jumped at her every word. She whispered something to one driver and he left with another one of the group. Michael gathered it had something to do with drugs for a party.

"So, how'd you boys meet?" she asked.

"I met them in a house of ill repute in Memphis," Michael deadpanned. Everyone paused, looked at him, and then burst out laughing.

Paul, one of her entourage, said, "That explains why Poncho (as they knew Ralph) likes to party with the coeds at Delta State."

Michael shot Ralph a quick look, and he looked away—red faced and guilty. That was a clear violation of Bureau regulations, and it could come back to bite him in court.

"No, we go way back to college. I graduated and became a politician. They flunked out and became dope dealers." Everyone laughed again.

"Yeah, he's the brains, and we're the mules," Ralph said.

"So, you back them?" Rosemary asked, her eyes now searching, probing, predator-like, still framed by a face and figure that models would die for.

"I do what I can to help. Say, I hope you've found these wild men satisfactory to deal with. We need your connections to get more pure powder. Goes quickly in the marketplace and I can't get enough of it."

"Oh, yeah, baby, we got the best and plenty of it." Rosemary looked at Michael coyly and purred, "We're all going to party in Memphis tonight. Why don't you party with me—see just how good our stuff is." She openly telegraphed her intent—a little speed fueling the way to party time. It was either a trap or part of doing business with her—just part of the drugs, sex, and rock and roll so prevalent—no harm they claimed, just meaningless coupling and temporary joining along the libertine highway, but with emotional and physical scars that might never heal.

"I would like nothing better, believe me, but I'm committed to a meeting tonight where I will speak and pretend to be a pillar of the community. I have to keep up my appearances, you know," Michael said as he rolled his eyes in mock disgust.

"I bet it galls you to hang out with those hypocrites," she said in sympathy.

"More than you know."

The girl was persistent.

"Well, I'm from Memphis originally, and we still go up to party there with old friends. So, the invitation is open anytime," she said, leaning forward as Michael kept his eyes on her, glued to her slender, classic nose, nothing south of the border.

"Oh, did you go to school there, Rosemary?"

"Yeah, at freaking Memphis State, can you believe it?"

It hit him like a ton of bricks and he took a chance. "Memphis State, huh? Seems I used to know a guy up there in the old days. Fredrick was his name."

Without missing a beat, she said, "Yeah, yeah, you knew him? I knew him, too. We used to score from him before we established our own network."

His pulse was racing and his hands picked at his gold chains.

"Whatever happened to him? He still owes me some smack from years ago."

Rosemary forgot her incessant narcissism for the moment and made circular motions around her right temple with her index finger.

"Well, he went from crazy to total out there and got strung real far out on politics. He got involved with some really bad dudes and dropped out of sight."

"Know where I might find him? Any haunts?"

"I don't know," she said. "No, wait. There was this one place down off of Beale Street…the Bottom of the Blues Club. Yeah, that's it. He hung there, and you could leave messages there for him. I'd be careful down there, though, if I were you. Fredrick may not be the same guy you used to know," she said.

"That's okay, honey. I'm not the same guy he used to know," he replied, flashing his best boyish grin.

She had come closer and her right hand kneaded his forearm, her nails brushing the back of his hand.

She smiled a big seductive smile. "Are you sure you can't come with us?" she asked, leaning forward again in her skimpy top.

"No, not tonight, but I'll take a rain check, and I'll definitely be back for you," Michael said, in all sincerity. She positively beamed, unaware of what that meant.

Paul told Rosemary he was going to take some of the boys back to Memphis and would meet them there. As they left, Michael, too long out from undercover, made a slip and used Poncho's real name.

In parting, he said, "So, Ralph will know how to get in touch with you?"

Everyone looked puzzled, except Ralph, who looked terrified. Rosemary asked, "Uh, who is Ralph?" A big semi drove by and the smell of diesel filled the air. Rosemary's companion stiffened.

There was horror on the face of the agents, but Michael calmly said, "Oh, I'm sorry. I thought that was the name of the guy who just left."

"Nah, that's Paul," she said.

Then came mimicked suaveness and charm conjured up as some amulet from countless old romantic movies that he could cite line by line. "Oh, my mistake, but I'd never forget your name, *Miss Rosemary.*"

She smiled, and said, "You'd better not. I want us to have a private party."

The agents raised their eyebrows and silently mouthed a "whew" to him. Michael grinned and winked. He took Rosemary's extended hand from the car, briefly kissed it, and said, "You are enchanting."

As Rosemary and her merry band pulled away, he waved goodbye and walked back to his car. He made a quick stop in the men's room for some soap and water. He suspected that pretty young thing's hand had been places an obsessive germ phobic just would not approve of. He could almost feel things crawling over his hand, burrowing between his fingers. She was a striking young woman, but he could already see the telltale signs that the drugs were having on her. She was in the beginning stages of a slide toward malnutrition, hepatitis, and severe weight loss that would all too soon ravage her good looks. She would shortly look older than her years. All the cool players deluded themselves into thinking they could handle it.

The lead on Fredrick was a bonus. Michael radioed Clay and asked him to run everything he could find on the Bottom of the Blues Club in Memphis where Fredrick once hung out. Clay said he would and told Michael that Theodosius Jackson, a Black Liberation Army assassin linked to Fredrick was rumored to be in Oxford, Michael's old stomping grounds. He was trying to recruit radicals at Ole Miss of all places. Hiding in plain sight, Clay suggested.

Jackson hated cops, and he hated whites. There was nothing worse to him than a white cop. He was dealing drugs, running prostitutes, and stealing equipment from the university. An unconfirmed rumor had placed Fredrick in Oxford some three months ago, just before three police cars were blown up at the downtown station. The MBN had been called in along with the ATF to investigate the bombings which weren't fancy. Someone had crawled underneath two police cars, used an ice pick to punch holes in the tank, and then inserted detonators. The detonators were activated from a safe distance away, and *boom*, the cars went up in flames. Regular MBN informants knew nothing that could help, and the case remained unsolved.

Michael's mind was spinning, thinking about the Oxford case, Rosemary, death threats, all of it, what next—then, he caught himself. Not today, time only for the woman of slow, gentle kisses and eyes that wished him a long, long life with her. Point the Mustang toward Memphis, embrace the woman who waited for him, ask her to set the date, and get lost in the king of rock n roll's concert from the paradise of the Aloha State. No sadness tonight, only tenderness and refuge in the shelter of Dixie's arms. The Bottom of the Blues Club could wait.

CHAPTER SIXTEEN

"There's a long line of mourners driving down our little street.
They've finally brought you home to me."
—Elvis Presley, Long Black Limousine

By the time Michael approached Memphis, the sky was cast in maudlin purple hues. The smells of the city in early evening—flowers freed from the heat of day, catfish frying, and a local bakery—crept into his small red Mustang. Off in the distance, past the Memphis skyline and across the bridge in Arkansas, he could see flashes of lightning in an approaching thunderstorm. It seemed a wonderful night. He loved storms and their violent reaffirmation that God was still there after all. Eager to see Dixie, he felt alive and could smell the sweet aroma of elusive happiness. She seemed the same girl he met and then lost almost nine years ago but all grown up and out of her penchant for restless adventure.

He smiled as he recalled the evening he had met Dixie. There'd been a party at his apartment complex in the suburbs of Washington and someone had thrown her into the pool with her clothes on. Her long hair was plastered to her head and her clothes clung to her. Some guy was trying to sweet talk her, but her big blue eyes were locked on Michael as he shot a game of pool. If he had ever seen a stare of uncloaked and telegraphed interest, it now rested in her eyes. Even a thorough soaking couldn't ruin the prize that stood before him. They had both smiled. It was the beginning.

Their first date was to see the epic love story *Dr. Zhivago* at the grand old theater in downtown Washington. They fell in love like Yuri and Lara in the film, and became inseparable, but just as the revolution had separated Yuri and Lara, Dixie's own little revolution eventually separated them.

All that had been a long time ago. Now, they were granted a reprieve to get it right. She'd already told her parents that she had been given a chance to rectify her mistakes, and they were happy. They'd told her years before that she was making a mistake. Michael was their favorite. They thought he was a good young man, the antidote to cure and tame their wild and headstrong Dixie Lee.

As Michael approached Dixie's condo building, he suddenly had a sense of foreboding. He didn't feel better when Charlie, the doorman, was missing from his guardhouse post, though his duty light was on. *Strange*, he thought, as he used his code to enter the private garage. Maybe Charlie had to relieve himself, and he was just being silly. They had become quite friendly since Michael became a regular at Dixie's place. Charlie confided that he liked Michael a lot more than he liked Mr. Community. He also said that the "dance" that Dixie's old boss and Michael had was a long time coming and overdue. He did not cotton to men who hit women.

Charlie, a retired boxer of the old school, looked at him one night and said, "Michael, you are deceptively quick and effective. You are disarmingly nice and peaceful in your demeanor, but after I saw what you did to that ole boy, I had to reassess you. You're all right by my book, son, and I can tell that you are good to Miss Dixie."

Michael hesitated for a moment and then rang the buzzer

at Dixie's door. There was no answer. Again. No answer! In the shower? He dug out his own key which she said meant they were engaged. She was already planning their wedding and picking out a dress. It didn't threaten him. It honored and pleased him. He would ask Clay to be his best man.

He entered the apartment. "Dixie?" he called to no answer. He glanced at his watch and saw that he was ten minutes late. The show had already started and Elvis was belting out the opening strains of "See See Rider." The smell of burnt popcorn wafted through the air mixed with the smell of a life-and-death struggle, a battle to cling to or to take life. He had encountered it before, and it was unmistakable. He came to believe it was dark energy, disturbances left in the air, residuals of a fatal and final dance.

He knew his mind was spinning out of control. Maybe nothing was wrong, maybe... But there seemed no simple explanation, and he was gripped by a cold, overpowering fear bordering on panic. His heart rate increased and his sweaty hand gripped his weapon. He thought, *Calm, boy, calm*, but his training and experience strained to overcome unthinkable visions of horror.

He heard something, a muffled scream perhaps from the recesses of the condominium. *God, no!* His revolver led the way now and he moved cautiously ahead. "Dixie?" he called. No answer. Popcorn was smoldering in the cooker and a ladle lay on the floor. He fanned his weapon over a wide-angle view of rooms and doorways. There was no dark, hulking figure, nothing...just some papers on the floor, magazines askew near the couch. One lampshade tilted hard to one side. He kept moving, low and in semi-crouch position, revolver gripped by both hands in a vise lock and pointing in sync with his eyes. A ceiling fan was swishing overhead in surreal tempo with a soft Hawaiian melody from the television.

Scuff marks on the tile leading from the kitchen. Someone dragged? Signs of struggle? "Dixie?" he called again with more urgency as he edged forward. Patio doors were open and the evening breeze blew the sheers wildly. The storm was closer now, and lightning illuminated the dark room with an eerie, electrical whiteness. He was startled by the loud clap of thunder that closely followed the brilliant flash and spun back toward the patio briefly. But there was no one other than Michael, his fear, and the smell of ozone.

He sucked up his dread and moved cautiously down the hall. Presently, he heard a new sound and moved toward it. The sound grew louder as he neared Dixie's master bedroom. The *thwack, thwack, thwack* sound repeated in a uniform cadence. "Dixie?" he called once more as he neared her bedroom with its beautiful view of the river. There was no reply, just the rain pelting against her partially opened patio door—the sweet smell of the freshening storm.

He slowly approached the door to Dixie's room and the *thwack, thwack, thwack* became more intense. His heart felt as if it were going to burst from his chest...he took three deep breaths...1, 2, 3. Go! He kicked the door open and burst into the room, rotating his weapon 180 degrees right, left, and back again. However, he could see little—the only light came from the nearby master bath until there was a brilliant flash of nearby lightning that lit the bedroom like day.

The boom of the accompanying thunder was deafening, but the source of the repetitive sound was revealed to him. The ceiling fan was turning in laborious motion, weighted by an object hung around one blade. It tilted the fan, and each time it rotated, the object hit the lighting attachments with a resounding *thwack*.

He watched in fascination for a few moments, and then he understood and looked down at the bed. Something inside him died ten thousand deaths. Even in the strobe like, flickering flashes of lightning, he could tell that it was Dixie Lee, and it was not good. She was on her back in her bed, but her body was not lying naturally. Her arms, body, and legs were out of kilter, a Barbie doll torn asunder by some petulant child.

He fell back against the wall, groping for light switches with his left hand, his revolver trembling before him. *Wake up, Dixie, I'm here now,* he thought, but part of him knew he was too late…

The light illuminated the room in a cold, clinical reality, and he lowered his weapon, oblivious to danger. Before him lay the woman he loved for so long—and it was wrong, so wrong. Her favorite baby-blue jumpsuit was soaked with blood, as was the bed she lay on. Blood dripped from the bed to form a growing, dark puddle on Dixie's expensive tile floor.

"Dixie?" he cried, as he moved to her.

Nothing.

"Dixie!"

Nothing.

He stopped just short of touching her. Her blue eyes were open and fixed in a death stare. Her lips were parted slightly with no signs of breathing. Her color was that of death despite makeup. Dixie's lips were swollen and bruised. Someone had struck her, toyed with her, punished her, before he… Michael couldn't finish the thought. *Need to fix her broken lips,* some part of him still in denial said. *Yes, yes, get her makeup. Touch them up. Make it all go away. She will be warm, sweet, and beautiful again.*

"Dixie," he whispered as he discovered the source of the river of blood. Her wounds were terrible. Trauma to her chest, repeated stabbings, an act of rage, the cop in him said. *Have to get some bandages from the medicine cabinet and stop that bleeding—make it right. Yes, yes, make it right.* But he knew he couldn't. The shock of his discovery had lifted, leaving him only with the cold, cruel truth. The one woman he had ever loved was dead—murdered in cold blood.

Now, he could see her as she was, and Dixie looked diminished in the arms of death. She seemed smaller than her larger-than-life presence, and shrinking before him. Her eyes were receding into her head, growing ever smaller. He reached out and touched her hand. It was still warm, but all life had drained from her. Clutched in the death grip of her right hand was the silver cross and necklace he had given her. Tears came and he cried out to God. "Why? Why her?" Michael knew he also meant, "Why me?"

The thwacking sound recaptured his attention and he looked at the whirling foreign object that was the cause of the irritating dissonance. It was a binder Dixie had purchased to keep her collection of his poems. It was suspended from a fan blade by a small chain she had used to hang it near her when she was working. He had told her she made too much of his poetry, but Michael's words were never far from her. Someone—the killer—had hung the collection on the fan blade for him to find. Message delivered.

Then he saw the torn piece of paper on her nightstand. It was smeared with blood and pinned to the stand with a blue-handled stiletto knife. It was a bloody page of his words—the last poem he had sent her, a poem about who she was and who she had become. The words jumped out at him from the blood-soaked paper, mocking his impotence.

Dixie

To love her was an arduous journey without end from the start;
She was illusive, a mystery that can break a man's heart.
A will of the wisp, a firefly on a summer's night,
She is too fragile to hold, too ephemeral for morning's light.
Tender yet remote, try to capture her to no avail;
She withdraws and is suddenly gone, hidden by her veil.
A puzzle that cannot be solved, a riddle without leads,
Handle her with care; lest she drive away all that she needs.
Bearing unknowingly a beauty too impossible to endure;
The essence of her spirit lingers and has no cure.
All she is to him fills him with fright, but brings him to his knees.

Stirring an unknown longing, a strange but familiar yearning;
She fills his heart with an aching and unbearable burning.
Painful, beautiful eyes beckon and plead from an unknown place,
He reaches for her, but the image fades into another time and space.
Dreaming the same dream, he waits and feels the distance narrow;
Eternity's bow aims at his soul, the welcomed sting of love's arrow.
Whispers on the wind carried by the mists from the dawn of time,
Speak of one soul split, searching for her mate, lost rhythm without rhyme.
This angel fallen to earth, not knowing she has what she seeks,
Pleads in his dreams; you are the one I've been waiting for, she speaks.
With every breath that he breathes, he calls out his plaintive cry,

For you I was born, my love; for you I will live and die.

Through the giant speakers connected to the television, Elvis sang, "It's Over." Michael felt dizzy, sick, his knees weak and rubbery, but he didn't fall or faint. He knew he had to get help, call Clay. He moved toward the telephone one step at a time, amazed that he could still stand.

Dixie's telephone seemed a living thing that changed and morphed into odd beings that would not be still. Though his mind was cracking, his body was functioning on automatic pilot. He grasped a tissue from her dresser to pick up the receiver. It was all hard-wired—preserve the evidence, be a good cop and help the pretty lady. As he grasped the receiver, he stopped. What? There, in the dimly lit corner of the room near the telephone was a little white ball of fluff. He felt sick again. It was the final blow. Little Geordie lay crumpled on the floor. Red stained his satin, white hair. His cute bangs were plastered with blood.

Made one last stand for your mom, did you, little man? He bent down, looked at him closely, and touched his throat. No pulse but still warm, wearing that look of a little soldier who died doing his duty.

203

Black marks on his side indicated a probable kick. Knowing Geordie, the little dog had rallied and charged back, latching onto the intruder. More careful examination revealed that a knife under the rib cage had ended the brave little dog's life. Michael pushed away a tear and wondered who could have committed such a foul deed to kill this beautiful woman and her innocent pet which was the size of a cat but with the heart of a lion. *Unconditional love… that is what you brought her, Geordie. At least you were here for her.*

"Clay?" he said in a faraway voice that cracked and seemed not his at all.

"Michael, what is it?"

"Clay, Dixie Lee is dead." Suddenly his words made it real.

"What? How? Are you certain she's dead? Called an ambulance? Where are you?" he asked.

"She's dead, Clay—her apartment, blood all over. I got here too late, Clay. Too late! I was taking care of Bureau business, or I could've been here for the concert and popcorn," he said.

"Michael, listen to me. Hang on, buddy. Are you secure? No one in the building?" he asked.

"I should've been here, Clay. I should've been here sooner."

"Michael, listen to me. Are you secure?"

"Don't know. Charlie, the doorman, was missing when I came in, or I didn't see him," he answered with a rote, drone-like efficiency taking over.

"I'm taking the chopper now. Brad will drive me to the airfield and I'll be there soon. You hold it together until I get there. Assume a secure position. Do you hear me?"

"Yes, I hear you," he numbly answered, succumbing to the narcotic of shock that tugged at his senses.

"I'm calling the chief of detectives at Memphis PD and briefing them on what is in their jurisdiction and bringing them up to speed. Are you with me?" he asked.

"Yes, I'll wait for them and you. I've preserved the scene, I think. There appears to be lots for forensics to work with."

"Michael? Are you okay?" he asked.

"Yes, I'll be fine. We'll fix everything, won't we?"

"Yes, we will, old friend," he said.

"Clay?"

"What, Michael?"

"Fredrick was here. He killed her, Clay," he said, comprehending the truth. "That monster killed her, Clay, I know it."

"I'm sorry, but we'll get him," he said.

"Clay?"

"Yes, Michael."

"Get the FBI, DEA, CIA, PTA, I don't care who, up here, and get us some answers. Please, would you do that?"

"Already working on it," he said. "God be with you and with Dixie. She is with Him now." And he was off and running, grieving for his friend and wondering who would accuse Michael of the crime.

He returned to her desecrated body and sat beside her, trying not to touch her, trying not to stroke her hair and contaminate the crime scene. Images flashed before him of times past and recent intimate and happy moments on the cusp of forever. A burst of images that would never be realized quickly replaced those— marriage, home and hearth, and little children who looked like her. That's when he began to cry in earnest for all that could've been and would never be, for memories unmade, children unborn. She was gone.

All the childish mischief and essence of life that resided within her had been snuffed out like a candle in the night. Evil had visited her, snatched her away, and nothing would ever be the same again. He was left with a sickening void in his gut—an aching emptiness. The river had been right—he was indeed worth no more than *the fall of a sparrow*. He suddenly felt alone and the ache of a frail mortality in his soul. Was that the storm's final clap of thunder or was it Old Man River having the last laugh?

The tear in the false security of normalcy that premature death brings, and the clatter and official noise of those hired to paint over the aftermath of evil in a pretty marketing shade of happy yellow awakened the sleep of denial. Residents of other condos peeked out in curiosity clothed in royal-blue pajamas and baby-pink nightgowns, so snug and safe behind locked doors, never knowing that death was near. Just slap another coat of paint on it all. There's an opening in the building. Tomorrow, it may be yours.

When the first units of the Memphis PD arrived at Dixie's condominium, they had been fully briefed by the chief of detectives whom Clay had contacted. Chief Drew supervised the investigation, offering his condolences when he arrived. Two of his best detectives took Michael to an adjoining apartment for questioning. That is what it was after all, *questioning*.

Michael felt like a criminal as the two professional, but cold officers pursued every possible angle while the crime scene experts worked the condominium top to bottom. He sucked it up and was about an hour into the interview when Clay entered the room. Before the door closed behind him, there was a glimpse of men who drew chalked lines around the dead and made coarse jokes about blood spatters and female anatomy—men with dead eyes which had seen too much.

"Can we take a break here, boys?" Clay demanded, more than requested.

"Sure," they said, rising and hitching up pants of cheap suits with sweat stains, cigarettes dangling from their lips.

After the interrogators vacated the room, Clay offered Michael a Coke and sat down near him, gripping his arm. "How are you holding up, buddy?" The pungent aroma of death and animal violence had wafted into the room along with a fine cadmium-yellow powder, a dust storm settling over the once pristine retreat, applied by earnest men brushing for the prints and tracks, the spoor of murder. The hum of the air-conditioning unit ceased, building an oppressive humidity in an apartment with too many people, too many camera flashes, and too many polyethylene walls taped up to section off areas of the crime scene.

"It can't be real, but I know it is."

"Are they treating you okay?" he asked.

"Okay, yeah, okay. Good cops—very efficient and methodical. They did ask for a set of my fingerprints, but I knew they were just trying to eliminate my prints. Worst case and this was a lover's spat, they would have them," Michael said in a rote and dispassionate recitation.

"That wasn't needed yet!" Clay exclaimed in a rare burst of anger, touching his side near his surgical wound as scar tissue tugged at him, reminding him of his own recent vulnerability.

"Sure it was. I want them to have everything, know everything about…" and he choked back a near sob that caught in his throat. "I want this by the numbers…by the book, nothing to chance." From a crack in the door, he saw solemn stretcher bearers in mortician gray en route to her bedroom.

"Forensics has lifted a good print from the bloody paper found near her bed," Clay said. "They also got some tissue from beneath her fingernails. She put up a good fight and may have left us something to work with," he said in a low voice.

"Charlie, the doorman?"

"Yeah, poor Charlie—they found him in a storeroom behind his guardhouse. He had been stabbed in the back and side of his neck in the guardhouse, and his body dragged to the storeroom. Lab boys think he was distracted and stabbed in the back and then finished off with a thrust to the neck. The guy who did this was a pro—he'd done this before," Clay said. He paused. "The guy that did this—liked it."

Sucker-punched him, Michael thought, *the only way a creep like Frederick could take Charlie "Cougar" Condon, the old middleweight who could still snap quick jabs. Lost his last match in a rigged fight that really was not his fight. The tough, old boxer thought he had escaped from the mobsters and the wise guys when he retired to his condo security job, but they killed him anyway.*

"Your new supervisor's here with me. Robert Wilson is outside." There was clearly irritation in Clay's voice.

"He's been promoted and given this area to supervise from headquarters?"

"I've brought him up to speed on pretty much everything. He's already rethinking his promotion, I believe," Clay said with a sarcastic laugh. "Boy's like a fish out of water. I don't think it will change anything or that you will see much of him. What I am saying is—nothing changes. We'll work this together and *dog these monsters to hell,*" he said with resolution.

"Okay, thanks. Gonna need some rest after these Memphis boys are through with me and I need to see Dixie's parents and make some final arrangements. Oh, can you and Chief Drew have everything ready for a full briefing sometime late tomorrow afternoon? Need to do that, too. Is it hot in here?" His voice trailed off, his desperate and futile attempts at order failing and falling before a world of chaos.

"Count on it, old buddy," he said.

As Clay got up to leave and let the detectives come back in, Michael asked, "Oh, one more thing. Are the Feds here? Are they cooperative? Will they give us what we need?"

"Just leave them to me," the former soldier said. "Just leave them to me."

Beyond the open door, Michael spotted five men with military-style haircuts. They all flashed credentials to the locals, and one young, ramrod-straight man looked like he could have been a Marine. He shot Michael a quick look, something in his eyes—recognition? They called him Tommy? They weren't local, he thought, and they didn't look happy based on their body language—Feds not from the same pot of bureaucratic stew. If ever he saw a group ready to point fingers at each other, all capable of lying through their teeth, these were the boys, holding to a tenuous truce—at least for the moment. As the door closed when the detectives reentered, he saw Clay's dark, brooding features approaching the Feds. They didn't know what they were in for.

Michael dropped his heavy head into his trembling hands in the darkened room, now only lit by the one small light bulb the detectives had used in the interrogation. His labored breathing was coming in gasping, gulping sighs aggravated by the yellow dust that the crime scene officers had dusted everywhere to capture evidence of the crime that fractured his world. It was on the walls, the furniture, the ceilings, and the very chair in which he now teetered. The murmured voices outside his smoke-filled mini-tomb faded just as the next rush of waves of numbing pain and horrific imagery crashed onto the shores of his psyche. He floated silently on this angry sea—bobbing, sinking, and rising like a storm petrel, a dark little seabird that lives its life constantly fluttering above a churning ocean of danger and death.

As the heavy condensation in the room formed a fine mist, it began to rain a yellow rain from the dust. As the droplets of yellow dripped onto Michael's face, the lost storm rider called out for superscription. "My Navigator, please tell me which way to go…"

* * *

Murky devil faces swirled and fumed in a sooty smoke from the fires of hell's furnaces. Rotting demon eyes were rolled like dice by a crimson figure with acrid breath and a snake-like tail, a serpent's arrow whipping and slashing the just and the unjust.

Michael was covered in sweat when he awakened from the nightmare that seemed to come every night now. It was always the same…he was back in Dixie's Memphis apartment and there in the shadows was the red-eyed albino stalking Dixie Lee. But he errs and makes a slight scraping noise and she sees him and calls out to Michael, pleading with her eyes—begging him to save her. But he is almost paralyzed and cannot reach her. He is moving in slow motion and the murder of the woman he had let back into his heart is playing out over and over again in front of him. "Stop!" he yells, and the beast smiles an evil smile as he raises the evil stiletto for the death thrust.

"It's on you, pig. You shouldn't have interfered," the beast says.

"Help me, Michael, help me!" she screams.

But he can't. He might as well not be there. Fate has hold of him, doesn't hear, and will not be moved. "Let me go. Let me go," he pleads.

Dixie reaches out to him as the last of her life-blood flows from her. Her clawing fingers leave a bloody print on the thin window that separates the living from the dead and she utters one final question: "Where were you, Michael? Where were you?"

As he rises from his tortuous visions, the vividness of her remains, a painful clarity of all she was, but also the smothering residuals of the sanguine monster with the white skull-head of death.

* * *

The news of Dixie's death had resonated in the tri-state area. The *Memphis Commercial Appeal* and the *Memphis Press Scimitar* carried editorials lamenting the loss of innocence in Memphis and the savagery thought impossible in the South as the sun set on what was left if old Memphis in 1973. All three network television affiliates battled to outdo each other in the ratings wars, and Dixie's death was the new measuring stick among all the news consumers who kept the viewing logs so vital to setting advertising rates for television and radio stations.

The vapid news anchors with blow-dried hair and suits from JC Penney, struggling to be Walter Cronkite, stared glassy-eyed at the black-and-white screens of Teleprompters with rolling tides of vacant words written by writers who only parody real tragedy. Man-on-the-street interviews by insipid reporters elicited responses from the average Memphian on the latest gruesome crime scene photos leaked to the "first station to bring you these exclusive photos."

Pulpits were ablaze with passionate pleas from pastors of all stripes who believed that Dixie's brutal murder was the result of judges who were soft on crime, and sermons on marquees around the city echoed a general theme—"Repent, it's later than you think! An eye for an eye."

Everywhere Michael turned, there was her face—fresh and vital—staring at him from dusk to dawn from every television set and newspaper. It was crass. It was theater. It was circus. Memphians wanted to look away, but couldn't. Lost in it all was the girl who had shed the chains of her past and only wanted to live, love, and be loved.

The day of the funeral, the crawling cars and motorcycles escorting the hearse from the funeral home to the Whitehaven church next to Graceland stretched as far as the eye could see under a bright, squash-yellow sun of a clear Memphis sky. The wind was cool and fresh. It was a new day but a different world. Leaks about Dixie's relationship with Michael and her cooperation with a police investigation spread far and wide, and police from several states came to show their colors. A sea of flashing lights from police cruisers and motorcycles provided escort for the procession of mourners, and salutes from members of the sapphire-blue fraternity paid honor to Dixie as the hearse passed each intersection.

Michael rode in the long, black limousine with Dixie's parents and her younger sisters. Dick and Martha Carter were a solid middle-class couple who produced three beautiful girls. They'd been inconsolable when Michael went to their home to tell them that their oldest daughter was dead.

He feared that they would blame him as he blamed himself. After hours of tears, prayer, and hugging, Martha summoned him to her room for a private talk. "I'd never seen her so happy, so full of life and expectation. Don't blame yourself, Michael. I don't know why or how, but I know that this is a part of God's plan," the woman, who looked too much like Dixie, said.

They hugged and cried again. Remnants of an almost family united in a sorrow of silvern luster of soft, dulcet tones where saline droplets poured from Michael's eyes as he rocked almost imperceptibly, mumbling "I'm sorry. I'm sorry. I'm sorry."

The grounds surrounding the church were ringed in vehicles bearing local and some national media outlets. The cavernous sanctuary of the old, white church with vaulted ceilings was filled with Dixie's co-workers from AT&T and friends and family who had come to mourn her passing and pay their respects to the Carters and to Michael. Reporters lurked in the corners and shadows, speaking in the hushed tones of a shallow reverence, and police uniforms dotted the congregation.

The director, a veteran of bloody homicide cases and unspeakable horror, came and laid his steady, big hands on Michael's shoulders, and his emotions betrayed him for a moment as weary basset eyes moistened and his fingers trembled. He looked very old at that moment, nearing his own end. Even though still weak from his own ordeals, Clay agreed to join the other men as pallbearers.

Michael could only sit and watch Dixie's coffin as it was delivered to the front of the church for the services, escorted by the one man who understood what a loss this was to him. Sounds of grief and sobbing echoed from the ceilings of the old church as Memphis mourned for the young woman they had adopted on television as almost a member of their families—a proxy for all of their fears and regrets.

Flowers ringed the sides of the sanctuary and filled the side room with red carpets. One large spray of white roses in the shape of a cross came from Graceland. The scrawl across the card read, "God bless and be with you. At peace in the valley, Miss Dixie Lee Carter. E.P." She would've been so proud.

Michael also found gaudy sprays sent by Frank DeVaney and Ace Connelly and instructed the stunned funeral officials to throw them in the trash. He tore up the sympathy cards so her parents wouldn't see them. No one would defile this sacred moment today. No one. His head spun in a daze, but somewhere between the bagpipers playing "Amazing Grace" and the final recitation of The Lord's Prayer, he heard the minister say that Dixie was in a better place. He requested that the congregation and the community of Memphis dwell on love and forgiveness to honor her life. Michael was numb, and forgiveness was not in him then. Perhaps it never would be, but he closed his eyes and repeated the minster's words, "Yea, though I walk through the valley of the shadow of death, I will fear no evil for thou art with me…"

Following the long trip that Michael would never remember to a rustic cemetery on the river bluffs overlooking the city, the crowd of mourners stood beside the gravesite, and the minister spoke there at the burial service of Dixie's life and her faith. The sun was lower now, and the light was fading, but the rays seemed to fall on the minister's face and pierce the gathering as he said, "Dixie believed in everlasting life. They tell me that they found her clutching a cross in her hand, reaching out to God in her hour of trial."

Michael nodded and tried to capture the feel and the smell of Dixie Lee. She danced through his mind in memories seared deeply into his soul. Intimate reality was exiled to that part of the brain that warehouses precious images and sounds of those gone…a place where desperate loved ones go nervously seeking to recapture the subtleties lost minute by minute to those left behind.

The 21-gun salute provided honor but not release to Michael and to Dixie's family. As the last sound of the final volley faded away into the distance and winds carried the smell of rifle rounds toward the heavens, he looked down the slope of the hill at the grieving people clinging tenaciously to her memory. He thought the light of love and unity from this hillside surely must be visible all the way to the celestial city.

He knelt beside her grave after the service, long after everyone had moved on to their private gatherings in homes where love and food were offered as Southern balms for broken hearts. The workers had arranged her flowers beautifully. Clay waited at a respectful distance, standing guard over the private moment. The poet, whose future prose was now silenced, wept once more and read to her one last time of prodigals come home—a girl who finally found herself and the boy who was delivered from death in Tylertown to rediscover love.

On an adjacent hill in the old cemetery with weathered monuments, a solemn man in dark glasses, with black hair and sideburns, quietly watched Michael's last farewell to Dixie. As Michael rose to leave, he saw the familiar figure point to the sky— once and then again—to emphasize "The One." He saluted crisply and held it, and then—framed by a pink coral sun that blistered the juncture of day and night at the skyline and branded the final resting place with sudden darkness—he turned and walked down the green hillside toward a waiting limo that would return him to Graceland.

An epilogue to common threads in a universal blanket of pain was finalized—a doxology for an absent actor in the prologue, lost to a merciless world where the loss of one girl can still darken all skies.

CHAPTER SEVENTEEN

"The dews of grace fall heavily in the night of sorrow…every hour has its duty; so confirm your calling as the Lord's servant."
—Alistair Begg

The months following the loss of Dixie Lee had been tumultuous. Michael drifted between deep depression and a burning anger that raged within, a fury that threatened to consume him. He retreated to his apartment where Katie the cat resumed her role as friend and giver of unconditional love. He returned home to family and Parker Grove but Pearl was no longer there, only reminding him of loss and the transient nature of life and the fleeting face of love.

The director insisted that Michael be given time to recover physically and emotionally. Clay was watching and consoling, distracting him from events that replayed in Michael's mind like ripples on the great waters of life created by the randomly tossed stone that was death.

As feared, the Feds had been obstructing, citing national security as an overriding issue in the investigation. Finding this unacceptable, Clay had raised so much noise up the line through old military contacts that they had opened up just a bit and had begun to cooperate. Some of what was revealed was off the record, spurred by competing agencies and a desire to pass blame. Fredrick had been an informant for at least three federal agencies, easily manipulating them and playing them against each other.

Fredrick had left home as a teenager for a commune near Mound Bayou, Mississippi, a primitive retreat of poor sanitation and shelter. It was a brief refuge of radical hippies and misfits that took on a paramilitary posture. It was there that he was first recruited after a story about him prompted a closer look. Fredrick had a run-in there with a big, burly cook over food. Fredrick took a meat cleaver to him, hacked him up, and floated him out in a big gator-infested slough. The big gators got the cook, wedged him deep, let him get ripe, and fed on him for a long while. Every now and then, a finger or toe would pop up and Fredrick would say, "Old Cookie's still feeding the masses." That's when they signed him up.

They had been useful to him as well—he'd given up some people who were no longer useful to his cause until he subsequently left the federal reservation. They no longer knew where he was, or so they said. The parents were to be left alone at the insistence of the Feds who said they were monitoring them. Chief Drew of the Memphis PD delivered a friendly warning to Clay about coming into Memphis without their knowledge and any attempts by anyone at retaliation.

Clay had smiled and said, "Sure thing," muttering, "That'll be the day," under his breath. A John Wayne fan, he frequently used the term that Wayne's character, Ethan, repeated in the classic movie *The Searchers*: "That'll be the day."

Clay had given the Feds just enough to get them to open up. He knew the game and kept some critical facts close to the vest—leads that could be followed in this new environment where friends weren't really friends and enemies often wore badges or carried government-issued papers. Clay and Michael shared an intense distrust of most federal agencies.

Dixie's death had churned up the cases in federal court. Ace Connelly's lawyers suddenly found themselves out of delaying tactics and out of political favors. The community was aroused at Dixie's death and demanded action. Ace was tried and found guilty of racketeering, bribery of elected officials, income tax evasion, and interstate transportation of narcotics and illegal weapons. He was sentenced to twenty-five years, and the IRS seized almost every penny he had. What they didn't get, Ace's attorneys relieved him of, prompting him to ask an associate, "What's the difference between an attorney and a catfish? One's a bottom-feeding, scum-sucking parasite. The other's a catfish."

Before his trial, Ace tried to tie up nagging loose ends. Michael's would-be assassins, the Tiller brothers, had been visited by state and federal agents and were pressured regarding the murder contracts Ace put out on Michael. But before they could testify in court, their bodies were found alongside the muddy banks and sludge of the Mississippi River. The first body, still bound in brown burlap, was discovered near Tunica, Mississippi, by Amos Jones, a very surprised commercial fisherman. Amos had thought the buzzards might be circling a deer carcass, but it turned out otherwise.

The second body was found twenty-five miles downstream by authorities. Apparently, the concrete block weights had come untied and the bloated bodies floated in the current until dumped along the river's muddy edge by an obliging eddy. Both bodies were in bad shape. It appeared that some of the river's hungry denizens—giant catfish and snapping turtles—had made several meals of the Tillers before local deputies fished them out. Each had a single small-caliber bullet hole in the right temple. The brothers had died neat, professional deaths before they became fish food. They'd slept briefly with the fish, but even the fish rejected the boys who had waited to kill Michael at Horn Lake.

Others involved in the case experienced milder forms of justice. The Hernando County Sheriff was defeated for re-election before he was charged. He paid out all the illegal money he'd gained from mobsters to his attorneys. In the end, he pled guilty to a reduced charge, and drew a year at a federal correctional facility near Memphis.

Frank DeVaney was arrested and hauled back from Arizona, eventually turning state's evidence against Connelly and Fredrick Hammel. DeVaney was instrumental in many of the convictions and was put in the Federal Witness Protection Program and whisked away. All of the *better people* in Memphis society were dismayed that someone like him could fool them so easily. "To think," the genteel, blue-haired chairlady of the Junior League said, "he was our United Way Chairman. Why, it's enough to give you the vapors. Pass the Grey Poupon, please."

The Memphis crime scene boys had pulled a fingerprint matched to Fredrick Hammel from the nightstand, and they also preserved some tissue from under Dixie's fingernails that typed out to Fredrick's A-negative blood. There was other damning evidence as well—a blood droplet of the same type, consistent with a cut to the lower leg, had been found in the carpet near the bed. Apparently, little Geordie had drawn some blood from the monster before he was done. Not disclosed to Michael was evidence of bite marks on Dixie's neck, reminiscent, said the coroner's report, of "a cinematic vampire attack." A state grand jury returned warrants for Fredrick for two counts of murder, Dixie and her doorman. The federal grand jury issued interstate flight to avoid prosecution charges, conspiracy to transport illegal weapons across state lines, and narcotics trafficking charges. But where was he?

Clay suspected that the intelligence services knew much more than they were telling, but they were in self-preservation mode, the obfuscation they did so well. Clay's shadow source did open up again in a rambling dissertation on responsibility and accountability in the netherworld and the Wild West law of espionage and counter-intelligence. "Highly compartmentalized," Clay told Michael. "Each cell is ignorant of the others with only one contact between cells. While most cells have many members, Fredrick was a one-man cell gone wrong, granted carte blanche authority. He was a killing machine in a giant chess game—agent, double agent, and triple agent serving his own master. Whom do you punish? Whom do you terminate?"

The source told Clay that the night of Dixie's funeral, Radio Havana issued a broadcast on shortwave: *Today a young innocent was laid to rest, a victim of capitalist imperialism. The fallow fields plowed by the pallid spirit seeks shelter. Welder the unifier welcomes.*

Clay said that they believed that was a message to Fredrick, the pallid spirit, to come in from the cold to the code-named Welder, the unifier, his controller on the other side. Clay never heard from his source again who told him that *"they"* were sorry.

While this was all transpiring, Michael was helping Clay's analysts update an organizational profile of all the players and potential players. He'd once had little patience for such mind-numbing tedium. He wanted to be out and about, things to do, scores to settle. However, there was little to argue—such quality work often revealed strategic areas of weakness, potential targets, and much more. It was exhausting work and he knew he had been dragged into it with forethought. Wear Michael out and keep him thinking about something else for a while.

Finally, he headed back north to coordinate the arrests of the dealers from whom Jimmy, Doug, and Ralph had purchased illegal drugs in their Delta-to-Memphis operation. Word on the street claimed that photos of Michael taken at the funeral were working their way around the city. A curious reporter had tried to identify the man in the long, black limousine. It was another reason to wrap up the operation before someone pegged him, and the marks flew the coop. Arrests would be made simultaneously from Greenville to Memphis.

Just before Michael went up to represent the Bureau on

the Memphis phase of the round-up with the local narcotics unit, a letter came in the mail from Dixie's attorney. Her last will and testament had been filed and probated. She filed an addendum to her will just two weeks before her death. She left Michael her condominium and Geordie in case anything happened to her. It was akin to hearing a voice from the past. He looked at the date on the will—it was signed around the time she had told him, "This time, Michael, it's until death do us part."

He was appalled by the thought of benefiting from Dixie's death and tried repeatedly to persuade her family to take it, but they would have none of it. Mrs. Carter said, "She wanted *you* to have it, Michael, and I'd never overrule my daughter's last wish. We couldn't bear to go there and would just sell it. I hope there is something good left there for you." He had grudgingly accepted the bequest, but doubted anything but death could reside there.

The Memphis Narcotics squad had chosen a conference room at the Howard Johnson's Motel on Elvis Presley Boulevard as their command center, the same motel used before the Full House raid, and where a room dubbed the "Powder-Blue Room" was maintained as a getaway for Elvis. Teams of officers were given warrants to serve, along with photos of their suspects when possible. Michael requested that he accompany the team serving the warrant on the residence where Rosemary Taylor and her band of merry men lived and ran a major methamphetamine operation.

About 11:00 p.m. they approached the old, two-story, wood frame house near Memphis State University, after verifying that cars registered to her and six other suspects were parked at the house. The neighborhood was a popular area for the counter-culture—part-time students, drug users and dealers, and true bohemian pretenders.

The place was rocking when Michael knocked on the door. The door opened, and he was taken aback at the sight of her. There, standing before him, was Rosemary Taylor, and as he had feared earlier, she was on a fast track to nowhere. The speed had wasted her, burning off twenty-five to thirty pounds in the few months since he had seen her. Her looks were just about gone. She was nothing but skin and bones, a wild-eyed, shriveled-up husk of a former beauty stoned out of her mind. She smelled like death, and her once healthy tan was now a jaundiced yellow.

He almost gagged, but spoke in his pleasant officer's voice, "Well, hello, Miss Rosemary." She blinked, not comprehending, as other officers stormed past, guns drawn, shouting everyone down.

She brought her hand to her mouth and teetered on her skinny legs for a moment. "Don't I know you?"

"Yeah, we met one night in Grenada when I was in my red Mustang."

"Oh, man," she said. "I think I'm going to be sick." He helped her outside and she vomited in the front yard of her little house of pills and needles. Her sides heaved and she shuddered, her skin clammy.

"Miss Rosemary, I have two warrants for your arrest for the sale of amphetamines and heroin. Doing some speedballs?" he asked, referring to the combination of speed to rev one up and smack to bring them back down to earth. He read her rights to her before she could answer. She had nothing left to say.

He said, "All right," and led the stunned woman to a waiting cruiser.

She sobbed most of the way to the booking—knowing it was over—that *she*—was over. Rosemary Taylor was no longer the object of anyone's desire, or disdain for that matter. She was a lost soul to be pitied, someone who needed help. She would be held accountable, but she was on the ragged edge, using her own stuff and likely suffering from one or more sexually transmitted diseases contracted in the midst of her haze. There was the likelihood of hepatitis from shared needles. She had fallen far and fast.

When she was booked at the station, Michael asked if he

could speak with her. He took her to an interrogation room with a witness sitting in with him.

"Rosemary, do you have a lawyer or someone you want to call?"

"Oh man, my parents are going to die," she sobbed, her body racked with violent tremors.

"Let's talk about some things and I'll see if I can help you. All right?"

She nodded yes, her once luxuriant hair now thinning, dirty, and caked with grime.

"Do you remember us talking about a guy named Fredrick, Fredrick Hammel, who used to deal at Memphis State?"

She struggled and said, "Yeah, I remember Freddie, weird Freddie. He had the good acid in the old days," she said. She wiped at the mucus leaking from her eyes and nose with the back of her hand and a soiled tissue.

"Yeah, that would be him, Rosemary, the pale rider with the dead eyes." He saw the pattern of marks on her arms, matching the needle tracks the police matron at the jail found under her breasts.

"He was messed up in the head, man. He used to try to sign us up for rallies when he sold drugs to us. He, he… Oh, yeah, now I remember you asking me about him. I saw him after that, and man, that dude had changed. He was really far out there—in another zone, you know?"

"Yeah, I know. Where did you see him?"

"Oh, I saw him coming out of the Bottom of the Blues Club late one night," she said, fading a bit, leaning forward, dulled eyes fluttering.

"When was that, Rosemary?"

"It was right after the party you missed the night I met you," she said.

"Are you sure?" A sick feeling gnawed suddenly at Michael's gut.

"Yeah, I'm sure, man. Because I wanted you to party with me

that night, remember?" she asked, smiling through dingy teeth and cracked, bleeding lips.

"Yes, I remember."

She giggled, and said, "Well, I partied without you, Mr. Cop, and you'll never know what you missed."

"No, I am sure it was my loss, but back to Freddie."

"Oh, yeah. Saw that freak at the club, and he was acting real strange, jumpy-like. I asked if he was having a bad trip." She was suddenly animated.

"You know, he was just downright mean, and called me a slut. You don't think I'm a slut, do you, Mr. Cop?"

"No, Rosemary, you're just a lost girl who was about to run out of luck when I knocked on your door, but you'll be all right now," he said. She began to sniffle, and he gave her a handkerchief and told her to keep it. Blood trickled at the edge of her ulcerated nose. Snorting, too?

She blew her nose and looked at him. "I'm in deep, ain't I?"

"Yes, Rosemary, but it may save your life. Now, tell me, did you see Fredrick again or remember anything else about that time?"

"No, uh—oh yeah, man. I remember one thing cause I thought he must be dealing. He came downstairs from the office of, uh, James Walker, the man we call Super Fly—you know, the dude who runs the club. Freddie was putting a fat envelope in his jacket, like money."

"Thanks, Rosemary," he said. He paused and then asked her, "Do you know Jesus?"

"Who's that?" she asked.

"Someone who loves you very much, and who is waiting to forgive you," Michael said. He held her bony hand and she wept.

A female officer led her away to help her clean up and make phone calls now that she was semi-coherent. She would require extensive detoxification and medical assistance. However, it didn't happen—an hour later, her parents arrived with their lawyer and bailed her out. Her attorney was bringing her out to face her parents when he spotted Michael in the hallway leaving another interview room.

In a little show for the paying clients, the lawyer, an intense, short man with black hair and a black wooly mustache, said, "Are you happy? Feel like a big man picking on this poor, young girl?"

Michael had encountered the lawyer before, but hid his disdain—almost. "If we hadn't arrested her tonight, counselor, she would've been dead within a month and you wouldn't be collecting your big, fat fee. Yes, maybe we kept her alive, and some of the kids she was selling her chemicals to as well. My advice—you had best get her to a doctor ASAP because she is going into serious withdrawal very soon."

The lawyer started to respond, but Rosemary's father, a large and imposing older man, waved him off. The old man and his small, withered wife looked at Michael with sad eyes that had run out of tears. The father nodded and closed his eyes, accepting the unacceptable—that they had failed as parents and their daughter was almost at the point of no return. Then they swept Miss Rosemary out into the night without another word. Though he often wondered about Rosemary, it was the last time Michael saw her until she showed up to plead in court many months later. Out of detox, she had regained her weight, and her skin was a good color. Dressed like a sorority sister at Ole Miss and radiating innocence and contriteness, she drew a short period of incarceration in a treatment facility.

* * *

As the long night became another day, Michael reviewed the outstanding warrants for Memphis. Pretty good—sixty-five of seventy-two suspects were in custody, but the rest were either missing or on the run. He was tired and there was nothing more he could do. He decided to call it a night and impulsively turned down a vacant side street and headed toward Dixie's condo—now *his* condo. He had seen senseless human degradation and destruction again tonight and the talk with Rosemary had stirred up the "Is this all there is?" voice in him.

Gone were the crime scene markers from the condominium, the police barricades, and the useless ambulances. There were no hordes of reporters descending on the scene like vultures, no pack of detectives or unpleasant federal agents. The distasteful harbingers of unpleasant events had disappeared as quickly as they'd assembled, moving on to new venues, to fresh bodies. A snot-nosed punk, maybe twenty-one, named Rick, had replaced Charlie. He said that if there was anything he could do, just call him, day or night.

The elevator music that mellowed original tunes almost beyond recognition annoyed Michael as the floors ticked by on the way up to the condominium. Recent events still swirling in his head, he hesitated and took a deep breath as he slid the key into the door. The last time that he had opened this door, his world had turned upside down. Maybe it was too soon to be here. A part of him was drawn to this place, however, and he knew that he was still looking for her.

As the door opened, he caught the pungent scent of room deodorizers and bleach. He felt nauseous from the burning odor of chemicals that had cleansed the abode of the last traces of her life. The condominium association maids had been in. An unknowing eye could never see or feel the horror that had been visited upon this place. Rooms once filled with Dixie Lee's bubbling vitality were now dark and quiet like a tomb. Michael listened intently, hoping for echoes of what was, but there were none.

As he searched through stacks of letters and personal belongings, he came across a picture of the two of them the night he'd met Dixie Lee in Washington. Dixie Lee, forever young, wet hair and all. There were other photos as well—photos of them in private, happy moments and with friends. He thought how innocent they looked, babes in the woods. Time stood still for a moment, and then he turned the first picture over. Written on the back in her then eighteen-year-old handwriting were these words:

> *Someday, I am going to marry this man. I just love him.*
> *Dixie Lee Carter, 1966*

His lungs gasped for air, but what did him in was the new Bible he found beneath the faded photos, a Bible he had no idea she had purchased. It was heavily marked in the margins, and a bookmark drove his eyes to the words she had underlined and highlighted. "For God so loved the world...." Next to John 3:16 was her cursive revelation, "Thank you Jesus for loving even me."

Then, it all came rushing back, and the well of tears he thought were long dry burst again. He fell to his knees and wept. He cried out to God demanding answers and then slumped onto the couch and slept the sleep of he tortured.

* * *

He rose the next morning, shaved the dark stubble of beard, squinted into a brilliant silver sky and uncharacteristically called in for a personal day off. He told Clay where he'd be in vague terms, packed, and set out for a forbidden destination.

The east side Memphis address of Fredrick's parents was in a report Clay had shared, but it could hardly have prepared him for the sight of the mansion he found there. The gated compound had tall, wrought-iron fencing mounted atop a white brick foundation that matched the palatial home's facade. The tree-lined brick drive wound up a gentle slope, elaborately landscaped with azaleas, camellias, and other flowering perennials designed to provide a year-round splash of blue, white, red, and yellow color. Beyond the fragrant blooms, the massive Colonial mansion had the cold, hard feeling of a fortress or sanctuary, but a sanctuary for whom?

There was a callbox by the gate. He punched the button and waited. "Yes?" the curt voice answered.

"This is Agent Michael Parker, Mississippi Bureau of Narcotics, to see Mr. or Mrs. Hammel."

Silence.

"Do you have an appointment?" asked the disembodied, metallic voice, challenging with the dismissive air of delegated authority. Michael's tedious studies on transactional analysis kicked in.

"No, but I'd like to talk to them about a girl at rest on a hillside named Dixie Lee Carter."

There was a long silence and he raised his voice. "This is in regard to a homicide investigation in case I didn't make myself clear."

There was no response, but the gates slowly creaked open. It brought to mind an ancient castle lowering its drawbridge and beckoning him enter. He hesitated for a moment. Had the Feds not warned him not to bother Hammel's parents? Sure, but when did that ever stop him?

As he drove up the road in his car, he marveled at the natural beauty and considered the material wealth that it took to create and maintain such a place. Gardeners were busy at work. Off to the left in a lush pasture nearer the house, several men rode sleek horses that pranced, danced, and spoke of fine breeding. He felt like an intruder in a world where he clearly didn't belong, a world he couldn't comprehend. However, wealth didn't excuse criminal behavior, and he swore he would find out how such a place could spawn the monster that had robbed him of the one thing he cherished. Then he would attend to the horror that was Fredrick Hammel.

As he got out of the car in front of the massive doors to the house, a courtly manservant appeared in tails and beckoned him to follow. He said, "Madam will see you now."

Michael nodded and followed him through the foyer with its massive crystal chandelier. They walked past two elegant staircases that wound upward, seemingly to the heavens. Finally, he was escorted into an impressive study filled with rich bookcases and ornately bound volumes, a library full of the best works of mankind. The bindings of the books suggested they had been there for a long time, long enough for a young Fredrick to have read these very volumes as a young boy.

As he waited, he browsed the titles, picked up a copy of *Romeo and Juliet*, and randomly opened the classic. His jaw muscles tightened, his throat became full, and his eyes squeezed back the moistness as he read Lady Capulet's judgment, "Death lies on her like an untimely frost, upon the sweetest flower of all the field." How could anyone read this wonderful literature and end up with a mind that seemed more a product of *Mien Kampf*, Mao's little red book, or Timothy Leary?

Then he thought about security and looked around the room. French doors off the study framed by expensive white curtains opened to a magnificent view of the grounds and stables. The horsemen in the distance didn't appear to offer any threat. Their khaki jodhpurs spoke of another time of British colonialism in India.

He walked to the phone and unscrewed the mouthpiece. There in the set was a piece of equipment that was not standard Bell System issue, but rather appeared to be standard FBI tech. Not surprised, he replaced it and pulled a small gadget from his briefcase. He surveyed the room, and the readings suggested that there were most likely more electronic surveillance devices. He quickly put the device away at the sound of footsteps on the hardwood floor.

An elegant-looking woman entered the room. He guessed her to be in her early fifties, although she could pass for much younger. She had dark hair, streaked a bit with gray, and reminded him somewhat of Jackie Kennedy. She wore a long strand of white pearls around her neck, and her walk and look spoke of the same good bloodlines that he had seen in her horses. He also knew from experience that looks could be deceiving.

"It is nice to meet you, Agent Parker. I am Clarice Hammel," she said with a genteel, Southern drawl, an almost regal bearing.

"I appreciate you seeing me on such short notice, Mrs. Hammel. You are very gracious," he said.

"You are the agent who was close to that girl who…?"

His raw emotions exposed, he couldn't finish the sentence. "Yes, I was. I am."

"That's why I agreed to talk with you. My deepest condolences," she said softly.

"Thank you, Mrs. Hammel. It's a beautiful day. I wondered if we might sit out on the patio and talk?" he asked, pointing to the light fixture above and then to his ear.

She paused and said, "Yes, that would be delightful." She rang an antique pewter bell for her servant and ordered lemonade, and they retired to the covered patio and piped music where Andy Williams sang, *"Moon River, wider than a mile, I'm crossing you in style some day."*

As they sat on the wrought-iron chairs, she turned to him and asked, "Agent Parker, are you here as an agent of the government or as someone seeking personal revenge?"

"Mrs. Hammel, I'm here as a seeker of truth."

"Aren't you out of your jurisdiction in Memphis?" she asked.

"Truth knows no boundaries," he replied without hesitation.

"All manner of government men have been here, and asked questions of us about our son, Fredrick. They think we know where he is, I believe. They suspect we are supporting him financially somehow, but we aren't, Agent Parker. I asked his father to cut him off after the investigators came and told us about Miss Carter," she said, with a catch in her voice. "I'm not saying I don't love him. He's my son, but if he could do such a thing?" There was a long pause, and lemonade was served. A mourning dove in a pink dogwood tree plaintively called, "woo, woo" in its sorrowful coo.

"This is very good lemonade," he said. "It reminds me of the fresh-squeezed juice my grandmother made for me as a child." He paused. "Pearl was her name. We often drank lemonade when we played 'Pollyanna' on days like today."

"We're all very innocent as children, aren't we, Agent Parker?"

"Yes, I suppose we are. Please call me Michael."

"Well, Michael, what do you want of me?" She looked at him intently, studying, assessing.

"I, I'm not sure." He watched the whirling blades of the ceiling fan above for a moment and it brought him back to the horrible truth and why he was there. "I suppose I wanted to understand how a young man of privilege could go so far astray of the life he was born to."

She looked across the broad expanse of all that her son had left.

"I would like to know the answer to that as well. He was a gentle child who one day became a stranger. It seems to be happening to parents all over the country now, what with the war, drugs, this sexual revolution, and corruption in government," she said.

They talked for over an hour and a half, and she became less guarded with him. He gained a sense of admiration and sympathy for her and decided she wasn't his enemy. Perhaps, she could be his friend one day, perhaps not. Sometimes the divide was just too wide, he reflected, but grief could make a sturdy bridge.

As he stood to leave, he gave her his card. "Mrs. Hammel, should you ever wish or need to contact me, I've written a private number on the back. The person who answers that line will be able to get you through to me wherever I may be, day or night."

She stood, took the card and extended her hand. "You're an easy man to talk to and to trust. Is that part of your training to put people at ease?" she asked.

"Yes, we're trained to be good interviewers, but today, the only training you've seen is that imparted to me by Pearl."

She shook his hand and said, "Call me Clarice."

As he drove down the drive and the big gates swung open, he thought of all she had said. He must write it all down and transmit it to Clay via a private channel. Lost in thought, he pulled out on Poplar Avenue and drove toward downtown Memphis. He glanced at his rearview mirror in time to see a brown sedan pull out of a side street. Its occupants were two men in dark suits and mirrored glasses. *Could you be any more obvious?* From the look of the car and their dress, he assumed they were Feds, not local cops.

Driving his Mustang on an official day off gave him certain advantages. The car was his. It had plenty of muscle with its 289 engine, two four-barreled carburetors, and a four-speed manual transmission. The car was like a part of him. He waited to see what his shadow's game was. After a while, it just appeared that they were content to follow him and see where he went. He slowed down, they slowed down. He speeded up, they speeded up.

He knew the streets of Memphis much better than these guys did. As he neared a one-way street that intersected with Poplar, he slowed the Mustang to a crawl in the far left lane of the four westbound lanes as the traffic neared a stoplight changing to red. He looked to his right. There was a Standard Oil service station on the right corner, and a break in the southbound traffic stopped at the light waiting to cross Poplar.

He dropped the Mustang into first gear, gunned it, and swerved through three lanes of traffic across Poplar. Still burning rubber, the Mustang flew through the service station with stunned customers and workers gawking. He bounced onto the southbound lanes of the one-way street heading north. Horns were blaring from all directions and people were shouting obscenities, or as close as the genteel people in Memphis could come.

He met a few cars he had to artfully dodge, but coming at him from the next light down the one-way street was a solid wave of vehicles. Then there it was, just where he hoped it would be. A narrow alleyway appeared off to his left. He hit second gear and accelerated down that street just as the oncoming traffic passed behind him, sealing off his pursuers. The g-men were beside themselves the last time he saw them—wildly gesturing, slamming their dashboard, still trying to get across Poplar. Michael was pleased with himself, although a certain part of him—the conformist—didn't approve of such showboating.

The driver of the red Mustang whistled for the first time since Dixie's music ceased to play as he passed through a cathedral of old cedars on either side of him, momentarily shielding him from the sun and from grief.

CHAPTER EIGHTEEN

"The bitterest tears shed over graves are for
words left unsaid and deeds left undone."
—Harriet Beecher Stowe

Darkness was gathering as Michael turned onto Beale Street. The faint glow in the western sky diminished on a palette of pink, purple, and lavender. The Bottom of the Blues Club was another two blocks on the left. A gaudy neon sign that sputtered on and off with a crackling buzz marked the club's presence. It was a contrast to the tones and timbres of the day's dying colors that refused to surrender above the horizon. Although it was a long shot, he had decided to take a run at the club. He figured he had nothing to lose.

No law enforcement agency that he knew of had informants covering the club, and from what he could pick up from Memphis Narcotics, they weren't interested in the character who owned this place. The MBN didn't have the manpower for permanent surveillance on the club or its owner, and he didn't trust the Feds when it came to Fredrick. The tail reinforced that feeling. He had found some information in Clay's report that could prove useful, his ace in the hole if he had to play it. He eased into the only available parking place, well lit to deter thieves and easily accessible for a quick escape.

After losing his escort, he had changed into street clothes and slipped into his leather jacket. Despite law enforcement's lack of interest in the blues joint, he had a feeling—call it cop's intuition—that he might encounter some heavy lifting when he walked through the door. He decided to take no chances and fully armed himself. The 9mm Browning automatic was in its holster under his arm. He had inserted a small .38 loaded with hollow points in the small of his back and a very small .25 caliber automatic in his left pants pocket. He carried extra rounds for all three weapons. Why? He didn't really know, except for a cop's intuition and the reputation of the man who ran the club. Clay said he'd been relatively clean for a long time, but you could never really tell.

The Bottom was a genuine blues club, and the music that thumped from the walls was B.B. King and authentic Delta Blues. He entered the darkened club with purple velvet trim without drawing so much as a notice. Michael wasn't the only white guy in the place. There were as many white faces as black and they all seemed to be into the music and the despair it conveyed. He suspected they could have found a more upscale venue for their cultural enlightenment, so why were they here? Finding an empty seat at the bar, he ordered a beer, even though he didn't drink. The big black guy on the next bar stool gave him a strange look but said nothing.

A band was already playing standards and mournful tributes to the hard times of life. He loved good music of various genres if it was authentic and not commercial pap. This was good music, and the patrons in the smoke-filled room were feeling the pain. Their "thrill was gone away."

Michael figured the tall, skinny bartender as a former junkie or worse, but took a chance and asked him if Freddie had been around lately.

Without looking up from polishing glasses, he asked, "Freddie who?" The blue haze of smoke swirled around his unique reddish pigmentation.

"You know, man, Freddie—Freddie the freak—the whitest white man anyone has ever seen!"

That made the bartender laugh and he said, without thinking, "You got that right. He's the whitest dude I ever seen. If it was snowing, you couldn't even see him." "Red" slapped the bar to punctuate his little joke.

Michael laughed, too, and said, "He's whiter than my lily-white behind." More laughter. "That little piece of crap owes me money."

"He owes everybody something," the bartender said.

"He still running with that big guy, what's his name?"

The bartender realized he was being played like a fiddle, became cautious, and said, "I ain't seen that boy in a long time."

The bartender shut up and went back to his work, but another deep voice came from behind Michael. "What's so funny and what boy y'all talking 'bout?" He turned to see a large, black man with prominent eyes and very dark skin. He could easily have tipped the scales at over 350 pounds and had the look of an old pro athlete gone to seed. He seemed jolly, but his eyes were hard. The bartender's reaction told Michael this had to be James Walker, "Super Fly," himself.

"We ain't talking 'bout nobody," the bartender said, clearly afraid of the big man.

"We are too. Talking about that freaky little pansy, Fredrick the albino," Michael countered with a smile.

"And who might you be?" Walker asked, fingering an old brown belt that held up his tan trousers. Extra holes punched in the old belt indicated he was fighting a losing battle of the bulge.

"I'm just a businessman that he screwed over looking to collect on a debt. J.T. is my handle." Michael extended his hand and Walker gave it a perfunctory squeeze in his giant paw.

"Well, well, Mr. J.T., you come on up to the office and let's have a chat."

"Mighty kind of you."

"First," he said, "I am going to have to ask you to check that big gun you got under your armpit there."

Michael looked at him, and saw the bartender tense with his hand on his billy club under the bar.

"You're very observant."

"Don't worry, you'll get it back when and if you leave," he said, and laughed uproariously. Michael eased the Browning out and handed it to the bartender.

"Nice," the big man said.

He followed Walker up the steep stairs as the blues pounded rhythm through the soles of his shoes, and he thought of Johnny Cash singing "Welcome to the Home of the Blues." The wooden stairs creaked and groaned under Walker's weight. He was a huge man, and Michael didn't know how to approach him. He figured Walker as an old pro who had seen everything and was as savvy as they come.

Michael's hackles went up as they entered his large office. There were two dangerous looking thugs lounging in chairs along opposite walls, monitoring bar conversation over a little speaker on the desk. The bar was bugged, and they'd picked up his every word. Walker settled behind his massive desk—had to have been custom made—and eyed Michael with a grin that made him think of a cat eyeing a trapped mouse. He walked over to the impressive photo gallery wall behind Walker's desk and studied the famous faces there with genuine interest.

Walker was irritated with Michael's forwardness and said, "Sit," motioning to the wooden chair in front of his desk.

Michael glanced down as he moved to the chair and spotted a sawed-off shotgun that Walker had bolted under his desk. It was aimed straight ahead, a deadly deterrent against armed robbery or other social disputes.

"Can we talk alone?" Michael asked, motioning to the other men.

"My boys get nervous if I'm alone with a strange man who carries big guns," he said, swiveling back and forth in the plush leather chair.

"Well, I understand, but this is confidential, and I really want to sit in that chair on the side away from that big, ole scatter gun you got under the desk."

The two goons tensed up and eyed one another, awaiting a signal from their boss.

Michael laughed, his left hand in his pocket. "No, no. Be calm. If I had to shoot one of you boys with this here .25 automatic in my pocket, it would ruin my leather jacket." As they looked at his pocket in horror, he slipped the second gun from his back with his right hand. "Worse still, I might have to shoot the other one with this .38." The words flowed with a confidence that made it appear not possible, but probable.

Walker laughed loudly, "Ha, Ha, Ha!" He motioned to his bodyguards to leave. "Get out. It's all right. I know this boy," he said. At that, the hoodlums left, and Walker locked the door behind them.

"Whew, glad that's out of the way. I would have hated to shoot a big man like you with a little .25. *That* would've been downright insulting," Michael said, with a big smile.

"Boy, you're all right," he said, "for a cop!" He smiled a huge crocodile smile accentuating the deep laugh lines around the whites of his eyes.

"What makes you think I am a cop, and why'd you say you knew me?"

"He told me that you'd be coming for him. I didn't know then that he had just killed your woman, or I might've killed him myself. He did that out of plain old meanness. Ain't no other reason."

Michael looked at him with surprise.

Walker shrugged and leaned back, interlocking his massive dark fingers and stubby nails.

"I done lots of bad things in my life, but killing women and children ain't among them. That boy's got innocent blood on his hands, and he brings nothing but trouble down on all of us. He brings people like you through the door. Are you here as the law or as a vigilante?"

Michael looked at him for a long pause, and said, "I am here for justice, Mr. Walker. *Justice.*"

"Well said, my man, but why on earth would I help you?"

"Because you owe me."

"How you figure that?" he asked, with furrowed brows as he propped his elbows on the massive desk.

"I took out Ace. Ace was your competitor, a man who had screwed you six ways from Sunday and your enemy. And you know what they say."

"What's that?"

"The enemy of my enemy is my friend."

He laughed long and hard. "So, that was you. Freddie told me he thought a narc who once messed with him in Jackson, Mississippi, was in Ace's club. Said he thought you were tight with one of the girls there."

"Not *one of the girls*. The woman I loved. The woman he stabbed to death." Michael heard his own voice come from far away. His words were one more confirmation that he had gotten Dixie killed.

Big James Walker, framed by black-and-white photos of Little Richard, Little Anthony and the Imperials, Muddy Waters, Fats Domino, and others not recognized by Michael, looked at him long and hard. "Mr. J.T., is it?"

"Michael."

"Like the big-guy angel. Uh-huh, yeah! Mike, I do owe you more than you know, but I won't say more in case you got room for a wire on your body underneath all them guns. I won't say more in fear of incriminating myself." He flashed his big, Cheshire cat smile.

"No wire…not interested in hurting you since I am your friend."

"Okay then, let me tell it like it is, and shoot straight with you," he said. "Ace going to prison was one of the happiest days of my life. As for that little Commie freak, I paid him some money I owed him for some transportation work and told him to never come back here again. He told me that he was going far away, and wouldn't be back to Memphis for a long time. He also told me that the revolution was coming, and that I would be free. Hell, I told him I may be black, and I may be bad, but I ain't no Communist!

"I saw he had blood on his clothes. I didn't know what he'd done, but told him to get out. When I saw the news, I knew he done it—had his trademark stamped all over it. Some friends on the force told me about the knife that he favors being found near the scene. If I knew where he was or who might tell you, I'd give him to you. You believe that?"

Michael stood up, and said, "Yes, I think I do. Thanks for your time, Mr. Walker. Here's a number you can reach me at any time if you hear anything a friend should know," he said.

"You never know. You never know." His deep baritone voice trailed off.

As Michael turned to leave, Walker said, "You mind an observation?"

"No, feel free."

"You don't look too good. You be all wound up like a wounded animal. Stay the night on me. I got some girls who can maybe help you forget for a while." A freebie from a kindly pimp.

"I appreciate the offer more than you know, because I know it is sincere. Not that I doubt the talent of your girls, but what I'm looking for—need—only one woman has ever brought me, and now she's gone."

Walker freed his bulk from the chair and escorted him to the door. He wrapped his giant mitt around Michael's hand and shook it firmly. "Take care, son. It's dangerous when you walk on the wild side, particularly when you walk alone."

Michael picked up his weapon at the bar and walked out into the dark of another Memphis night. The sun was now sleeping on the other side of the world. Music blared from a dozen clubs, competing for customers and their money. Though he didn't need any more clubs, the friendly women of the night were harder to avoid. Several scantily clad, young women asked him if he was looking for a good time. Ironically, he was, but happiness didn't reside there. The old movie he had watched with Dixie late one night had it right: *The Heart Is a Lonely Hunter.*

* * *

The inefficient air-conditioning unit groaned and rattled in the darkened waiting area outside the Jackson, Mississippi, Ramada Inn conference room. Housekeepers came by with carts loaded with towels and soap and stared at Michael in curiosity. He waited impatiently to be called for an interview with a panel of police executives from the Interview Board of the International Association of Chiefs of Police.

It was to be his final interview for promotion in the Bureau, and he wasn't only impatient to get it over with but uncharacteristically nervous about the whole thing. He sweated, and it was more than the bad air conditioner. Perhaps he now wanted this more than he had confessed to Clay, more than he had wanted anything. Things had changed and this was his chance to immerse himself totally in a commitment that knew no end and had no room for emotions and memories. A hiding place?

Six months had passed since he lost Dixie and much had happened in that time. The holidays had been the worst times. He tortured himself too often with images of snowball fights on a cold morning in the fresh-fallen powder, opening gifts, and Dixie running to fling her arms around him in delight. He'd gone to the family gathering for her parents and sisters, but he left early, sensing that his presence somehow reminded them of her. He could see Dixie in her sisters' eyes and walk. They, like him, dwelled in the land of what-ifs. He prayed they didn't blame him for her death...

He'd declined his concerned mother's invitation to move back home. Rather, he remained in his apartment in Batesville, staying up late with the cat and watching TV. He was still emotionally labile and cried as Clarence got his wings and Jimmy Stewart found out what life would be like without him. He was beginning to learn what life would be, *was* like, without Dixie—without the gifts of her smile and the smell of her near in the night. He resolved to never let life hurt him this way again, but prayed this was not a resolution to no longer live it. It was not "a wonderful life" now.

As he waited for the interview, he thought about why he was here—why this seemingly lost opportunity had presented itself. Robert, his supervisor, had found the rigors of command as daunting as the appeal of a young female agent under his tutelage was irresistible. He'd surrendered his rank when it all came out. Clay had been right about Robert, and now Michael competed with forty other agents for that one glorious command slot. The odds weren't good, but the Bureau was desperate for success in the Northeast sector, where crime was rampant and the agents were lacking.

In the last five months, a gang of dope dealers had tied an informant to a tree, whipped him with a bullwhip, and carved their initials on his chest. They'd strutted into a restaurant at noon and laid a hangman's noose before the foreman of a grand jury that had indicted a member of their gang. The county prosecutor's home had been burned to the ground, and the chief judge wouldn't send dope dealers to prison and that was just the trouble in one northeastern county.

In Michael's hometown of Tupelo, local enforcement was

generally weak. Some tried, but the system wore them down. Some were just short on ethics. The relationship between officers of the court and a local lawyer was just too cozy for comfort. The whole area needed a boat rocker, someone who would push the status quo until it squealed. Some of the MBN agents in the area were lazy, others were boozers and womanizers.

The team of men with prominent bellies born of desk work and too much fried food finally called him in. He'd already endured three days of in-box management, endless role-playing that he despised, and group sessions designed to see who was interested in problem solving and who in cutting throats for this promotion.

The board of police veterans said they wanted to give him a chance to change his answer to one of the questions posed to all the candidates. He tried to remember that once they were all young, baby-faced rookies.

"Why would I want to do that?" he asked.

The chief from Maryland, a fifty-something, balding, intense man, leaned forward, and said, "Son, you were the only candidate who said you wouldn't authorize your officers to reward those who had been friendly and supportive of law enforcement efforts. You also answered a question indicating that you would challenge a prosecutor if you thought he was wrong even though you don't prosecute, you enforce." Subterfuge, trying to provoke anger?

The others crossed their arms and looked at him accusingly.

"Why is that, and do you want to change your mind now that you know that you are alone in your thinking? Perhaps you think you are somehow so special that you know more than everyone else?" grumbled the tanned and grizzled chief from Texas, testing and provoking him. "Who do you think you are?"

"I can't change my answers even if you had the whole state of Mississippi saying I was wrong. The first question is crystal clear to me. We don't reward people who do favors for us, and by inference, are slow to help those who don't. We're hired to enforce the law for all, to serve and protect. I won't get on that slippery slope. I know the difference between right and wrong."

They looked at each other and raised eyebrows a bit. Then the Florida chief, a man with hawk-like eyes, who had been listening intently, asked, "Well, what about you trying to be police and prosecutor? Don't you know your place?"

"Respect is a two-way street, and just as I would respect the prosecutor, he must respect my people and our mission. We aren't inferior to a prosecutor or superior. Our allegiance is to the safety of the public, and if it was in the public interest for me to challenge a prosecutor, then I would do so with respect but without hesitation," he said. "We can't be cowed by the system or the fraternity of lawyers when we see that justice isn't being served or palms are being greased."

"You don't like lawyers very much, do you?" the Maryland chief asked with raised eyebrows.

"There are good lawyers and bad, like good cops and bad, but no, I have a healthy suspicion of them all," he said with candor. "I believe in compassion and don't believe in one-size-fits-all sentencing, but the mechanics and technicalities of the law too easily obscure the real victims in many cases. The defense too often wants to cut deals with their fraternity brother, now a prosecutor, or vice versa. Often, the prosecutor worries more about his win/loss average than about real justice. Justice may be blind, but many of the officers of the court aren't."

That was the end of it. He couldn't read them, but then they all began to smile. The interview team members stood up and shook his hand, and he left there not knowing, or caring anymore what happened. He drove slowly back to his hotel in Jackson and was fast asleep by 5:00 p.m. After three days of running what seemed an exhaustive and tedious assessment gauntlet, he needed sleep. And sleep he did, mostly escaping his chronic nightmares until the telephone jangled him awake. Marcie, the director's personal assistant, was on the line in her usual crisp, efficient mode.

"Michael, the director would like to see you ASAP," she said with a hint of her assumed delegation of authority.

"What time is it, Marcie?"

"It's seven a.m. We were here late last night and back early this morning."

"How long do I have?"

"You're late *now*, darlin'," she replied, sighed deeply, and hung up.

He stared at the receiver in his hand. "Now what?" he exclaimed aloud. He splashed some water on his face, put on a fresh change of clothes, grabbed a tie, and left for headquarters. As he entered the townhome-style row units off Lakeland Drive, he thought how glad he was to be away from headquarters, the office politics, gossip, and endless mind games played out here. Seeing Clay and his people was the one exception.

He punched in the code and entered the building. Judy, the receptionist, sat in her usual place, polishing her nails. "Hi, Michael," she said with her best fake smile. The office secretarial pool had been rumored to be infatuated with whoever appeared to be in favor or in command at the moment. He didn't think they viewed him as a prime, grade-A cut for management or power. He was just the serious loner, the weird guy who always disappeared into the bat cave upstairs, that mysterious place no one else was allowed to go.

He wished everyone a good morning and swung around to trot up the winding, wrought-iron staircase to the director's office. As he neared the top, Marcie Jones was sitting at her large desk outside the director's office. The ever-vigilant woman with the blonde pixie haircut and hazel eyes was like a guard dog when it came to those seeking access. Today, it was a different story.

"You're late," she said. "They're waiting on you." She opened the door and said, "He's here." As he passed her, he thought he saw her wink.

He entered the director's office and there was the old man,

looking as inviting as a pit bull, sitting under a giant painting of the Bureau shield, flanked by state and U.S. flags.

"It's about time. Come in, boy," he growled. Clay was there along with the newly installed chief of enforcement for the state, Larry Burnside, a competent, fair man whom many of the shirkers in the Bureau didn't care for.

"Well, this looks serious," Michael said, with a smile. "Am I going to be fired, or is this a court-marital?"

"Sit down," the director ordered in full general mode, motioning toward the conference table where Clay and the chief sat. The director rose and then sat next to Michael across from the others. He squeaked when he walked. More new cowboy boots?

The director flipped papers in a folder and looked at Michael over the top of the rims of his wire rim glasses resting on the end of his bulbous nose.

"It's the opinion of the IACP team that you placed first in the assessment," the chief interjected. Clay shot Michael one of his "be serious, don't blow it now" looks.

"However, I'm not so sure," Burnside said. "We have the final say in this matter, and I'm not sure that you have put this thing in Memphis behind you."

"This thing?" he asked, bristling a bit.

"Sorry," he said, softening. "The loss you have experienced and any desire for retribution might distract you from command responsibilities."

"Oh, I see."

Trying his best to appear impartial, but not quite making it, Clay leaned forward and asked, "Michael, as they said in *Cool Hand Luke*, *'Is your mind right?'*"

"Right? I can't say if I'll ever be…right, but…I'm much better, and need a challenge," he answered. "I won't lie for this job, and say I'm a hundred percent, but I think the position is what I need. I think I will be good for the agency and the position will be good for me."

245

"You're somewhat of a lone wolf. Can you run with the pack?" the chief asked a bit perfunctorily.

"I can as long as they toe the line on the standards written in our *Manual of Conduct*," he said.

He paused and took a deep breath.

"I want full control of the Northeast division and the freedom to resurrect it. Right now, the whole thing is just a disgrace."

Clay grimaced at Michael's harsh words and started to speak, but the director cut him off and spoke for the first time. His deep voice resonated throughout the room, reminding Michael of Bear Bryant again atop his tower in Tuscaloosa, shouting at some errant quarterback.

"There're some good boys up there," he snapped defensively, as if Michael had impugned his judgment.

"Yes sir, I'm sure they are, and they'll be given every opportunity to quit chasing bar lizards, develop some informants, and make some significant cases. It's gonna be shape up or ship out—if you appoint me, that is."

"Michael, you're the best we have when it comes to developing informants. It's a gift you have. It's not something we've taught you," the chief said. "We want you to take what you have done and teach the rest of the agents how to do what you do."

"I've worked closely with Michael," Clay said. "I know he can bring his success as an investigator in the Delta-to-Memphis sector to the Columbus-to-Memphis division."

"I agree," said the chief, who had always let these two wild cards run their operations up north unencumbered. He had many agents to nursemaid and Michael wasn't one of them.

The director arose to his full 6'5" height, and said, "All right, boys. I appreciate your input. I want a word alone with Michael."

The agents took their cue and left. The director ambled back to his black, high-backed chair behind his massive desk and motioned Michael to a chair in front of him.

The boom was gone from his voice. He sounded tired, resolute. "Son, I need someone to go in up there and bring order to chaos. The agents are good boys but weak, and you won't have many allies. The local chiefs and sheriffs are mostly no good, but we have to be careful working around them. A few of the prosecutors are respectable, but most people will want to see you fail or dead." He paused and looked deeply at him for what seemed a long, pregnant moment.

"I understand completely, Mr. Collins."

"You are going to make many enemies. You've shown that you know how to do that, but you can also be persuasive with the public and taxpayers. They like you. They think you are sincere and wholesome," he said, and laughed a deep, belly laugh, breaking the soberness of the serious tones.

"Why, I *am* wholesome, sir," Michael deadpanned. They both laughed then.

"I know, but behind that choir-boy image lurks a determined and resourceful agent," he said. "I'm giving you command, son. Hard times are ahead for all of us if certain politicians get elected. I hope I can shield you boys from that. You'll have your hands full righting the situation up there. I'll back you as long as you are right. As long as I'm certain that your duty comes first, I'll empower you with this new shield to pursue your own personal demons and make things right. Let them all know that the long arm of the Bureau knows no bounds and backs up from no one."

He stood up, handed him the glittering, new gold shield, and said, "Congratulations, boy!"

"Thank you, sir. I won't let you down." *Starting quarterback. Thanks, Coach, for sending me in. Do you want to grind it out on the ground, three yards and a cloud of dust, or do you want some razzle-dazzle?*

"Marcie," he bellowed, never bothering to use his intercom. "Get in here, please, ma'am." With that, Marcie came in with cake and punch and kissed Michael on the cheek. He was now one of the chosen few, it seemed. Strange, very strange indeed.

"Stop by my desk before you leave, I have a hundred forms for you to sign," she said, with a broad smile and wink.

Clay came in smiling ear to ear and said, "Way to go, buddy. It's about time."

"Batman, you're going to have to show me more respect commensurate with my rank."

Clay laughed and said, "You just agreed to take on a hundred times more stress, longer hours, and supervise a bunch of yahoos for very little money."

"I guess I was railroaded, huh?"

"You never stood a chance," he said, and they all laughed.

The announcement was posted with the expected reaction. A number of Michael's peers who thought they had played all the right games and had the right connections felt screwed and made it known. The director saw himself in some of them, and he liked their company, but that did not mean he would promote them. He wanted results, which took a relentless agent of change. It simply was not in these boys and never would be.

Michael pressed the accelerator and felt the surge of the powerful V-8 engine. The new car had been his first surprise after receiving his promotion. It was still a Ford sedan, but there was a dynamo under the hood that no ordinary citizen could buy. On the seat beside him were new surveillance toys, a stack of briefing papers from Clay, and a secret log and checkbook with carte blanche authority to write coded, encrypted checks to informants. They'd be known only by numbers and receive checks from an account that no one could trace. Last, but not least, he received new, admiring glances and smiles from the secretarial pool. Ah, it was good to know who your real friends were.

Driving up I-55 that night in the dark, he thought of the many changes coming in his life, and how proud Dixie would've been. He wondered how things would work out, and he wondered if he would ever find Fredrick. Being the obsessive perfectionist, he also mentally wrote new directives and formulated an action plan for his new command.

His folks were happy that he was coming home, but Katie, the cat, greeted him at his apartment with the same love and devotion as always. He didn't need a new shield or title for her to rub against his leg, purr like a Geiger counter, and gift him with the long, slow blinks of her eyes known as cat caresses.

He leaned down in the dark and picked her up. "We're going home, girl." The Geiger counter buzzed louder and began to bathe his hand, sensing his need to be clean and tidy in his new position.

CHAPTER NINETEEN

"Grief melts away, like snow in May,
as if there were no such cold thing."
—George Herbert

A grueling gray rain streaked the window obscuring his vision as Michael catalogued the comings and goings of the people of Tupelo. There were soft, elephantine people of baggy pants and swollen faces; the kind and gentle with hearts as soft as a baby's bottom; and the Celtic descendants with coarse brown hair sprinkled with a burnt red. The passing parade included the chiseled weightlifter types gulping brown protein powder; the backsliders who cursed like sailors, but crowded the front pews to repent and reload; and those empty travelers who sailed on windless seas of doldrums, trying in vain to fill a void within them through bed-to-bed histrionics and soap-operas of temporal indulgence.

But, none were Dixie. He often imagined that if he looked long enough, he would finally see her, the smiling beauty with laughing eyes and tousled gold hair who never met a stranger. *But no*, he thought as he turned from the window. *Time's run out. I can't fix it. I can't fix it.*

He and Katie the cat rented a duplex on Church Street

in Tupelo with hardwood floors, space heaters, and beautiful neighbors. The sisters, Glenda and Linda, two comely nurses, lived next door and Michael considered them fringe benefits. These tall, robust amazons with legs from here to yonder soon fell in love with Katie and offered to care for her during Michael's sudden and unexpected absences. Katie was a flirt and charmed both girls on their first visit. She strutted, purred, and bumped and rubbed against them. "Oh, pretty kitty. She's so sweet," Glenda cooed. Katie peered at Michael over her shoulder with her Asian eyes, classic wedge face, and a look that said, "They're so easy, and by the way, aren't I doing good?"

There would come a day when a waddle-walking government knacker would probably show up to condemn and raze the aging, dirty white duplex. It sat high upon a hill, just across from Robbins Field, the site of what had come to be called his immaculate discus throw in a high school track meet.

Robbins Field, with its granite-gray, graveled track and weathered bleachers, became a field of divine intervention for Michael that day. His school track team was hosting the conference championship, and he was likely the skinniest discus thrower in the conference.

As the day wore on, the meet had become a tight four-way race for the conference title, and he was informed that the point system now rested with him alone. He wasn't comforted as he watched the competition warm up, those with arms like his chest who could've been Greek discus hurlers of old. The first seven discus throwers had already exceeded their best career efforts with spectacular throws. It was looking like eighth place for Michael and just a matter of whether he would be lynched or drawn-and-quartered.

He came to the small circle on a windless day where the throwers were already congratulating the apparent winner. Everyone came to watch as Michael sucked it up, twisted his body, and grasped the edge of the discus in his right hand. With a grunt of effort and good follow-through, he released the discus and watched in slow motion as it sailed in perfect spin, upward and onward…a tiny disc headed toward the early moon that brightened in the sun's last rays.

But, it reached its apex too soon and began its slow descent, far from first or second place, but then Michael heard the flags above the stadium flutter and pop before he felt the gust down below. A sudden, powerful wind found the field—cheerleaders squealed as their skirts billowed up and their carefully styled hair blew around their faces. Programs and cups took to the air and airborne grit stung his eyes. Hats blew from the heads of spectators, and the press box was in bedlam.

The gradual descent of his saucer suddenly ended as it was lifted ever higher by the swirling tempest. The discus then incredibly began to advance downfield, and a hush fell over the crowd as it continued to sail until the wind stopped as suddenly as it had begun.

A lump was in his throat, and his heart pounded. The first cheer broke the silence as the discus neared the distant goalpost. "He's in first place!" someone shouted. There were more shouts and then the onlookers were all standing, cheering for *him* and throwing hats up in the air. As he walked through the crowd in disbelief, he paused in the wake of the miracle and looked back at the field, feeling for a moment that something…that someone was following him.

Michael remembered that day so long ago as he walked down from the duplex to the stadium, now in need of maintenance. It had been neglected and forgotten. He stepped inside the circle under a honeydew-orange haze and heard the roar of the ghost crowd. He let go a mighty throw of an imaginary discus, and victory was assured once again. It was good to be home, but Tupelo was also home to some bad people, including several who did business with Fredrick Hammel.

Mob lawyer Reggie Morris operated out of Tupelo, as did his

lackey, handy wiretap specialist, and all-around gopher, Detective Howard Floyd who'd become head of a regional narcotics unit made up of local police officers in three counties. Part of Michael ached to do nothing more than watch them full-time and try to pick up Fredrick's cold trail, but he had promises to keep and duty to be done and would have to bide his time.

Northeast Mississippi had been running wild, and the director had every right to be concerned. An element of lawlessness dominated the region, much of it fueled by the lucrative drug trade and payoffs. Clubs ran wide open as they did in Desoto County, though not connected in the same sense as those were. In neighboring Chickasaw County, the Harland gang ran the county with an iron fist, and the torture of the Bureau informant and threats to kill the grand jury foreman had become a part of the mythology of lawlessness in Michael's new territory.

Aggravating it all was a judge who wouldn't imprison any connected offenders and empowered those who no longer feared prison time. Martial law had been threatened in one county. Too much had gone unanswered, and now the stage was set for a hard case to right the wrongs. At least, that was the hypothetical plan—a tall order for the former diffident kid from Parker Grove.

The day he arrived at the makeshift office that was the new regional headquarters for the Tupelo district, he found the dimly lighted place sloppy and unkempt, just like the cadre of agents it housed. The motley crew was all present and accounted for in the third story suite of a dank, old building off Main Street. Most were reared back in their chairs, feet on their desks, and talking up a storm when he entered the offices. Walkie-talkie units in chargers and manual typewriters crowded the corners of their desks.

Their case production matched the damp, lightless lair in which they languished. Michael saw very little to be excited about that day. The new agents promised by the chief were his only source of solace.

He'd done his homework before he arrived. Agent Chuck

Henderson was a giant ex-jock with oxen-spread, overweight but big and strong, and not the brightest star in the sky but streetwise and very political. "Hey, boy" and "Yeah, boy" were the main staples in his vocabulary. He seemed affable to the extreme, but a violent temper simmered just beneath the surface—a bully who loved nothing better than to thump people in confrontations or arrests when it wasn't necessary. A confidante of Detective Howard Floyd, he had compromised himself riding at night with him, sharing pints of booze left in mailboxes at liquor stores as gratuities for Floyd.

Michael knew Henderson would approach him with some offer from Floyd, and given a hard choice, would choose Floyd above his team, above the Bureau, above honor.

Jackie Moreland, a prematurely bald man with bug eyes, was close to Chuck. He talked a good game, but was desperate for peer approval. He also could be quick with his fists, but a poor investigator. Like Henderson, he wanted to play cop but not do the hard work. Though he was not dangerous, he was best kept on a short leash and given specific instructions. Henderson was a corrupting influence on all the agents, thought that he should have been named supervisor and resented Michael.

Jimmy Riley, a pragmatist with long blonde hair, could be a fair officer when a fire was lit under him, but it had to be initiated by someone else. He was a wild card and generally played along with whoever seemed to have the upper hand. He was cleaning his sidearm when Michael entered. He waved slightly and continued oiling his weapon, a purposeful show of disinterest.

No one rose to help Michael as he struggled with his heavy box of "essentials." However, once in his dusty private office, he found what appeared to be a hint of generosity—a large, elaborate fruit basket rested on his desk. The basket was decorated with a large, red bow, and a card was attached.

He smiled as he opened the card. It read:

Dear Michael,

I was so happy to learn of your promotion. Good to have a local boy in charge. I'm having a little quail barbecue and pool party at my country home this weekend. I hope you can make it. I want to introduce you around to some folks. Sunday evening, 5:30 p.m.

Sincerely,
Reggie Morris

Well, they wasted no time, he thought—predictable, tried and true. Buy, corrupt, nullify in man's nadir.

Michael glared at the telephone suspiciously when it rang, but fortunately, it was Clay. "Michael, remember Theodosius Jackson, the militant in Oxford who was an associate of the Ice Man? We have an informant who says he is back in town."

"I'm all ears."

"We know he's holding drugs for sale as well as stolen equipment from the university. Might know where Hammel is... I'll call you when we get the probable cause for a search warrant and a little more information." Clay paused and asked, "Can you handle this?"

Handle this? Dixie was confined to the brown humus at the end of an empty grass patch in Memphis. The dirt was packed tight and tidy around her, tamped and sealed like his heart. Be good. Be patient. Handle this?

"Sure, can do. Just tell me when and where."

"I'll get back to you, buddy."

Just as Michael wondered how Clay was handling his cancer, Chuck ambled in, swinging his arms in a private rhythm as Michael was hanging up. "Hey, boy," he said.

"Hey, Chuck, what's up?"

"Well, I know you're gonna have a meeting with us later, and you got a lot on your mind and all, but if I can help in any way, just tell me how."

My new best friend. "Appreciate that, Chuck."

Chuck's grin revealed two front teeth that had serious cavities. "In fact, I was talking to some locals 'round town about us needing to hire a secretary for our new field office. Sure 'nuff, they recommended someone who could start right away. Great typist and such," he gushed in his feigned gosh, gee-whiz manner that he could manufacture so well.

"Barbara Smith really wants to interview with you, Michael. She could come in today for an interview. I know you're anxious to hit the road running," he said with a big, dumb smile he didn't have to fake.

"Who told you about her, Chuck?"

"Oh, you know, just some of them local law boys who want to help," he said, dodging a direct answer.

"Would one of these boys happen to be Howard Floyd?"

"Uh, yeah, I believe Howard did mention her to me," he stammered.

"This the same Barbara Smith that Howard has been 'dating' for the last ten years?"

"Uh, you know, uh, I wouldn't know about that," he said.

"Chuck, I'm from Tupelo and know just about everybody here or some of their kin folks. I know a great deal about Howard and his associates…and his methods," he said with a feeling of coldness rising up in his tone.

"Chuck, you think I would hire anyone that worthless skunk recommended? You think I'd trust his mistress to see every enforcement and intelligence file that goes in and out of this new headquarters?"

The big man of bad color and considerable jowls stammered and stuttered, "Uh, oh, well, I can see your point, but I don't think…" he said, fumbling to recover. Both he and Floyd had grossly underestimated Michael.

"Furthermore, from this moment forward, none of the agents—especially you—are to ride with Floyd or give him any

information on our activities and whereabouts. Is that understood?"
Storm the castles. Breach the ramparts.

"Well, yeah, but I think you're wrong about Howard. He's just a good ol' boy," Chuck said, struggling to recover, jaw sagging.

"Listen to me, Chuck. Floyd is no good, tied to the mob in Memphis and to Reggie Morris. If you've associated with them— ever—you'd better keep your distance from now on. Understood?" Scatter their armies. Sink their navy to a bottomless blue grave.

"Well, yeah...sure," he nodded, bobbing his head up and down and shrugging his massive shoulders.

The sound of the front door opening was surrounded by a syrupy sweet female voice. "Hi, everybody. Where's Chuck?"

It was Barbara, Howard's main squeeze, in a red dress too tight for normal breathing and make-up that appeared to have been applied by the local paint and body shop—extra glossy.

Jimmy said, "He's in the office with the new boss." Alert now, they all were sensing drama, entertainment.

Chuck, aware that bad had gone to worse, turned a little pale, and said, "Gotta go." He raced into the outer office and intercepted his latest problem. "You gotta leave right now," Chuck said to the girl. All the agents stopped to watch the show.

"Leave?" she squealed. "Howard said this job was all set for me."

"There's been a change of plans," he said.

"But, Chuck, honey," she cooed in her best coquettish inflection.

"Get out. Now!" he yelled. Chuck led the struggling girl to the door by her arm, her red hair courtesy of a bottle, bouncing violently. The door slammed, and an eerie silence fell over the new office. One agent began emptying his trash basket and another tidied his desk.

The office remained solemn until Michael walked out and announced that he was ready for the team meeting. They shuffled

257

into his office with looks of wariness and apprehension. He looked at each of them for a moment before he proceeded. "I'm proud to be here. I plan to be fair to all, but I intend to fulfill the director's instructions to the letter. We're in poor shape right now, but in time, we'll be the top producing region in the state. The good times of coasting and rousting hapless low-level dealers are over."

He remained silent for a moment, letting the hard words sink in, studying the stunned expressions and the unfrequented intellects and curiosity for life. Idle hands were indeed the devil's workshop.

Then, he passed out pocket copies of the U.S. Constitution to all. To questioning stares, he said, "Next to the Good Book, this is our guidepost. Read it. Believe it. Keep it close. We'll enforce the laws given us within the confines of what the founders gave us. We aren't judge or jury. We don't frame. We don't abuse our authority or our neighbors. The ends don't justify the means."

After that bombshell met with gaping mouths, he proceeded to set goals, parameters, and rules of conduct, most outlined in the Bureau manual but generally ignored. He told the agents that he wanted a list of their informants on his desk by the next morning. They squirmed, balked, and looked as if he'd asked for their firstborn child. Registering the resistance, he said, "They aren't *your* informants. They belong to the Bureau. They'll be issued a code number, and their efficiency will be tracked. They will be rewarded accordingly, and you'll be given credit for what they produce."

They weren't angry or anxious because he was violating their proprietary relationship with their informants. They were flushed out from their sloth and vulnerable. Most didn't have any real informants or any worth a hoot. Even the potentially good informants weren't producing because they weren't worked, directed, or encouraged. They were going to have to come up with some names…even if they were fabricated.

At the conclusion of the meeting, they all rose to leave.

"Chuck, please take this contraband fruit basket down to the ladies at the Easter Seals office and tell them to enjoy it." Chuck looked at Michael as if he was a creature from another planet.

"Oh, yeah, I'll keep the card. We wouldn't want the nice ladies to wind up at any wild party this weekend." Chuck shook his head, picked up the basket, and left. Michael was sure that Floyd and Morris would soon hear the bad news, and sense that the lay of the land was changing. The first gauntlet had been thrown down.

After a disappointing call from Clay saying that the trail in Oxford had gone cold, Michael excused himself and drove down to the local sheriff's office. The Sheriff was a retired highway patrol ticket-writer in over his head, reportedly getting a little money under the table from club owners, bootleggers, and prostitutes. His jail was dingy and dirty with a reputation for beatings, bribery, and bad food.

Sheriff Jack Mullins, a gray, balding man with an unhealthy pallor, remained seated at his desk when Michael walked into his private office. Mullins looked old and tired, like he should have been on a creek bank somewhere warm with a cane pole and minnows trying for the big fish he'd never caught. Eric Clapton played in Michael's brain, singing, *"I shot the sheriff, but I did not shoot the deputy…"*

"Morning, Jack," he said as he slapped at one of many flies drawn to the man's fertile buffet of toxic delight.

"Michael," Mullins returned, finally rising to meet him. "I heard about your new title and the Bureau's expansion into field offices. We're so glad to have you here. I've known your family for a long time, and it's good to have you home, boy."

Michael remained standing after the portly man shook his hand and settled back down into his leather chair with a groan. "Jack, I'm glad to be home, and I don't know any way other than to be direct and honest with you…" He let his opening words hang out there briefly before he carried on.

"We are receiving complaints that your department is lax in the enforcement of state laws in general and are especially slow to move on certain violations when the people are your political supporters. I don't know why you tolerate these clubs, but I'm putting you on notice that, as our mission demands, we won't tolerate any drug dealing at these clubs by the owners, their friends, or anyone associated with them."

Mullins' jowly face reddened as he spit out the words, "Better be careful, boy. You're the new kid on the block, you know."

"Yeah, I know, but Jack, I don't have the time or resources to do my job and yours, too. But if citizens keep calling the Bureau for help, I'll do what I have to do."

The sheriff appeared to search for words. "It's you college boys who're the problem!"

"How do you figure that?" Michael smiled and asked.

"Watergate!" the sheriff blurted.

"Watergate?"

"Yeah. It was them college boys who caused all that," he declared with self-evident exasperation.

Michael had to laugh at that one—hard. The sheriff began to laugh too, and finally turned apologetic, assuring him that they were partners against the forces of evil.

By the time Michael left, they seemed the best of backslapping buddies. He was moving fast, maybe too fast and hard, but he felt he had done the right thing. He had taken the shortest route, the straight line from A to B. Either he had recruited an ally, or another gauntlet had been thrown down. Time would tell.

From there, he went to the office of the *Tupelo Daily Journal*, and gave his first detailed interview as an agent—another step in his belief that there had to be a public face of the Bureau. In a profession where secrecy reigned and where identities were protected at all costs, part of the evolution of the Bureau would depend on someone stepping up and saying "We represent the people." Those who want someone to trust, to confide in, here are your poor evangelists of the new way, the paladins of law enforcement.

The interview came out that weekend in a special insert and fold-out article. It was complete with a profile shot of Michael looking at a large map of the state, pointing at Tupelo—*Normandy before the invasion,* he joked privately. Some would say he was a hotdog, a publicity seeker, but all of the successful role models he had studied first won the confidence of the "silent majority" that Nixon had cynically but successfully invoked in political campaigns.

The reporters for the influential newspaper had listened and accurately described the drug problem and its cost to society. The phones began to ring, the intelligence reports flowed, and the agents listened as the callers and visitors filled in all the blanks.

His theatrics and melodrama were working, much to the dismay of critics with vested interests in the status quo. All the fuss and action was also a distraction to his depression and duct tape to a broken heart.

Driving back to the office, he saw a mutt meticulously marking his territory and felt a certain kinship with him. As Jerry Lee might have said, *"There's a whole lot of spraying going on."*

* * *

The faint pallor of dawn peeked in his window as he awakened to the gentle rain and wind in the giant pecan trees behind the duplex and the mist of a Mississippi morning. He no longer had the bad dreams in which he failed to save her. Sadly though, she visited less often now, just enough to remind him that she was still there in some spiritual sense and that he had unfinished business. Though infrequent, her appearances seemed increasingly real. He could still feel the touch of her when he awoke and the smell of her perfume.

The dreams were particularly vivid when he got away for a night at the Memphis condo—the purple twilight fading over the city as he watched from the balcony and thought of Dixie. After he fell into restless sleep, she would come to him there and then finally fade away, whispering that danger was near. He would beg her to stay but she would go, and he would remember to be vigilant. He would also remember the shape and sway of her when the sun was behind her, burning her silhouette into his memory banks, and the intense hugs she gave him when she ran into his arms with abandonment and joy.

After these dreams, he would take long, hot showers with Dial soap to scrub away the pain. *Aren't you glad you use Dial? Don't you wish everybody did?*

The first few months of command had gone by quickly. There had been so much to do. The agents coped with his frantic pace. Some sought routine and sameness, but they were death to him. The house he lived in was on fire, and he was frantically bailing water as fast as he could.

People were eager to help, some too eager. Informants had become a particular issue. Public relations had attracted potential informants in droves and the valuable contributors had to be weeded out from the infiltrators and well-meaning but useless blabbers.

A certain mythical status was forming around the unit as they scored surprising raids and made stunning arrests. Still, Michael was not satisfied with the pace. He needed fresh agents sooner than later, soldiers in the war capable of pulling their own weight. Unencumbered by a family or a lover, he did little other than work. Only the unfinished business with Dixie's murderer distracted him from his mission.

After extensive interviews with potential secretaries, Michael finally selected Arlene Davis, a dainty, fragile young lady with olive skin. Arlene was quick-witted, spunky, and a tad neurotic but trustworthy. It was a match made in Heaven because she had that ability to anticipate his needs, knew how he wanted things done, and kept her mouth shut outside the office and with the agents.

The good ole boys in his group complained to the director about his demands. One claimed that he was "supervising them to death." Indeed, he was a perfectionist, but was trying to educate and empower them while encouraging them to accept the responsibility that came with it. It was his intention to give them the tools, skills, and the required vision and then let them sink or swim. He wanted some to swim, but others he just wanted to push until they asked for a transfer—he knew they would never change.

One day, the director called about what he was hearing and said, "Boy, the mark of a good supervisor is knowing how to work with what he inherits and make good worker bees out of them."

Michael smiled at the thought of ever making a worker bee out of a drone like Chuck Henderson, but respectfully replied, "Yes, sir, I believe that, but I also know that a good supervisor knows when the time comes that he is spending ninety percent of his time on the bad agents and ignoring the good ones who want to learn and grow. Sometimes, you just have to write them off as lost causes and not deprive the rest of the team."

After a long silence at the other end of the phone, the old man sighed and said, "Keep stirring the pot, Michael," and hung up, the obligatory caution out of the way, green-lighting Michael to keep on keeping on.

And so he did.

All the troubled agents eventually requested transfers, and the frustrated chief asked him if they could go in exchange for the first five draft picks out of the new academy class. He said other supervisors wanted experienced agents, not green rookies.

Michael laughed and said it was a deal, the one he had wanted all along. The chief chuckled knowingly and said, "The other supervisors don't have a clue what you have pulled on them, do they?"

"No, not a clue," Michael replied. He had lectured at the academy and seen the bright cadets who had no bad habits to unlearn. He had pushed them to see if they could think and reason outside the box and was pleased at what he had seen.

Then came the call he had hoped for from an intense but jubilant Clay who also sought diversion from his own special pain through work. He was unusually excited and said the Oxford project was now red hot—Theodosius Jackson was in town and holding. Clay had the goods for a search warrant and it was time to move.

As Clay was reeling off his information and his urgent timeline, he stopped cold to say, "There are some reports of a white male militant staying with Jackson. It could be Fredrick—we just do not know. If he's there, you know it's going to look bad if you have to kill him, even in a clean shootout."

Clay had once told him that you can't kill a committee, but *this monster was flesh and blood,* Michael thought. The hum of machinery broke his thoughts.

"I know. I know. Your directions and information for the warrant are coming through on the fax as we speak."

"Wish I could be with you," Clay said.

"Yeah, I wish you could, too, but it'll be fine. This is the first break we've gotten and I'll be careful and not blow it."

He summoned two of his agents, Moreland and Riley, and after some discussion, they headed for Oxford late that afternoon. The farmland around Tupelo and Pontotoc soon gave way to the rolling forest land of Lafayette County and Holly Springs National Forest—Faulkner's Yoknapatawpha County where courageous soldiers who had fought the great battles of the Civil War rested peacefully in Oxford's Confederate Cemetery. He wondered what Pearl's dad, Captain Patterson, and the Confederate warriors of the past would think about the current enemy he was about to meet. Not much, he suspected.

They reached Oxford around 6:00 p.m., and just as the agents felt the last warmth of a fading, deep-pink sun, the JP looked over their affidavit and issued the search warrant for the premises now occupied by Theodosius Jackson.

Clay's contact called the agents on a payphone at a prearranged time, saying that Jackson was out but would return sometime before midnight. The nervous and rapid speaker said he had just left Jackson's place and could confirm that stolen items and a large stash of marijuana and hashish were on the premises. The informant repeated the warning that Jackson always carried a two-shot .38-caliber derringer in his jacket pocket. He said Jackson was crazy and mean and would not be taken alive unless the cops got the drop on him. He confirmed that an albino-looking guy had been in and out of Jackson's place, but didn't know if he was still in town.

En route to their destination under the first purple blush of twilight, they passed the Ole Miss campus rich with young beauties who were blissfully unaware that such ugliness lurked so near their fields of social and academic dreams.

It was a short drive to 38 Oak Street which appeared dark and deserted—time to do what they did best—hide and wait. Riley was posted on a little rise above the scene with his radio. Michael and Moreland approached what once had been a fine old home, but the years hadn't been kind to it—it was rundown, unkempt, and had been divided for duplex rental money.

Jackson's apartment was on the east side. His neighbor's wind chimes tinkled a wandering, metallic tune in the breeze, reflecting silver in the rising moon. Jackie and Michael, along with a local officer, knocked on the door and received no answer. Michael tried the door, and surprisingly, it was unlocked. They entered with flashlights and quickly determined no one was at home in a place so filthy that habitation seemed almost unthinkable.

The stolen equipment was there—expensive items—high-powered microscopes and other scientific paraphernalia, clearly identified as University of Mississippi property by blue and red background stickers and serial numbers. Little effort had been made to hide twenty-five pounds or more of marijuana in clear plastic bags.

Anti-American literature in various languages was scattered about the filthy, jumbled apartment. The walls were papered with trendy hate material, and stacks of documents were found hidden in a closet in an old box, covered with dirty blankets. Tutorials on recruitment of new converts, which targeted the gullible, helpless, and innocent as fodder for revolutionary machinations, had been marked and highlighted in yellow.

Some of the documents were in diary form and many were communiqués from a leader in the movement. The hairs on the back of Michael's neck stood up when he saw the initials "F.H." at the bottom. His mind was racing when his walkie-talkie crackled with word from Riley. Jackson had just topped the ridge. Flashlights blinked out. Michael assumed point position by the door and ordered Jackie to back him, though the thought of the excitable agent in the rear with a loaded and cocked double-barreled scattergun wasn't comforting.

They heard the car screech to a stop, but it remained quiet for what seemed like an eternity. Michael noticed the stench of the place for the first time—a combination of stale marijuana smoke and human excrement. It made him nauseous. His heart raced. Would Fredrick Hammel walk through that door? Michael's finger tightened on the trigger of his weapon as he squinted in the dark and peered through a break in the front window curtains.

Eventually, a car door slammed, and then the thump, thump of approaching footsteps. Jackson was alone, wearing ragged jeans, a sleeveless army jacket, and military boots. However, the big black man appeared formidable—even in the dark, he looked rock hard on the outside and, from reports, even harder on the inside.

The hyperactive alert cop waited for the doorknob to turn slightly and then jerked the door open. He yelled, "State police, put your hands up!"

Jackson's eyes went wide and wild. He bolted down the front of the duplex like an Ole Miss safety on a full blitz as a chorus of green tree frogs punctuated his flight in synchronous croaks.

Even in the dimness of the moonlight, Michael could see his right hand reach into his jacket pocket. He stepped out and took aim at Jackson. He heard a voice that sounded like his, but far away and different, one on the edge between life and death. "Freeze or you are dead!" The hammer was already pulling back on his Magnum as his finger squeezed the trigger.

Jackson froze at the last possible moment, and Michael felt the shotgun on his back as he had stepped into Jackie's sights. Jackie, who nearly shot Michael, was on the perp like a dog on a bone. Even spread-eagled on the wall, Jackson was trying to slide his hand down to the derringer. Jackie kicked him under his rump and lifted him off the ground, and fished out the derringer. His neighbor turned on the porch light and ventured out. The old lady was advised to go back inside.

As he was cuffed, he looked into Michael's eyes with nothing but pure hatred and a reflection of the garish, 100-watt General Electric porch light. He spat, "If you'd been just a bit slower, honky—I woulda killed you dead." Michael had never seen such evil, such danger in anyone's eyes, except Fredrick's. He didn't look at Michael, but through him with a total piercing consumption.

"You'll have time to think about that in prison. By the way, where is Fredrick?"

"Oh," he said, nodding and grinning. "Yeah, yeah. You're the man after Freddie for killing your woman, ain't you? Yeah, Freddie told me she was one nice—" With that, Jackie jabbed him hard in his rib cage with the steel barrel of the shotgun.

"Where's he now?" Michael asked again.

Theo laughed in the house of evil where he lived and preached in his church of hate.

"Freddie is everywhere, man. He's white—like you—and I forgive him for that, because both of us…we hate everybody. We hate da man in all forms. Freddie'll find you when he's ready. You won't be findin' him."

"Haven't you heard, Theo? The war's over."

A mosquito sang in Michael's ear as Theo said, "The war against the man will never be over," he said.

Several patrol cars had arrived and they transported the twisted revolutionary to the county jail.

As Michael watched the taillights disappear into the darkness, he said, "Let's put this place under surveillance for the rest of the night and hope he doesn't bail out or drop a call to Fredrick if he's around."

Jackie said, "I got the evidence tagged and bagged."

"Good deal, Jackie. Good show by all tonight."

Jackie beamed at the heartfelt compliment and sheepishly confessed, "I'm sorry. I almost shot you when you stepped up to call out Theo. I still don't know why the shotgun didn't fire. Somebody's protecting you upstairs."

He paused and said, "Sorry, too, that snake Hammel wasn't here. I know how much it means to you." The agents had all heard the stories about his woman's death.

"Thanks, we'll get him sooner or later, and as for Jackson, he's gonna be a hard nut to crack. We may be able to deal with him, but I doubt it. He's driven by the deepest hatred I've ever seen. He's stone-cold—a zombie that feeds on irrational hate."

As it turned out, Jackson made his one call to none other than Reggie Morris in Tupelo. Reggie was tight with Circuit Judge Hillburn, the same one who was refusing to imprison drug dealers in Chickasaw County. Morris filed an immediate request to suppress the evidence against his client on the grounds of illegal search-and-seizure.

In a move only possible through political corruption, Hillburn, an old aristocrat with a penchant for hard liquor, agreed to hear the motion to suppress and dismiss the following day. The prosecutor was furious but helpless.

When Michael entered the courtroom in the giant, old courthouse on the square in Oxford, he knew it was a stacked deck from the get-go. Jackson was grinning at him and Morris, the effeminate dandy, gloated, "You should've come to the barbeque, Michael. Learn to loosen up and respect the system if you want to survive around here." Then he actually winked.

Michael's fears were confirmed when the judge called the kangaroo court to order. "Counsel for the defense has a motion to file?" The prosecutor tried to object, but the judge dismissed his complaint outright.

Reggie strutted back and forth in the courtroom, wearing a silk suit that cost more than Michael made in a month, maybe two months. The lying started right away—Morris claimed the evidence was planted.

He said, "Agent Parker has a grudge against my client and, in fact, there was no real informant giving the information, and if there was one, he's not reliable."

The prosecutor put Michael on the stand, but it did not matter. The fix was in place. He testified that there was indeed a reliable informant used by the Bureau many times and that the items were found where he said they would be.

"Produce him, then," Morris responded.

The judge nodded in agreement and said, "Counsel has a good point. Produce your informant if you have one."

"I can't do that, your honor. It would be signing a death warrant for him. I gave him my word that I would protect him."

"Well, then, you give me no choice but to grant the defense's motion, and give the defendant a one-year suspended sentence on misdemeanor possession. You would do well to remember, Agent

Parker, that the rule of law must be upheld," the judge ordered and slammed his gavel.

Everyone was stunned, and Michael said some things in anger within earshot of the judge. The prosecutor urged him to be quiet or face contempt charges, but as Michael passed him, he said, "I have nothing but contempt for this court." *A pants-wetting judicial bully,* he thought.

As they turned to leave, Jackson smiled, showing lots of teeth. "Better luck next time," he said. "You ain't half the man they claim you is."

Sweeping his hair from his forehead, Reggie had just turned around as Michael said, "That's all right, Theo. It was well worth the trouble. The information you gave me on Fredrick, Reggie, Ace, and Hal Davidson was invaluable!"

That little incendiary floated around like an errant horsefly, buzzing in the ears of its recipients, finally exploding with atomic force. Morris, stunned and shaken, looked at Jackson, wide-eyed.

"Man, I don't know what he's talking about—the cop's lying," Jackson protested, gesturing wildly. Actually, scared?

Michael thought, *Damage done, no need to interrupt these boys. They have lots to discuss.*

"You gentlemen have a good day. Reggie, I will be by to see you on official matters."

The district attorney tried to pretend he didn't hear it all, but couldn't suppress a smile. The judge looked as if someone had just confiscated his last tin of hard liquor at an Ole Miss halftime.

Then, as Michael walked away, it was his time to grin when he overheard the angry lawyer ask Jackson, "What did you tell him?"

Less than a month later, two fishermen running jugs for channel cats found the body of a large black male floating in the backwaters of the Sardis Lake near Abbeville. The decomposing body had been snagged by the supporting structure of the Tallahatchie River Bridge. The man had been knifed repeatedly and his tongue had been severed.

The death photos from left, right, and all angles were sickening and a testimony to savage brutality. Though identification of the body was difficult, it was finally confirmed as that of Theodosius Jackson by prison dental records. The murder was never solved.

Likely, the only white man Theo trusted—the whitest man he could ever cast his lot with—had terminated his tenuous contract as the devil's advocate and rendered him so much fatty fish food.

More butchery, ironically by a man as white as lard.

CHAPTER TWENTY

"I will make justice the measuring line and
righteousness the plumb line."
—Isaiah 28:17

The singsong pitch and nasal twang of the Southern preacher on Michael's car radio droned on in a classic, hued-homily of AM radio commentary. "So many people enter this world in pain, and it never ceases until the final pain of death. They want to be 'somebody', to be loved. Absent any real moral compass, they begin to seek power for power's sake. They begin to compromise to get the 'right people' to love, accept, and validate them. One day, they wake up and realize that they are prostitutes. They finally arrive at the gates of the club they sought so desperately, but the very people that they have prostituted themselves for now refuse them entry. Why? Because, as the club members whisper mockingly from behind their gated world, 'After all, you are but a whore!'"

Michael turned the dial, but wondered if that was how it all began for Reggie Morris and Hal Davidson.

The afternoon sun burned brightly over the old town with the Indian name. Pontotoc, west of Tupelo, wasn't much of a

272

place, but it had long been a frequent stop for Michael on his many jaunts between Tupelo and Oxford. A place called the Dairy Bar still made chocolate malts the old-fashioned way and he had a real weakness for them, but this visit to the shop was about more than malts. Michael arrived at the Dairy Bar soon after the discovery of Jackson's body.

As he waited, a prim and proper young woman walked into the almost empty establishment. He knew from her descriptions that she had to be Margaret Snelson, a well-respected community leader and organizer from Chickasaw County, a rural area south of Tupelo. She was country pretty, well dressed, and obviously uncomfortable being there. Underarm sweat stained her white blouse, and when she extended her hand, it felt as hot as a country plum in the Mississippi sun. She had phoned and asked for the meeting, but now appeared nervous.

With a look of uncertainty she asked, "Are you Agent Parker?"

"Yes, ma'am, I am. Have a seat. Care for anything?"

"No, no," she said, "I'm fine, just a little nervous, that's all."

"No need to be. Everything we say stays right here, just between the two of us. I appreciate your offer of help and your courage to stand up to some bad people in Chickasaw County."

"I won't mince words. We're just so tired of the hooligans running our community and threatening honest citizens," she said. "The judge won't lock anyone up and that lawyer from Tupelo—that Morris guy—represents them all."

The young woman looked at him intently, "Please tell me what I can do. I'm just one lone woman." She ordered tea from the waitress who seemed to know not to intrude.

"Maybe, but one who's obviously fed up and ready to act. You have immense power, Margaret, through your grassroots organization to put pressure on the courts and other public officials to do their jobs.

Public meetings where citizens can gather and organize, petitions to Judge Hillburn, who needs the votes of the people in your county to get re-elected position, guest editorials in the local paper, media coverage of your meetings—these are all things we can do. You take the citizen side, as I take the enforcement side and gradually the judge, the sheriff and others will respond as the voices of the people are multiplied. We aren't impotent and without power. Get the judge's attention, and we'll handle the rest."

"You make it sound so easy," she said, taking a long drink of her mawkish rose-colored tea.

"No, don't mean to, just confident that it'll work. You're the kind of lady who can get people to follow your lead."

They talked for the better part of two hours, and laid down their game plan of future meetings, petitions, and press interviews. As they parted, they shook hands, and he told her, "Margaret, today marks the end of business as usual in Chickasaw County."

It was the end of business as usual in his office as well.

The veteran agents had departed Tupelo. Jackie was the only one who had anything to say before he left. He said he would miss Michael, and apologized again for almost killing him in Oxford. Michael meant it when he told him that he would miss him.

There was no vacuum, though. The new recruits had begun to arrive—all young and fresh, eager beavers. The only exception was a seasoned veteran of police work who'd gone through the academy with the "cubs" as he called those that he mentored. Jack Denton, a personable man who loved honky-tonk women, would provide immeasurable help to the rookies, and invaluable counsel to Michael if he could keep his mind off what agents called "road lizards," the euphemism for seasoned bar women.

In the pristine regional office, there was a new sizzling energy that reflected order and efficiency, but also an intermittent crackling silence that lazily nibbled at the edges of Michael's mind, whispering that a parade was about to leave that he best run to get in front of—to pretend he was leading. At the first team meeting, he was struck by how different it was to look out at all of those innocent faces and see the eagerness in their eyes. It stirred his soul and he could see far, far into a future of endless possibilities for this group. They saw in him a manic drive that didn't offend, but drew them in to join in his mania. Jack would laugh and tell the kids, as he called them, that "Michael could sell snowflakes in hell."

Michael had a secret weapon, too—one that no other supervisor wanted—Merlene Jones, the state's first black female agent. Their bigotry, or ignorance, had cost them the one person that gangsters of all stripes and colors believed didn't exist in the Magnolia State of the 1970s. Merlene, a cocoa shade just over five feet with big brown eyes, had grown up in an educated family that didn't suffer fools. She could genuinely charm the birds from their trees and if necessary, just cut the bad boys off at the knees.

Michael's other secret weapon the others didn't want was Sandra "Sandy" Jean Smith, white with a long pretty face, a wan pallor and long, almost waist-length hair. The bad guys always dropped their guard around pretty women. They didn't fear or respect women. These two ladies could sneak up on a lot of outlaws.

Robert "Bobby" Jenson was a tall, good-looking guy with high scores on his tests, but nervous with darting eyes. Michael instinctively felt that he would challenge his authority and leadership. He had inherited a great deal of money and didn't have to work. Maybe he was here for other reasons—wrong reasons— power, glory, thrills. Time would tell, but if it was only a game to him, it was a dangerous game.

Jim Riley stayed with the team, and was placed in charge of the Columbus section of the golden triangle. Michael told him he wanted informants and good intelligence reports. He liked what he saw in the new and improved organization and decided to come along for the ride.

Lonnie Peterson, a short powerhouse with small, sparkling black eyes and a full handlebar mustache, was one of those rare guys whom everyone liked. Always smiling and truly thrilled to be where he was, there was not an ounce of guile in his body. He would require minimal supervision, and only a deserved "well done" now and then. He reminded Michael of himself at that age. That age! Only a five-year difference. Just a pat on the head and a "good job" and he would be ready for another 50,000 miles. Michael knew what it felt like to know you were appreciated, and he planned to let them all know when they'd done well.

Ray Bullock, a transfer from another region, rounded out the team. He was about to be fired by his supervisor, who knew as much about empowering and inspiring people as he did about quantum physics. The chief called and said that Ray would be fired unless Michael wanted him. Michael didn't hesitate. He knew that Ray had a good heart and was honest, and when you start from that premise, everything is possible. Ray would go on to become a good agent and one day be promoted after the man who wanted to fire him was himself fired.

Time for talk was short and the agents were issued weapons, cars, radios, buy money for undercover operations, and their own copies of the Bill of Rights. Assignments were passed out that sounded a lot like their college exercises but were the real thing. Meetings were set at discreet locations where they'd be introduced to their informants, who would, in turn, introduce them to the world of drug dealers and outlaws—the things that college didn't prepare them for.

While the agents dispersed into the wilderness of the undercover world, Margaret Snelson had been busy in her county. She wrote guest articles in local newspapers on the state of their community and had arranged a large gathering at the county seat. Michael would be the keynote speaker for the newly founded Parents Against Crime.

The event had been planned for the county courthouse, a beautiful, three-story domed structure that dominated the town square. The meeting room could seat several hundred people who wanted to come to hear Michael. When rumors surfaced of contracts on his life, Clay insisted that he bring his team in to provide security and gather intelligence—photos, tag numbers, and watchful, armed avengers—the full treatment. The meeting was like a baited trap, and Chickasaw County was full of hungry bears.

The steady drizzle and the darkness of the meeting night provided a somber setting for the "showdown" as angry citizens had called it. Cars and pickups were parked everywhere and others sloshed through the puddles seeking a rare parking place. As Michael crossed the street to the courthouse, he recognized a dark, unmarked van that circled with the crush of cars. He smiled as he considered the small army of Clay's troops that rode inside, peering into the rain and darkness, missing nothing.

When he entered the noisy courthouse, it was packed to the rafters, standing room only—browned-by-the-sun farmers, pious pastors, pasty-white factory workers, grandmothers with blue hair, nervous merchants, and three suits that didn't seem to fit in with the locals. It was because they were not local—Clay's boys armed to the teeth to make sure no one shot the speaker. Michael's own Secret Service stood out like sore thumbs—the little earpieces and tiny mikes they used so cleverly in their cupped hands to talk with other agents shouted, "I am not from here." Some locals thought they were imported hit men for the local branch of the Dixie Mafia. Others figured rightly they were cops—well meaning distractions to locals and Michael.

He was introduced by Snelson after an opening prayer, and stood there quietly for a moment, making eye contact with his audience until a hush fell over the cavernous room. *Worst case—they kill me, but if that happens, Clay's boys will get them*, he thought.

He launched into a speech about the community. He told them that Chickasaw County had become a haven for drug traffickers and that each time law enforcement made a case, the courts found a reason to turn the dealers back to the street, and as in one case, to threaten the foreman of the grand jury that had indicted him. "Ladies and gentlemen, this is your home. I'm just your guest, but if this were my home, I'd be up in arms. I'd take back my streets from the people who think they own this county, and I'd do it block by block if necessary."

Someone from the back of the crowd yelled out, "He's right. We know who they are, and where the Harlands live. Let's get our torches and burn them out!"

"Yeah, let's go," several others shouted. Affirmatives echoed throughout the hall. Green Frankensteins powered by inflammatory words were on their feet, shaking angry fists.

Michael was stunned. He hadn't sufficiently weighed the situation, and his words had been reckless and provocative. His ill-chosen words had been just the match to ignite an audience already pushed to the brink of vigilantism. He, as an enforcer of the law, had empowered the people of Chickasaw County to commit crimes. Now, he had to do something about it and quickly as some already headed for the exits. The local sheriff, who was in the pocket of the gang, was there with several of his deputies and clearly frightened.

Michael held his hands high and walked away from the podium. "No, no, my friends," he almost yelled. "That is what *they* would do. We can't let them drag us down to their level. What we must do, along with the leadership of people like Margaret, is make it plain to all officials that we want a safe county once again. Margaret has a petition up here for you to sign, and all of you who want action, get on up here and let your elected officials know where you stand."

There was some grumbling, hesitation, and some disappointment, but they came one-by-one—first the brave ones, then the timid few, and then they flocked to the front by the dozens. Finally, hundreds of signatures were collected with promises of more to come from ill and infirm neighbors who couldn't make the meeting. The newly empowered came by to shake hands and thank him. Though they had been "saved" in a different way, it reminded him of a tent revival meeting he'd gone to as a child where a loud, almost hysterical evangelist had mostly frightened Michael, but had been effective in his own way. People were passing out from the heat of the sermon, and everyone wanted to come down and confess their sins. Michael vowed to choose his carefully in the future.

When the masses had departed and gone their separate ways, he walked outside into the wet street, still watchful for the glint of cold steel. There were no killers lurking in the mist, just Clay leaning up against a light pole swigging a Coke, remarkable in his endurance despite his lingering battle with cancer in remission.

"Well, Reverend, that was some sermon you gave tonight."

"Yeah, I guess, and I learned some lessons, too…"

"I'll just bet you did. Got a little bit touchy toward the end there, but you rallied pretty well." Clay looked pensive and asked, "What do you think will happen now?"

"Call me a cockeyed optimist, but I believe things will never be the same down here and all we need to do is step back, let Margaret do her thing, and then feed some fresh cases into the judicial system."

"I think you're right, buddy," he said as his old friend, now gaunt with bad color, patted him on the back and disappeared into the darkness.

The next morning, the *Houston Times* headlines shouted: *"SLEEPING GIANT OF PUBLIC OPINION AWAKENS IN CHICKASAW COUNTY."* In the following weeks, Margaret's group presented petitions to Judge Hillburn, the local sheriff, and the district attorney.

When the first new cases were presented, the judge had

found the light, and off to prison they went, dealer after dealer. The unraveling of the grip of terror from the Harlands and their affiliates had begun. Michael was pleased but didn't trust the judge, a lackey for Reggie Morris and rumored supportive of his former fellow judge, Hal Davidson. After testifying in court, he ran into Judge Hillburn who called out to him in a loud and annoyed voice, "Well, Agent Parker, is it safe to assume you were pleased with the sentences today?"

He turned to the judge with a dry recitation, "Judge Hillburn, as a wise man once told me, the rule of law must be upheld." Michael walked away—as the judge stood speechless in his judicial robes, facial muscles popping out along his jaw.

When he returned to the office, Arlene had a note for him from an informant inside the Harland gang. The note said, "You've stirred things up. Old Frank Harland said, 'Every time I get these people whipped into line, he comes down here, and stirs them all up.'" Progress.

CHAPTER TWENTY-ONE

"Night brings our troubles to the light,
rather than banishes them."
—*Seneca*

Outside the darkened pharmacy, a fresh breeze moved the tree branches like waves on water, and the moon was so full and bright that it seemed to rob the sky of its stars. But inside, the dark was blacker than night. The searing, almost volcanic heat, trapped a persistent and pungent amalgamation of odors—old coffee grounds, dirty ashtrays, and an ancient, undisturbed dustbin where Jack and Michael waited, shotguns at the ready.

Except for the deafening chirping of a cricket, all they could hear was a low and ominous transmission of the original *War of the Worlds* from a local radio station playing a staticky version of the original Orson Wells broadcast—not something to choose late at night when perched in the storeroom of a large pharmacy in Houston, Mississippi. The old radio play that had so terrified Americans in 1938 still had its power, especially for two anxious watchmen awaiting the arrival of several drugstore burglars.

"This radio station is giving me the willies, big boy," Jack whispered.

"We can listen as long as we keep it low. The agents outside will let us know if someone comes our way. After seeing some of the women you date, Jack, I never thought you could be bothered by a few ugly aliens."

"Very funny," he whispered again.

The cricket ceased his chirping as the radio crackled softly. "You got company moving round, 816."

"10-4," Michael answered, and immediately killed the Martian invasion, readying for the real invaders.

Only the hum of the pharmacy refrigerator and the odd creak of an old board broke the silence. The building had a high ceiling with an old skylight boarded over. An informant had infiltrated the worst of the drugstore burglar teams linked to the Harland gang, a group that previously had used a machine gun in a brazen daylight bank robbery in Tupelo. The informant was with them, along with Ray Bullock who was working undercover on the case. The leader of the group had vowed never to be taken alive. Now was a chance to take them off the streets and pump them for intelligence. Agents knew that Michael was not only aggressive, but that he was looking under every rock for leads to the demon that haunted him, no matter how unlikely.

They sat, listened, and waited. Finally, the silence was broken by the ka-thump, ka-thump of footsteps on the roof. Michael smiled. It brought back all of the childhood fears of things that go bump in the night and memories of an old *Twilight Zone* episode on a lonely, country Saturday night. The burglars scurried around the rooftop like large rats amidst their muffled chatter—human rodents out foraging for cheese…forbidden cheese of the dope variety.

The silence was broken by burglarious grunts of effort in the night and the loud screech of a crowbar prying up the lumber that covered the skylight. He whispered into his radio for everyone to hold their positions and to get ready. Yes, Rod Serling was right.

They had just crossed over the line. Up ahead was the signpost, "Now entering—the Twilight Zone."

Just as the last of the boards had been pried loose, the metallic jangle of the phone in the pharmacy rang loudly like a deafening wake-up call to the dead. The sound of running feet and the clanging of dropped tools joined the clatter of the phone. Michael cursed under his breath—he had forgotten to kill the phone, a key detail.

Jack exclaimed, "Who's calling at this time of night?"

"Ten to one odds, it's that pharmacist," Michael said.

He'd had his concerns from the beginning when they had told Bobby Bradfield, the pharmacist, that he was going to be hit, and asked him to close as usual and leave them inside. He'd appeared very nervous and possibly unpredictable. Enough so that Michael considered that he might be in on it, a set-up to allow a burglary to account for unexplained losses of narcotics. He didn't think that was the case, though—more likely, nervous about his family business.

As the sound of scurrying feet stopped, Michael unplugged the phone and radioed agents to hold their positions. They'd wait and see, and pray that the burglars would come back. They probably thought the phone was an alarm they'd tripped. After what seemed like hours, but was only a few minutes, the sounds of feet on the rooftop returned. Then the lead rat dropped almost twenty feet from the roof onto the floor of the pharmacy, landing with a loud crash. Jack and Michael were inside a ring of high boxes in the storeroom, invisible to the intruder.

The nocturnal shopper limped around with his bag, taking stuff off the shelf and shouting back to his partners. "Hey, man, you should see the stuff here. Just like picking apples from a tree—Dilaudid, morphine, downers, uppers—oh, man, what a night."

The man walked right by them, and with the boxes as a screen, he never saw a thing. His eyes were transfixed on the pharmacy shelves where the goodies were. As Michael watched the man move from bottle to bottle, he wondered why the pharmacist hadn't locked the narcotics in a large safe that stood open. Presently, a rope and a bucket were lowered from above and the man dumped his bounty into it. Time to move!

Jack rose up, and said, "Freeze, State Narcotics! You're under arrest, dirt bag!"

"Don't shoot, don't shoot," he cried, as the sound of running feet on the roof commenced after hearing their partner cornered.

"Down on the floor!" Jack ordered as he pulled a .38 from the burglar's belt.

"Going out the rear, Jack," Michael shouted. He weaved through the boxes and hit the emergency exit bar. Just as he slammed out into the back alley, there was a muzzle flash and the buzz of a round as it hummed past his ear like an angry bee, splintering the doorframe. He ignored the burning on the right side of his face.

The informant and Ray should be with them, Michael reasoned, and he didn't want to return fire for fear of hitting them. He ducked back into the doorway just as he heard the feet land on the next building, and then down to the large garbage container out back.

He then broke out into the alley and ran to the corner of the building. "816, we see the perps," the radio crackled.

"Hold your positions and don't fire," he answered as he rounded the corner. He looked out into the open field where he saw four figures running. He could see the informant and the agent running and veering off to the left. They were wearing the distinctive clothing with a strip of light-reflecting tape that he had given them.

The pair veering to the right were running hard and fast, but threw two shots over their shoulders at him that whistled just over his head and bounced off the building behind him. They were out of range of his shotgun, but he didn't want to kill them anyway. He knew who they were from undercover agents, but he couldn't let those rounds go unanswered because there were other agents outside who might catch a lucky running shot from the burglars.

He aimed at the shooter, elevated his 12-gauge at wild guess angle and hesitated. He realized his hands were sweat-wet and shaking—one of the heavier elements of the periodic chart had just come within inches of his head and he had splinters in his face to prove it. He elevated the angle of the shotgun an unlikely 45 degrees and fired. After a short delay, one of the running men went down, hard. "Oh, man, I'm hit!" he shouted, but he got up limping and disappeared into the darkness. Likely, a few of the pellets had caught him in his behind or his calves. There was no need to venture into the darkness to chase them and risk being shot. The shooter was marked. There'd be no more random shooting by him.

They took the suspect, Boo-Boo Anderson, a skinny black kid with a full afro, to the county jail to be booked and interrogated. Michael called the pharmacist and told him that his store was safe. Bradfield admitted he had called. He said he just couldn't wait any longer to see what was happening and apologized profusely for the stupid call. Michael chastised him for not locking up dangerous drugs of interest to criminals, and he agreed to do so in the future.

They brought in Ray, who had "surrendered" to outside teams, and "interviewed" him in an adjoining room after the real perpetrator saw him in handcuffs. Wanting to maintain Ray's cover, Jack would shout a question, and Michael would shout "liar," and clap his hands together as if he slapped Ray hard. He would groan mightily—an Academy Award performance.

By the time they got to Boo-Boo Anderson, the man who "wouldn't be taken alive" and leader of the drugstore ring, he was singing like a canary. He copped out to nineteen burglaries of area drugstores, named his partners, and provided reliable information as to where they might be found.

The one night's intervention would dry up the street trade in stolen prescription pharmaceuticals for a few weeks. Large pharmacies, like Bradfield's, kept huge quantities of prescription painkillers on hand for hospitals and terminally ill patients. The street value of the drugs they would have taken from the store would have been worth well over $100,000.

As agents packed up to go round up Boo-Boo's partners, the crime-spree leader asked, "Is Ray all right?" He referred to the agent.

Michael just said, "He's fine," stifling a laugh.

They made a quick trip to the east side of the county to a dense field of evergreens that surrounded a rundown white farmhouse. There in the gang's headquarters, they arrested two more suspects and the informant. The runner was found in the back of the house in a filthy bed, face down, with bandages on his right buttock and both thighs. Charges of burglary and attempted murder did not lessen his pain.

Michael felt exhausted, but drove on to Tupelo, arriving as the first rays of sun penetrated the darkness and greeted the light, early morning traffic. He was thinking how good his own bed would feel when the radio crackled with Arlene's sleepy voice. Michael figured she had just arrived and hadn't consumed her morning's dose of caffeine.

"Base to 816," she growled. *Yep, no coffee yet*, he thought.

"Go ahead," he said. "This had better be good."

"Two things—*The Daily Journal* called and wants an interview on what y'all did last night, and the Tupelo PD wants you to come by 1224 Jefferson Street, Apartment C-3, as soon as possible. Didn't say why. Just said it was urgent."

He sighed. "All right, Arlene. Can you patch me through to the *Journal?*"

"Will do, please stand by."

As tired as he was, he knew he couldn't ignore the media. Good coverage on successful operations like last night's bust produced big dividends—made them look larger than life.

By the time he said goodbye to the reporter, whom he'd come to know well, he was nearing the Jefferson Street address.

He parked beside some of Tupelo's blue and whites with the indispensable shotgun racks and equally important coffee mug holders, and walked up the flight of stairs to the apartment in question.

He smelled it before he entered the door—the odor of human excretions almost knocked him down. Nearly gagging, he entered the hovel and looked around. Dirty diapers were scattered about the room and in their midst was a pale, malnourished infant. The baby was quiet, perhaps too weak to protest the filth it survived in and the mother it had been dealt. Two police officers stood off to the side, shaking their heads.

Thomas Kennedy, a juvenile officer and pleasant enough guy who looked a bit like Elmer Fudd, walked up to Michael and shook his hand. "Can you believe this, Michael? A neighbor tipped us."

"No, I can't. Whose baby is this?"

"Charlene Carson is the mother and nowhere to be found. She's fifteen, and has been turning tricks for money and drugs for Alvin Portis. Didn't you boys make a sale charge against him a while back?"

"Yeah, we did, but his cases have a way of being continued forever and then quietly disposed of. It's something we need to address. I can't believe this child was left here, alone like this. We've got to nail that guy, but more importantly, what are you going to do about the baby?"

"I don't know…the welfare department is reluctant to come and take the child from the girl despite the fact that she's an underage prostitute who doesn't take care of it," he answered.

"Who'd you talk to?"

Although Michael was against the taking of children by the state except as a last resort, this certainly qualified. He got the young woman at welfare, Sylvia was her name, and had a heart-to-heart talk with her. He asked that a caseworker be sent to take the baby out of what could only be called deplorable conditions.

Perhaps his insistence was fueled by exhaustion, but it was effective and a caseworker soon arrived to rescue the child just as Charlene arrived.

Michael muttered, "Great timing." They were met in the stairwell by the infant's mother, a chubby teenage girl with acne, a short skirt and a blue and gray Dallas Cowboys cap.

Charlene staggered up the steps toward them and brought her hand to her mouth when she saw the social worker with the child. Then she comprehended and pointed at the baby. "Hey, that's my kid. What's she doing with my kid?"

"They're taking her to a clean and safe environment, Charlene, and unless you shut your mouth, you'll be hauled off by these nice fellows who are considering child endangerment charges against you," Michael said.

"Me? I didn't do nothing. That babysitter must've left my baby."

"I suppose she left all of this squalor as well?"

"Listen, I been working hard, and the guy I was with last night, he, uh…" she said as the juvenile hustler caught herself and stopped short of confessing to prostitution, one wandering eye offset from the other.

"So, you were with some john last night that Alvin set up for you?"

"Alvin's just my friend. It's not like he's some kind of pimp," she said petulantly.

"Oh," Michael said, grabbing her wrists, turning them over, and pushing up the sleeves of her blouse. The telltale track marks of needles were those of a heavy user. *Another Miss Rosemary*, he thought.

"Is this how Alvin pays you? Help me help you."

Anger sparked in the pitiful girl's eyes and she started to speak, but no words came. She wrapped her arms around herself and started to shake. Charlene's next fix was obviously late. She began to cry.

"I think we'll have to take you downtown for some long interrogation," Michael said.

"No, please don't do that, baby. I'll be so good to you," she said, caressing his arm.

"Sorry, that won't work here, Charlene. I want you cured of your addiction and back in shape to be a real mother to that little girl. You can trust me. Tell me about Alvin," he said.

Her terrified, but otherwise empty eyes darted to and fro.

"I won't have to testify?" she asked, shaking more by the minute but remembering the other devil she was accountable to.

"Not if I can help it, and if you do, we'll set you up somewhere a long way from here."

The social worker assured the sick mother that her baby would be fine, and Michael and the officers escorted Charlene back to her apartment to the cleanest room they could find. Confronted by the filth, the stench, and her own wretched condition, she started talking. The more she talked, the harder he listened.

"Alvin ain't such a bad guy, really. I met him when I was in junior high and we dated some. He turned me on to Quaaludes and stuff. Then I started buying from him and got deep into debt with him real quick. He offered a way for me to pay him what I owed and get more drugs on credit. I know… I know I'm not special. I've seen him with lots of other young girls, and most of them are doing exactly what I'm doing. I shouldn't have had no baby. I slipped up and got pregnant. Alvin wanted me to go to see this doctor and have an abortion, but I couldn't kill my baby. I just couldn't. I felt her move inside me and I just couldn't kill her. She wasn't just a blob of tissue like Alvin said, and I'd heard of other girls who went to them doctors and couldn't have no more babies. Now, I don't know whether I did right, or not." She gave Michael a pleading look, seeking reassurance, anything…

He sighed, put his hand on her shoulder, and said, "You did a good thing."

She grabbed his forearm, rested her head on it, and began

to sob. She was little more than a child herself, shaking from withdrawal and the pain of the hell she lived in. She was just another lamb who had lost her way. He asked her what she had in her large purse.

She raised her bloodshot eyes up to his, and said, "There was something special about that trick last night. Alvin wanted me to tape him, and get some pictures if I could. I shouldn't be telling you this, should I?" Her tremors increased.

"Right now, I'm the only real friend you have, Charlene," he said. "Show me what you have, please." She pulled out five poor yellowish Polaroid photos of her john, but there was no mistaking the face in her photos. Michael was stunned. The grainy figures were of none other than Hal Davidson, leading candidate for governor, in various poses. Michael swallowed hard as his heart rate accelerated. *Oh, Lord, oh Lord*, his mind repeated.

"Got anything on the tape?" he asked a bit too casually.

"Oh, I got it all, but I don't want you to hear it in front of me. It'd just make me sick."

"That's okay. I'll just take the photos and tape and you tell Alvin tonight that the old geezer didn't give you a chance to photo or tape him. By the way, how'd you get away with it?"

"He was drunk as a skunk. But please, Alvin will be coming by tonight to give me my stuff and collect any goodies from last night. He said our lawyer wanted to see and hear it all. He is kinda strange that way. He likes to watch—you know. I made a bunch of tapes for Alvin and Reggie, some when Reggie was in an adjoining room."

With that moment of candor, she took his breath away. It just got better and better.

"Tell you what—we'll copy the tape and return the originals to you this morning. You can give him this one Polaroid shot that is slightly out of focus. How about that?"

"That'll be okay," she replied, sounding uncertain.

"What's the baby's name, Charlene?"

"Jane. Agent Parker, will I get to keep my baby?"

"That's something that we are going to work together on real hard," he said.

Suddenly, he was no longer sleepy at all. He was charged with a burning energy to seize this moment that God had given him. He was ready to shake the gates of Hell itself.

As he walked down the steps, he felt the hunger again—hunting them to find Dixie, perhaps. He had put a fragile, tenuous divide between him and yesterday. Now, he was at the edge of the world again trying not to look down for that is where the dead and lost ones were, buried in their own private hotel of horrors. What was it the Eagles said? *"You can check out anytime you like, but you can never leave"*? Yeah, that was it. What else? Oh, yeah. *"They stab it with their steely knives, but they just can't kill the beast."*

"Vanity of vanities," he heard Solomon say. "There is nothing new under the sun." *Am I, then*, he thought, *no more than Narcissus of Greek mythology staring at my reflection, singing in harmony with Sinatra, 'I did it my way'?*

No matter, he thought. *While I breathe, I fight.*

CHAPTER TWENTY-TWO

"The Prince of Darkness is a gentleman."
—Shakespeare

Pigeons, gray with white rumps and black wing bars, seem to be the official bird the world over in courthouses and places of power. They were in abundance as Michael sat at a red light looking up at the giant old gray Lee County Courthouse in Tupelo. The gray stone statue of a Confederate soldier stood vigil in the yard of the courthouse. Captain Patterson's name was there on the statue which the pigeons had innocently defiled.

So many people had passed by the statue and into the courthouse over the years seeking truth, an elusive justice, or conviction versus acquittal. Through the courthouse doors entered the outcasts and would-be aristocrats seeking a temporal salvation, and those some would call the godforsaken, the desperate, the profane, the pampered, the guilty, and the innocent.

But who were the guilty, and who were the innocent?

He had no sleep, no rest for the weary—burning the candle at both ends now and losing weight he couldn't afford to lose. He came to see the district attorney to tell him that he had to get Alvin

Portis off the street, that he was addicting young girls and turning them into hookers.

Jimmy Hinton, a slick, condescending twerp with gold-rimmed glasses, was a transplant from up North with elitist tendencies that Michael didn't particularly appreciate. Why would any Yale lawyer come to Mississippi? Hinton was characteristically unenthusiastic about trying Portis on the old marijuana sale. Michael reminded the DA that it was only old because he had continued it about six times and that Portis was already out on bond from a drugstore burglary in New Albany. "That's all very well and good," the DA said, "but I need something stronger and hard drugs this time."

Michael smelled a rat and figured it had to be Reggie Morris who was muscling the DA for Alvin. Someone was intervening on this. From what Charlene said, Reggie had to be the prime suspect. He could feel it, but told the DA that he'd get what he asked for even though it got harder every time to make a new case on a suspect as they learned agency methods.

Since Charlene had spilled her guts on Alvin Portis and Reggie Morris, Michael had arranged for her to get into rehabilitation where she spent two months. Her baby had been placed into temporary foster care until Charlene was drug-free and employed. She stuck to her job and kept clean. Child Welfare returned her baby after five months of separation. She was grateful and Michael was happy for her and more than grateful for the information she had given him.

***

Almost six months had passed since Charlene's revelations. Merlene had done wonders in her first undercover operation. She'd purchased amphetamines from truck drivers bringing back supplies from Mexico, made cases on some of the top black dealers in and around Tupelo, and purchased drugs of all types from street-level and mid-level dealers in the area in a six-month investigation. Old Dixie Mafia types dropped their guard around the black girl they just knew couldn't be an agent in Mississippi. These old rednecks took her bait—hook, line, and sinker. Michael marveled at her ability to keep men—black and white—in line when they tried to buffalo her or came on to her.

He waited until she and her informant were maxed out on buys before they rounded up the hundred or so people in the warrant pool. It was a long night, and the media coverage enhanced their image as the omnipresent but unseen guardians of the streets. The round-up dried up the streets temporarily, steeply driving up the prices of drugs. It was the law of supply and demand and a number of buyers went bust and paid their own price for their sins in withdrawal. And, Alvin Portis was arrested for the sale of morphine—something stronger.

Eventually, the last of the miscreants was rounded up around 8:00 a.m., just as Michael was called again to the courthouse from a long night of arrests. As he walked down the hall toward the courtroom, he spotted a knot of local officers speaking in whispers, buzzing like flies. They stopped when they saw him, which wasn't a good sign.

"Okay, guys, what's going on?" he asked. A big, meaty deputy named Jerry, who was conversing with Detective Howard Floyd, said, "Uh, well, Michael, you ain't gonna like it."

"Just spit it out then." He was their morning entertainment.

He looked at the others, and Floyd said, "They just let Alvin Portis free on two thousand dollars bond."

"*What?* Who made that decision?" Michael snapped.

Howard Floyd smiled an evil smile and said, "The DA did it. Guess you don't run everything round here, college boy." A scornful laugh of derision punctuated his words.

He started to reply when he spotted bigger game—none

other than Jimmy Hinton was walking down the hall toward the group, steam rising from a hot cup of coffee he was sipping, the *tink, tink* of spoon against ceramic as he stirred and walked so precisely. Michael asked to speak to him privately. The DA evidenced smugness, and his tone wasn't friendly.

"Well, I suppose so," he said. They went to an adjoining jury room. Michael was unhinged and ready to call out this court jester. All eyes in the hall were on the closed door concealing the two combatants to see who would emerge from the tiny room still standing. Just like the old-school boxing days.

In a rush of barely concealed rage, Michael heatedly asked, "Jimmy, why'd you release Alvin on a low bail when he is already out on three other bails? He is ruining the lives of so many young girls."

Nose-to-nose, gloves off.

Jimmy frowned dismissively at him. "I'm the DA, and that's my jurisdiction." Bob and weave. Jab, jab.

Michael took one step closer and hit the Yale lawyer right between the eyes. "That's all fine and dandy, Mr. DA, but what if someone leaked it to the press that you're coddling a man who corrupts and prostitutes young, underage girls with sex and drugs? I think it'd be hard to defend." Political blood now drawn, defenses down.

"Now, now, wait…wait just a minute," he stammered, knowing of the paper's relationship with the Bureau. Backing into his corner. Bell ringing, fight over.

"Jimmy, I'm just your friend stating a hypothetical possibility. I'm really worried about your election campaign." He left him there alone with his conscience, if he had one, wondering how he had lost this bout.

Within forty-eight hours, Alvin's old case had miraculously been called up, and he was on his way to the state pen. News of the little victory made the rounds and added another layer of mystique to the stories about the Bureau and the power they wielded. He knew that it paid for others to know you have the media card and to believe you would play it. Hinton complained to the director that Michael was trying to muzzle anyone who didn't agree with his personal crusade. The director wryly replied, "Well, what are you going to charge him with—aggravated shushing?"

The graphic photos and tape received from Charlene were another matter. When Michael first came into possession of them, he'd called Clay. Clay picked up the director, and they came for a meeting in a remote place just off the Natchez Trace Parkway. It was kept on a need-to-know basis only. After he viewed the photos and listened to the tapes, they waited for the director's reaction.

They were certain that this could be used to knock Davidson out of the race and eliminate the threat he posed to the state with his criminal associates. The director sighed, looked at them, and said, "Boys, what you got here is political dynamite, and I'm going to pretend I've never seen it. I'm not saying that you shouldn't have it or consider dropping it on some aggressive reporter. It's the kind of stuff that I've wanted to protect the agency from, to keep us from becoming involved in gutter politics even for the best of reasons.

I have faith in the people of the state that they'll reject Davidson for governor without us intervening in the political process. I pray I'm not wrong about this. What I'd suggest is that you boys keep this evidence somewhere where nobody can get to it. You save it for a rainy day in case I am wrong about the good people of Mississippi."

Michael stewed over the decision. It was personal, too personal to him, but in the end, Clay took the damning photos with him for his safe to which only he and Michael had the combination. They weren't as sure of the people as the director was, but understood his motives and respected his sense of honor. Still...

Under a mauve night sky, where clumps of snow dripped and fell from pine boughs like shavings from ice-blue glaciers, they parted. As he neared Tupelo, Michael blinked at the sight of a brand-new, lighted billboard just as he exited the Trace Parkway onto West Main. There, larger than life, was the smiling face of Hal Davidson in a hard hat with a lunch bucket. *"It's time to throw out the fat cats... Elect Hal Davidson. He's one of us..."* The populist appeal of Davidson was undeniable. Already up with his billboard, and the race was still a year away. He hoped the director was right about the people.

If not, Michael thought, *what was it Dickens said? The director's 'spring of hope' could become Davidson's 'winter of despair.'*

CHAPTER TWENTY-THREE

"No man is an island, entire of itself; every man is a piece of
the continent, a part of the main…"
—John Donne, Devotions

The year 1975 was a watershed year for the revolutionaries and the boomer children who populated the anti-establishment movement. The Black Panthers were disintegrating and only the splinter group, the Black Liberation Army, was still operational in any real sense. The Weathermen, the violent spin-off of the SDS, Students for a Democratic Society, was also imploding, and many of the violent revolutionaries were on the lam. Infighting, legal fees, and world events sucked the shelf life out of the radical left. The apocalyptic arm of the Weathermen that Fredrick adhered to had also run out of steam and money, although some random robberies and rather insignificant bombings continued sporadically.

On April 21, 1975, a bitter and emotional President Thieu of South Vietnam resigned in a heart-rending ninety-minute television speech to the people of South Vietnam. President Nixon, retired to San Clemente, was lost to Watergate, and U.S. troops were long gone. Thieu read an excerpt in a letter from Nixon in 1972 promising "severe retaliatory action" if South Vietnam was threatened. "The United States has not respected its promises. It is inhumane. It is untrustworthy. It is irresponsible," Thieu charged. After allowing Thieu his moment of theater which few would ever remember, the CIA whisked him away into exile in Taiwan.

Graphic, grainy images on television captured a mission or a myth unraveling that began many years and many lives before in a disputed provocation in the Gulf of Tonkin. Communists shelled Tan Son Nhut air base in Saigon on April 29, 1975. Two stoic Marines died while guarding the gate as President Ford ordered Operation Frequent Wind, the helicopter evacuation of 7,000 Americans and South Vietnamese from Saigon. The operation began with the signal of the radio broadcast of the song "White Christmas."

Terrified civilians swarmed the choppers, refugees fleeing a red wave of Communism that would imprison and indoctrinate tens of thousands. The compound of the American embassy, secured by U.S. Marines in full combat gear, was a scene of chaos. Thousands of civilians attempted to get into the compound, and only a few made it.

U.S. aircraft carriers off the coast of Vietnam waited to receive the helicopters and handle their cargo of the displaced whose nation had just died. Theirs was to be a no-return trip and American helicopters were just pushed overboard to make room for more arrivals. Images of the choppers being tossed into a foamy white splash of the sea became a metaphor for the war in general. It was not so much the expensive helicopters sinking to a deep, dark, watery grave, but the soul of America lost in a Herculean battle against the Hydra of Communism.

On April 30, 1975, ten Marines from the embassy departed Saigon, ending American troop presence in Vietnam. Communist troops poured into Saigon and encountered little resistance. By noon, the red and blue Viet Cong flag that so many protestors had flaunted in demonstrations at home was flying over the presidential palace.

It was all so poignant and soul-numbing to see people desperate for freedom clinging to the ramps of the choppers as they tried to take off. It was an ignoble end, this retreat from a country America had now washed its hands of.

Dissidents and Christians were rounded up, thrown into the squalor of primitive prisons, tortured, forced to study Marx and told that their temporal god, America, had abandoned them and that their Christian God was dead.

In a tragic echo of the distant drums of defeat, the war claimed its last soldier. Billy Hull was found dead at his home in Tylertown. He was slumped in his wheelchair, a .22 single-caliber wound in his right temple. Scattered around him in his front yard were three dead bony-plated armadillos—stand-ins for the Viet Cong. A lone bugler played solemn "Taps" at the funeral for the stooped and broken jungle gladiator freed from the prison of his chair and the torture of his mind. But what about good men like Clay?

The war was indeed over, and the cause so many gave their lives for was lost, but not all was in vain. At home, the last of the radicals were on the run, their groups and funding on the wane. They would soon become curiosities from the period and mere caricatures of the serious militants many were. Fredrick's great revolution wasn't to be, but he had to be found and held accountable for his savage killing of an innocent who was apolitical.

In the MBN's little corner of the world, Clay's analysts had scrutinized the documents that were seized at Theo's apartment and worked hand-in-hand with some of the more capable analysts from the federal agencies. Fredrick was indeed still alive and well, but where was he? The documents and some intelligence information suggested he was in Oxford for a time and may have been the one who bombed the Oxford police cars out of boredom or as mindless revolutionary recreation. It was also almost a certainty that Freddie had killed Theodosius Jackson after the raid. Did he act on his own out of random madness, or did some people want Theo silenced forever?

True to her word, Hammel's mother contacted Michael and confessed that she'd heard from her son. She had received a postcard from Cuba with a likeness of Che Guevara on the front. All the note said was, *"I am well, Mother. Viva la revolución!"* It also listed a numbered Swiss bank account for donations, but Clarice wasn't inclined to send him any more money.

More than two years had passed since Dixie Lee's death. The Northern region was out-producing the others in the state by a large margin. The agents were getting better each day, and recruitment of quality, high-level informants had begun to forge a fundamental change in the local landscape. Michael accepted the director's praise for their work, but the fact that he hadn't brought Dixie's killer to justice gnawed at his insides constantly like some hungry rodent, and his self-flagellation cannibalized his core. It kept him awake at night and increasingly, he ruminated during the day. His group of young lions worried at his dark divinations, but he knew that vermin lived beneath stones and if he turned over enough of them, he would find Dixie's killer. It kept him going.

In the midst of the dog days of his stagnation, he looked over the quiet streets of Tupelo and pretended for a moment that the memory of her was not spread over everything like the sky-blue blanket above him. Then he saw the new church billboard across the street from the Bureau office, which read, *"By perseverance, the snail reached the ark."*

So, he would press on, polish his rusting and pitted tin armor, take down the old crooked lance from the rack, and rightly divide the Sword of the Spirit.

CHAPTER TWENTY-FOUR

"Yea, they are greedy dogs which can never have enough."
—Isaiah 56:11

Michael was deep asleep, his mind reliving recent events in the disordered chaos that marks the dreaming mind. Somewhere far away, a telephone rang and rang. His brain said that someone should answer the phone. It wasn't part of this dream that was more real than the less vivid reality of wakefulness. He was dreaming bits and pieces of battles mostly won in the last few months. They had slain many dragons in a short time, though the sleep-dragons were often things mixed with his distant past-childhood. The knights of Tupelo reigned supreme in his dream and he could see Dixie's furtive figure in the brilliant sunlight with angels all about…

He was always reluctant to abandon his vivid dreams, not from some masochism or desire to be punished but his certainty that answers to his burning questions were embedded in the shadows of his dreamscape.

The phone jangled again and Michael was half-awake. His mind wandered through a twilight version of a recent arrest. Ginny, a young nurse, phoned Jack from the ER of the top hospital in the

Golden Triangle and whispered that a well-known drug trafficker that Michael had sent to Parchman Farm, had been paroled. She said that he was in the ER overdosed on his own wares. On admittance, he had been in possession of probably two ounces of coke. His doctor, Melvin Greenberg, a well-known psychiatrist and close associate of Reggie Morris, had ordered the coke secured and directed the staff not to leak a word of this to anyone. He had said that he would take care of it...

Jack showed up immediately and made an arrest of the dealer who was an associate of Fredrick Hammel. Greenberg was furious and wanted to know who had called the state. He'd narrowed it down to two people on the staff and was determined that one or both of them be fired. Jack tried to intervene but found high-level interference. The doctor had threatened the president and board of the hospital, claiming he would take his lucrative practice elsewhere if they didn't fire the nurse with the big mouth.

Michael called the president of the hospital and told him that he had a choice—keep a good employee and citizen or bow to the wishes of a corrupt "physician." He could risk losing the doctor's patients, or endure a news conference in which Michael would inform the public that his hospital punished law-abiding citizens who tried to do the right thing, but coddled cocaine dealers who were trying to enslave local children to drug addiction. It might even be possible to charge Greenberg.

After remarkably little discussion, the board decided that the nurse was a citizen-patriot after all. They came down hard on physicians who consorted with drug dealers or handled illegal drugs. Michael had been correct in his belief that the management of the hospital was "principled" and would make the honorable decision.

All these residuals danced like green and gold fireflies at the edge of his waking-sleeping mind. He was slipping back into deep sleep again ... But this time the persistent telephone and the purring cat on his chest won out.

"Hello," he mumbled into the receiver.

"Michael, sorry about the early time, but I have a patch-through call for you marked urgent," said the polite voice of Cliff, the headquarters dispatcher.

"Hmmm, okay, Cliff, put it through."

"Agent Parker is on the line," Cliff said, and dropped off the line with an electronic click.

A slight pause, then a deep voice said, "Did I wake you, Mike, or has all this walking on the wild side done wore you down and made an old man out of you before your time?"

"Well, well. Long time since I've heard *that* voice. To what do I owe the pleasure of this call?" He was wide-awake now in anticipation of what this call could mean for the one fire that burned within him—justice, revenge—call it what you will.

"How about you joining me for breakfast here at the club, my man?"

"What time is it, anyway?"

"The shank of the evening for people like us—three-thirty in the a.m., to be exact. Not too early, not too late," Super Fly said, and laughed his deep, hearty chuckle.

"You're right. I'll be famished when I get there. Hope you got lots to eat."

"How you like your eggs, son?" he asked.

"Over easy, Mr. Walker."

"Son, you won't do. I'll see you at six."

"Six it is."

He rolled out of bed, anxious to hear what the big man had to say after so long without contact. His heart rate was up. He was now wide awake, jumping into and out of a cold, quick shower. He dressed quickly, excited and filled with anticipation about Walker's call. He had his .357 Magnum, but to be safe, he added an ankle holster with a .32 automatic just inside his right boot. The sides change like the wind, and he didn't want to walk into the Bottom of the Blues without a plan B.

Thirty minutes or so after the call, he was dressed and on U.S. 78, headed north for Memphis. His wiper blades only smeared the bugs on his windshield in a light drizzle that passed quickly. He radioed Cliff and asked him to call Clay about six and tell him that he had the blues and was going to see Super Fly and to send in the cavalry if he had not heard from him by nine. As usual, Cliff asked no questions. He was accustomed to receiving such cryptic messages which he dutifully and efficiently followed.

Michael thought that Memphis sunrises were becoming routine as he neared the city. Still, it was a beautiful morning and purple hues mixed with the promise of golden rays outlined the horizon. Michael's red pony car wove effortlessly through the sparse traffic—he would be on time. He didn't want to be late to what he hoped was going to be a fruitful meeting. He approached the meeting with a certainty of purpose not supported by any solid information.

Beale Street was almost deserted when he arrived. A shifting wind whipped paper cups, food wrappers, and the usual urban debris down the dirty street. Two hookers and a wino were either passed out or dead in a darkened storefront and were the only evidence of the nightlife that had so recently departed. One of the hookers stirred and moaned as Michael passed, alive at least for now.

The Bottom of the Blues Club, like the windswept street, was nearly empty. In a bit of eye-jolting outdoor "art," he saw that Walker had installed an oversized old electric-blue mailbox in front of the place, with the club name spelled out in black metallic letter. *Hmmm*, Michael thought, *Ah, yes…black and blue.*

A smell, like an old wet dog, hung in the air. A singer and two backups on the stage continued—the joint seemingly never closed. The lead singer, a tall, skinny, black man wailed a slow and mournful rendition of Otis Redding. *"Sittin` in the morning sun, yeah I`ll be sittin` when the evening comes. Watching the ships roll in, and I watch* *'em roll away again…just sittin` on the dock of the bay, wasting time…"* Michael thought the singer looked vaguely familiar, but dropped the thought when he heard the boom of Walker's voice.

"Come on in, son. The music never stops here at the Bottom. Just like the blues, they keep wailing night and day." He motioned him over to a big table where his cooks were laying out a breakfast big enough for ten people on a fresh white linen spread.

"Please check that oversized peashooter you're wearing at the bar," he said, and laughed in his haunting, baritone sound of merriment or amusement at his own private joke. "You got to get comfortable to enjoy a good meal."

Michael grinned at him and the smiling bartender and checked the Magnum. Just as he handed him the big revolver, the bartender reached across and patted the jacket and the small of his back and smiled again. Had he been serious, he would have checked Michael's boots, but he was too busy collecting forgotten glasses of stale, discarded liquor from the night before.

"Leave the boy alone. Breakfast is gonna get cold," Walker bellowed.

"You mean all of this is just for us?"

"Well, son, about eighty percent of its mine, I figure. You skinny as a snake, boy, and don't look like you eat too much."

Michael grinned again—he was right, especially at that moment.

He watched Walker dig into the spread of eggs, bacon, sausage, biscuits, gravy, grits, hot Memphis coffee, fresh-squeezed orange juice, ice-cold milk, bread pudding, and sliced pineapple while Michael picked at his eggs.

"Mr. Walker, you know how to live." The big man motioned for a fresh pot of coffee, announcing that he liked his coffee like his girls, "hot and black."

Midway through the breakfast, he stopped and asked, "Tell me, boy, have you ever found you another good woman?"

"Not looking."

"Yes, you are," he said. "You're still looking for that girl you lost. You're still hoping to wake up and find that this has all been one long, bad dream. That's what you're doing, boy."

"Maybe so," Michael muttered.

"Anyway, that's not why I called you here." His mood changed. When he stopped smiling, everyone stopped in the club where he reigned supreme.

"The beast you hunt, my friend, has returned to your turf. He came by here. You barely missed him at Theodosius' apartment that night. You must've said or done something to upset him because he came back and cut up poor ol' Theo, and dumped him in Sardis. Am I right?" he asked, leaning forward a bit, his mouth half full of hash browns.

"Yes, I dropped a little grenade at the trial that stirred the pot, I think."

"Ah, I thought it was something like that," he said. "He's back now, roaming in your neck of the woods. Still too hot for him here, and I understand Mommy and Daddy don't have the welcome mat out, anyway. You know, when the prey is trapped, the hunter has to be careful, lest he become the hunted. You follow me, son?"

"I'm with you so far. Pass the biscuits, please?"

"Signs of an appetite," he laughed. "We might fatten you up some yet...build a whole new man around that skinny frame."

In the far corner, two intent and very professional men played what appeared to be high stakes nine ball. The squeaking of blue chalk on cue tips was almost ritualistic, leaving their hands a grape blue.

"You say he's trapped. What do you mean?"

"Your friends at the federal level have been lying to you and the cops. They had him in some kind of witness protection all this time!" he declared bluntly.

Michael's jaw clenched and acid reflux burned his throat. Sweat beads broke on his upper lip, but he remained quiet as a cold, serious voice called, "Nine ball in the corner pocket."

Walker continued, "Kinda makes you lose faith in your side, don't it?" The clang of the cash register at the bar chimed out the news—*everything and everyone is for sale.* Cha-ching.

"They needed him to make cases on some of them radicals and he was working 'um like a charm. He'd give them someone he was on the outs with now and then or someone he felt had betrayed the cause. But the truth is, he just kept on killing, bombing, running drugs, and living off the fat of our po' ole Uncle Sam, and whatever other governments would pay him."

Michael sat there slowly chewing, but feeling a deep rage welling up inside him. He closed his eyes, and his breathing became shallow.

"I see the wheels turning in your mind, son, but don't let 'um grind in the wrong direction and deter you from the project at hand."

Walker made chocking motions with his big hands. "He called here desperate for some cash and a place to lay low. Ace's old mob won't touch him. His fellow radicals have mostly gone straight or are dead from overdoses. Fidel caught him double-dealing him and banned him from Cuba. He is lucky Castro didn't Castro-ate him," he said, laughing heartily at his play on words. "Get it son? Cas-tro-ate him!"

He continued after his humor fell flat. "So, the Feds are looking for him now 'cause he's left the reservation with a pile of their cash. He missed some trial dates when he was supposed to testify for them. Give him his due. He has screwed everybody equally. He done got the Feds after him, the Commies after him, and he got you always on his trail. You always back there someplace, he told me. He was there up on a hill watching when you almost killed Theo. Told me he thought you were gonna kill Theo and save him the trouble. He said you're too formal, too good to be in your line of business, and that is *your weakness*. You'll hesitate. He won't. It'll get you killed."

Michael continued chewing the mouthful of eggs, which seemed to be getting bigger all the while. He needed to spit them out, to get busy.

The jovial man continued even though he couldn't miss Michael's discomfort.

"You hesitate before killing. He don't and won't the day you two meet eye-to-eye. So, you gotta be careful, man. That boy was never wired right in the head, but now, he has really done lost it. Got no grasp on no reality other than the one he lives in. He began to tell me about his Father Lucifer. You know, Mike, he told me that when he was in Cuba, he'd play a little game with the kids that the Commies liked. He'd tell the kids to pray to Jesus for candy. When nothing happened, he'd tell them to pray to Castro. When they opened their eyes, there'd be candy all around. But, when the Commies walked off, he'd tell the children to pray to the devil and then he'd produce the really good candy and tell them that Lucifer, not Castro, was their Father. I told him to get his sorry self out of my club, or I'd kill him myself. Would have, too—in my younger days."

"I appreciate the good counsel, the good food, and the good company, Mr. Walker. How much do I owe you?"

He rolled his eyes. "Now, son, don't go insulting me. No gratuities needed. These are just pleasant exchanges between two old friends."

"Fair enough. Until we meet again, then."

"Boy, if you start singing 'Happy Trails' to me like some Roy Rogers, I'm gonna slap you," he said, laughing and slapping the table.

Michael had to smile at that one and laughed, too, on the outside. On the inside, he was churning. He retrieved his big gun from the bartender, checked the load of hollow points, and bid them farewell.

He walked to his car and noticed that he was subconsciously scanning the area for danger, even more so than usual. A gospel tract blowing down the street asked, "Do you know Jesus?" That warning about becoming the hunted had taken root. He turned the Mustang toward Tupelo and used the radio concealed under the seat to bounce a radio call off the first tower he could reach. Cliff was still there working double shifts and patched him through to Clay.

"Go ahead, 816," Cliff said.

"Hey, where are you?" Clay asked.

"I am leaving River City."

"Roger that."

"Know this conversation isn't secure, but our friends have been protecting our big game all this time, but now the game is off the reservation. The big cat is in our jungle. Copy?"

A bit of silence followed, which meant he got the gist of the conversation and was cursing a blue streak. "Ten-four, 816. Know which friends?" he asked.

"Figure it to be J. Edgar's old crowd, but who knows? It may be someone that we don't even know exists. I'll give you more when I get to a secure line, but wanted you to know that their rabbit is running, possibly headed my way."

* * *

When he arrived at regional headquarters in Tupelo, there was a visitor, none other than Reginald Morris, Esq. "Morning, Michael. My, you look like you've been very busy for such an early hour. Do you boys never sleep?" he said, dressed in his seersucker suit with a red bow-tie. Reggie was slender in build and had rather delicate features for a man, but his eyes betrayed a shrewd manipulator. He exuded a latent energy and cunning.

"I'm just a humble public servant doing my duty, Reggie. Just earning the big bucks they pay us. To what do I owe the pleasure of this visit?"

"A few words in private," he said, nodding toward a stern-looking Arlene.

"Step into my office then."

The courtroom style of presentation began in his plantation Southern accent wrapped in an almost girlish voice when he was excited, punctuated by a slight lisp.

"You and your folks have cut a wide swath across this area in a very short time. You've made many enemies, but you've also impressed many people, including the man who will be our next governor, Hal Davidson," he said.

"That warms the cockles of my heart, Reggie."

"It should, because we can make you the director of the agency, and you'll have all the power, then." He looked and sounded at that moment like some earnest TV game show host saying, "Just risk what you have and spin the big wheel for the jackpot," as he whispers, "Don't worry. You'll win, for we've rigged the game."

"I have all the power I want right now, Reggie, especially if you'd tell me where I could lay my hands on Freddie."

A deer-in-the-headlights look. A flicker of panic?

He looked momentarily stunned, but recovered quickly. "I don't believe I know which Freddie you are talking about, Michael..."

"Ah, but you didn't hang out at Ace's old club in Memphis with any Freddie but one...the pale one with the bleeding eyes. Fredrick Hammel."

The lawyer studied him for a bit, and said, "My, my, you do get around, don't you?" Cold appraisal. New respect?

"What can I say? I am an insomniac. I see all kinds of things in the dark of the night—lawyers, radicals, mobsters, crooked politicians—all bloodsuckers that live under rocks during the day."

Reggie's face reddened and he said, "Just who do you think

you are, going around upsetting things that took years to put in place?" He was so angry, he was spitting and a globule stuck on his bow-tie. The moist mucin bubbled and stained the perfect red threads.

"I'm just a humble government employee who doesn't like quail."

Reggie nodded, biting his lower lip.

"Well, I must be running along now. You've indicted so many of my clients, I suppose I should thank you for the business," he said, recovering a bit of his composure and going into what could only be described as a curtsy as he held the tips of his jacket by his fingertips.

"Glad to be of service to hard-working counselors like yourself. Come back and see me when you want to give me the one person I want."

As he turned to go, he said, "I know who you want, but I don't think it would buy your friendship even if I could give him to you."

"No, I suppose not," Michael said, and Reggie was gone.

"Arlene," he shouted, "get that Lysol spray and fumigate the place. It suddenly seems filthy in here."

"Already on it, Michael," she said, with a smile and holding her nose.

The next call was from Clay, and he'd been busy. "Everything that Walker said was dead on. The Feds finally coughed up the fur ball that prevents them from speaking the truth. They had Fredrick staked out in central Florida with a new identity and home. He was given enough slack to go back and forth to Cuba, ostensibly to gather intelligence information on Castro and drug-running activities in that area. He'd given them some low to mid-level operatives in the radical underground. He was set to finger a major operative when he just vanished into thin air. One minute he was in the house, and the next, he was gone to parts unknown.

"They were contrite and red-faced about the whole issue. Did they lie? Yes. Are they still lying? Probably. Did they break state laws by aiding and abetting a murderer? Yes, but they said the big picture trumped the emotional aspects of his other crimes. They swore they were going to give him up as soon as they'd squeezed the last bit of juice out of him."

Michael shook his head and said, "Right," under his breath, not knowing how Clay got all this out of them, and he'd never ask.

"The only reason they decided to come clean was that they knew he represented a clear danger to you and to others. They couldn't afford more domestic violence with the Senate hearings now underway on the counter-intelligence operation, COINTELPRO. He'd made it abundantly clear that a personal vendetta existed between the two of you and that he would settle up one day. They said they would place him on the 'Ten Most Wanted' list and privately refer him to the CIA's covert 'Elimination File.' The thing is, they have no clue where he is, or whether he's in this country or a foreign land. All the embassies in suspect countries have been notified, and if he suddenly wants to come in from the cold, the controlling agent will be notified," Clay said.

He went on to say that they graciously told Clay that Mississippi drug agents had their blessings to eliminate him if they came across him first. That generosity could only mean that he possessed information that would be embarrassing to his handlers.

Clay also told Michael that the polls and the political alliances that were being formed didn't bode well for the honest candidate for governor, the man who would retain Mr. Collins as director. Clay's fresh intelligence update indicated that Hal Davidson could very well win. With him, he would sweep into power such people as Reggie Morris and even Hammel, unlikely as that seemed. Fredrick, it appeared, funneled money from Central American despots to Davidson through Reggie. That flow of money had most likely stopped now. Morris and Fredrick had become quite chummy at Ace Connelly's old club and shared some deviant sexual appetites. Ace was in prison, but the remnants of his group and the crime families in New Orleans were backing Davidson. The loose confederations of career criminals labeled the "Dixie Mafia" were also solidly in the camp of the old judge.

Clay said the director had been fully apprised of how bad things looked, but that he still didn't want to leak the photos and tapes. Clay argued passionately for a pre-emptive strike, but to no avail. The election would take care of itself. He assured him that there was only one thing they could do. "Pray, Michael. Pray hard."

Michael hung up and peered trance-like out his window at this vale that shapes our souls. He thought that Clay must be right. The weaker we feel, the more we lean.

* * *

He was up early on a chilly Thanksgiving morning. He watched the thin pink-red line on the eastern horizon. There was not enough light yet to see, but he had all the ugly clarity he needed. An ill wind had blown into Mississippi on election night and brought with it a huge upset in the governor's race. The unthinkable had occurred. In one of the last gasps of the kind of vote that had elected Huey P. Long in Louisiana, the people of Mississippi had reached down and breathed life into someone or something who surely must've been Long's illegitimate offspring.

The Magnolia State embraced the populist message of Hal Davidson. He was a "cracker" if there ever was one, but one who was able to mold a strange coalition of black voters and old segregationists into an uneasy truce and then ride it right into the governor's mansion.

Watching him on television accepting his accolades was a painful thing to Michael. He said there were going to be many changes now that he was governor-elect. As if he were speaking directly to the MBN, he said, "Some state agencies have gone off the reservation and are going to be brought to heel."

Michael was angry with Mr. Collins. Why hadn't he used the tape and photos? As he reached for the telephone to call Clay, it rang. It was none other than a jubilant Reggie Morris. "I told you that you boys should get on board this train. Think about it. Got to go party and cook quail."

Sure, Michael thought. *Go get the quail, the drugs, the booze, the prostitutes, the young girls and the young boys, and all the other commodities Reggie's parties are famous for at his country estate near Columbus.* He put his customers first. He gave them whatever they wanted.

The agents' hard work had tilted the playing field in favor of law and order, or at least "equal justice for all," a rare thing in Mississippi, but now it would rapidly swing back the other way. Davidson had already pronounced on election night that he was "tired of hearing about the bad things in the state," and that there was "no organized crime in Mississippi." That was "just talk by junior G-men who wanted to scare the people, and get more and more of the people's hard-earned tax dollars appropriated for their agency." In a moment of true eloquence, he also said that it was time for "the great state of Mississippi to move up in prosperity, and take "our rightful place at forty-ninth." Michael thought it would've been funny if it wasn't so tragic, and the stakes weren't so high.

The list of names being floated about for political appointment in the new administration was like a who's who from MBN intelligence files. They were a mixture of outright criminals or their facilitators cloaked in the trappings of fancy law offices or old hangers-on and go-along types from previous administrations safely ensconced within the "in crowd."

Let the good times roll! Walter Billingsly, the bookish candidate that Collins had hoped for, and who was the favorite in the race, had bit the dust. On election night, an exasperated

Billingsly asked, "This is what you want for your governor?" He was the last victim of a Mississippi that made another in a long list of uninformed choices. Now, the state would pay a terrible price.

Clay went into a long strategy session with the director to discuss the fallout from the election, how Davidson's mandate for change would play out, and what, if anything, could be done. The director's reappointment had to be blessed by Davidson's administration. He might hang on if he bowed before Hal's throne, but—at what cost?

Michael shifted his focus to a sudden source of brown heroin in the region. Some new dealers were dusting the highways and byways of Columbus and Tupelo with what they called "smack" or "horse." It was unthinkable that the streets of his Saturday night drag races with "horses" under the hood were now lined with a different "horse" in a syringe.

Tupelo was a wholesome, little slice of Southern-style *American Graffiti* just a decade before. Now, bad people were trying to mainline the new generation of kids who played on the runways of Main Street, USA. Did the new crooks already feel empowered by the recent election? Michael thought so, but figured the first arrests would tell the story.

It all seemed just too much at times, overwhelming even. He had begun to question his purpose and place and if he was little more than a government jack-in-the-box—wind him up and the smiling clown head pops up. Pop goes the weasel, even as, drop by drop, they flavor the foundation of your soul with the hemlock of doubt, poisoning those like Socrates who had the temerity to seek truth and declare that "an unexamined life is not worth living."

Forget it all for now. Think of Christmas. Get your axe and roam the hills of Parker Grove. Find that perfect cedar tree for the agency party, and make that special blend of holly leaves and mistletoe for wreaths for the resting places of his best girls...Pearl and Dixie.

CHAPTER TWENTY-FIVE

"Everything intercepts us from ourselves."
—Ralph Waldo Emerson

Michael was in the grip of an untimely crisis—a heroin deal gone sour on Christmas Eve. As he walked out of the emergency room of the Northeast Mississippi Medical Center in Tupelo, a blast of the cold winter storm wind hit him, rocking his lanky body and stinging his tender eyes. The innocence of the season seemed suddenly a thing of dreams, and even the frigid air didn't register in his emotionally numbed state.

Life had him, and those close to him, by the throat. He looked at his trembling hands and saw the unmistakable stain of dried blood that had resisted all scrubbing. He wondered if it was there at all or if he was losing his mind. He searched for answers but didn't even know the questions.

He wiped his hands against his coat, his rapid breathing forming clouds against the frigid night. Blinking, mesmerizing lights on the hospital Christmas tree flashed on and off in a surreal strobe-like rhythm, sirens from approaching ambulances split the night, and a nurse startled him as she scurried to the warmth of the hospital with a quick smile and "Merry Christmas."

317

He pulled the collar of his coat around his ears and tucked his chin into the warmth as he tried to squelch the ulcerous pain in his belly. Today's horror seemed to punctuate the terrible toll that the last six years had wrought on him and exposed him as a twenty-eight- year old, going on fifty cop married only to his job and the ghosts that haunted him. It was almost Christmas Day in the heart of the Bible Belt where God-fearing red, white and blue patriots still put drug dealers and Communists in the same category of evil, and the question of mothers and wives, fathers and brothers hung over frozen fields of regret—Do you know that your protectors bear unbearable sorrow?

***

Christmas Eve began as countless days before—children filled with youthful anticipation and innocent excitement, anxiously awaiting the arrival of the man in the red suit and imagined sounds of tiny hooves on rooftops. Salvation Army volunteers rang bells for donations for the less fortunate, department store loudspeakers blared familiar Christmas standards, and local radio stations played non-stop cheer. Parents rescued long-hidden presents to place under trees that illuminated their homes in hues of red and green, and the war on drugs seemed far away except to all but a few anonymous souls.

Michael anxiously awaited a heroin deal and had been out to find $20,000 in flash money. A reflection of his search for Dixie's killer, such deals had become metaphors for his quest and all dealers were in some fashion…Fredrick or possible leads to him. The quest became all-consuming, and his group reflected his obsessions to find the illusive enemy that he searched for. Like an addict himself, he needed more and more to sustain his relentless search and to fill the void within.

Presents were stacked under the tree in Parker Grove,

awaiting the family gathering, but Michael sent his regrets on Christmas Eve morning to say that he was sorry, but couldn't let this one go. The Parker clan was accustomed to his no-shows when he would disappear for days.

In his tiny apartment, he cleaned his gun, checked his ammunition, and made other last-minute preparations for the drug buy and bust he would supervise, and watched Katie.

"What are you doing, sweet girl?" he asked the sleek little feline. She had his attention, looked at him as if she knew exactly what he said, and rolled over and over in a fight to the death with a vicious toy mouse. He'd found her his senior year at Ole Miss in a pet mill where the conditions were deplorable. He was smitten and paid ten dollars to free her that day. She'd become the bearer of unconditional love in those moments when the world seemed to close in on him. When others thought differently, she still believed that he was the best man on the planet.

As Katie played, glancing at him to see if he was watching her, he counted the flash money he'd located for the buy on short notice. He was strapping on his .357 Magnum and loading his 12-gauge Remington pump shotgun with buckshot when the phone rang.

"Michael, it's Jack," said Agent Jack Denton.

"Yes, I have the money," Michael said, anticipating the question from his senior agent, the "old man" of the Northern District group at thirty-five years of age, a confirmed bachelor and self-professed ladies' man.

"Where'd you get it?"

"I went to see Mr. Shrecker, my boss in college when I worked nights at his movie theaters. He had it in his safe from last night's receipts and was anxious to help."

"Today'll be routine," Jack said.

"Don't freak me out and say that, Jack. You know I'm superstitious."

"No, man, I've bought from this punk, Rodney Harris, before. We just set this large deal up to draw out his suppliers who won't trust this jerk with a nickel's worth of smack. We go in, make the buy, and take them all down quick and easy," Jack reasoned.

"Maybe we can get them to point us to their suppliers and mules in Texas and Mexico. It might yield some conspiracy charges on some of their political protectors." He was playing to Michael's obsession. "Who knows? What could go wrong? You worry too much," he said.

"Someone has to, Jack, and you always tell me that I do it so well," Michael retorted. "I'll meet you and the others at the motel at 1600 hours and we'll go over this thing one last time. Oh, by the way, Clay's coming to work with us on surveillance and backup."

"Clay's coming?" Jack asked. "I thought he was too..." and he paused.

"Yeah, his cancer, I know, but I can't refuse him, and I'll feel better having him with us even though the weather folks say that a hard freeze and storm is headed our way." As if on cue, a sharp blast of frigid air rattled the windows in the old duplex. Katie edged closer to the heater.

"Okay, I'll get the others and we'll meet you at the Holiday Inn. "Oh, hey, big boy," Jack said, employing his favorite phrase.

"Yeah, what?"

"Merry Christmas, guy," Jack said, laughing.

"Merry Christmas to you, too, he said. You're just happy because of all this overtime pay you can spend on the honky-tonk women that you find so fascinating." Michael joked.

They both laughed because they knew that they didn't get overtime pay for anything they did, just compensatory leave that no one ever took.

Even as he hung up, he couldn't escape a feeling of foreboding, an itch you cannot scratch, a sixth sense that all good cops develop. He convinced himself that it was the Christmas blues...too many memories of times long gone, stirred into the mix of the stress and adrenalin of what passed for a normal day in his world, and, as always—Dixie.

His concern for Clay was tugging at his heart. His cancer had showed up again, and the treatments were taking their toll. Michael's mother loved Clay and had made him promise that he would look out for her son. When Michael called with his Christmas Eve regrets, she cautioned the son she'd allowed Pearl to raise while she worked long hours for modest wages.

"You'll be careful, won't you?" she had asked.

"Sure, Mom, you know that I'm always careful," Michael had joked.

He knew he'd disappointed her by not marrying, settling down, and giving her lots of grandchildren to compensate for the closeness they missed, to form bonds such as he and Pearl had shared. After the loss of Dixie, she didn't push him—maybe one day. Today, her words had been tinged with a bit of intensity. Maybe it was all the loss. Dixie, Pearl, and now Michael's father recovering from a stroke. People look back at Christmas, look ahead, hear the clock ticking and imitate the Norman Rockwell images of the perfect family and the ideal life, trying to hold on to that which they complained about but which they feared losing with all of their hearts.

Clay, through it all, was still Michael's mentor in the Bureau at thirty-six years old, and his best friend. He'd saved Michael's life at least once and deflected political fire directed at him countless times. Clay was good and decent—strong in those moments when impulsive young agents foolishly thought they would live forever and needed wise counsel.

When Clay fell ill again, Michael thought of the loss of Billy Hull, consumed by the shadow of Vietnam that darkened his world in Tylertown. He thought of the army spraying those cursed defoliants to eliminate enemy cover. The chemicals were the now silent enemy, the source of the cancer that had ravaged his friend's strong body. Now it was back along with his combat nightmares.

Michael knew that Clay shouldn't be out in the field, much less in this weather, but it was important for him to feel normal, useful, and essential.

"You need me," Clay said when he first called. "This is a buy-bust. Anything can happen. Who else would want to be stuck with you for hours on Christmas Eve, anyway?"

"Well," Michael said, "how can I resist an offer like that? A man who eats pork rinds and onions on surveillance shouldn't talk, you know?"

Clay still loaned Michael his gadgets, covered his back against the gatekeepers and small minds at headquarters, and called with coded messages on a new and improved scrambler that allowed the two conspirators to speak freely on a scrambled pathway. Even the hated wiretap squad in the current governor's security detail wouldn't be able to hear conversation, only gibberish. This private little army trolled for political intelligence and blackmail material to compromise uncooperative legislators, and it was sure to run wild under Davidson. That prompted Clay's upgrade of his scramblers, a bracing for the storm to come.

"Well, come on up then, cowpoke," he said to Clay, the western enthusiast. "Let's look the enemy in the eye once again."

"Pardner, I'm revving up the batmobile as we speak. I'll be there armed to the teeth, ready to take on the outlaws," he quipped. "Just have Elvis on your eight-track player, singing 'Lonesome Cowboy'!"

The sick man sounded better immediately and his optimism was infectious, but Michael sensed that he, too, could smell something ugly in the air that day. Engaged fully in life with a purpose, you can deny death and control destiny for a time. He sounded, appropriately, like a kid on Christmas who just got that special bike that he wanted.

After alerting Glenda and Linda, the vivacious next-door nurses, who looked in on Katie during Michael's often long and sudden absences, he drove to the office to secure body mikes for the agents.

He passed beneath Tupelo's Christmas lights, and past the Confederate statue bearing the Captain's name. The lighted tree atop the Bank of Mississippi twinkled a yellow-white and looked a bit like the star of Bethlehem if you squinted and used a bit of imagination. Parents were out with kids, already loading up for Grandma's house.

He briefly envied their rosy innocence, or was it their indifference? He remembered Christmas mornings long ago, waking to find that Santa had left that special bike, those hit 45 records, or ironically, his favorite *Have Gun Will Travel* pistol set—"A knight without armor in a savage land." Paladin rides again.

As he drove to his office, his mind raced ahead, planning for every possible contingency and assigning agents to cars that could swoop down instantly to the scene of the arrests in case they needed backup. Lost in this obsession, he entered the northern headquarters, still searching for the perfect plan in an imperfect world. Having gathered surveillance devices and other materials for the operation, he raced from his office to his haphazardly parked car. Always running close on time, he jumped in, cranked the car, and placed his hand on the gearshift.

It was at that moment that the strangest thing happened—something that would change him forever, in ways he couldn't grasp and remind him that he wasn't alone. An unidentified presence filled his car. It was more like ether than fog, a spectral breath that permeated every nook and cranny of the big Ford—brushing his senses and pouring through every cell in his body. His hands were frozen to the steering wheel at this sudden convergence of all of his yesterdays and tentative tomorrows, a place he sensed that he came from and was going to.

A portal seemed to open up to the gates of heaven itself and divine providence. In a burst of mind-numbing clarity that threatened to overwhelm his fragile mind and heart, Michael heard the clearest and sweetest of voices caress him and say, "Go back and get the bulletproof vests." A momentary knowing of the unknowable echoed in his ears and became metallic in character as it faded away. He was stunned. Where had the voice come from? Was it the voice of God, or was he losing his mind? Jack had said it was routine, so no reason to think more danger lurked than usual. The undercover agents didn't like wearing the bulky vests so hard to conceal. The presence receded, but when he tried again to leave, the enigma swept over him anew like a tidal wave with the command that wasn't optional—"Go back and get the bulletproof vests."

"Okay! Okay!" he said aloud. He hurried back to his office, shaken and seeking answers within a paradigm that had just been shattered on the Rock of Ages.

There he selected two second-chance vests. The vests had no armor and could only stop the equivalent of a .38-caliber weapon, but they were the best available. As he ran downstairs, a brisk, cold wind hit him at the door and chilled him to the bone. Somewhere off in the distance, a church bell chimed a Christmas hymn.

The seemingly supernatural experience left him with an ominous feeling that this day would be controlled by powers much greater than one obsessive agent. He felt as though he and his agents had somehow become instruments of a higher purpose. Perhaps it was just Clarence, the angel in *It's a Wonderful Life*, earning his wings again, and Michael was but a poor man's Jimmy Stewart being taught a lesson in a revealing of alternate realities.

He glanced at his watch and then hit the gas—hard.

CHAPTER TWENTY-SIX

"If all the world were just,
there would be no need of valor."
—Agesilaus

The vast arch or vault over the earth seemed alive. Peering up at the swirling, billowing dark clouds, it was easy to see ominous signs and distressed faces as the celestial hierarchy peered down at humanity and all of its folly. Perhaps it was a day such as this in ancient times when Noah ventured forth to cut the shittim wood for the ark.

Serious precipitation looked imminent on the drive to the rendezvous site. Just enough of a mist sprinkled the windshield to make the wipers scrape with annoying persistence. He waved to the uniformed officers in state highway patrol cars, knowing that he'd just pegged their radar units as he whizzed by them in the cold drizzle.

As Michael wheeled into the Tupelo Holiday Inn, he glanced up at the Big Star flashing out front. Some letters were missing as the neon popped and hissed. A tired housekeeper pushed her cart from room to room as the wheels wobbled and squeaked.

The worn hotel was a favorite meeting place for foot soldiers in the "war" on drugs. Drug deals, meetings with informants, and planning sessions such as these were all fine-tuned and birthed in the musty, cramped rooms.

Once, a careless agent, who was a fan of the Dirty Harry movies, accidentally discharged a .44 Magnum in one such room. The errant round passed through three adjacent rooms and agents ducked and cursed. Miraculously, no one was killed or wounded, but the director banned the "most powerful handgun in the world."

Another agent discharged his .357 Magnum after cleaning it in his apartment. Thinking it empty, he "dry fired" the weapon, taking careful aim at the bad guy on *Gunsmoke* pictured on his new color television set, recently bought on credit. The television was blown to bits and the sound of the discharge and exploding TV was deafening in the small apartment terrifying his wife who locked herself in the bedroom, convinced that her husband had lost his mind. It took Michael an hour to coax her out, a harbinger of destruction to come as her husband descended the slippery slope of ethics in the drug netherworld, wounding and killing their marriage just as surely as he had "killed" the bad guy for Marshal Dillon.

All the memories seemed far away and indulgent on this night of promise and destiny as the dealers of chance flipped coins of fate in a rigged game. Heads we lose and tails they win.

Entering the musty-smelling, smoke-filled room, the noise level was deafening—too many people talking at once and too much loud television that no one was watching. Michael scanned the motley crew with a grin—they wore every manner of beard and affected bad-guy look they could muster for their dual roles in undercover work and topside investigations—pretenders all. Michael knew that he'd never see their match. They were the best, tops in seizures and arrests. They apprehended both the low and the mighty, irrespective of position and favor, and were the only unit never sued. The theory that there was a direct correlation between busted heads and effective police work was discredited by these effective agents in the north.

These kids—and that was really what most of them were—were not judge and jury, and wanted convictions, not the momentary indulgence of an urge to slap some hapless kid with a roach. Only if threatened or fired upon would the response be swift and massive to protect their lives, those of comrades, and the lives of innocent bystanders. Though they followed Michael's lead on the Bill of Rights, they never stopped to consider the deeper, longer-lasting collateral damage to liberty by merely enforcing drug laws, so sure they were of the rightness of their crusade.

Jack was there, joking and calming the others who were younger and less seasoned. Jack had a full beard and was balding near the front, which seemed to bother him. After hours of practice, he'd mastered the art of the comb-over from just over his left ear to the right side of his head. Some local sheriff called him "patch head," and Jack wasn't pleased.

Sandra "Sandy" Jean Smith was quiet and a bit shy, but as good as the gold in Fort Knox. Lonnie Peterson was gentle, solid and dependable, one of Michael's favorites. Jim Riley and Robert Jenson wore their best bored "bah humbug" looks, but it was mostly faked. Gaunt and too thin, Clay arrived from headquarters wearing his old army jacket and carrying his favorite Blackhawk pistol. He also had on his Nam hat, and looked as if he could've just walked out of some stinking jungle. Jungle Jim indeed, a latter-day Johnny Weissmuller.

He nodded, and gave Michael a firm handshake with a thumbs-up. Always cold from all the cancer treatments, he wandered back to his spot near the heating unit that was on full blast.

Michael was overcome by a feeling of sadness as he looked at the group. He was in conflict. Several had already succumbed to the desire to live in the arena rather than be with their families. So, the numbers they posted looked good, but at what price? It was a sad commentary on the profession and a reason the divorce and suicide rate was so high. Michael also knew that it was why this group was so successful. These erstwhile and unquestioning Boy Scouts often left hearth and home at inopportune times to counter their adversaries in a chess game of sorts. They were young, immortal lions, or so they thought, and these cubs felt they had all the time in the world, but it was late for those so consumed by living in the mornings of their lives.

"Listen up," Michael said. "Today we are going to remove some heroin dealers from the street and end this supply of smack going to area schools. This will be a typical buy-bust. We have two buys on Rodney Harris and need to take him out. If we get lucky, his suppliers won't trust him with this large amount and will be with him as well, and it will be a very Merry Christmas for all!

"Except," he added, "for those eating the lousy chow at the Lee County jail on Christmas Day!" Everyone laughed heartily, confident to the point of cockiness.

"Sandy will be working on the undercover buy with Jack. She's played Jack's lady friend in previous buys. We all know that's above and beyond the call of duty."

Sandy fluffed her hair, blushed, and nodded her head in agreement. The group laughed as Jack rolled his eyes.

"Funny," he quipped.

Sandy narrowed her eyes, cocked her head to one side, and put her hands on her hips. "Michael, Jack's kinda cute sometimes… for an old man," she said as she smiled and bowed. The agents laughed again and clapped.

"Sandy, you're too kind. Jack couldn't make a buy without you. He's just too ugly to go it alone!" Michael offered.

"Funny, funny," Jack muttered again. "Y'all slay me."

Everyone whooped and Jack feigned hurt—the usual

horseplay and boisterous, nervous bonding before something serious. Michael was never comfortable with such foolishness, but he tolerated it because they seemed to need it. Whatever brought the cohesiveness that made them a team, he encouraged…up to a point.

"Folks, put on your body transmitters. Surveillance units, test your receivers, set to frequency Bravo. Jack, yours will be primary and if it fails, Sandy can switch to hers." The click, hiss, and buzz of electronics ensued along with playful mock questions, "Can you hear me? I can hear you."

A hand went up as Sandy headed to the small bathroom, and Jimmy said, "Uh, I would be willing to help my fellow agent secure her transmitter…"

"No, Jim, Sandy doesn't need any help taping the mike to her chest, but I'm sure she appreciates your thoughtfulness," Michael said, somehow keeping a straight face. More juvenile whooping and horseplay ensued. These rituals were akin to those in wolf packs that establish bonding and rank within the group, the complex structures of socialization and order.

"Okay, Jack and Sandy will meet Rodney—and hopefully, some friends—at 1700 hours. We keep the buy in the city so we can stay close on surveillance and have buildings as cover. When we hear the signal on the body mikes that the money and drugs have changed hands, we'll swoop down on the scene like avenging angels.

"What's the signal?" Michael asked again.

"What a Christmas to have the blues," all answered in unison, a chorus of questionable angels.

"Correct. I also want Jack and Sandy to wear these bulletproof vests along with the body transmitters." Eyes began to roll in the room.

Jack and Sandy groaned. "Oh, not those vests, man. They're bulky and ruin Sandy's figure," Jack said. "This is gonna be clean and routine."

More laughter erupted, nervous this time. "Clean and routine, clean and routine," the group chanted.

The specter of the voice from beyond the temporal echoed in their leader's ear. "Go back and get the bulletproof vests."

"Michael's right. It doesn't hurt to be careful," Clay agreed.

Jack looked at them and laughed. "Man, I think you guys have been into that spiked Christmas fruitcake again. But, hey, if it makes the boss happy, let's just do it." All the agents grabbed their gear and filed out the door like fearless paratroopers hooking up and jumping into the unknown. White McDonald's bags were tossed into gray garbage cans. Cigarette butts were stubbed after one last drag. Voices faded, car doors slammed.

And with that, Clay and Michael were off with their fledglings. Christmas Eve's light was fading under a pewter sky as modern-day errant knights went forth in search of an elusive and questionable holy grail. In those days, they still believed that they could change the world and that they could win, unaware, even in the abstract, what constituted winning. Michael suspected that some of them secretly still believed in Santa Claus.

"Is that a windmill up ahead? Charge then, Sancho," said Don Quixote.

CHAPTER TWENTY-SEVEN

"Be sober, be vigilant; because your adversary the Devil, as a roaring lion, walketh about, seeking whom he may devour."
—1 Peter 5:8

As Clay and Michael followed the agents to the agreed-upon meeting place with the heroin dealers, the weather looked ominous. Images of forgotten faces and places formed and disappeared in the tempest above seeming to offer clues to life, but there were no answers. It was only a mirage.

A lone, bright-red cardinal fluttered into the shelter of a dense evergreen as they passed. The sky grew darker by the minute and the rolling clouds had their way and carpeted the winter sky, squeezing the last ray of light from the heavens. Michael believed in signs and this brooding, dark storm added to his sense of foreboding. It was almost as dark as midnight, though only dusk and suffocating in the sudden stillness.

"It's going to be a long, cold night, buddy," Clay offered as he looked up at the sky.

Zipping his blue parka up to his throat, Michael answered, "You feel it, too, don't you?"

"You mean this hair standing up on the back of my neck? I just thought it was the radiation and chemo cocktail they gave me for the holidays!"

Michael looked at him for a moment, sadness tugging at him, but then they both broke out laughing. That was why Michael needed him there. Clay had the calmness and sense of humor Michael often lacked in his intensity and tendency to force things and "guarantee" outcomes. Clay possessed the true gravitas that many laid claim to, but only a select few actually possessed. Both men were quiet on the short ride to the meeting place in East Tupelo near the birthplace of Elvis Presley.

Rodney Harris was a young man with no eyebrows, a pockmarked face, and Indian-black eyes. He stood beside his car, well back in the shadows, as the undercover agents approached him. His rapid bursts of hot breath were captured in mini-clouds of icy air. Michael's premonitions began to materialize as soon as Harris spoke through the cigarette he nervously puffed. The ground around him was littered with evidence of a chain smoker.

"You guys follow me. I have a good, private location to conduct our business," he ordered, dropping another unfiltered butt and working it into the cracked pavement with his black army boots. Clay and Michael listened on their receiver from Jack's body mike.

"All right, lead on," Jack said, in typical deadpan tone with almost slight impatience or boredom implied.

"No, no, keep it in town, keep control," Michael shouted at the receiver, but it was too late for such orders. The agents and the dealer moved off under the rumbling sky. The surveillance teams fell in line like clockwork—closing and falling back in a choreographed dance of leap-frogging cars, shadowing on parallel streets, and listening to the messages from the radios. They had done this many times since they honed their skills as students in DEA exercises in the foreign suburbs of Maryland. It was soon apparent that the two cars were heading toward the country in a circuitous route to check for tails. The dealer was also no novice. Cat and mouse, but who was the cat and who the mouse?

"See if you can get ahead of them on old Clayton Road," Michael radioed to Jimmy and Robert, suggesting the parallel route.

"Will do, 816, we're just ahead of them now," Jim answered as the radio crackled and growing interference from the storm hampered communications. Agents began using special switches to cloak their look. One minute they were a car with two headlights, the next, only one.

Clay and Michael dropped back since they had been on their tail for too long. Lonnie took point as the surveillance vehicles came to an area in the backcountry and stopped suddenly for the deal. Lonnie radioed that they'd stopped, and he was passing them to join up with Robert and Jimmy on the opposite side of the scene. There were now units on both sides of the position occupied by Jack, Sandy, and Harris...the chosen stage where the final acts of this drama would unfold, where all of the actors would take their marks and play their roles.

The radio chatter and body unit conversation between Jack and Sandy ended, and a prolonged silence ensued. The silence before a storm? The radio's static was broken by Lonnie's voice. "Michael, they've stopped on a high portion of the road that overlooks swamps and lowlands on either side. The suspect pulled down into the depression on the north side. Sandy and Jack parked on the shoulder of the rise on the far side of the road and are walking down the slope toward the violator. I only see one perp."

A clump of pine needles, cones, and branches tore free from a nearby tree in the wind and banged on the roof of the command car. Clay and Michael strained to hear the choppy reception hampered by the storm and the limited range of the body mikes. They cursed the technology and the central procurement officer in charge of vendor products who tended to buy inferior products to cut corners. He was confident that the field agents could "get by" with any cheap model on special. The same MBN procurement chief, Arthur Pender, had actually gotten these pieces of junk "for free" as an incentive on an AR-15 rifle deal—not to mention an expense-free weekend at a Biloxi resort paid for by the vendors, meaning taxpayers.

Jack and Sandy were now at the fringes of the range of the weak transmitter at a time when every word was precious, and life and death often rested on the quality of these impartial devices. The slightest inflection of tone could indicate imminent danger, and every second of delay could mean victory or a ticket to the hereafter. Getting a word now and then wasn't nearly enough to assess the scene unfolding just out of sight.

Fading in and out now like a faraway shortwave station, they heard Harris ask, "You got the money?"

"We got the money if you got the good stuff," Jack said.

"Show me," he said.

"No, *you* show *me*."

"What the [inaudible] does this [inaudible]…?" Harris exclaimed, his metallic voice chopping up. Michael leaned closer to the receiver and pressed his ear to the speaker as the unit light cast an eerie orange glow on the car's interior.

"Give me a sample for my little tube of chemicals," Jack said, referring to the field tester agents now used openly in large deals.

"Hey, dude, look at [inaudible]…blue color," Harris said.

"Here [inaudible]….money," Jack said, as they envisioned Jack handing Harris the money to complete the standard hand-to-hand transaction so favored by prosecutors.

"You [inaudible]…arrest, get down!" Jack ordered.

"No, don't, don't shoot!" Harris said, screaming.

Then there was a deafening silence in the conversation as the reception died. Only muttering and the whistling wet wind were audible.

"I can't hear it, Clay," Michael said, banging on the receiver, sweat forming in his palms.

Grabbing the mike as Clay adjusted the directional antenna, he asked, "Anyone receiving the mike transmission?"

"Negative," Lonnie said.

"We're flying blind, 816," Jim responded.

Suddenly, the speaker came alive once more, like Dracula rising from his coffin, and erupted with sounds, argument, and tension too fuzzy to fully decipher. Raised voices shattered the momentary silence. Then what sounded like "da tow, da tow."

With his heart in his throat, Michael rasped, "Clay, was that a gunshot?"

Before he could answer, all the agents could hear bloodcurdling groans and muffled impacts of incoming rounds against bodies or vests as the mikes began to work. At that moment, all things that go bump in the night became real. The boogey men were near. Death's shadow penetrated the cloud cover and cast a pall along the pale palisade.

"All units close in," Michael shouted into the radio as the body mike erupted with more shots—da *tow, da tow.*

The burning rubber of the state car formed a pungent dark blemish of ambiguity.

"It doesn't sound good," Clay said, as he shifted the gears, and pushed the limits on the 289-horsepower Ford V-8. The sounds of silence they had cursed only seconds before were now broken by the cries from torn flesh and the impact of heavy weapons.

Jim said, "They're in a fight, Michael. There's more than the one violator. Sniper somewhere—we're screwed!" Real desperation and panic was now evident in the voice of the still green and naïve sunshine soldier dragged into this howling winter of darkness.

The few seconds it took Clay to close on the scene of chaos seemed like forever. Tall evergreen and bare hardwoods zipped by the window. Suddenly, there was the elevated rise in the road.

Michael struggled to get a fix on the situation—who was where? How to rescue as first responders and live to tell about it? An open field stretched to the swamps on both sides of the depression. The field was split by a railroad track and a clump of pine trees off to the left.

Eyes flicking desperately left, right, tracking, seeking to arrest his own growing panic, Michael yelled, "I see the cars, Clay, but no bodies."

Clay nodded and scanned for suspects and agents. Where were the good guys? Where were the bad guys, and how many?

Something there—the agents to their right. As they passed where Jack and Sandy had retreated up the rise to take cover, Clay saw a muzzle flash from the clump of pine trees near the railroad trestle, then the crack of the rifle that rent the night.

"Incoming!" Clay shouted, as a high-powered round bounced off the roof of the car like a rock skimmed on a pond. Clay swerved to the shoulder in unison with the "spee-yong" sound of the ricochet. As they rolled out of the car on Michael's side, small arms fire from Robert and Jim up ahead answered the last incoming round.

Scrambling to the cover of the car, Clay and Michael joined them and rose to fire rounds at the last muzzle flash as Michael heard the buzzing sound of a tumbling round whistle past his ear. The marksman had missed but just barely. The smell of gunpowder filled the air, and sleet began to pour from the opaque sky.

A look of horror on her young face, Sandy rose up behind Clay's position. Her eyes were white, wide, and wild. She pointed to the same clump of pine trees to their left near a railroad trestle about seventy-five yards away. "Sniper!" Clay said. Robert, Jimmy, and Lonnie were up ahead like anxious referees, signaling a time-out on a Saturday afternoon at Ole Miss so the team can regroup.

"Both exits covered, no way out," Clay said, "except through the swamp or through us."

Jack appeared down, slumped against Sandy. From Michael's vantage point some forty yards away, it didn't look good. *God help us, oh, God…please help us,* his mind cried.

Sandy radioed, "Jack's hit bad, Michael, and I'm taking him to the hospital. Right now!"

"Go, go. I'll meet you there."

"One still on the bridge," she answered.

"When we saw the heroin and arrested Rodney, someone opened up on us from the trees. Rodney tried to pull a gun then. I shot him, Michael. I shot him," Sandy said in a calm, but little girl's voice, strained by sudden bloody realities altogether unlike classroom exercises. Michael knew that the violent tremors and sweats would come soon, and her voice would become a stranger that she wouldn't recognize as her own.

"Should be two loose on the ground," she mumbled, as she threw rock and gravel, speeding away with her precious cargo— the growing curtain of the darkness enveloping her car.

A sudden stillness fell on the scene as the violent rupture of tranquility mocked them.

"No movement in the green or the gray," Clay said, referring to the pine trees and the swamp. "It's so dark." Ice formed on the car that they used as a shield, and the sleet rained down like angry ice pellets.

Switching to the local police channel, Michael radioed for backup in a voice edged with fear, near panic. "Officer's down! We request backup! I repeat, officer down, need backup. Old Clayton road, near railroad tracks!" Michael said.

After a moment of silence, the sheriff's dispatcher answered, "Units on the way, 816!"

Then there were no more shots. Though ears still rang from the reports of high-powered weapons, it was quiet, eerily quiet… deafeningly silent. Agents moved tentatively behind the cars, sneaking looks.

In the heat of battle, everything slows down, and surreal images bombard the senses—distant shouts, the smell of gunpowder on a cold winter evening, and Sandy's car racing from the scene with a look etched on her disturbed face that left no doubt that someone's life depended on her and her alone. Though the battle was over, agents still scanned the trees for targets, firing the occasional nervous rounds at perceived movement. A thousand thoughts bombarding his mind, Michael radioed everyone to stop shooting at shadows. They knew better, but one of their own was down. They'd been violated, and the enraged officers were looking for the foes that had now crossed the threshold from suspects to enemy combatants. They were also covering their own abject fear that had just seized them and toyed with their false bravado.

The front money, all that cash, was blowing in the wind and down the hill in slow motion. Strangely, Michael thought about how many presents that would have provided for poor children for whom Christmas would bring no joy.

Suddenly consumed with an obsession to recover the money, he stood and moved out from the safety of the car amidst distant cautions to leave it. A death wish? Wanting to join Dixie Lee? He made his way down the slope, watching the trees for danger— perhaps a movement, a strange shadow, but time moved slowly again and he could taste the air, hear the wind, see the molecules of all that was, and felt one with that place and moment. A sudden wind blew his hair across his numb face. Somewhere off in the distance, a crow cried a commentary on the folly of man, and he thought of Poe's raven crying, "Nevermore."

A myriad of thoughts raced in his mind competing for dominance. He felt more alive in those dangerous moments than at any other time in his life. He now understood those disturbing stories Clay had told him about Vietnam, when the Grim Reaper was near, perched like a vulture waiting, patiently waiting. Scooping up the blowing bills that tumbled down the slope like dried leaves, Michael saw a blood trail leading off into the swamp.

"Blood trail, Clay," he shouted, pointing toward the trail leading off into the darkness of the big stand of cypress trees. Thick cane grew along the trail, a convenient hiding place for killers, but it now appeared the curtain had come down on Act One of this unfolding drama. All the players had retreated to freshen their makeup and check their lines. There seemed to be nothing there except icy winds and empty air. Michael paused, his hair wet and ice-filled.

The wailing of pulsing sirens signaled the approach of local police units, fire trucks, and emergency vehicles. Michael returned to the top of the ridge. "Clay, I'm on my way to the hospital. Please take charge and secure the area, and get some tracking dogs in here before dark—if any can be found on Christmas Eve."

He paused, looked up, and smelled the air, seemingly drugged or in shock. What was that smell on the tempest? Death? Or life…?

The look in his eyes made Clay uneasy.

"You go on. I'll handle things here and then meet you at the hospital as soon as I can," Clay said, sensing his friend was frayed and on overload.

It was clear to Clay that the adversaries were long gone. This crime scene needed preserving for supporting evidence like shell casings, blood and such, but Clay knew where the action would now shift. The shooters were on the run. Every moment was now critical to apprehend known and unknown felons before they slipped away into this storm from Hell. This battleground was now past tense. Leads and justice lay elsewhere.

Michael raced to the Tupelo Hospital, hoping to find life and not death in the same halls where he was born twenty-eight years before this dank day. It was the only place for a violator to go when a young female agent has shot you. He needed to see about Jack and Sandy and felt he would find more than friends in the emergency room. He raced back down the route they had traveled and dodged police and medical units flying low with sirens and lights flashing. All were headed toward a little piece of real estate between Heaven and Hell that had trapped them all in a schism at the intersection between history and eternity.

Entering the emergency room, the smell of disinfectant, despair, human suffering, and stale air peculiar to hospitals was overwhelming. Then he saw her. Agent Sandra Jean Smith leaned against the cold concrete wall, her long, auburn hair resting on her shoulders. Her chin was on her chest and her wrapped arms tried to comfort her. He thought Sandy looked more like a scared young girl than a seasoned agent at that moment. Not even the cold of this dark night could put color in her pale cheeks. Michael squeezed her hand, and put his arm around her shoulders as large drops of tears overflowed the well of her eyes.

"They have Jack over there," she said, in a far-away, trembling squeak of voice, unable to blink her tears away.

"Everything's going to be fine, Sandy. Are you okay?" he asked.

She nodded an unconvincing, "Yes," and shivered, not from the cold but from seeing too much. Jack's blood stained her jacket in droplets of drying crimson.

"Just stay put. Clay'll be here shortly to debrief you, okay?" No answer.

"You did good today, Sandy. You protected your partner. I'm very proud of you," he said. He was only a few years older than she was. He knew at that moment that he should've tried to tell them all how it was in Tylertown. How it *really* was.

Methodical voices barked code calls in cryptic hospital jargon and attendants scurried along practiced routines to stave off death in what would ultimately be a swing battle for all earthly travelers. Sandy nodded again, but clung to his hand tightly as he turned to go. Finally, she headed off with an attendant who promised good strong coffee. Well, maybe strong, anyway.

Nothing could have prepared Michael for what Sandy had already seen up close. Jack lay motionless on a gurney, and emergency medical personnel were cutting away his blood-soaked clothes. The *bink, bink, bink* of a heart monitor beeped methodically, oxygen tubes were in his nose, and a saline drip was fixed to his arm. Michael's heart was in his throat as he looked horror full in the face. He had never seen so much blood. The white bulletproof vest was soaked in a purple-red pool. As a child, he had felt faint when Pearl would chop a chicken's head off for Sunday lunch. Here there were no feathers, only broken skin.

Jack was always so full of life, and unlike Michael, he lived in every moment, not consumed by worry about consequences of every action to the point of losing the moment. If Michael was the Puritan, Jack was his counter-balance who reminded his boss to laugh now and then. Now, he couldn't laugh—here he was, his body riddled with bullets by anonymous assassins. He wasn't moving, and Michael fought the urge to look away.

A blur of sturdy Nightingales pushed past him.

"Please stand back, sir," one of the efficient nurses said to Michael as the professionals went about their business in blue scrubs soiled with the burnt copper smell of fresh blood.

Another nurse called to him. "One of 'them' in the other room," she said with venom in her voice, snapping her tightly-bunned head toward the back.

Michael walked toward the adjacent room. He found the dealer the agents had met bleeding from a shot through his hand, now temporarily wrapped. Harris had reached under his coat as the agents attempted the arrest, and the gun battle ensued. Sandy had shot him right in what would've been his black heart, piercing his right hand as he drew his weapon.

It was obvious he'd live, and as Michael approached him, he could feel the tension on his inner trip wire. Control was the key word. He lived a life with too much control, too much the perfectionist and idealist, myopic in his narrow world where monsters roamed treacherous terrain waiting to consume Boy Scouts.

While growing up, rescuing the weak from the strong and the hopelessly outnumbered from torment on the schoolyard, had become a way of life for him. To goad and cajole him into a fight was a difficult thing. He would walk a mile to avoid a fight, but when that tripwire was broken, the one that indicated that right vs. wrong was in play, friends said his brown eyes grew black, sometimes unleashing his own long-suppressed darkness in tsunami-like waves.

Michael paused for a moment and looked around at his surroundings. Several of the overhead fluorescent lights flickered, producing strobe-like effects on the stained, concrete-block walls of the secured examination room. Then his eyes locked onto those of the wounded violator before him. *The empty eyes of a man who has no soul*, he thought. Michael said, "Rodney Harris, you're under arrest for the sale of illegal drugs and the assault of a state narcotics agent with a deadly weapon."

"Screw you!" Harris said with a venomous scowl and ink-black eyes.

A nurse supervisor in starched white peeked in for a second and then retreated.

"You have the right to an attorney. If you cannot afford one, one will be appointed by the state, and anything you say can be used against you," he continued.

"I want to see my lawyer," Harris whined, clutching his hand. "That girl shot me."

"You can call your lousy lawyer as soon as we're done and you're treated. Please don't attempt to leave this room or this facility," Michael said, barely suppressing the growing rage in his heart.

Harris smiled a twisted smile, sarcasm dripping from his mouth. "You'd like that, wouldn't you, so you could kill me? Cops! You're all alike."

Grinding his teeth, his jaw muscles popping from his face, Michael glared back at him through narrow slits. "My friend's fighting for his life in there because of you. Now, please don't make a good cop go bad!" An unattended small ball of saliva flew across the room like a deadly projectile, hitting Harris in the eye.

Harris, feeling threatened, looked at Michael directly in the eyes and whatever he saw chilled him to his bones. He grew pale and shrank into the hard chair as he turned as green as the ragged foam cushion on which he sat. He retched in a dry heave and then was silent.

Michael was unable to stand the stench of him any longer and left the interrogation of Harris to his less emotional colleagues. He could only think of Jack at that moment.

He fought tears and a growing nausea as he walked through the big hospital, surrounded by the sickening scent of disease and death. Doctors and nurses hurried by ignoring Michael, thinking only of preventing the inevitable. Jack's corner of the ER lay just ahead.

An older emergency room physician, who'd been a family friend, was working on Jack with the assistance of the nurses. His sad beagle eyes matched his pallor and jowls, and he motioned to Michael to come closer.

"Michael, here's where one round passed through Agent Denton's right arm," the doctor said in a coldly clinical, matter-of-fact voice. Jack lay comatose, blissfully unaware of the men discussing his alarming condition, but the rhythmic rise and fall of his chest seemed somehow reassuring at a moment when Michael was clutching at straws.

The doctor pointed to Jack's privates.

"Another round left a burn on his scrotum, and had it been a quarter inch higher, your friend's chances for a family would have been severely diminished," the portly doctor said, appearing a bit cavalier but only trying to ease the tension.

However, Michael was not amused. "Yes, go on."

"Unfortunately, the final round hit him right in the chest..." He inserted his gloved finger into the entry wound in the chest, making some point lost on Michael. The gaping hole was obvious. Michael wanted to look away but couldn't.

"Darnedest thing. The round penetrated his vest, but it deflected its trajectory and took some of the punch out of it. It entered behind his right breast and skittered around his rib cage—finally exited behind his left breast. It tore up a lot of tissue, but no vitals."

The doctor paused, sighed heavily, and said, "I've never seen anything like it in twenty years in the ER. If not for this vest, it would've taken out his heart and lungs, and he would've been dead before he hit the ground... Michael, do you hear me? Agent Parker?"

But Michael was far away, hearing Pearl say of the world, "None of this has anything to do with us, son." He closed his eyes, remembering and feeling the presence in his car, the command to get the vests, and what his childhood pastor had said one Sunday long ago—*"The Comforter is near—never leaving us or forsaking us."*

He shuddered at the thin line between life and death, and cold chills racked his body. He knew they weren't alone that day. Michael felt a presence in that room of life and death—standing vigil, the soft fluttering of angels' wings almost perceptible, an almost discernible murmuring of words he couldn't hear and embraces he couldn't quite feel. He staggered to the small chapel, fell to his knees, and said a prayer for goodness and mercy, for Jack—for them all.

CHAPTER TWENTY-EIGHT

"My mother groaned, my father wept,
into the dangerous world I leapt."
—William Blake

Late on Christmas Eve, the restless rain and sleet had become all sleet, then small and large hail and snow, and it seemed as if the fountains of the deep had broken and the windows of heaven had opened to paralyze north Mississippi.

Golf-ball sized hail pounded Tupelo like the stones from heaven cast down on the Amorites, but these rained down on the just and the unjust alike and they all agreed that they'd never seen such a storm, such a persistent winter. Preachers called it the icy breath of God as the earth groaned.

The cold didn't matter to Michael. He was already numb from all that he had felt when he had looked at Jack and saw the skeleton-white skull of death where his head should be.

Scientists use a test called the "absolute threshold of pain" to measure the beginning of pain. Pressure is applied to a sharp needle and increased incrementally until pain registers: 20 grams on the forearm should produce pain, 100 grams on the back of the hand, 200 grams on the sole of the foot, 300 grams on the fingertip, and so on. Such a test would not produce pain tonight. Michael's physical pain sensors were desensitized or turned off to the emotions and mind by endorphins, like morphine or a temporary leprosy, anesthetics to allow him to function and do what must be done and to feel later when sensation was not a luxury.

A luxury at that moment would be a jumper cable. The extreme cold had numbed his car battery, and it barely gave him a whump-whump. He flagged a passing wrecker doing good business and sparked life back into the car.

The wipers wouldn't move the heavy layer of ice on the windshield. While the motor ran, he used a hand scraper to free the rubber blades which finally began to move in a swish-swish to clear the glass. He radioed Clay, who was coming in from the plain of death they had been on, and told him that Jack was not good and in surgery. Sandy would call with any change, and Rodney was under guard.

The crime scene had been secured as much as possible in the storm and darkness, and further work there would have to wait. They agreed to meet with the agents at the sheriff's office, but only after Clay asked the question that Michael did not want to think about.

"Have you called the old man to brief him?"

"No."

"You'd better. You don't want him to find out from someone else or the TV."

"Yeah, I know."

So, en route to the meeting, Michael asked that he be patched through a static-filled relay tower to the director's home number.

"Hello," answered a familiar gruff voice, a bear just kicked in his warm cave of hibernation.

"Mr. Collins, it's Michael." He sighed and launched into it. "We had a buy-bust heroin deal late this afternoon in Tupelo.

During the deal and arrest, a sniper opened up on Jack and Sandy from some trees. Jack was hit bad and is in surgery. Sandy wounded the perp at the scene. He's under arrest. We're about to meet and serve search warrants." He breathed deeply after his long, uninterrupted exhale.

Silence. Then, "Where was the violator hit?" A dreaded question.

"In the hand."

"Well, hold that scum until I get there, and maybe I can do better!" Connection broken.

Cliff, the radio wizard, asked, "Uh, 816, do you want me to try to get him back?"

"No, Cliff. It wasn't the storm." The ice storm, anyway.

All the agents were there at the meeting, except Lonnie, whom Michael had dispatched to the hospital to assist Sandy in debriefing and securing the wounded perp. The sheriff's office and jail was an ancient gray building with more horizontal and vertical slits than actual windows to let some faint light into the cells, offices, and interrogation areas. As inadequate and primitive as it was, it would be home and the center of all activity for the crucial hours to come.

A hastily drawn, but detailed search warrant was signed by a justice of the peace judge whom a sheriff's car picked up and brought to the jail in the blinding storm. Extraordinary circumstances.

Agents paired with deputies and city police went out into the frigid night two-by-two in modern-day metal arks to search for evidence and weapons at various locations but primarily at the home of Rodney Harris and his brother, Ray.

Agents arriving at the old clapboard house with peeling blue paint found a card game in progress. Present were Ray Harris and three others, two men and one girl—poker faces for all sorts of games. Ray was about six feet, thin with a long angular face and a sour and bitter look of contempt for everyone.

He swore that he and his friends had been home all day playing poker. He had no idea where his brother was or what he had been doing. All the players backed him up and nodded vigorously in affirmation to each profession of innocence. The female punctuated every sentence with a salutation of profanity.

Michael "invited" them all downtown for questioning and left agents to search the home. Each suspect traveled with two officers and was kept separate from the others from that moment on. Whatever alibi they'd concocted must now stand without refreshment.

Clay and Michael would do the interrogation and agreed to save Ray until last. They believed he was most likely the shooter. He and his brother were inseparable, reports revealed, and he was a marksman in the Marines. Whoever had been firing that rifle at Jack knew what he was doing.

First up in the small but bright room with no windows was the female five-card stud player, Shirley Anderson. Shirley was a slightly chubby girl of eighteen going on fifty with blonde hair and black roots. Her short dress and low top accentuated what she clearly felt were her best assets, not counting her foul mouth. She launched her blue invectives from atop her red, spiked heels.

Michael knew of her by reputation. Her mother had brought her to the rough clubs of Lee County to troll for men when she was only twelve years old. She'd lost all innocence long ago and was a first-rate grifter and liar and capable of severing a man's masculinity—physically and emotionally. She was known to give cops a tumble in the squad car and to be a main squeeze and informant for Reggie's favorite detective, Howard Floyd. No lady.

As she sat in her chair, Shirley purposely didn't pull down her short skirt and made constant challenging eye contact. She had her own psychology and body language.

"I don't know why y'all drug me down here. Howard's not going to be happy when he finds out. You know I help him on cases." Smacking her pink Double Bubble gum, she slowly pulled back her lips from her teeth in a grotesque imitation of sensuality.

"Miss Anderson, we just want to get you on record formally, and give you a chance away from the others to tell us what really happened today," Clay said. "What you say can be used against you, and if you need a lawyer, one will be appointed."

"Yeah, yeah, you oinkers keep on grunting. I done told you boys the truth. We was playing cards for hours and hours," she said, cackling as she leaned her elbows on the table to create more cleavage, cupped her face in her hands, and stared at Michael. "I know all about you," she said, purring like a feral cat in heat.

His eyes fixed on hers above her display, he said, "I know all about you, too, Shirley, and Howard can't save you this time. Your animal instincts won't work here. This is your last chance to avoid prison."

Shirley reared back, bristling, sudden anger making her dull eyes come to life. "I don't know nuttin', Mister Po-lice!"

They excused her, but only to the outer area where she was still isolated. Next up was James Miller, a twenty-three-year-old white male with long black hair to match a black moustache tucked under a hawk nose. He had the vacant eyes of a chronic marijuana user and a false confidence about an inch deep. It took each question an extra moment or two or three to penetrate his fog.

"James, do you understand your rights?" Michael asked and proceeded to give him his Miranda warnings.

"Yeah, dude. I understand all that, but I ain't got nothing to hide, man. You can't touch me anyway cause I'm a citizen of the world." He grinned a foolish smile.

"So," Clay said, "you were there playing cards for hours? Since two or three? And Ray Harris was there all that time?"

"Yeah, man. That's about it."

"Funny, James. That's not what Shirley just told us," Michael said. Divide and conquer.

349

"What?" Surprise. Hurt?

"Yeah, she said you just came in before we got there. Are you lying to us?"

"That slut, man, don't know what she's talking about." Angry now, defensive—a little sweat beginning. "Oh, man, you're confusing me."

"So, who's right? You or her? She thinks you might've been helping the Harris brothers. You a dealer or a shooter?"

"No, man, I was there longer than she was. She only just come up. It's her that's lying."

"This is your last chance, James," Clay said. "Do you want to change your statement?"

"Uh, no. Well, I don't know. I need to think."

"The officer will take you back to your room for a while, where you can think about Shirley putting it all on you," Michael said. They let him leave. They had done what they wanted without pushing so hard that he would lawyer up. Their real target was next.

Joey Jenkins came in to fatherly greetings from Clay and Michael. He was nineteen, but looked fourteen. Nervous as a long-tailed cat in a roomful of rocking chairs, he picked at the pimples on his face and pulled at his thin brown hair constantly.

"So, son, we understand that you had been in the game with the others since one or two p.m. Is that right?" Clay asked in a soft tone.

"Yes. Yes sir, it is."

"And Ray Harris was there the whole time, correct?"

"Uh-huh. Yeah, sir!"

Michael leaned forward and locked eyes with Joey who tried not to look at him.

"So, Joey, how old are you?"

"Nineteen. Just had my birthday," he said proudly.

"That right? Well, the agent that the Harris brothers shot today is in surgery right now. Did you know that?"

"Yeah, I guess. Uh, no, I didn't."

"Nineteen, huh? If he dies, Joey, we are talking murder, son—murder or accessory after the fact for you. You should be maybe forty-five or fifty when they parole you from Parchman Farm."

Joey was picking furiously at his face. Blood ran from his pimples, and he was gnawing his lower lip in what looked like self-cannibalism. The odor of fear hung in the stale air of the small room.

In an adjoining room, the director and his driver, Chief of Enforcement Larry Burnside, had arrived, and were listening with the sheriff and a sullen Detective Howard Floyd, who had joined them.

Michael knew Joey was ripe for the plucking, like a plump yellow plum about to fall from the bush.

"Joey, now what I think is that you wanted no part of this. You just got caught up in the Harris brothers' scheme and they forced you to alibi for them. Isn't that right?"

Poor young Jenkins came undone in a burst of uncontrolled emotions, a dam bursting with pent-up stress. He saw a man on the far shore toss him a life preserver and he took it.

"Oh yes sir, yes sir! They made me do it! They made me do it!"

"I know, I know," Michael said. "Captain Strickland will take it all down in this statement for you. You did the right thing. It's going to be all right."

When that bit of news was purposely leaked to the others, they couldn't get back quick enough to recant in a sudden case of repentance or clairvoyance.

That only left Ray.

They brought a sullen and surly Ray to their room, but some of the fight seemed to be diminished by the betrayal he sensed. His right eye was now his betrayer. It twitched and spasmed, and he couldn't arrest it. It was a billboard revealing the stressful stew that simmered and boiled in his soul.

Michael felt sorry for him for a moment. He was a wounded bull, but this bull had gored Jack. So, like a good matador who had failed to slay his bull with the thrust of the sharp sword, he pulled out his death knife and stuck it right behind the ear.

"Ray, I just want you to know that we have you…I don't need to talk to you. I don't *want* to talk to you. They've all given you up. You're going to prison for shooting Agent Denton."

The words pierced Ray like the sharp knife of a real matador. Looking as if he wanted to run, he said, "I ain't saying nothing."

"Fine. Clay, take him out of my sight."

With that, Ray suddenly hung his head and said in a low guttural whisper of agony, "I shot him. I shot him, but I didn't know he was an agent."

Clay pulled out his pen and paper and nodded to Michael. It was over.

As Michael left the room, the observers next door were leaving, too. The director said, "Well done, Michael."

Larry patted him on the shoulder, but Howard Floyd looked at him as if he wanted to kill him then and there. His hand even moved involuntarily to his sidearm before he recovered. The director saw it and said in a deep, accusing voice, "Howard, you got a problem?" He said "No!" and scurried away quickly like a rat exposed in a sudden light.

But he did have a problem. He was supposed to protect the Harris brothers as the Regional Narc Unit Detective. Reggie would be furious. Worse, the people who fronted the heroin would be looking for their money.

Howard fled to Reggie's office early that morning for emergency Christmas Day instructions, but Michael's agents were waiting—and watching—and documenting.

The snow and ice mix still fell, but after bringing the earth to its knees with brute force, the ice fell in dainty patterns like Tony the Tiger's Frosted Flakes. Sandy called the jail and told Michael, "Jack made it. He's going to be all right, Michael. He's going to be all right." Then she began to sob in a heaving release of all that was and might have been.

Clay and Michael talked until first light, tidied up all loose ends, and arranged to take Ray back to the scene to recover shell casings and the rifle he hid in the swamp grass.

Clay told him, "You did good, buddy."

"No, Clay, *we* did good. Someone was watching over us. Just a misstep here or there and Jack would be dead."

He then told his friend about the voice, the warning, and it cast all of their mortal dithering in a different perspective.

"Maybe, Clay, we send some low-frequency distress signals to heaven even when we aren't aware we're doing it, but if the whole earth blinked out in the universe, it would only appear a brief flicker of a match in the cosmos." After a long silence, they agreed that it made their heads hurt worse than they already did.

The glory of a citrus-orange sun rose to relieve the moon that had presided over a long night and a frozen earth. The blue-white snow and ice took on a golden tint, as Michael squinted against the stinging light and walked out to a new world full of second chances.

A Christmas Day mockingbird serenaded all its neighbors in a celebration of the sun's life-giving heat and light, not knowing or caring that another storm was forecast for New Year's Eve. Michael could have sworn that it was singing "Joy to the World."

A desperate Howard Floyd told the district attorney that he would testify that Michael and Clay denied Ray an attorney. The DA told him that if he did, he'd be prosecuted for perjury. The surveillance photos of his meeting with Reggie were produced. Howard was fired and cut loose from his pension and his usefulness to Reggie. He was left only with his booze and bitterness. His female companions moved on in search of new sugar daddies.

The Harris boys decided to plead out as an angry citizenry

demanded life in prison. They were given twenty years. Rodney sued the sheriff's office for inadequate medical treatment for his wound and the partial loss of function in his right hand that Sandy had pierced with one slug from her .38 lightweight. He lost his suit.

Sandy received *Parade* magazine's Police Service Award for her actions on that cold Christmas Eve to save her partner. She looked positively angelic in the annual *Parade* magazine police edition. Jack recovered sufficiently to attend the awards ceremony, accompanied by one of his many female admirers who seemed to want to mother him since he was wounded.

And in a cosmic tying of dangling threads, Reggie Morris, member of the Mississippi bar in tenuous good standing, was found floating in the pool of his country home on New Year's Day. His throat had been cut from one teardrop-pink earlobe to the other.

Like Theo in the backwaters of Sardis, the Tillers in the muddy Mississippi, Ace in prison, Frank DeVaney, broken and hiding from mob hit-men, and Howard drowning in his bottles, Reggie's time had run out. He would never reap the rewards from the man he worked so hard to elect governor. No, Reggie was now filing briefs in a court that heard no late appeals.

The murder remained unsolved, but Reggie's nearest neighbor, an old farmer, swore that on New Year's Eve in a blinding snow, he saw a man who appeared to be a creature of the snow itself—some sort of yeti.

He said that the thing was there one moment, but when he blinked his eyes against the wind and snow, he was gone. Gone back to the white—the nothingness from which it came.

CHAPTER TWENTY-NINE

"I can't see my reflection in the waters...
I can't remember the sound of my own name...
If tomorrow wasn't such a long time."
—Bob Dylan

The vast grid of gray over Jackson had subdued a dull sun, and it seemed as if the heavens were at war with the heathens below asking, "What've you done?"

Governor Davidson was inaugurated on a cold winter's day in January in an abbreviated ceremony to spare the crowds outside the old capital building. Most knew who and what he was, but came anyway to hold their nose and curry favor. Some came precisely because of what he was. Just as soon as he sobered up from the parties, he started the New Year with a long list of priorities—enemies to get even with or eliminate. His supporters had leaked it that Davidson would "get the MBN" if he was elected, and now it seemed likely that he would make good on his pledge. It was just a matter of how and when.

While his aides ushered in his plug-ugly coterie, a who's-who of Mississippi outlaws, chosen for key appointments, Davidson and his wife constantly fought in the governor's mansion. His chimera, as he called her, eventually shot him in one argument. The mother of his children had tired of his illicit liaisons that she once turned a blind eye to, but now, he had hired all these easy and eager young women. He was like a kid in a giant candy store, indulging his lecherous sweet tooth courtesy of the taxpayers and ignoring the cautions of his nervous aides. It was reported as an attack of appendicitis and covered up in the press. Some lamented the fact that she wasn't a better shot, but the governor was unable to sit without a cushion for some time.

They refused to fly on the same state plane. They ordered the MBN plane to fly her into Hattiesburg on an official trip and land right behind his plane, simply because they didn't want to fly together. The MBN pilot was designated to tell the governor that his plane was purchased strictly for drug enforcement with federal money, and that the state could lose the plane if it was used for other purposes. There would likely be fines and penalties as well.

Davidson screamed, cursed, and threatened the pilot until his staff and handlers finally calmed him down and thanked the shaken pilot for informing them of the law. Even as the pilot made a quick exit, the governor ranted and jerked about, a wild, fish-eyed madman flopping on the bank of this polluted political pond—demanding, gasping for respect. The governor's exercise of power and arrogance bordered on insanity and scared even his own staff. The door closed behind the MBN pilot as Davidson continued screaming, "I am the governor! I am the governor! You don't mess with me!"

Davidson was cautious about one thing—making a direct run at Collins. His reputation with the Mississippi legislature and his national reputation as a cop and administrator was a temporary shield. Instead, they went after Larry Burnside, Chief of Enforcement, and the top merit system appointment in the agency. His position was theoretically beyond the governor's grasp, but Davidson didn't care. In its own way, this was a bolder move than going directly after the director. His strategy seemed to be one of chipping away around the edges and destroying the agency from within, poisoning the well until it was dry.

Former MBN supporters developed a terminal case of hear-no-evil and see-no-evil. The director was powerless to stop the governor from removing the chief who immediately resigned from the agency. The merit system had strict guidelines for the replacement of such a position. Michael was the odds-on favorite under the rules to become chief, but the rules had been thrown out the window. The governor wanted someone he could control, and he knew that was not Michael. He told his staff that he would get to that thorn in his flesh later. Then he added, "Why, that makes me sound almost Biblical! Can we use that?"

He brought over a flunky, John Thompson from the Mississippi Highway Patrol, to become chief, and Michael was left where he was. Thompson later accused Clay and Michael of having a secret pipeline for funneling politically sensitive intelligence to the director—intelligence that he would have gleefully given the governor for political blackmail.

After they were castigated, Michael turned to Clay outside Thompson's office, and said, "That was a heck of a thing for him to accuse us of. We both know it's true, but it was a heck of a thing to accuse us of." Clay laughed until he hurt. It was one of the last genuine belly laughs Michael would hear from him as his treatments continued.

A new arrival to the Bureau, courtesy of Thompson, eyed them red-faced and spitting. Margaret Davis, black hair in a flip, held in place by a ton of hairspray, and generously endowed, humphed at the two and scolded, "Mr. Thompson was sent here to clean up this place, and you two—you, you *juveniles* just make it hard on him."

Michael walked over to her brand new and seldom used

Royal electric typewriter and said, "Maggie, this is the 'on' switch." He and Clay walked away laughing as she ran to Thompson's office crying—black hair bouncing despite her heavy-duty Final Net.

The governor's henchmen had not yet shown any inclination to go after field supervisors. Political odds-makers bet that the director would not be around for long. It was clear that the governor was putting as much pressure on him as he could to force him to resign out of principle, avoiding direct termination that might have legislative repercussions.

The next move came swiftly. Once the personnel director's position became vacant, the governor's team vaulted their boy, Patrick Barnes, over twenty-five more qualified applicants to name him chief of personnel to bring the "right" people into the Bureau. He had a background that disqualified him and had failed to clear an investigation of his past when he previously applied for a job as an agent.

Sensing that change was coming fast and that his own time was running out, the director sent for Michael late one evening. They met at the Shoney's Restaurant on I-55 in Jackson and found a quiet corner booth where there would be no worry about wiretaps.

The political hurricane was fast approaching, the Bureau was sucking up energy from the heated political waters in Jackson, and Collins was to be in the eye of the storm.

Collins walked over to Michael's table in the busy restaurant, shook his hand, and popped a match with his thumbnail to light the first cigarette Michael had seen him smoke in years.

"It's good to see you, boy. I appreciate you coming," he said. "I want to talk to you about some things that are happening and things I want in place while I still have the authority to make them happen. The legislature passed authorization for twenty-five more agents, and we need to rearrange the command structure of the agency. I'm naming you the first captain in the agency. You'll be given control over the north half of the state and have two supervisors reporting to you," he said.

Sensing what was happening and retreating into denial that the old man could ever be taken out, Michael said, "I appreciate it, but I don't know if the timing is right—if I'm ready yet."

Collins looked impatient, but weary, and his features softened.

"This isn't open for discussion, son. We don't have the luxury of waiting for the right time as you did when you postponed your first promotion. The chief is gone, and his replacement isn't to be trusted. The head of personnel is bringing me resumes of people we don't want—can't have—in this agency. They are going to tear down all that we've worked for. I've expanded Clay's organization and his authority. I'm establishing a little beachhead where you and Clay can make your stand and defend the integrity of the agency from within," he said with a deep sigh, a raising and lowering of his massive shoulders. The old veteran looked like he knew he was about done—the guard was changing.

"I asked you long ago, when you came down from Ole Miss to test for an agent, if you were a man of faith. You seemed not so sure or felt unworthy. Despite all that has happened to you and even because of all that pain, you are a different man. You don't walk alone. You'll need your faith more than ever now for there will be a shaking of things and we can't fight alone. It is He, the Unshakeable, who must and will remain."

Michael had never heard or seen this side of the old Korean war vet and peace officer. He wanted to reach out and tell him that he had been like a father to him, but gave him a simple "Yes, sir. I'll do my best."

"Watch over Clay, son," he said. "He's watched over you for a long time, and he's going to need you now."

"Always, Mr. Collins," Michael assured him as wetness welled up in his eyes at the enormity of the world that pressed in on them.

He left that meeting feeling more than ever that the agency was now like the Alamo, and this was the gathering of volunteers and officers to man the walls of the old mission. The news spread quickly of Michael's promotion, to the delight of some, and the horror of others within and outside of the agency. Soon, an influx of new agents began to arrive from the academy class who'd been hired before the new personnel director arrived.

Michael's area named acting supervisors and resident agents for some major centers. They were at full strength from the swamps of the Delta to the Golden Triangle of Columbus, Starkville, and West Point and up to Corinth and Memphis. They were running fast to produce informants capable of working new agents into positions to buy drugs from major dealers across the northern half of the state—to counter operators now emboldened by Davidson's election.

Soon, there were active undercover operations and a few sting operations working across the district. Old limits were pushed and agents, posing as fences for stolen goods, were soon buying stolen airplanes and Cadillacs. Michael believed that if they couldn't take criminals off the street through the front door, then they would take them through the back door. Major criminals believed no one was working these clearinghouses for stolen goods in Mississippi. The agents found the going pretty easy on that side of the street and had more business than they could keep up with. The Bureau had to lease giant yards to house planes and luxury cars by the dozens. They were knocking down some major career criminals, affiliates of the Dixie and Italian Mafias who sold drugs, but also hijacked trucks for high-end appliances, moved hot items from burglaries, and stole everything drivable or capable of flight in the Tupelo-to-Corinth run.

* * *

Violent death stalks law enforcement officers and Michael's team wasn't exempt from its reality. He'd sent Lonnie Peterson to Corinth to be resident agent. It was home for him, and the young man was overjoyed by the opportunity. It was a steamy August day that Lonnie answered what seemed to be a routine call to back up a local officer.

There was nothing alarming about the scene. A seventy-five-year-old man accused of abducting a young woman sat peacefully in an old car beside the road. The uniformed officer, who'd called Lonnie for help, stood beside his patrol car with lights flashing. Beyond the two cars, a long stretch of black asphalt simmered in the intense heat as Lonnie and the officer approached the car. Lonnie saw that the old man had his hand behind him, possibly concealing a weapon. Lonnie drew his revolver and tried to coax the old man to pull his hand out slowly. Lonnie was a gentle spirit and likely not cautious due to his concern for the old man, who inexplicably whipped out a concealed .38 Derringer and shot Lonnie dead at age twenty-six.

"No—don't!" was still on Lonnie's lips as he grabbed the car and crumpled to the hot pavement.

Michael was devastated. *What next?* The director came and the officers went to the little wood frame church nestled in a country field surrounded by green oaks. It overflowed with hundreds of mourners and police officers from many states. Michael fought to hold himself together. It was one thing, he lamented, to go to the funeral of someone you loved who had lived a long life and was perhaps diminished by age and disease. However, Lonnie looked as if he were merely napping in his coffin. His gold shield with the black band across it shined from the pocket of his coat. Michael had to stop himself from involuntarily reaching out, touching the fallen officer, and saying, "Wake up, Lonnie."

He had run out of words for Lonnie's widow and young boys and just sat with them and held their hands as the agents and other honorary pallbearers filed by. Lonnie's death seemed particularly hard on Jack, still nursing his own wounds.

It was a dark day and gray thunderheads grumbled their own disapproval of a promising life cut short. Mourners in dark suits and long gray dresses rode in black limos coming to carry the young man home. His young widow and children were inconsolable. Sweat poured from the Baptist preacher as he bowed before God, kneeled to pray, becoming almost prone before the pulpit. His sweat on the floor of the pitted plank chapel matched the tears of the mourners—so many moans, some speaking in tongues. Lonnie's mother fainted. The choir struggled mournfully through "Take My Hand, Precious Lord" as a sea of handheld fans bearing a painting of the Last Supper waved to a gospel beat.

Swing low, sweet chariot. Lonnie was one of the good guys who left a big hole in the hearts of all who knew him.

The ending of Lonnie's young life in this chance encounter with a deranged old man suffering from alcohol-induced dementia seemed to make it all the more tragic and maddening, a sideshow that came out of the shadows, leaving only questions of—the end, or the beginning?

Michael's radio played softly in the background as he drove away from the cemetery. As if on cue from somewhere beyond this life, normal play was interrupted for the solemn announcement that Elvis had died at Graceland, and Michael knew that we were all mortal after all.

He couldn't push away the flood of tears for Elvis's death. It seemed that Dixie, who loved Elvis so much, had also died again. She was gone like Lonnie. Pearl was gone, and now with Elvis, another closing of all that was in "Old Tupelo." And Clay and Collins, two more essential pillars that held up his world, were threatened.

As he wept, he finally understood that there were only so many days left in this life to get things done, and there were certain sins that could not go unpunished.

There was a loud clap of thunder and rain fell in sheets. He pressed harder on the accelerator and moved off into the growing storm.

CHAPTER THIRTY

"He who does not prevent a crime when he can, encourages it."
—Seneca

Stacks of morning newspapers were thrown out to vendors by carriers moving rapidly along their routes just as the dim rays of dawn broke over the Capitol. These were not just any papers, and they went like hotcakes, the fresh black ink marking the hands of eager readers.

The *Clarion-Ledger's* bold headlines shouted the message, *"Man Given Job Despite Background Check."*

Someone had leaked enough to the Jackson, Mississippi newspaper to let them know that this was a major story and they ran with it. Patrick Barnes' life and sordid times were now on public display in the state's largest newspaper. The governor was jogging that morning with his security detail when they handed him the paper. They said as he was reading, running, and cursing, he inhaled a huge green bug that almost choked him.

The new chief of personnel was forced on the director, on the heels of the firing of the chief of enforcement. It was more than the old man could take, and he called a news conference and resigned, rather than oversee the dismantling and abuse of all that he had built. Clay was out for treatments and struggling, and Michael's world was imploding. He felt like a lone sailor in a windless sea full of sharks and dragons. He didn't have to go in search of them. They were everywhere, and some wore government-issued costumes.

The governor quickly moved to stem the bleeding at the agency and appointed Timothy Charles, an Ole Miss Professor with long family ties to the Southern Baptist Church, as the new director. He was a good and decent man and one of Michael's advisors while at the university, but in for a rude awakening. The political scavengers sought to use his good name in the midst of controversy and he deserved better. Still, there was every reason to believe he would try to hold the line. The press had been given enough background information on the new personnel director to fill the front page of the *Clarion-Ledger*.

It wasn't a pretty story. Patrick Barnes, a former teacher and coach, had been previously rejected as a candidate for agent due to numerous allegations regarding his past, and the media seemed to have acquired them all. Some thought Michael leaked the information, but he didn't, and Clay swore that he wasn't responsible. Perhaps it was Larry Burnside, the deposed chief of enforcement, or Collins himself.

Sensing a way to compromise the new governor, a cry went up from public figures for an Internal Affairs investigation. Some agents in Jackson wanted the assignment to whitewash the governor's boy and "earn" advancement that they could not have otherwise achieved. Charles, to his credit, rejected some very bad nominations to head up the investigation and asked Michael to run the project.

"The press likes you. They view you as a straight arrow, and will buy into whatever you find," he said. "And if I know you, you'll be thorough. Won't you?"

"Absolutely," he said. Then Michael paused and said, "We never studied this at Ole Miss, did we?" It was a rhetorical question.

Many of the allegations had to do with abuse of underage girls. So, Michael asked Sandy Smith if she would accompany him to several states to conduct some very sensitive interviews that would dredge up a past that many were probably trying to forget. She agreed, and he was glad to have her along. People relaxed around Sandy...opened up, spilled their guts. She was tight-lipped and would never compromise anyone. Her actions in the Christmas gun battle were a confirmation of her character.

He had wanted to avoid Barnes until he had some idea where the truth lay on the continuum of actual crimes, lies, hype, and ballyhoo. But this luxury came to an end one morning when Michael was working alone in his office.

Barnes burst in unannounced and demanded that they talk unofficially, neither a proper nor safe procedure. He came in as if he owned the place and smelled of alcohol. He was a brutish man of imposing size with an air of volatility about him. Some thought the man an altogether scary contrivance. Michael had seen him once lift and move a file cabinet that would have taxed three men.

"Michael, it's good to see you," he said. "I've heard so many good things about you." He looked at him through designer glasses that magnified small, dark, savage eyes, nestled under a $200 hairpiece.

"You been talking to my mama?"

He laughed, and Michael sensed that he could play him. Barnes launched into a discussion of the numerous allegations by young girls. He said more than he should have, so Michael let him talk...and talk.

Barnes gestured with hands like a catcher's mitt.

"You know, Michael, how those little girls are. They wanted it and I gave it to them." An old linebacker maybe going to seed a bit. Too much gut, but broad shoulders with a resonance of power.

Michael felt physically sick in his presence, but he managed to retain his cool and to speak in a business-like manner. "Pat, I agreed to head up this investigation and you'll find no one who will give you a more impartial and truthful investigation of the facts."

Michael's face darkened. "But let's understand one another. I don't like what the governor is doing to this agency, and I don't have to personally like you," he said, in a moment of reckless and self-indulgent candor.

The locker room familiarity and façade evaporated like snow under a hot sun.

Barnes' temper showed immediately. His giant hands were clenched into red balls of fury and Michael knew he wanted to come over the desk and attack him.

Barnes rose from his chair in a barely controlled rage. His face was blood-red as he said, "I want you off this investigation."

Michael paused and put on his best poker face, never revealing how weak the hand was that he played.

"That would be fine with me, Pat. As I said, I will be fair to everyone concerned, but hey, here's my phone. Call the director and we'll notify the media that I have been removed as head of the investigation." He slammed the phone on his desk in front of Barnes, making the ringer sound a chime, much like the opening bells in a boxing contest, but this was more a contest of testosterone.

Barnes was literally shaking with rage by now, but something in him saw the danger of alienating his benefactors with more bad press, and he realized that Michael had been baiting him.

He tried to recover and backpedal.

"No, no," he said. "You'll do right by me, I know. Sorry, I just let my temper get away from me. I know the director picked the right man for the job."

In poker, bluffing is essential, and the pair of deuces trumped the pedophile's royal flush given him by King Hal the First.

Barnes left, and it was easy to see how the big ape could've dominated and terrified young girls. Michael realized that he was sweating. He'd thought Barnes was coming after him in a blind rage. If he had shot Barnes with his .357, that would've been difficult to explain since Barnes was unarmed and there were only two witnesses. He gave a deep sigh of relief and mentally prepared himself for what he knew was going to be a nasty assignment.

He also thanked the Lord that he had not gotten involved with Davidson, a creature who seemed to become more unhinged with each passing day. His aides reportedly said that he had become more and more incoherent and they were having trouble covering for the man that they said "is a sociopath, but *our* sociopath." He was speaking in tongues, but it was not the kind the Apostle Paul had in mind.

* * *

Michael and Sandy arrived in the Boot Hills of Missouri just as the sun was setting behind blue hills tinted golden by the leaves of a brilliant fall. The humidity of Mississippi was behind them, and the air seemed cleaner there. It didn't seem a place where girls recalled their nightmare pasts in their dreams, now fodder in a power struggle on a political field far, far away.

The subjects were wary, and rightly so. They'd been visited in the past by other representatives of the Mississippi government who weren't seeking the truth. Michael had to convince them that they were somehow different, and the first step had been the phone call. The Applegate family, who had gotten an old warrant issued for the statutory rape of their daughter, Cissy, was most helpful. After a long talk, Cissy detailed the abuse by her basketball coach.

More girls, now young women, gave statements of their relationship with the man who had once been their teacher, and it was the stuff that would make hardened investigators weepy. By the time Sandy and Michael returned to interview a young woman in Memphis, they were emotionally drained. This last stop would be it, they agreed.

When Marcie Jones met them at the door, she looked pale and frightened. When contacted earlier, she seemed willing to cooperate. Now, she was tentative, visibly shaking and didn't want to meet. He asked Marcie if anyone had contacted her, and she said, "I'm just a little person, and they're so big and powerful." She finally admitted that the governor's chief of staff had called her. Finally, Michael agreed to forego the interview and rushed to a phone booth to call Director Charles.

"Tim, the governor's boys have tampered with one of our witnesses."

"Michael, I don't think the governor would allow such a thing," he said in his calm and measured way, and Michael knew he believed it.

"Call them, and tell them that if they ever contact anyone else in this investigation, I'll go to the press."

"Stay where you are. I'll call you right back."

Michael fumed until the payphone rang. The director was shaken. "The staffer said he just had to hear it for himself. He said he was after the truth, but there would be no more calls made. They understand your position," he said.

"Truth?" Michael said. "That staffer is all heart. They should bronze that heart and put in on display in the Capitol for all time."

"There's just one more thing," Charles said after a long sigh. "Sex isn't going to be enough. You've got to bring me more for us to fire Barnes."

"*Not enough?*"

He knew that they had the director over a barrel and he didn't want to do anything that would get him fired, too, but he clenched his jaws in a sign of the nightly bruxism that left his face and bones sore each morning now.

"Okay, if these are the rules, then if there is more, I'll find it." Michael slammed down the receiver and steamed back to his car.

Sandy took one look at Michael and knew it hadn't gone well. She remained silent as he slammed the Mustang into gear and headed back north. They once again pulled into the gravel drive of the little Missouri farmhouse. Though Michael knew they wouldn't receive an enthusiastic welcome, he prayed that no one had compromised the young woman.

"Cissy, I know this is hard going through this again and again, but I am going to be honest with you. I am looking for something that may have happened to violate the law besides what you have already told us. It may be something you just were too embarrassed to admit, but if there is something—anything— I need it, honey."

Cissy looked at him and then her husband with her big, blue eyes. The husband pondered the obvious question, rubbed the stubble on his chin, and then nodded to her. "You can trust them."

She swallowed hard and said, "Well, he did run away with me for a while."

"*Run away?* But where, Cissy?" he asked.

"Well, he took me down river, and we wound up someplace in Mississippi. We lived like, in the forest for a while," she answered.

Michael looked at Sandy. His mind was already thinking interstate transportation of a juvenile, a federal charge.

"How'd you live, Cissy?"

She looked at the floor and said, "Pat broke into some hunting cabins, and we stayed there and lived off of what they had put up. We went down to some farms and stole some chickens and a hog that Pat gutted and hauled off."

He knew they had just hit pay-dirt. Sex is not enough, huh? Will breaking and entering, larceny, trespassing, theft do? "Now, honey, this is a very important question. How do you know you were in Mississippi other than he told you so?"

"I know right where we were. We camped just outside of a

little town called Tunica. I know because we slipped in there at night and he stole stuff. Sometimes he would send me in to the stores during the day to buy provisions, you know. Mr. Crowley at the feed store took to me and would remember me."

He thanked her and took her statement, and he and Sandy pulled out of the Boot Hills for what they hoped was the last time.

"Michael, you think the governor will let Tim fire him now?" Sandy asked.

He sighed. *We shouldn't have to clean up the governor's mess*, he thought. *Or bother these young women.* "I don't know. I hope so, but I'm going to relieve you from duty on this assignment to protect you, and if they don't fire him, I'm going to resign and call a news conference and lay it all out, every bit of it."

They turned over their completed investigative packet to the director. He read the executive summary, nodded and asked Clay to arrange for Barnes to come to his office that night. Then, he cleared the room so he could make the required "political calls."

Barnes arrived at seven that night, as requested. The director asked that Michael not be in the room. It might cause violence or otherwise complicate things. Michael patiently waited across the hall and listened. It was quiet for a while, and then there was a great deal of yelling by Barnes, who said, "Michael is just a hatchet man for his old boss, Collins. These little boys can't stand to have a criminal in their ranks to stain their precious reputations."

It was loud. It was ugly. It was almost out of control. Everyone at headquarters could hear every word. Clay recorded it all.

He threatened to sue. He threatened to call the governor. The director told him that option was no longer available. Oddly enough, Barnes began to whine about what he had to eat and how hard it was when he was on the run with that girl. Finally, all the emotion and outrage was drained from the man, and they escorted him out of the building.

There was a knock on the door and Clay came in to inform Michael that it was finally over. "The Director didn't ask the Governor, just informed him that he fired Barnes. Not many could've gotten away with it, and not many would've tried it with this Governor, but Tim has the credentials to make the politicos hesitate, and he has the right stuff at his core. Davidson's staff squealed, but the Governor just asked if he could get help for Barnes."

Michael sighed a deep sigh, "Well, now they won't have a liability like Barnes to contend with in the Governor's run for the Senate."

"How're you?" Clay asked.

"How're *you*?" he countered.

"Boy, I'm tired, and I'm not well. I go back in the hospital next week for more treatments, and I just don't know if this old horse hasn't run his last leg," he said, with a diminished twinkle in his eyes that didn't quite obscure the sadness. He was brooding lately and swallowed almost constantly from the treatments. His prominent Adam's apple moved up and down laboriously, trying to swallow saliva that was diminished.

"You need to watch your back, Michael. I worry about you. You've made some serious enemies this time."

"It seems you are always telling me that, Clay. I'll keep my guard up," he said with a weak smile.

Clay was thin as a country split-rail. His color was just above mortician gray. "Michael, I think it's time that we drop the atom bomb."

Knowing he meant the photos and tapes, Michael said, "Past time, Clay."

"I plan to have a clear conscience on the matter if things don't go well for me," he said. There was conviction and honor in his voice.

"It's the right thing, and I'll leave it to you how it is done."

Clay looked at him with eyes old and weary, but drew himself up pouter pigeon straight and smiled.

"Have you ever read *Beowulf*, Michael?"

"I remember something about it from English Lit. A poem?"

Clay smiled, "Yep, just an old Anglo-Saxon poem about a young warrior who slays the monster. That's all. An ancient Danish poem about the man who finally slays Grendel. You're like him. Like Beowulf."

"How so?"

"You're what they called an eotanweard, a watcher for monsters. Your monster, your atol angengea, the terrifying solitary one, is coming one day as a sceadugenga, a night walker..."

"What does this—"

"Listen. The Grendel often slays the eotanweards in his silent approach in the moonlight. On one night alone, he killed thirty watchers, Danish warriors that he surprised and ate. But not Beowulf. He knew the monster was mortal and found the monster's one weak spot and tore off his claws and evaded his bite of death."

"Okay. What're you saying?"

"Remember, he is what they called godesansaca, God's adversary and a feared on helle, a devil in Hell. Find his weak spot, like Beowulf did, and the deathscra, death's shadow, will fall."

"We're just talking about an old poem, right?"

"Go home, Michael. I'll be in touch. We've earned our pay and tomorrow is another day," he said, as he clasped his friend's hand.

Michael sighed, and thought, *Yes, tomorrow is another day. A new sun, another celestial candle to burn away the lingering darkness.*

CHAPTER THIRTY-ONE

"There are only two kinds of people in the end: those who
say to God, 'Thy will be done,' and those to whom God says,
in the end, 'Thy will be done.' All that are in Hell, choose it."
–C.S. Lewis

It was a long and lonely drive up the Natchez Trace at two in the morning. Mottled brown nighthawks swept past his car diving for nocturnal meals, and the white barn owls, which ancient people thought were spirits, stirred from their roosts and floated moth-like through the night. Michael could almost feel the ghosts, the spirits of the lost Indian tribes whose burial grounds were along the darkened historic trail. He had enough ghosts of his own. The natural was deadly enough without the supernatural to contend with, and Clay's tales of Beowulf and monsters were beautiful poetic language but strangely unsettling.

He was dead tired, but determined to limp home and let the events of the day play out in Jackson. He barely missed two bounding, white-tailed deer just outside of Tupelo but rallied a bit and made it home. He willed himself up to the door of his duplex, knackered and ready for bed. As he looked up, a dark cloud covered the moon and a whippoorwill called its plaintive cry in the hollow below.

A wrinkled note was attached from his neighbors and cat-sitters, Glenda and Linda, on Michael's front door. He smelled the smoke from their fireplace where they roasted nuts and marshmallows. The scrawled note said they wanted to see him before he went to bed, probably—hopefully—to share a plate of their delicious leftovers from dinner or special roasted delights, he thought. They said he didn't eat enough, and they were right. He knocked on their door, and heard one of the girls say, "Come in."

Their curtains were all drawn tight, and the light was off outside their door, casting their apartment in shadows. It was unlike them not to greet him at the door with their usual flurry of charm and jubilant hospitality. Feeling something was amiss but too tired for caution, Michael wearily opened the door and saw Glenda sitting in a chair across the dimly-lit room. Linda lay limp and sprawled across the couch as if she were asleep, but one arm dangled disjointed to the floor—a Siamese moan of distress emanated from beneath her couch. He glanced back at Glenda and saw too late the bruises, swollen lips, the terror in her eyes, and the ropes that bound her—just as he felt the blow from behind and to the left.

Cold steel stabbed at his heart and cut through his shoulder holster ripping open the skin under the pit of his arm and sending his Magnum flying across the apartment. The blow and force knocked him to his right, and he tried to go with the force and pull his assailant with him, but the man was cat-quick. That effort earned him a slashed forearm as the attacker withdrew his first attempt to stab him. Michael lost him and went crashing into the television stand which overturned and sent the television set and a vase of flowers smashing and thundering in the small room. The late news commentary regarding the extraordinary firing of Patrick Barnes in Jackson came to a violent end.

Blood gushed from the first wound and spurted from the second. It seemed to be raining in his head, and a roaring river of pain sought to wash him from the earth. Michael's left arm felt numb, a mile long and thin as a straw from the cuts and dizziness. Nausea swarmed around him from the long night, punctuated by the sudden attack and loss of blood.

His vision blurred, but he could still distinguish the pale visage from hell that stood in front of him. Wondering and waiting so long, and now hell had coughed up this vermin to kill again.

"You're too late again, Parker. I'm going to cut up these lovelies after I kill you, you pig!" Hammel screamed with deranged delight. *No, no,* Michael thought, *that could not happen, no matter what!* Somewhere in the distance, he heard Glenda make a dry, gagging sound.

The Ice Man's face became a demonic force powered from Hell, and he lunged again with a wide sweeping left-to-right motion of the stiletto that sliced Michael's shirt open as Michael arched his back and sucked in his belly at the lunge. Stinging pain left new trickles of blood to ooze down his white, button-down oxford. It was a near-miss and the assassin lost his balance, giving Michael the opening he needed.

As he leaned in from the sweep, Michael thumbed him deeply in his pale throat socket, grasped him by his collar, and banged his head against the wall. It was a blow that would've disabled most men, but Hammel groaned and lunged forward to recover the knife that had skittered across the floor, a knife just like the one he had used on Dixie. As he rose with the stiletto, Michael willed himself past his primal fear of the cold steel and hooked him under his right rib cage, driving for his spine. Fredrick gave out a rush of air and Michael followed with a backhand across eyes and nose. Fredrick coughed, and blood ran from his nose, but on he came.

The man had to be wired up on speed to take such blows

and not go down. *Shoot him! Must shoot the monster!* Michael reached for his .357 on the floor that the first lunge had dislodged from his shoulder holster, but Hammel was quicker, and came down heel-first on the back of Michael's left hand. *Snap! Pop!* Bones broke in his hand and Michael almost fainted from the pain. Hammel laughed and kicked the gun away and stomped at Michael's head as he rolled away.

His white face hovered above him, inspecting the damage. "Are you playing possum? No, no," the madman said mocking, taunting. "You know you have to die, and you know *how* you must die—just like your sweet little lady in Memphis."

Michael tried to rise, but his body was shattered. He tried to breathe, but sounded like an old man with a wheezing death rattle. His heart seemed as empty as smoke, and he could hear the mournful whimpering of the sisters.

The edge of darkness tugged at him, his body wanting to shut down, *but mustn't or he wins, I lose*, Michael thought. *I lose, the girls die. Too many girls have died. The hunter has become the hunted. Help me, Lord.*

Hammel threw back his head and said, "Father, I now pay my dues!"

Then he came again and Michael improvised. He grabbed a full quart bottle of 100-proof vodka that had dislodged from the nearby bar and with a desperate swing, hit him across his left shoulder and neck. The bottle shattered and the liquid spilled over Fredrick, but still he stood—unaffected, smiling as if he were hit with some prop bottle out of a bad western movie fight.

Michael was near blacking out and spots danced before his eyes. He saw two of everything. *Two monsters.* He slumped, awaiting the madman's final thrust. The buzz of summer insects in his ears was replaced by soft music that he did not recognize from an eternal jukebox, and then Dixie Lee's whispering, ethereal voice. "Put on the full armor. Save me, Michael. Save me." She spoke with a celestial clarity not of this earth, and Michael found the inner strength for one more desperate move.

He plunged his numb right hand into the fireplace and found a flaming log. He grasped it and flung it with his last ounce of strength. The flaming brand hit the Ice Man in the chest, but bounced away harmlessly. Fredrick looked at the log, laughed his deranged laugh, and took one step toward Michael. Then, a lone ember that had stuck to his shirt flamed brightly for a moment before his alcohol-soaked garments exploded in a blue flame.

Suddenly, the Ice Man—this denizen of Hades—became a human torch. He cried out first in insane amusement, then panic, and began to swat at the flames, only spreading the fire. His hair ignited with a great searing sound, and Hammel became a flaming medusa running for the door and fighting the flames in vain. Michael crawled to the door, and there he was, rolling on the dry leaves, starting new fires along his path. Suddenly, Fredrick fell still, flat, and heavy—eerily limp.

Then, as Michael watched in horror, the unrecognizable, charred figure of a man rose from the ground and staggered back toward the doorway. He had to be near death, but the speed had released a final surge of neurotransmitters, and the chemical zombie from a burning inferno came for Michael with an upraised stiletto, the cords in his charred neck visible and alive in spasms of pain.

Michael raised his right hand, grasping the madman's knife, turning it back toward him as he collapsed on Michael. Michael had no strength for a death plunge, but the inertia of Hammel's falling bulk drove the stiletto deep into the heart of the man he had met so long ago in Jackson.

He was repulsed by the flow of his assailant's blood and the stench of burning flesh and pushed him away. The two men lay side by side. Michael was breathing hard, a spreading red stain soaking his clothes as he lapsed in and out of the darkness. He knew the silent and motionless figure was finally dead. But no! His eyes popped open, and through charred lips, he gasped for one last breath, which had the aroma of rot, looked at Michael from another time and place, and said in a guttural hiss, "This was all because of...*her?*"

Michael saw for the first time on his hairless face the telltale pits and marks of the teenage curse. He had once had acne.

Michael said, "You killed my woman," but Freddie was now beyond all reply and all knowing. This time, the Ice Man was dead, a once pale but now blackened servant of his prince bound for the lake of fire. Michael could almost hear the shrieks of demons as the gates of Hell swung open to welcome one of its own.

Michael tried to rise, but he was wobbly and dropped to his knees. He sat on his haunches, his face resting in his burned and broken right hand. Somewhere, Pearl scolded him for jumping too high to pluck the forbidden apples in the orchard, only to find them bitter. Then, she asked, "Was it all worth the price you've paid, son?"

Then, someone in the heavenlies turned out the lights and slammed shut the big door to the hereafter with a clang.

CHAPTER THIRTY-TWO

*"Hold on to what is good, even if it's a handful of earth. Hold on to what
you believe, Even if it's a tree that stands by itself. Hold on to what you
must do, Even if it's a long way from here. Hold on to your life, Even if
it's easier to let go. Hold on to my hand, Even if I've gone away from you."*
—Pueblo poem

In those first long days and nights in the intensive care unit,
a man with piercing eyes, who some thought must be a physician,
was often seen by Michael's bed. Dressed in snow-white, he sat
by the bed holding Michael's hand, praying and whispering in
his ear... "Not yet, not yet. It is not your time." He came and
went undisturbed. ICU nurses, who normally were bulldogs when
protecting their fragile patients from intruders, did not question
the stranger, but his voice was not a stranger to the young police
captain who drifted at the edge of the sea of forever. Michael had
heard and trusted that voice before...in his car the day of the
ambush. Each time the man left, Michael's vital signs improved
dramatically, until one day—he came no more.

In the months that followed, Michael healed in the
Northeast Mississippi Medical Center ICU under the care of the

two traumatized sisters and Katie the cat that they covertly brought to his room. Glenda and Linda had recovered physically, if not emotionally, from the night from hell, and stepped in to practice their nursing skills as private duty nurses, shoving away the regular staff. He was seldom alone. The sisters had quite the time getting rid of some "nurses" from Memphis sent by Super Fly himself to heal Michael's soul. Michael vaguely remembered a cute girl named Janine coming to him one night, and telling him that she knew of his pain and loss. She offered her personal healing powers to soothe his broken body and his heart when he was ready. She kissed him softly on his cheek, and left him in his twilight world to mend physically and emotionally. To say the least, Glenda and Linda did not approve of that brand of nursing.

Multiple surgeries sought to repair bones broken like sticks and tissue mangled almost beyond repair as Michael lived in a haze of morphine and other potent painkillers for months, drifting in and out of a foreign landscape.

People came and went that he would not remember. Perhaps he remembered Collins' visit and the doctors with their needles, and a volunteer, an angel named Susan with brown hair and brown eyes that were filled with the same love that Michael had seen as a child in the eyes of Jesus in a painting that stared down at him each Sunday morning in the sanctuary of his small Methodist church.

He existed in a sleep where light seemed diffused and gray, and more hallucinated than dreamed scary versions of what he had experienced and survived. Wild-eyed albinos chased him with long knives and all were consumed by the fires of their personal hells. Lawyers drifted in pools of their own depravity and greed. Gangsters fed the fish in the depths of the muddy Mississippi while corrupt officials suckled at the public tit. Shadow-box figures from dark swampy places ate razor blades and breathed fire. Young men died as snipers gave them deadly Christmas gifts. A giant black man in Memphis watched as he struggled with demons from Hell.

A golden-haired beauty stood silently in the background watching over him in his terrible dreams, perhaps waiting for him to join her, and visions of Pearl's boys fighting for one last "lost cause" swirled within his fevered mind. And, somewhere—Beowulf felled Grendel...

As his wounds healed and doses of mind-numbing drugs became less frequent, friends and well-wishers came by to see him, and someone told him that John Wayne had died. He knew that would crush the one visitor he wanted to see. Friends were evasive about Clay, but even through the drugs and pain, he knew that it was not good. Clay was far worse off than he...

Finally, Tim Charles came in to the hospital one day, threw back the curtains, and said, "Look at you! Don't you look pretty?" Michael attempted a smile, but it hurt. "I've got the front page of a newspaper that's about two weeks old that I want you to see," he said.

The banner headline shouted, *"GOVERNOR DIES OF SUDDEN HEART ATTACK."*

"You were out of it when it happened," he said. "I told them to let it rest—all of it. The governor was at his ranch retreat, planning his run for the Senate with his aides. That's the official story. His chief of staff brought in a big envelope marked private, priority mail that the governor had to sign for. Seems as though it was filled with pictures and tapes of Davidson in all sorts of compromising positions. His chief of staff told me that his eyes bulged out of his head. He turned red and coughed loudly and then choked to death on the big mouthful of barbeque he was eating. He fell over right into his plate, they told me. Oh, it was all cleaned up, and everything was proper and everyone mourned the loss of this public servant, but it's over for Davidson's bunch. They've already packed up and left Jackson, for the most part."

He paused for a long time, as Michael tried to reconcile this and all that had happened. It was hard to believe.

Michael was numb and remained speechless for a moment. "So, it's over?"

"It would seem so for the moment. The lieutenant governor is vowing to clean house," he said, and he laughed his famous country laugh. He looked at Michael for a long time, smiling a clever smile, and asked, "You wouldn't know anything about those photos and tapes, would you?" Before a reply could be made, he started laughing in a cackle that harkened back to when Michael was his student at Ole Miss. "I gotta go, but there's someone who wants to see you," he said.

As he left, Michael looked at the door, and there stood the gaunt figure of Clay himself.

"Welcome back to the world," Clay said. "I know that you're still trying to absorb what you just heard. I thought I wasn't going to make it out of the hospital, so I dropped the package in the mail with a note saying it would be copied to all the major media outlets. Then, the darnedest thing happened. Doc walks in and says I'm in remission again. Who knows how long it'll last, but I couldn't very well withdraw the mail, now could I?"

Michael looked at him and felt the sob choking in his throat. "The bad guys, they're all dead, Clay," he said. "But Dixie Lee is still gone."

"I know, and you have this guilt that God killed her to punish you for not being there, for not being as perfect as you think you should be. Of course, you aren't perfect, but you try harder than anyone I know. You can start healing now. Dixie Lee has long since forgiven you, and I know she waits somewhere for you when it's your time. Now, you must heal your physical wounds. We have new dragons to slay. It may be a little dull after all we've been through. As someone said, 'they just ain't making grails the way they used to,'" he said.

Laughter and tears followed. They told bad jokes and outrageous lies. The two old friends were euphoric. Being alive against all odds was something to savor, something to hold on to.

Long after Clay had left, and Michael was alone, he saw a card Collins had left on his nightstand. He opened it, and the message was a quote from John Leonard.

"He will wonder whether he should have told these young, handsome and clever people the few truths that sing in his bones. These are:

1.) Nobody can ever get too much approval;

2.) No matter how much you want or need, they, whoever they are, don't want to let you get away with it, whatever it is; and

3.) Sometimes you get away with it."

You boys got away with it. You have *"true grit."* –John Edward Collins

Michael pushed away a tear. *Yes,* he thought. "We outwitted the monsters, and have gotten away with *it,* whatever *it* is."

When he finally left the hospital, he made his way to Parker Grove. He wetted his lines as he sat in the lazy sun on the banks of the pool where he learned to swim. Katie the cat jumped to and fro over tall spring grass in cat-bounds synchronized with the leaps of a large green grasshopper she was chasing. He thought that from death comes life and that maybe chivalry was not extinct.

He felt a tug on his line and hooked the monster bass of the lake that had eluded him for so long. When he finally got the twelve-pounder to the bank, he released him in kinship, a nod to all things ancient and endangered.

He thought he was getting better. He hadn't thought of Dixie in a long time, maybe half an hour.

THE END